He's Amish.

His mouth left my skin, and he pressed his ear against my heart. His breathing was hard and hot. I could feel the heat from his entire body penetrating the thick polyester dress. A dress that I really wished I wasn't wearing at all.

"Oh, Rose—my Rose, I love you so much." He stuttered the words out between breaths with such strong emotion that I felt guilty that I'd become irritated with him at all.

He went on, "I don't take a single step all day without thinking about you—wanting you. And here you are, finally in my arms."

She's not.

He pulled back, locking his eyes on mine. "I couldn't live without you. I couldn't survive a world with you not in it—so you have to be good, and very, very careful."

I understood what he was saying. But I still felt way deep down, beneath all the raging hormones, that I hadn't done a thing wrong this night.

"I think it was sweet of Suzanna and Timothy to do this for us. I mean, I would do about anything to be with you. Being here together like this is a real gift," I whispered, my words mumbling into his hair.

"I know, sweetheart. But the quicker the bishop and the church allow you to join, then the sooner we'll be officially courting. I thought I was done with all this sneaking around."

Is love enough to bring their two worlds together?

Praise for *Temptation*

"Wonderfully compelling, becoming highly emotional
with an interesting ending."
—*XpressoReads* blog

"*Temptation* is a beautiful, forbidden romance....
I highly recommend [it]."
—*I Heart YA Books* blog

"I completely adored this book."
—*The Book Blog Experience*

"I loved this book!...Readers who enjoy books
with forbidden or secret romances will be riveted."
—*Mrs. ReaderPants* blog

Books by Karen Ann Hopkins

The Temptation Novels

in reading order

TEMPTATION
BELONGING

belonging

Karen Ann Hopkins

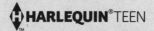

Recycling programs
for this product may
not exist in your area.

ISBN-13: 978-0-373-21081-7

BELONGING

Printed in U.S.A.

For my father, Anthony Lanzalaco, and my brother, Tony Lanzalaco, who've always been there to rescue me with their wisdom and unconditional support.

1

Rose

Peeking out the window, I watched Noah limp down the pathway behind his mom. The sunshine caught the golden highlights in his hair, making him look like a grungy angel fallen from the clouds—an injured one, that is, with the metal brace that was attached to his leg glinting in the sun.

Seeing the brace sent a chill down my back when I remembered the buggy wreck that had nearly killed Noah. A few weeks had passed, but my knees still felt like jelly when I pictured that rainy night on the road and the blur of the giant truck heading straight for Noah and his horse, Rumor.

I shivered, closing my eyes. If I'd lost Noah on that fateful night, a part of me would have died also. I couldn't even imagine a world without him—it would be as if the sun disappeared from the sky. My heart wouldn't have recovered, and that's why I had to be brave right now. I couldn't live without him, and somehow I had to make my decision to become Amish work—so that the two of us would never be torn apart again.

When I opened my eyes, Noah was gone, and I suddenly felt very alone in a foreign world. The murmurings of the strange language behind me didn't help the feeling of displacement I was experiencing, either. If my ears and eyes weren't deceiving me, I really was in some faraway land.

Dad's voice drifted into my mind, *You know, Rose, no one is holding a gun to your head to do this. You can back out anytime.*

My belly tightened at the remembrance of his words.

It still amazed me that my dad was allowing me to move into the Amish society to be with Noah. Of course, his reasons were less than honorable for sure. Tina, Dad's girlfriend, had talked him into believing that his baby girl would run home after a week or two of living the harsh and restrictive lifestyle of the Amish. They'd both be in for a big surprise, I inwardly vowed, despite my uneasy feelings.

Whenever the little doubts would eat away at me, I'd think about the first time that Noah had kissed me, and liquid warmth would coat my insides, giving me strength. Even now, with the heat of sunshine through the window warming my face, I could smell the leaves and the pine of the hidden forest clearing—and feel his lips moving on mine. Our secret rides into the trees, which I'd nicknamed the fairy wood, because of the hazy, magical feel of the place, were the most wonderful moments of my life. Knowing that there would be many more of those times waiting for us in the future made me smile. As long as Noah and I were together, everything else would be all right.

The sudden stillness in the air told me that they were all gathered, waiting for me to turn around.

Trying to be brave, I sucked in a quick breath, cleared my mind of anxiety and turned to face my audience. I was immediately met by six serious faces. Five men and one lone woman greeted me with what could only be described as wariness.

I recognized the bishop straight off with his Abraham Lincoln features and long, snowy beard. His eyebrows were as white as his beard and were bushy on his jutting brow. I'd hoped that the sight of him wouldn't instill as much fear in me as it had the first time I'd seen him, so long ago now. Unfortunately, he still gave me the jitters.

Really, this whole scene wouldn't have been as bad if I'd had some warning. I couldn't blame Noah. He had been taken by surprise as much as I had to learn that mere moments after I'd arrived at the Hershbergers, who, for lack of a better description, were my new Amish foster parents, I would be ambushed by a meeting with the bishop and ministers. I didn't even have time for a proper get-to-know-you before Ruth Hershberger, Noah and his mom were being hustled out the back door only a minute following the sight of the three black buggies making their way up the driveway.

I had no idea who the woman standing off to the side was, but she immediately struck me as a happy person. When my eyes met hers, she smiled warmly. The smile was genuine, if the deep wrinkles at the corners of her pretty brown eyes were any indication. Because of that smile I felt a bit more at ease.

And of course there was Noah's dad, Mr. Miller. He wasn't usually a scary guy, but seeing him standing there with his buddies, all grim and uptight, prickled the hair on my arms. The image flashed in my mind of Amos Miller astride his black horse in the rainstorm, fury distorting his features.

From firsthand experience, I knew Mr. Miller could be intimidating. Upon learning that his son was having a secret relationship with an English girl, he'd been incredibly angry. And he sure hadn't been shy expressing his displeasure at the discovery that stormy day, either.

I only had a few seconds to register the faces of the other three men in attendance before Mr. Bishop broke the silence. One was old Mr. Hershberger, who, up until that point, I'd only had a chance to say hi to. Rebecca Miller had informed me upon arrival that he wasn't really an active minister any longer, being in the process of transitioning away from the duties of the job. But I guess, since I was his new *daughter,* he wasn't going to miss the excitement.

The other two were middle-aged guys with no gray showing in their lengthy beards, beards which, despite their length, didn't hold a candle to the bishop's Gandalf-inspired do. The tall guy put me in mind of Ichabod Crane with his skinny face and large nose. His blue eyes were friendly enough, though.

"Miss Cameron, I'm Abram Lambright, the bishop here in the Meadowview community." He looked me straight in the eye. Although I wanted to turn away, I managed to keep my gaze locked with his. I definitely didn't want to give him the idea that I could be bullied.

Funny that he didn't offer his hand for a shake, though. That would have been the polite thing to do. Taking charge of the situation, I stepped forward, thrusting my hand out.

"Hey there, Mr. Lambright, you can call me Rose."

Bishop Lambright's mouth twitched at the one corner, maybe in amusement or perhaps he wanted to ring my neck. No telling, but he humored me by shaking my hand firmly. Then he did spread his mouth in an attempt at friendliness. Seeing the almost-smile made me relax a little more, pushing more of the tension out of me.

"I've heard much about you, Rose." He paused as if trying to pick his words carefully. "And to put it frankly, the other ministers and I would like to talk to you personally about your presence here in our community. We don't often find ourselves in the situation of taking stray English children into our lives."

My hackles were up, but before I said something unpleasant to the charming Bishop Lambright, the woman made her presence known. "My dear, I'm Martha Lambright, Abram's wife. You can address me by Martha, though." She flowed across the floor smoothly, and before I knew what was happening she had me locked in a hug, tight against her slender body. "We are so pleased to have you with us."

Seeing Martha up close I was shocked that she was the bishop's wife. She must have been twenty years younger than him, showing just a few gray hairs at her temples and flecking through her root line. Her round face and wide-spaced eyes hinted at the beautiful girl she must have been in her youth.

"Glad to meet you," I murmured, startled by her swift dousing of the flames.

She went on to introduce Mr. Marcus Bontrager, the *Sleepy Hollow* guy, who nodded several times in my direction and smiled awkwardly.

Then she said Mervin Weaver's name and I felt a tickling of recognition before realization dawned on me, hitting me like a brick. *Ella's father*—there was no mistaking the family resemblance now that I gave him a longer appraisal. He'd passed on his large eyes to his daughter—the girl who was supposed to be courting Noah, instead of me.

Besides his attractive eyes, Mr. Weaver was completely ordinary in height, stature and coloring. But those eyes were bright with thought, and my mind quickly processed that I'd have to tread carefully around him.

"Rose, why don't you have a seat here at the table, my dear?" Martha ushered me to a chair, and although she didn't really shove me into it, somehow her hovering presence got my butt seated in a hurry. She pulled a chair out beside me and made herself comfortable. Maybe I was wrong, but Martha Lambright appeared to be highly entertained by my situation. Of course, who could blame her? Without TV or the internet to occupy a person's time, community gossip would be the next best thing. I was the show.

While the five guys were arranging themselves across the table from Martha and me, I resisted the urge to scratch at my bun, which felt itchy under the cap. Sitting there all dressed up Amish was quite strange. I felt as if I had a Halloween costume on.

"I'll not beat around the bush on this matter, even though my wife would like to coddle you like a weanling." Bishop Lambright eyed Martha with distaste before focusing on me again. "There is much more to being one of us than just wearing the dress and covering your hair. Our way is the old way. The traditional way. The difficult way."

My mouth began to form words, but the bishop raised his hand, cutting me off before I even got started. He leaned in a bit closer and said darkly, "This is no trifling matter that you've gotten yourself into, young lady. I've only consented to you being allowed to live among us under the pressure of Amos Miller, here, who has vouched for your honest intentions and good behavior."

I glanced at Mr. Miller, who, catching my gaze, nodded his head reassuringly. His smile was controlled, though. The poor guy was my bond man, and if I screwed things up, he'd be the one paying for it—and me, of course. I didn't even try to say anything this time. Bishop Lambright obviously had a bunch of things he wanted to get off his chest, so I slouched back in the chair, preparing myself for the long haul.

The bishop let out an annoyed huff, and after looking briefly at his comrades and then his wife, he fixed on me, saying, "I can't teach you all you need to know in the brief amount of time we have this afternoon. Obviously, this will be an ongoing learning experience for you, but there are a couple of issues that you must be fully aware of *now*." After a more agitated breath, he went on. "Like all the other young people in our community, you will not be allowed to begin courting Noah Miller until you have become a member of our church."

At this point Bishop Lambright's eyes narrowed, and again, he leaned across the table.

Yep, he was scary. I resisted pushing still farther back into the chair.

"And I will not have you joining the church until you have had ample time to acquaint yourself with our rules and customs."

It suddenly occurred to me that I might be waiting years before I could even date Noah and I blurted out, "Excuse me, sir, but...ah...how long will that be?"

"Ach, you are an impetuous child, aren't you? You can't even hold your tongue for a moment while you're being spoken to." The bishop's eyes sparked while his mouth tightened.

Somewhere deep in my mind was the feeling of utter confidence as I looked back at Bishop Lambright. After all, my Dad—or even Sam—would get me out of here in a heartbeat if I called. Still, I would not let this puffed-up old guy get the better of me. And he was not going to keep me and Noah apart. I would do what I had to do to gain the bishop's trust.

I'd walk the line—and I would not fall.

"I'm sorry, Bishop Lambright," I said meekly, lowering my eyes. Yes, I could play the part when needed.

"There, child, it's all right. We understand that it will take a bit of time for you to know how to behave properly," Martha said, squeezing my shoulder for good measure.

"First things first, Martha—Rose, you are a young woman, and you will act accordingly with our customs. As spoken in first Timothy, 'A woman should learn in quietness and full submission.' Therefore you will not be interrupting me again, and you will always show respect to the men in this community. The womenfolk will fill you in on all the details about following our customs and being obedient in time. Do you understand?"

His words made my feminist side dizzy with anger, but I was up to the challenge.

Peeking my eyes for an instant, then dropping them again, I answered, "Yes, sir."

"All right, then." The bishop leaned back and breathed evenly, seeming satisfied with my response. I hardly even noticed the other men, the bishop's type-A personality was so blasting.

"To answer your question, I do believe a few months of living our ways will be sufficient for you to join with us. That is, if you obey our rules and don't cause any trouble." The tone of his voice deepened. He took advantage of my full attention, and strengthening his voice, he said, "And be advised, young woman, that I will be watching you...we all will be watching you."

The warm air in the kitchen seemed to tingle with his words. I looked away from the bishop, staring at the burgundy-colored curtain swaying above the sink from the breeze.

The desperate need to be with Noah had been at the forefront of my brain since the accident. I hadn't seriously considered all the other stuff that came with him—like a pack of grumpy old men telling me what to do.

My tummy felt rocky again. I summoned a picture of Noah before me, and seeing his handsome face drove the fear and anxiety back. Reaffirming my decision, I knew in that instant that I'd do anything to be with Noah.

"I will be good, I promise," I said, hardly above a whisper.

"Our idea of *good* and your view are probably entirely different." His voice oozed sarcasm, causing me to raise my head and meet his gaze again. He held my eyes for several uncomfortable seconds before he seemed to crack. Or maybe he was simply growing bored with me.

He said resignedly, "Fair enough—for now, anyway." The

bishop stood abruptly, inciting the others to rise quickly from their chairs also. "We all have work to get back to, so let us end this meeting."

Before I could start celebrating inwardly that my tormentor was about to leave, Bishop Lambright once again locked his piercing stare on me and said, "You would do well to heed what Paul spoke in Romans, 13 verse 1. *Everyone must submit himself to the governing authorities, for there is no authority except that which God has established. The authorities that exist have been established by God.*"

With that, he forgot all about me, reverting back to his language as he walked with the men to the front door and out.

Despite feeling quite reserved and thoughtful from the encounter with the bishop, I still shouted a silent *yippee* in my mind. I'd survived. And I was on track to being with Noah.

Hopefully, I'd only be seeing the pompous Bishop Lambright on Sundays.

"Child, are you still so willing to turn Amish after all that?" Ruth Hershberger appeared out of nowhere, and I instantly knew that the old woman had been eavesdropping. Her hands were placed rigidly on her plump hips; her eyes, camouflaged by the thick glasses, told me that she was expecting me to be heading out the door.

I'd show her—and the bishop—that I was dead serious.

Martha was still sitting in the chair with keen interest emanating from her body. I remembered to keep my response subdued and not say the first caustic thing that popped into my mind. "Mrs. Hershberger, I know that this will be difficult, but I'm committed to being with Noah, and I'm ready to begin my new life in your community to do so."

Ruth's stance softened a bit, while Martha's mouth spread into a broad grin.

Ruth said, "If you'll be living under my roof, I'll be having you call me Ruth. We best start on the potatoes. With all those young'uns of the Millers coming for dinner, we'll need an extra pot."

"I'll help you get started on those, Ruth," Martha chirped as she stood. She reached out and gave my hand a squeeze before she followed Ruth over to the pantry.

Potatoes—I could peel potatoes. I was abruptly very happy knowing that Noah and his family were coming back that evening. I followed the two women to the counter with extra lightness to my step.

Moodily, I scraped the remnants of dinner from the dishes into the pot. Sarah was alongside me working in the sudsy water, and Rachel was busy clearing the last of the water glasses from the table. We were the only inhabitants in the kitchen besides Ruth and Rebecca, who were sitting leisurely at the far end of the table chatting away like busy birds. At first, it struck me as odd that the older women weren't helping with the cleanup, but then I realized that they had the teenagers well trained for the job. And, unlike their English counterparts, these girls didn't even dream of arguing about the chores.

I had been blissfully happy the entire afternoon. Peeling and cutting up the potatoes was no big chore, and the time had gone quickly, helped along by a bombardment of nosy questions from Martha and Ruth about my pre-Amish life.

After Martha had made her exit, Ruth had given me the grand tour of the two-story farmhouse. It was so similar to the Millers' house that I'd been hard-pressed to find many differences. The house was large and I could imagine a time, long ago, when its rooms were full of the stomping of little feet and the laughing of children's voices.

Ruth had asked me to sweep the downstairs while she

picked some tomatoes in the garden, and I'd perkily went about my work. I wanted to impress Ruth, show her that an English girl could work as well as any Amish girl.

Being alone in the house had given me the opportunity to gather my thoughts and recover from my earlier encounter with the Amish law. I thought I'd handled myself admirably, but I was pricked with lingering doubt about what I was doing among these people. Would I ever really be okay with all the subservient crap that these women had to put up with?

I didn't know, but as I'd made my way around the house I'd curiously spied into the Hershbergers' lives. Of course there weren't any portraits displayed anywhere, but there were quite a few pretty framed pictures about the walls, most of them with Bible verses inscribed on them. Touching the blue-and-tan quilt that was draped over the back of the sofa, I'd admired its designs before I'd wandered to the corner of the family room to check out the books that lined the shelves of the bookcase there. Most of them were spiritual in nature, but there were also some cookbooks and a few books of fiction that had struck me as the Amish equivalent to romance novels, with their covers sporting women with white caps and buggies in the background. After flipping through the pages of one, I'd placed it back on the shelf, smiling at Ruth's pastime.

Having the opportunity to spend the rest of the afternoon with Ruth had settled my nerves down a few notches. She was a "say it like it is" sort of person with a very down-to-earth vibe. And, unlike the bishop, she didn't quote any scripture to me, which I was relieved about. I sensed that she wasn't the type of granny you'd want to tick off, but she was definitely a fair woman. I was betting that the two of us would get along just fine once we got to know each other.

By the time Noah and his family had finally come up the drive in a collection of three buggies, my insides had been bubbling with excitement. I was going to spend the entire evening with my guy, and my heart had beat frantically at the sound of the clip-clops pounding up the gravel.

The floating-on-air feeling had lasted about ten minutes more until I'd realized that Noah wasn't coming straight into the house to see me. Instead, he'd hung about outside with the men, while the ladies had gotten the food put on the counter and finished with the water glasses. Even *that* hadn't irritated me too much. What had caused my insides to shrivel was that Noah hadn't looked at me, not even once, during the dinner.

He'd appeared exactly the same as he had earlier in the day when he'd taken me for my first buggy ride ever. The bruises on his perfect face were shrinking away to the point where he now looked as if he'd gotten into a fistfight, instead of being hit by a semi. His hair was still gloriously thick and sexy, and even though he was getting around on a walking cast, he managed to look cool, with no hint of clumsiness.

Noah was the same guy on the outside that I adored, but it was as if his brain had been snatched by an alien; he seemed like a completely different person. For instance, instead of flirting with me as he'd done hours before when his mom had allowed us to sit beside each other on the buggy seat, he was now acting as if I wasn't even in the same room as him. I recalled how he'd caught my eyes only briefly enough to flash a wink at me before he'd followed Jacob out the door after the meal, abandoning me for masculine companionship.

Now, as I attacked the little bits of food clinging to the plates, I boiled inwardly. The only way I would survive this situation was if Noah helped me. If I had to play love games with him, I'd go mental for sure. The worst part was that all the indecision from the days before came flooding back in. I wouldn't exactly call it regret that I was feeling, for I was still happy that I'd been able to see the guy that I loved for a little while, which would have been impossible had I not chosen this path. No, it was more of a quiet panic spreading through me that this was what all my days would be like—that I'd forever be chasing after Noah, unable to catch him.

Sarah and Rachel worked silently yet efficiently, and mostly distracted from the chore, I hustled to keep up with them. I was actually glad for the lack of conversation. But I couldn't help but listen to the older women behind us.

They seemed perfectly content to relax, speaking Pennsylvania Dutch—a dialect of German—for a while, then abruptly switching to English. It was odd to my ears the way the languages flowed into each other with hardly a break. I'd perk up when words burst forth that I actually could understand.

"Yes, I am a trifle worried about dear Emilene. She issued all her previous ten children in the home, but with these twins and her difficulties this time, I do believe it would be wise for her to plan on a hospital birth," Ruth said, concern cushioning the words.

My gloomy thoughts were interrupted; ten—*twelve kids?*

I stopped the scraping, turning to the women swiftly. "Did you just say ten children and she's pregnant?"

Ruth looked at me, and there was that *oh, I had forgotten all about you* expression on her face.

But she recovered. "Why, yes, that is what I said. Emilene is my only daughter and my oldest. She is due to have her eleventh and twelfth in about a month now."

Rebecca was watching me carefully, and even Sarah and Rachel had stalled their labors to listen.

"How old is your daughter?" My brain just couldn't comprehend that many kids coming out of one woman. Mrs. Miller had blown my mind with eight kids.

"Oh, let's see, Emy will be forty-three in a few months."

"Does she live here in this community?"

"Our church split about a year ago. She's part of our greater community, but she lives just a few miles away, over the line to the North Road Church community."

I couldn't stop myself, I was on a roll now, and after answering all of Ruth and Martha's questions about my home life, I figured it was high time I got a few in myself. "Why would your church split?" I was envisioning all sorts of nastiness.

My question seemed to please Ruth, who smiled and motioned me to take the seat beside her. I glanced at Sarah, who nodded her head toward the chair, pushing me lightly with her free hand.

"When our churches are blessed, growing very large, they are split, usually separated by a boundary such as a road or small town," Ruth said once I was seated.

Rebecca added, "You see, we don't want to have too many families within one church since our services are held in our homes. Most Amish can only handle a gathering of about, oh, fifteen to twenty family groups, before it becomes too crowded."

Crossing my arms on the table and leaning forward, I asked, "Does every family host the service at some point or do just a few families divvy it up?"

"Oh, each family within the church takes their turn," Rebecca went on, seeming to enjoy the flow of the conversation. "In our community, there are sixteen...or is it seventeen families?"

Here, Rebecca looked to Ruth who quickly nodded firmly, and said, "Seventeen. But with Jacob and Katie marrying in a few months and Lester and Barbara shortly after, our numbers will jump to nineteen right quick."

Oh, yeah, Ruth was proud of the fact that her community was successful.

"Ruth, you ought to know better than to be talking of the weddings," Rebecca scolded in a harsh whisper.

I felt as if I'd missed something, and I glanced at Sarah who had taken the seat beside me. She shrugged her shoulders nonchalantly at my questioning eyes. Rachel was less subtle, barking out a short laugh before plopping down in the seat beside her mom.

Ruth raised her tone a bit louder than I would have expected. "Land sakes, Rebecca, I didn't even think about it since Katie's been spouting her mouth for weeks."

Rebecca let out a huff, but nodded her head in agreement. "Yes, you're right. Katie has been overly excited about the news."

The remembrance that Katie, Ella's older sister, was marrying Noah's brother, Jacob, suddenly popped into my mind. I was definitely lost and couldn't help butting in again. "Why is it a big deal if Katie's been talking about her upcoming wedding?"

Ruth and Rebecca telepathically sized each other up as to who was going to answer me. Ruth won.

"Oh, my, there is so much for you to learn, my girl," she informed me. "It is our tradition to keep our engagements and the date of our weddings secret until a couple of months before the union."

"Why?"

Ruth stopped to think, then looked at Rebecca again who raised her shoulders lightly, but left the question to Ruth.

"It's just our way. There are many things about us that might not make sense to you, but there's no reason to question it if it can't be changed anyhow."

"Oh, Rose, our community is a lot better than some of the other churches where the bride and groom are given only a month to announce the big day," Rachel threw out, with the scrunched-up expression of distaste.

Unlike Sarah, who'd become my instant friend upon our first meeting, Rachel acted aloof around me. On the outside, the two girls looked nearly identical, except that Rachel's hair was a shade darker than Sarah's and she was an inch taller than her sister. Inwardly, though, Noah's sisters were very different. Sarah was shy, but when she did lift her face, it usually framed a wide smile. She was always helpful and polite to everyone. Rachel, on the other hand, was more reserved—or even grumpy. Thinking back on it, I couldn't recall ever seeing the younger girl sporting anything but the same droopy frown she had on now.

"When I was married to your da that's how it was. My poor mam was in such a state trying to keep my brothers and your papaw's mouths tight." Mrs. Miller shook her head, smiling when she added, "Right glad that we don't have to wait to such a late date to make the announcement now."

"It was so long ago I can't remember, but I reckon I only had a few weeks to openly make plans myself," Ruth said, turning her attention back to me. "Have you ever been to an Amish wedding, Rose?"

"Can't say that I have," I told her.

"Our weddings are huge events, sometimes with over five hundred guests attending. Rebecca, what about Katie and Jacob, how many do they intend to invite?"

"I think the list is at four hundred and fifty-five right now."

"Four seventy-two," Sarah piped up.

"Oh, my, Bessie will have her hands full," Rebecca said.

As the conversation moved to the details of Katie's choice of server gifts, dishware and pies, I decided that I couldn't recall a time when I ever sat for so long with a group of women. Even when my mom was alive, and we'd be at Aunt Debbie's for a visit or holiday gathering, there would always be a guy around or the TV would be on or we'd be driving somewhere. To actually sit down and talk like this was unique—and nice, in a way.

My mind drifted, and I couldn't help but wonder what Mom would have thought about these new women in my life. Somehow, I knew that she'd like them both. But whether she'd be okay with me becoming one of them was another story altogether. When I thought too much about it, my heart tightened—Mom wouldn't like it one bit.

A loud sniff at the doorway turned all our heads. Butterflies fluttered in my belly at the sight of Noah leaning against the door frame. He didn't look at me, though, directing all his attention to his mom instead.

"Noah, you best wait outside," Rebecca said flatly. Her quick look to Sarah and Rachel had them up in a hurry, heading for the door.

Noah lingered for a few seconds after his sisters had slid by him. His eyes *finally* met mine, and they were round with anticipation before he disappeared out the door.

"Rose, dear, I must tell you that Amos and I were unaware of Abram's intended visit today. Else, I would have prepared you ahead of time."

When my eyes skipped to Ruth inadvertently, she said quickly, "Or I, child. James was as surprised as the rest of us to see them heading up our drive. It was a shame that you had barely stepped a foot in the kitchen when that whole business was thrown at you."

The tone of the women's voices had lowered, probably unconsciously, as if they worried that they were being listened to. The change of atmosphere was tangible, and I straightened up in my chair, leaning in closer so they could drop their voices further.

After a deep breath, Rebecca said, "It was Amos's and my intention that you would join the church swiftly, followed closely by your courtship to Noah." Here she hesitated, looking to Ruth for support. Ruth's nod and firm face gave Rebecca the courage to go on. "Ruth and James are also in support of you and Noah moving forward."

Ruth interrupted, "I see no reason that the two of you should not claim each other now. Humph, it seems to me that having you unattached in our community is more trouble in the pot. But then again, nobody asked my opinion on the matter."

Ruth was obviously irritated, showing more emotion than I'd seen from her all day as she continued to press the tablecloth flat under her fingers until the material looked a lighter shade of blue.

I waited, not wanting to do anything that would sidetrack the women from what they wanted to say to me. Somehow, I knew it was important.

Rebecca was the one to continue. "Marcus Bontrager, although a kind man, lacks spirit and would not stand up to Abram on any count. And...Mervin Weaver is firmly on Abram's side in the matter." She didn't need to clarify the reason on that one.

Ruth showed her impatient nature by cutting to the chase. "What Rebecca is saying is that the issue of you joining our church is not up to us. You *must* convince Abram...and the rest of the community to allow you to do so in order for it to happen. And frankly, my dear, you need to be quick about it."

"How do I do that?"

"You must behave yourself, Rose. I'm sure it's hard for your young eyes to imagine looking at my aged body now, but I was once soft and vibrant like you. And in those days I could hardly keep my hands off James." Catching my widened eyes, Ruth laughed at my expression. "But of course, I did keep my hands off him...for the most part anyhow. What I'm trying to impress on you is that Rebecca and I understand how difficult it will be for you to sit back and watch Noah from afar. But if you are good, obedient and chaste, then Abram and the rest of our people will have no choice but to allow you to join with us and thus begin your life with Noah."

"What about Mr. Weaver—will he accept me?" my body tensed, waiting.

"Oh, it won't matter what he wants if you get Abram on your side. Along with my James and Amos, it will be settled. The other families will follow their lead...trust me on that."

Ruth captured my eyes. Not letting me look away, she said severely, "But if you stir things up in any way, child, that will the end of it." Then she breathed in deeply, and I could tell she was playing with some serious thoughts in her head. "And another bit of advice you'd best heed, my dear, is to be careful around Martha Lambright."

My face must have lit with confusion if her hasty follow-up was any indication. "Now, Rose, this is not something you need be talking about to anyone, especially the other girls. It's just a fair warning that a pretty smile isn't always a sincere one."

Rebecca was uncomfortable with the territory the pep talk had gone into, and she took both my hands softly between hers. "I'm sure you'll do fine. But, please, please be good." There was almost a look of desperation on her face.

What was her angle? Was she worried, if I got kicked out of the community, that Noah would go with me—and what about the warning from Ruth about Martha? Could my initial instinct about the woman be so wrong? Martha had clearly been on my side during the laying down of the law by the bishop. I decided to file away Ruth's words to be on the safe side. But, I wasn't going to count Martha as an enemy until she proved to be one.

"Noah looked like he wanted something—what was his deal?" I asked his mom, a little worried about what she'd say.

"Oh, yes...well, he wants to have a few minutes alone with you to discuss this matter. Really, it's mine and Amos's fault that we allowed him such free rein immediately after the accident—calling you on the telephone and behaving as if the two of you were already courting. Now, though, things must be different."

"Can I spend any time with him at all?" I hoped I didn't sound as if I was whining, but the thought of being separated from him while I was learning to be Amish was almost too much to bear.

Before Rebecca could say a word, Ruth took over. "It's not only up to Rebecca and Amos. Now that you're under mine and James's authority, you'll be looking to us about the rules you must live under in this household, which are the Church's Ordnung, but not solely."

I slouched down in my seat. I knew a parental lockdown when I saw one coming. Only, I also knew that Ruth wouldn't be as easy to manipulate as Dad was. I adjusted my voice to sound resigned, I needed both these women on my side.

"What are the rules?"

"After this evening you will not be allowed to spend time alone with Noah unless there is a chaperone present." And for good measure, Ruth added, "And the two of you will not be acting like a couple, either. That is exactly the kind of thing that will get Abram's beard in a tangle."

My optimistic personality chose to hear only the part about *after this evening.* "Do you mean I get to talk to Noah, tonight—in private?"

Rebecca answered, "Yes, but only tonight, until you're officially a courting couple. Ruth and I understand how things have changed suddenly from what you were prepared for, and we feel it is best to let you do your talking with Noah now. Hopefully, this will keep you from mischief later." She held my eyes for a significant few seconds before pushing her chair out.

"I do believe Noah is waiting on the front porch for you." Rebecca pointed toward the hallway. "We'll be out back on the porch."

I caught Ruth's wink from behind her glasses as she walked by. One second of solitude and I was sprinting down the hallway.

I didn't even have to touch the knob, for Noah had the door open just as I reached it. We stood a few feet apart, both breathing deeply and both waiting.

Maybe it was the dress and cap I wore that suddenly made me feel as though I really was an Amish girl. Or perhaps it was Noah's eyes, wide with anticipation that raised the tingling waves of nervousness from my belly.

For the first time in a long while, I didn't know what to do with Noah.

2

Noah

As soon as she walked through the door, her lovely scent hit me—the familiar smell of warm lavender. My heart thumped, excitement coursing through my body, making me almost too weak to stand proper.

Under normal conditions, feeling this weak would make me think I was ill, perhaps with the flu, but Rose making me feel like this was all right, wonderful, to be exact.

She looked anxiously at me, rocking softly on her feet, unsure of what to do. Was it the talk with the Elders that was holding her back? Seeing her tug her dress down from her waist with an annoyed expression briefly lighting her face, I decided that it was probably the unfamiliar dress causing her shyness. I couldn't keep the smile from pulling at the sides of my mouth.

Even though my mind was swimming with questions about the meeting, my body wanted only one thing. I stepped forward, pulling Rose into my chest. I bent down, burying my face in her sweet-smelling skin. I couldn't help it; even though I should have been more careful, I nuzzled the curve of her neck, feeling her warm pulse flutter under my lips. I breathed her into my soul.

Rose was perfectly content like that; me holding her tightly on the front porch, open for the whole world to see. After a minute or so, sanity regained hold of my mind, though.

The last thing she needed was to be seen hugging me so romantically.

I disengaged from her glorious arms but didn't release her hand. I pulled her over to the porch swing and down beside me. Feeling on edge and fighting my body's desire to press her against me again, I began pumping the swing vigorously with my legs until we were moving back and forth briskly.

"Gosh, Noah, if you don't tone it down, we're going to be airborne in no time at all."

Rose sniffed and grinned at me. She was so beautiful it made my heart ache.

I resisted grabbing her up again, although that's what I wanted to do more than anything in the world. Looking at her face, I was once again amazed at her beauty. I knew that beneath the cap were long, brown locks that were soft and sweet-smelling, but even with her luxurious hair hidden from me, her face still took my breath away. Her skin was smooth and her cheeks were always slightly flushed. The small nose and wide mouth reminded me of the girls I'd seen on the magazine covers at the grocery—but it was her eyes that made her truly striking. They were large, and the lightest blue—the color of a robin's egg.

Even more than her beautiful face, the playful tilt of her lips and the fiery sparkle in her eyes tightened my insides.

Glancing away, I took a breath of air in an attempt to gather my wits and calm the hot desire that pushed through my veins at the sight of her. "Sorry about that. I've just been a wreck all afternoon worrying about you." I smiled and risked a sidelong look before continuing, "Guess I'm still on edge."

The puppy, Hope, appeared at our feet and whined, staring up at us. Rose reached down and gathered the squirming fluff into her arms. Once she had the puppy settled onto her lap, she looked up at me.

She held my eyes in a serious gaze. The look was out of place on her usual flirtatious face.

"Yeah, I bet you were worried—it was pretty intense."

I leaned into her, deciding it was better to get caught sitting too close to her than to be overheard saying something we shouldn't be saying. "What happened?"

"I was thoroughly warned to keep my paws off of you until I'm allowed to join the church, for starters," she said with a twinge of resentment, but not as much as I would have expected.

"Mother was so upset when she saw what was going on. Bishop Lambright picked Father up from his worksite and brought him directly here."

"Seems like a whole lot of inconvenience for several grown men on a work day—and all for little old me." Rose sighed, a hint of a smile playing along her lips. Her eyes were shining, showing the spunk that I was accustomed to.

I loved that reckless spirit, but it also scared the hell out of me. Rose might look the part of the obedient Amish girl in her new getup, but I knew that under the material she was still a plucky English girl.

Letting my eyes wander over her beautiful face, the bright blue eyes, arched brows and high cheekbones, I realized that I would love this girl forever, whether she was difficult or not. It was her wildness that was most endearing to me of all.

"My family expected there to be a meeting in the next week or so—maybe a dinner together or a visit around the neighborhood to make introductions. Not this kind of ambush. Father was furious. He'd already spoken to the others and thought matters were set." I stared at the road, expecting to see the bishop's buggy appear from around the bend at any moment.

"So, uh, doesn't your dad get to make the decisions around here?"

Her small hand clamped between my bigger ones made Rose seem unusually vulnerable. I wished that I could tell her that my folks had some say about her future, but they didn't. Unless they got others to side with them…and it went to a church vote. That was the last thing in the world we needed. Way too unpredictable. But I didn't want to get Rose more riled up than she already was by filling her in about all that.

"No, Father can't make the decision on his own to allow you into the Church. That will be decided by the bishop, ministers and the deacon."

Confusion flashed across her face.

"Who's the deacon?"

"Marcus Bontrager. He's only been in the position for a few months. You see, he's taking over the job for James Hershberger, and he certainly doesn't want to ruffle any feathers so early on."

While I was talking I could see that as her fingers stroked Hope, Rose's mind was working on things.

"What does he do?" she whispered, having caught on early about the need to keep certain conversations secret.

"Oh, I don't know everything, except for the main job. That's to be a messenger of sorts."

By the pursing of her lips and raised eyebrows I could see that she was not getting me.

"Marcus is the fellow that will go to a family's home if there are any problems that need dealt with. He'll talk with them about it, maybe dish out some advice, and then report back to the bishop and other ministers."

"So let me see if I got this straight. Bishop Lambright is the head honcho, and if he says that I can join the church, then it's okay…right?"

If it were only that simple I wouldn't be so worried, but Rose didn't need to feel my anxiety. I lied, "Yeah, for the most part." Even I didn't understand all the technicalities of the process.

Still leaning in to me, Rose glanced around to be sure that we were alone. I could hear the kids playing in the distance, and softly, the voices of the older folk were carrying to my ears also. Hopefully, we had enough time to talk everything out thoroughly, but I highly doubted it.

"What if the bishop won't have me—then what?"

Her voice had the sound of solid resolve that gave me hope that she'd be willing to do anything to make it work out. "If Abram supports you joining, then the rest of the community will go along with it, but if he's against the idea, then Father, James, Marcus and Mervin could go against him, and you could still be allowed. But really, we can't trust how that would go. Marcus is just not the type of guy to stand up for something that might get him into hot water, and then there's Mervin…"

"Yup, I know. Miss-spoiled-rotten-Ella's daddy probably isn't too happy that you picked a heathen over his perfect little daughter."

The way she said it, all jealous and uptight, made me smile. She was adorable. Here she was the prettiest girl I'd ever seen, and she felt threatened by a cold fish like Ella Weaver.

"Yeah, you get the idea."

"But if your dad and Mr. Hershberger sided with us, and Marcus abstained, then we'd be tied," she said, sounding all hopeful and cheery about it. She had no idea what she was saying, she didn't know what she was dealing with.

"Ahh, look, I don't know about the abstained thing, but

the best situation all around is if Abram just goes along with it. I don't think anyone, except Mervin, will give us a hard time otherwise. And he's only one minister."

While Rose was mulling over what I said, I started to think how I didn't want to spend the entire time I had alone with her talking about the problems we still faced. I was worn out from the mess and wanted nothing more than to forget it for a little while.

"So, it's up to me to be a good girl and win the crusty old bishop over, huh?"

Rose fluttered her eyes a bit and turned the side of her mouth up into a smile. I started to forget everything.

The hell with everyone; I caught that crooked smile in my mouth, pushing her lips apart with my tongue.

She pushed closer into me, her mouth working against mine hungrily for a blissful moment. But too short a time, before she wrenched away from me looking around with a guilty face. And here I was worried about her behavior. Rose was the one with some sense that evening.

"Noah, really, we need to be more careful about stuff like that."

The worried look on her face transformed into satisfaction that we hadn't been spotted, and she settled herself back against my chest and under my arm. She understood that we *couldn't* be caught kissing, but she didn't seem to get it that sitting this cozily would get us into a heap of trouble also.

I didn't have the heart…or the willingness…to separate from her, though. Into her hair I murmured, "It'll all work out. We just have to be patient a while longer, that's all."

I only half believed it myself.

3

Rose

My heart skipped against my chest as I stared out the back window trying to tell who was in the buggy following us. All I could see was a black hat, the glazed pale shadow of a face and a bushy beard beside an equally hazy woman with a white cap and dark-colored dress. Maybe she had glasses on; I wasn't sure. Leaning back on the green stiff-as-a-board cushion, I sighed out irritably. It probably wasn't Noah's family. With all the Amish people in the community whisking along on their way to Sunday church service, the chances of Noah getting behind us were slim at best.

"Is everything all right, Rose?" Ruth asked pleasantly.

The woman was way too perceptive for her own good.

Mr. Hershberger, whom I hadn't been invited to address by his first name, was in front of me, only inches away, in fact, and I could smell the faint scent of his pine-scented cologne.

Who would have thought that old Amish men would try to make themselves smell nice?

"Oh, nothing, I guess," I answered as I fidgeted with my hands. I held them closer to my face to examine the rough, dry skin. They were certainly clean, though.

Out of all the work I'd done that week, the laundry was the

worst. And I only had to care for the clothes of three people; I could only imagine what it was like for poor Sarah and Rachel. But then, they did that chore together, so maybe it wasn't so bad.

My adventures with the laundry had started with Ruth showing me in animated detail how to separate the colors and types of clothes. I'd made a pile of Mr. Hershberger's pants, a pile of dresses, another for whites and the last for towels.

That was the easy part.

I had been fascinated at first with the large old-fashioned washer that was set up in Ruth's basement corner. There were two white tubs beside the washer, all neatly organized to be as efficient as any woman could put together. Ruth had filled the washer with almost scalding-hot water and the other two with cold water—one for the fabric softener and the other for rinse.

She'd done most of the talking early on before she'd turned on the incredibly loud generator, which started the spinner in the washer. At that point, seeing the washer was power-generated, I thought the project wouldn't be difficult. I quickly learned differently. My first rude awakening had come when Ruth told me to fish one of the pants out of the sudsy water— with my hands. The water had been so hot I'd had to snatch one up quickly. Gingerly, I'd held the sopping-wet material in both hands and looked at Ruth expectantly. She'd impatiently taken the pants from me and squeezed the excess water from the material with her own strong hands. I'd watched in horror as she'd worked with the pants until they were still dripping wet, but not as much.

Then she'd shown me how to feed the pants through the antique-looking ringer that was above the washer. After I'd asked, she'd informed me that the washer was actually only about twenty years old—a specially built one that Mr. Hershberger had put together for her.

Mr. Hershberger hadn't worked all the kinks out of his invention in all those years, and the ringer, which should have sucked the pants in and spit them out in no time at all, decided to eat them instead.

That's what it felt like, anyway, as I'd tugged on the legs, trying to free them from the clamp. With Ruth's help I'd managed to get the pants, but not without a torn crotch. My foster mom had explained to me that it was usual for such things to happen and that I'd have the opportunity to do some mending. Up until that moment in my life, I had never really known what the term *mending* meant. Now, I knew.

After the clothes had gone through the ringer, they then had to go into the tub with the fabric softener and then into the rinse water—all by hand. Not only had my fingers been dried out, but my muscles were still aching from the exertion of manually squishing the water from the clothes.

In all, we had done ten loads, an "easy day" I was told, but it still had taken over two hours to complete. My dress had been soaked through by the time the last pair of socks was hanging on the line.

Although Ruth had seemed impatient with me when I'd balked at putting my hands in the wash water after she'd added the bleach, she'd praised me in the end for my hard work. She'd also informed me that I'd be in charge of the laundry from then on. I couldn't help but slouch down on the seat in defeat at the thought of doing it all again on Monday.

Ruth pulled my mind back into the buggy when she asked, "Rose, how long did you tell me it usually took you to do a load of laundry?"

Funny question, considering where my thoughts had been.

"Ah, a few minutes of actual work time. You know, I didn't have to stand around and wait on the washer and dryer while they did their thing. I was free to go do other stuff...."

I trailed off, not wanting to sound as if I was bragging. But, really, in hindsight I now felt pretty dumb complaining to Dad when he'd ask me to do the chore at home.

"Can you imagine that, James? I wouldn't know what to do with myself if I had that much extra time on my hands," Ruth spoke with a laughing bark at the end.

"That's right. You'd be bored with nothing much to do, and then what, eh? You'd get yourself into trouble." Mr. Hershberger's voice was kind and gentle—the type of man you couldn't imagine yelling, but what he'd said made me want to punch him just the same.

"I doubt that. I would just spend more time in the garden or cleaning...or cooking up some of your favorite recipes, I would." Ruth snorted.

Mr. Hershberger chuckled, patting Ruth's hand. "Whatever you say, Ma."

As we slowed to a walk and turned onto the winding driveway that led down from the road, I leaned forward between James and Ruth to get a better look. I caught Ruth's amused expression for a second before I focused my eyesight on the place that came into view.

Church was being held at none other than the creepy Levi Zook's farm. I had passionately told Ruth about what I thought of him when I'd learned where we were going. She'd laughed at me and agreed wholeheartedly that Levi was a rebel of sorts, getting into mischief time and again, but hardly the crooked boy I saw him as. She was entitled to her opinion—and so was I. I knew Levi was in a whole different league of rebel, especially after the way he'd galloped off to tattle on Noah to Mr. Miller when he'd seen us kissing in the field.

Anger still bubbled within me when I pictured Levi's smirking, pale face on that stormy afternoon, and his slippery voice making the suggestion to Noah that if he shared me, Levi would forget what he saw that day. He hadn't been kidding, either. I sighed deeply, saying a silent thank-you to the universe that Levi hadn't gotten his way.

We bounced along on the gravel between a stand of tall, neatly placed trees before the scenery opened up again to expose grassy hills surrounding a small homestead. I had to admit I was surprised by the sight that greeted me. The farm's home was smaller than the other Amish houses I'd seen, but what it lacked in size it made up for in cuteness. The house was gingerbread-like, with intricate woodwork designs along the top of the porch. Above the porch was a triangle roofline pointing to sky that was decorated in hunter green, matching the rest of the trim. There were a few flower beds here and there in front of the home, but nowhere near the blooming display that many of the Amish seemed to go for. Then again, the place really didn't need any help being pretty. The natural lay of the land and adorable old house was enough to do the trick.

I wasn't expecting the demon boy to live in such a place—just proving that Ruth was right when she'd warned me that looks could be deceiving.

"Pretty place, don't you agree, Rose?"

"Uh-huh," I mumbled out.

We continued on past the house heading to the large gambrel barn at the base of one of the hills. The barn wasn't painted, but not a board was popped out or rotten.

I really wanted to go with Mr. Hershberger to help take the harness off Dolly and put her in the barn with the other horses, but as usual, I was ushered away by Ruth to spend time with the women. Even though it was still early in the morning, sweat was rising to the surface of my skin under the dark maroon dress that I wore. It was a present from Ruth, a more formal outfit befitting church service. To me it looked about the same as my blue one, only this dress had an extra covering of cloth over my upper body. No chance of anyone checking out my boobs.

I followed Ruth past the parked buggies that filled the yard as if it were an old-fashioned parking lot. The day was warm, and already the sun was burning off the morning cloud cover, peeking out softly from its dewy cloak. Still, even with the perfect weather conditions, the rain from the night before was causing the buggy highway to turn to a yucky mixture of sticky brown mush and pebbles. I took light steps close behind Ruth while I held my dress up out of the mud.

I watched where my feet went, trying not to get my black Nikes too caked up and at the same time attempting to keep as low a profile as I could—another first for me. I usually enjoyed making an entrance, but not today. I figured that the less anyone noticed me, the better—especially Mr. Bishop. I definitely didn't want to be attracting his attention.

I still felt the eyes on me, though. Like—*all the eyes.* And it wasn't just my imagination, either. When I'd glance up, I'd catch old women, young guys, middle-aged men and their wives staring.

Even the toddlers sensed that there was an intruder in their midst, stopping to gawk at me as I sloshed past them. How anyone could tell that I wasn't Amish when I was dressed identically to the rest of the girls milling about was anyone's guess. Was it that I was with Ruth, and they knew that she'd taken me in? Or maybe they were all so tight genetically that they could automatically pick out an imposter in their midst.

Whatever the reason, I was noticed by everyone—and they were incredibly solemn. No boisterous greetings flying around the yard, and no kids acting like kids. I was inwardly relieved that everyone was wearing shoes. When I first squished down in the muck I envisioned being surrounded by nasty feet. I didn't know if shoes were required for church or if the icky conditions restrained the kids and girls.

Ruth nodded and said a few unknown words as we converged into a larger stream of women making their way toward a glorified garage-looking building near Hansel and Gretel's house. I let go of the smirk that must have appeared on my mouth as the thought slipped through my mind. That cute cottage must have a witch inside that birthed Levi.

An irrational chill swept through me when I thought his name. I picked my head up and scanned the crowd, ignoring the eyes that were locked on me. Pretty much when I'd return the stare with any of the Amish people, they'd immediately look away.

I guessed I could win all the staring contests with everyone in attendance—except *him*. When my eyes met the evil carrot-top himself, I was the one to glance away quickly, nearly stumbling into Ruth who'd stopped in front of me for a second before continuing onward again.

I took a long steady breath and didn't look back in the direction of where I'd spotted him staring at me. He'd been surrounded by what appeared to be all the men and teenage boys of the community hanging around the front of the makeshift church. Unfortunately, in the seconds that my eyes had scanned the crowd of beards, I hadn't seen any of the Miller men.

Apprehension spread through me as we approached the men. At that moment, they seemed more closely related to aliens than human beings. Some of the men were talking quietly to each other, but the majority of them were just standing there, saying nothing, doing nothing.

The women, on the other hand, moved with single-minded determination toward and into the white building. I should have just kept my head down, but, no; I couldn't do that, because I needed to see Noah, needed to feel his reassuring gaze on me. Ignoring the guys, I searched for Noah in the crowd.

I wasn't surprised to receive a hard look from Mervin Weaver when my eyes passed over him, but I didn't pause to give him fuel for his witch pyre. Instead, I quickly broke contact and dropped my gaze right before entering the dim light of the building.

I took a few seconds to quickly size up the dynamics before me. There were two sections of benches set up facing a dark, wooden wall that lacked any windows. Besides the benches, a line of tables on one side of the room and the throng of women, the space was empty.

Of course, all the girls and women, young and old alike, were seating themselves together on what I assumed was the girls' side. I dutifully followed my guardian to the middle of the benches where she seated herself close beside a gray-haired lady I didn't know. Still there were no introductions. I basically felt as if I were Ruth's unwanted shadow, but I wouldn't have complained about her behavior. I was glad to quietly observe the weirdness around me.

While I was mouthing O's to the wide-eyed baby a few feet away who was resting on her mama's shoulder, I got a big bump on my open side, causing me to swivel quickly. My irritation disappeared instantly when I saw Suzanna's bright smile. The blond Amish girl had struck me as being feistier than the other girls the first time I'd met her at the singing that seemed so long ago now. She'd definitely left an impression on me, and as she squeezed onto the bench, pushing me closer into Ruth's soft plumpness, I sighed out happily that she was there.

"Hey, Rose—fancy meeting you here." She winked at me, and much of the strangeness of the day disappeared.

"Hey, it's good to see you again," I said.

Suzanna whispered back, but I worried that her enthusiasm was bringing her voice up to an unacceptable level, "Do you know what you're in for, girl?"

"What do you mean?"

"Our church services are like, almost three hours long," Suzanna informed me gravely.

"Yeah, I'm kind of prepared." I brought my lips to Suzanna's ear. "Ruth warned me that Bishop Lambright tends to ramble."

"Oh, that's putting it mildly." She giggled. "But it'll be even worse for you, 'cause you don't even understand our language."

I was pretty good at daydreaming, especially these days with Noah on my mind, but I didn't tell Suzanna that. Instead, I whispered back, "Hopefully, I'll pick some words up in time."

"Hey, maybe I could teach you," Suzanna exclaimed, again her excitement getting away from her.

But I was so happy for the offer that I thanked her and said, "I already asked Ruth about a language book I could study."

Suzanna grinned, "What did she say to that?"

"She laughed at me and said that there weren't any such books. She told me that you all learn the language from your families when you're babes, and you start speaking English when you go to school in first grade."

"Yeah, I've never heard of any Pennsylvania German language books." Again she laughed softly, totally amused by the conversation. A wisp of blondish-white hair escaped from her cap, and she blew it out of her eye.

The mousy china doll face peeking around Suzanna's shoulder caught my attention. I hadn't even noticed the girl before. Her skin was pale, as if she'd just arrived from a faraway northern place that hadn't seen the sun in a while. I immediately noticed her teeth were darkish and shrunken.

She had rotten teeth. I quickly moved my eyes away from her teeth, not wanting to stare rudely, only to be trapped by the darkest set of sad brown eyes I'd ever seen. I was immediately overcome with emotion toward the girl. Was it pity? Maybe a little, but also an instant fondness and protectiveness swelled within me for her, too.

"This is my best friend, Miranda Zook." Suzanna pointed cheerfully at the little sparrow sitting beside her. Miranda at first glance appeared to be twelve or thirteen, but now, really looking at her again, she probably was the same age as me and Suzanna. I could barely make out the bumps beneath her sky-blue dress indicating a full-fledged teen girl. And those haunting eyes again—they looked old and tired.

"This is the crazy English girl I've been telling you all about, Mira." Suzanna grabbed my shoulder, squeezing and pushing me slightly at the same time.

I ignored the *crazy* comment and said, "I don't believe I've seen you before, Miranda."

"Oh, that's 'cause she's been...ah, living away for a time," Suzanna said in a subdued way, actually trying to think about her words before she released them, causing my curiosity to spike.

I had to know where *away* was, but before I got a chance to interrogate the poor girl, a bustle at the door tore my attention away.

While I was in the conversation with Suzanna, I hadn't realized that all the women and girls were now quietly seated around me. The side of the building was packed full, with most of the women's shoulders rubbing. There was almost no sound except the thump, thumps of the men's feet on the floor as they came through the doorway.

The sight of all the darkly dressed men with their black hats entering in an orderly fashion and taking their seats on the side opposite from the women was impressive—and downright bizarre.

Most of the women looked straight ahead, ignoring the men,

but Suzanna, along with myself and a few of the other young women, were watching the guys make their grand entrance. Miranda wasn't, though. She was staring straight ahead, like a frozen statue. My glance skipped over the men, up and down, back and forth. It was difficult to recognize one plain-clothed man from another, especially with all the bushy beards in the mix. Finally, I spotted Jacob, right behind Amos. My heart thudded hard until Noah came into sight and then almost stopped when his eyes met mine.

He had been searching for me, too.

The sixty or so men took no time at all situating themselves on their benches, and just as the last butt was getting as comfortable as it possibly could on the hard wooden bench, Bishop Lambright appeared in front of the congregation.

I had to give him credit—he had a natural sense for the dramatic. He stood still, yet appeared relaxed. He surveyed his tribe carefully with his focused eyes. I was sure he was imprinting to memory who was in attendance...and who wasn't. His face didn't alter its expression as he gazed briefly at every face in the crowd, even when his eyes slid over me. I didn't look away, but deep down I really wanted to slip under the bench.

When the bishop did speak, it was loud and steady. And in a language I couldn't understand. He wandered around the building while he talked, making sure that he paid attention to everyone, keeping them alert and awake. He was definitely not the type of preacher to tolerate snoozers while he had the podium.

I couldn't help it, maybe if I knew what the man was saying I'd have been able to stay in the room mentally, but my mind began to wander within minutes, lulled to another place by the drone of the bishop's voice.

I wondered what Sam and Justin were doing. Was Dad at

the hospital that morning or sipping his coffee over the news-
paper in the kitchen? It had only been a few days since I left
them, but it felt like much longer. I'd called Dad the first night
to tell him I was settled in and getting along with the Hershbergers. I didn't mention anything about the whole meeting
thing to him. I knew his game plan and he'd have liked nothing better than to hear I was being given a hard time straight
out of the gate.

Talking to him, even for a few moments, had made me feel
better, but it did bug me a little that he hadn't called me again.
Wasn't he going insane with curiosity over what I was doing?
Maybe not—perhaps Tina was keeping him so busy that he
really didn't even think about me.

I liked Dad's girlfriend now, really I did. Tina had been my
savior: the only reason that I had this opportunity to be with
Noah was because of her advice to Dad. Even now, I could
hardly believe that he'd listened to her at all.

But my doubts remained. What was Dad thinking? Oh,
yeah, he thought that I'd be running home in a week or two,
begging for my old life back.

I did miss that life: my brothers, even dopey Sam; my computer; and especially my phone. I didn't watch TV that much,
but it was comforting to know that the thing was there in the
family room, waiting to be turned on and stared at on a boring evening. I'd never get my license, either, which was the
worst part. And music...the sweet sounds floating to my ears
were gone, too.

But all of that wasn't really important to me. After almost
losing Noah, I knew that the one thing I couldn't live without
was *him*. I glanced over to the men's side, letting my eyes linger over the back of his luscious head. In the quiet dreariness
of the building I couldn't see his bronze highlights, but the
thick dark brown hair was in its usual untidy state. I wanted

to run my fingers through the strands, and I daydreamed for a quite a while about doing other things to Noah while the bishop made his laps around the church.

The rustling of movement and the shoving of something into my hand brought me back to the boring reality. Suzanna had handed me a book that said *Ausbund* on the front cover. Quickly, I flipped through the pages and my instant suspicions were correct: it was in a foreign language, of course. Ruth pointed to the number on the bottom of the page of her own, and I did the best I could to fake it through the sad, lonely sounding song.

There was no beat or tempo, just the unexciting harmonizing of the men and women. There were some interesting variations when just the men would sing a part, then the women, followed by everyone. How they knew what to do and when with their voices, I had no clue.

After the tune ended, there was a procession of ministers talking, more songs and even a couple of times where we got down on the floor, kneeling to the benches. I didn't understand the rhyme or reason to it all, but they all knew the drill.

I had to admit that none of the other ministers were nearly as commanding as Bishop Lambright was. Mervin Weaver stayed rooted in one place, speaking almost too softly to be heard at all. Regardless of the language barrier, he would have been a hard one to stay glued on.

I saw that several of the old men on the other side and even a few of the women in my sight had heads that were dropped, chins resting on their collar bones. *They were asleep.* The bishop never would have tolerated that, I was sure.

Amos did all right, shifting around the room a bit and speaking in a firmer voice, but poor Mr. Bontrager was a nervous wreck. I felt sorry for the poor guy; he wasn't a born speaker, that's for sure.

This all went on for an excruciatingly long period of time. My butt was sore, my back was aching and no matter which way I turned or leaned or shifted, I was assaulted with little pains.

Surely, it must be almost over, my mind screamed. If Ruth had allowed me to wear my little black watch I'd have had a clue to how much more torture I'd have to endure. But watches weren't allowed.

I always used my phone for the time, and already knowing that cell phones weren't permitted, I'd packed the most inconspicuous watch I could find in my drawer. Ruth had caught me just before I went out the door that morning, informing me that I couldn't wear watches or jewelry of any kind.

"But how am I supposed to know what time it is?" I had complained.

Her answer was simply that, "You don't need to know—things happen in their own good time, and since you can't control the flow, anyway, you shouldn't care about it."

My mind had gone blank. What could I have possibly have said to the woman? In some warped backward way, she was correct, but it still made no sense at all. I had just kept my mouth shut and taken the watch off my wrist, dropping it into Ruth's waiting hand. What she did with it I had no idea.

The service went on and on and on. Bishop Lambright took up the reins again, waking all the weak souls who had drifted away to slumber land. The songs were all so similar that I didn't even need to change the page, although Ruth continued to guide me with the hymnal by pointing to her numbers briefly, then forgetting about me again.

I had to give Suzanna credit: she sat still as stone beside me, not slipping up and trying to whisper to me through the agonizing minutes that just kept going. I had to pee so badly by the end that I had to tightly cross my legs. Even though many of the women with babies or young children would get up and leave for a few minutes, returning after the crying stopped or the bathroom break was over, I just couldn't bring myself to get up and walk out in front of everyone.

As I observed the comings and goings of only the women with babies or small children thoughtfully, it seemed to me that unless I grabbed the sleeping baby from the shoulder in front of me, I would have stuck out like a sore thumb making an exit to the bathrooms, wherever they might have been.

It was also becoming stuffy in the room, what with all the overdressed bodies squeezed in together as the sun was climbing higher into the sky. Body odor and nasty cologne smell drifted to my nostrils, putting the icing on the cake for my first Amish church experience.

I would have been able to handle an hour—or maybe even two—with no problem at all, but I was sure it was now pushing three hours that I'd sat on the torture bench, wedged in between Ruth and Suzanna.

Just when I thought I couldn't take a minute more, the song ended and everyone began to move around. Unlike the singing I had been to, there was no jumping up and running for the door this time. Everyone quietly handed their books down the line and leisurely rose from their seats.

My first order of business was to find the nearest bathroom. As far as I was concerned, even Noah could wait until I accomplished the task, but Ruth had other ideas. In her mind, the acceptable time to introduce me to the neighbors had arrived.

I stood uncomfortably for several more minutes while I met Iva, Mary Jane, Lilith and a few more whose names glazed across my mind only to be instantly forgotten. Some of the ladies were reserved, and some were friendly in a curious sort of way. They all were carbon copies of each other in dress, manner and speech.

I couldn't take it any longer. "I'm sorry, Ruth, but, ah, I need to go to the bathroom. Could you point the way?"

"I'll take her," Suzanna piped up behind me at the same time she grabbed my arm, pulling me away from the group of women that reminded me of a gathering of hens in a coop. Suzanna waited just the second it took Ruth to nod her blessing and mumble something in German before she turned and headed for the door.

I caught a glimpse of Miranda following behind us, but I didn't turn her way. I was too busy searching for Noah as we broke through the shed opening into the bright midday sunshine. The light hurt my eyes, and I shielded them with my hand while wishing I'd brought sunglasses. Could I have worn them? I certainly didn't see anyone wearing any right then.

We turned the corner and proceeded up the wooden steps to the cottage house. Suzanna passed everyone in silence, intent on her mission to get me to the bathroom quickly. I was thankful when we cruised through the busy kitchen and turned another corner into the large bathroom.

To my surprise, both Suzanna and Miranda followed me in.

Before I could protest, Suzanna was at the mirror telling me she wouldn't look and Miranda was peeking through the corner of the blinds of the sole window.

Necessity won out over being prudish, and I did my business quickly. The second I was decent, Suzanna turned around. Leaning back against the vanity, she said, "So how'd you enjoy that experience?" Her voice was dripping with sarcasm, and I couldn't help but grin back at her.

Sarah was an instant friend, and I loved her dearly, but I felt drawn to Suzanna. Her wicked sense of humor and playfulness would be entertaining for sure.

I really wanted to be my blunt self while I had the chance. Deciding to be honest, I told her, "It totally sucked."

"Ha. I knew it," Suzanna breathed out excitedly. "Noah's a good-looking guy and all, but really, what are you thinking, subjecting yourself to all this when you don't even have to?" Her arms shot out exaggeratedly encircling the world.

Slightly defensive but still understanding exactly what she meant, I retorted, "Noah is worth it to me. And besides, it must get easier with time."

Seeing her amused expression, I glanced at Miranda who had turned from the window and shook her head softly.

"Right?" I asked slowly, dreading the answer.

"Nope, it doesn't. As a matter of fact, it gets worse and worse. But, I guess if you're bound and determined to do this to yourself, I'm not going to stop you." Suzanna took my hands and pulled me toward her before saying, "'Cause, after all, we're going to have so much fun together."

My conscience started to peck at me then. Perhaps Suzanna and I together would equal big-time trouble. This girl was the polar opposite of the obedient Sarah, and she even made moody Rachel seem subdued. But, seeing how thrilled she was, the spark shining in her bright blue eyes, I couldn't help but succumb to her charms.

Miranda moved into our bubble and whispered, "Why don't you invite Rose tonight?"

Suzanna's face lit up, and I got the feeling that something significant had just happened. Even though Suzanna may have been happy to invite me to whatever Miranda was talking about, she seemed genuinely grateful that Miranda had been the one to suggest it. Miranda was giving her blessing to Suzanna making me a part of their little gang.

Suzanna asked with flourish, "Rose, do you want to spend the night at my house after the singing tonight?"

"Ah, I don't know. I mean I'd love to and all, but I guess it's up to Ruth." Then a thought occurred to me. "So you have slumber parties?"

Suzanna laughed, "Of course, silly. Miranda comes over the most, but sometimes I'll have Maretta and Summer, too."

Miranda made a little huff noise that got my attention and Suzanna's. Something hidden passed between the girls. I remembered that Maretta was the friendly girl who'd said the silliest things, but the name *Summer* was new to me.

"Who's Summer?"

"Oh, trust me, you're going to like her," Suzanna assured me before shuffling me out of the bathroom on a mission to find Ruth and ask her permission.

My mind was racing as we sailed through the crowded kitchen filled with women, children and babies. I couldn't shake the feeling that hanging out with these two was going to be problematic for me. But I wasn't ready to toss them aside. I'd need to keep a level head, though, if my instincts were even close to being right.

Again the eyes were all on me, and I couldn't help but slow to a leisurely walk when Suzanna put on the brakes. A glance to the side proved my earlier reservations were right on when I saw the group of young men gathered by the side of the house, checking us out as we approached. I really wanted to hurry around the corner and not attract any more attention from the pack of hounds, especially when I judged that Noah wasn't with them, but Suzanna seemed to be taking extreme pleasure in the interest. Glancing at Miranda, I was shocked to see that she was also moving with purposeful slowness, her hips swaying beneath her dress that seemed a bit tighter than the rest of the frumpy smocks I'd seen so far.

I couldn't have been happier to get away from the hungry eyes and back into the shed.

My stomach growled, and I realized how hungry I was.

I forgot my stomach pretty quickly when I saw Noah again. He was leaning against the wall, flanked by his two buddies: Timothy, who I'd personally nicknamed Volleyball-Boy; and Matthew, whom I would probably be calling Bashful in my mind, because of his red, chubby cheeks.

Noah noticed me at the same second I spotted him, but he didn't approach. Instead, he raised his eyebrows and nodded his head in acknowledgment. His smirk made me think that he was imagining doing things to me that he shouldn't be. I continued to watch him over my shoulder, unable to let go of his eyes as Miranda guided me behind Suzanna with her hand on my shoulder.

"What's this now?" Ruth said, pulling my attention back to the mission.

"I was wondering, Mrs. Hershberger, if it would be fine with you for Rose to come over and stay the night at my place?"

Ruth's eyes narrowed at me, considering. "Would you like that?"

Happiness began to spread through me at the amicable tone to Ruth's voice. "I'd love to. I mean, if it's okay with you and Mr. Hershberger."

Ruth turned to Suzanna, pointing a pudgy finger at her. "It'll be fine with me, long as you—" she pointed at Miranda "—and you, keep it a quiet and well-behaved evening."

"Of course we will." Suzanna smiled big. Almost too big; I worriedly looked back at Ruth, thinking surely she'd see through the exaggerated smile.

"All right then, girls," Ruth added, "Suzanna, if you will be a sweet girl and take Rose under your wing this afternoon, I'd much appreciate it."

I was beginning to think that all the adults in my life were clueless.

Suzanna answered in a honeyed voice, "Of course I will."

Then we were turning and heading back out of the building once again. I looked forlornly at Noah who frowned when he saw that I was leaving so soon.

I found myself in the kitchen once again, only this time I chatted with Sarah and Katie as we filled water glasses. I felt safer by far with the two of them. They were what I imagined Amish girls should be like—all quiet and obedient. No rebellious thoughts or plans were in their timid minds that was for sure.

Suzanna and Miranda fell into work with the other girls, putting on their "good girl" disguises again. I couldn't help but wonder about them. They certainly seemed to have a wild side, but maybe my imagination was getting away with me.

Then Ella Weaver snaked in front of my vision, coming straight at me. Before I had a chance to turn and pretend I hadn't seen her, she was on me.

"Oh, hello again, ah, Rose, right?"

Ella's voice was level and well planned. I had no idea what she was up to, but I was bracing myself for pepper spray when I answered her. "Yeah, that's my name."

"Would you please help me carry the water to the tables?" Her voice oozed pleasantness, but I wasn't fooled. She probably had a knife under her lavender dress ready to slice into me when no one was looking. A girl just didn't get over losing the opportunity to be with a guy she liked that easily, especially a guy like Noah.

I hesitated for a few seconds, studying the oval face before me that held a frozen, perfect smile. Blowing out a breath softly, I decided to get it over with.

"Sure thing." I picked up the tray and carefully made my way past the other girls, ducking between the few stray moms who were supervising the preparation of lunch.

I wasn't surprised when Ella turned left instead of right, taking us around the corner of the house that was well away from the shed and barn. Adrenaline pumped through my veins, making me feel invincible. The smart part of my brain was being pushed back behind the possessive part. I hadn't figured out how I was going to knock Ella silly without getting caught, but I was ready for a fight.

Ella didn't stop until we were behind a large, wild-looking bush that afforded plenty of cover. Then she slowly turned and looked me straight up and down with a grimace on her mouth. Still holding her tray steady, she said, "You look ridiculous."

I placed my tray on the grass, rather abruptly, causing several of the glasses to tumble over, spilling their contents. Later I probably would care, but at that moment I could have cared less about it.

"How can you say that when I'm dressed the same as you?" I hissed.

Ella's doe eyes narrowed, but she continued not to flinch with her tray. "Because you are a fraud, and I'm betting that you won't make a week with us."

Just at the second that Ella's tray was about to be knocked into her chest, Suzanna and Miranda appeared from the foliage.

"That's funny, Ella. I think Rose has more than enough incentive to accept our ways," Suzanna said.

"You must be kidding," Ella shot back, but a bit more respectfully than she'd been talking to me.

"If you really are taking bets, Ella, then I'll put my money on Rose. I mean, gosh, kissing a guy like Noah would be enough to convert most English girls, I'd reckon," Miranda said in a soft, yet sly, way.

The kissing part registered in my mind briefly before I was overcome with admiration for the two girls sticking up for me. If not for them, I'd surely have sent Miss Ella flying, and then Bishop Lambright would have had good reason to kick my butt to the curb.

Ella's face turned a deep red, and her hands clenched the tray harder, her knuckles whitening. She said coldly, "We'll just have to wait and see, won't we?" She let her scrunched-up gaze settle on me and said, "But I'm a patient girl. And I know how this story will end."

With that, she swept by me. Glancing at my messed-up tray on the ground, I had to begrudgingly give the bitch some credit. How Ella got though that whole soap opera scene without spilling a drop of water was a mystery to me.

"Rose, I thought you had more sense than to follow that girl into a secluded place," Suzanna said with hands on her hips. She was playing at a disappointed mama, but the twitching at the corner of her lips told me she was actually quite amused.

"I just wanted to get it out in the open, that's all," I said as I knelt to pick up the cups. Miranda joined me in a flash while Suzanna knelt, too, but instead of helping, she looked around for spies and said, "So you knew that Ella Weaver hates your guts?"

"Ah, yeah, she made that pretty clear the first day," I said, getting ready to stand with what was left of the contents of my tray when Suzanna's hand whipped out and held me down.

"It's because she's in love with Noah," Suzanna whispered while Miranda stood up acting the bodyguard.

"I didn't think that reptiles were capable of love," I said in a serious tone.

Suzanna erupted in a giggle, then quieted. "Seriously, you need to watch out for her. Ella is going to be looking for ways to make sure that you aren't accepted into the church."

Miranda glanced down and nodded solemnly, backing up Suzanna's words. It was strange that this girl whom I'd just met that morning was dishing out advice and I had been willing to pay attention to her. She had a very odd quality about her that I couldn't figure out. Suzanna's concerned eyes were sincere, though. I felt certain of that.

"I'll be careful."

"Come on, we need to get back," Miranda urged us as we stood up. Suzanna took my tray and led the way, giving me a chance to brush the leaves from my skirt.

By the time we arrived in the building with the refilled water glasses, all the adults were seated and eating. There weren't enough tables for the young people who had lined up neatly along the walls, girls on one side and boys on the other.

I ended up standing between Suzanna and Maretta, hoping that my rumbling belly wasn't noticeable. Surprisingly, instead of the yummy spread I was expecting, it appeared the midday fare was plain sandwiches.

"Are those peanut butter and jelly?" I whispered into Suzanna's ear.

"Just peanut butter—sometimes we have bologna," she chirped back into my ear.

The crowd was more relaxed than before the service. The conversations were certainly not boisterous, but there was a drone of voices filling the space. Looking around the room, I was surprised that couples were eating together. Bishop Lambright, Mervin and Amos were at the same table with their wives. Ruth was beside Martha, acting as friendly as could be, along with Rebecca, who was conversing with some of the women I'd met earlier. I remembered Ruth's warning from a few days ago and took the opportunity to study Martha without being caught. She was giggling like a schoolgirl, certainly not sending off any spray of evilness. Still, I would take Ruth's advice seriously and keep an eye on the woman.

Noah was positioned between Matthew and Timothy again. He stood solemnly against the wall, and I could only see him if I craned my neck his way. When I did, he was watching me. I could tell that he was thinking some deep thoughts. He did smile at me, but again, his expression was frustrated.

I felt it, too. The tightness in my chest made me catch my breath. I wanted so badly to be close to Noah. My body felt as if it was drowning, and he was air that it needed to live. When my eyes touched his again, my heart slowed and I knew in that instant that he felt the same way. He blew out his own breath of longing, and the invisible string that held us together sprang tightly between us.

The idea that I would hardly ever get to talk to him was too terrible to consider. If I thought too much about it, I'd go nuts. I turned away from Noah, not being able to stand the torture of looking at him while being unable to go to him. I tried to focus on an evening with the girls and not the fact that I'd much rather be hugging and kissing Noah in the barn loft. Blushing, I couldn't stop myself from stretching my neck again to see him. There was a mischievous grin on his lips now.

Could he read my mind, or what? A different kind of tingling rolled up my arms, and I shifted my gaze around the room to locate the source. It wasn't difficult to spot Levi. He stood in the far corner, and when my gaze reached across the room to him, he smirked back at me. I quickly looked away while my belly did a somersault. My mind registered shock at what I saw, and to make sure that I wasn't hallucinating, I glanced back again and met Ella's stare.

The girl, who would forever be a thorn in my backside, was standing beside Levi against the opposite wall. She was at the end of a line of girls, and he was at the beginning of several boys. To anyone else, their positions would appear to be a random thing. But I wasn't fooled. The way they were each turned slightly toward each other and the similar obnoxious twists of their lips gave me the heads-up that they'd been whispering to one another.

I certainly didn't want to be paranoid, but from the looks they'd given me, I was sure they'd been discussing me. The realization caused my skin to cool, and I blew out a breath of frustration. All I needed was for the two of them to join forces... I'd be screwed for sure.

Lunch was uneventful. I munched on my sandwich while the girls chattered away about all kinds of stuff. Sarah pointed out to me the boy she had a crush on. His name was Edwin. His straight, blond hair was thin and he had a hooked nose, but he was tall like Noah, and, unlike many of the other boys, he hadn't been leering at me. Since he was sitting in the same cluster that Noah was, when I looked to check him out, Noah winked at me. I one-upped him, sending him an air kiss. That widened his eyes briefly before he closed them, puckering his lips to receive my kiss.

"You two need to stop doing stuff like that or someone will see," Sarah warned me.

"Oh, I think it's cute," Suzanna threw out for good measure.

Silly Maretta, with her chubby face turning pink, said, "Youuu are soooo lucky, Rose."

Then the subject quickly changed to the material Sarah had found to make new purses, and I zoned out trying to catch Noah's attention again. Unlike earlier, when I'd felt as if I was about to have a nervous breakdown at the distance that Noah had to keep from me, I now felt calmer, and even flirty. The grown-ups were distracted, and for a change, Noah was able to pay some attention to me. Whenever he got the chance, he stared at me, and our eyes played games across the tables, causing the flutters to attack my insides. But all too soon, lunch was over, and I was once again working alongside the girls.

An hour or so later, I disappointedly watched Noah head out the driveway behind a procession of buggies as I stood beside Ruth waiting for Mr. Hershberger to bring our own buggy up. I really wanted to help him with Dolly, but Ruth only shook her head when I'd offered. Although I'd seen Katie driving an open buggy on the road the day before, I could only guess that since the women prepared the meal and cleaned up after it, the men were expected to work with the horses on Sundays.

Oh, to be such supreme masculine beings, I thought dryly, deciding that I certainly couldn't mess with tradition.

Luckily the sun had dried out the ground, leaving hard clumps mixed in with the wetter places. I dug my toe into the clayish stuff, disgruntled and exhausted at the same time. Seeing what I was doing, Ruth elbowed me, and I instantly straightened.

My mood was dark as I recalled what Ella had foretold. Maybe she was right. The idea of going through this kind of ordeal every Sunday for the rest of my life was enough to sap anyone of the strength to fight.

But there was still the evening singing later. And this time, I'd be on the team and not watching from the sidelines. The knowledge that I might have the opportunity to talk with Noah made me feel a little better, along with the warm breeze that was drying the dampness around my neck and under my dress.

And then, I also had the night with Suzanna and Miranda to look forward to.

4

Noah

"Just go ahead and spit it out, Jacob," I nearly shouted, surprising myself at how quickly I got stirred up when Rose was involved.

"Don't play dumb with me. You know exactly what I'm talking about. I'm trying to help you out." Jacob grunted after he threw the last bale from the loft. He proceeded down the ladder, with me stepping nearly on his head as I followed him.

I grabbed his arm, forcing him to turn and face me. "Maybe you better spell it out for me," I growled.

"Okay, then. If your girlfriend continues to hang out with the likes of Suzanna and Miranda, there won't be a chance in hell that she'll make it into our church."

"No—no, brother. That's not what you said up there. You were implying that Rose was a tart for falling in with those girls so quickly."

"Whatever, but don't you think it's interesting that out of all the girls in our community, she ends up hanging around with *them?*"

"There's nothing much wrong with Suzanna—she's just a bit unsettled," I said trying to convince myself.

"Yeah, well, what about Miranda? You know about her reputation."

"Are you really going to believe the crap that Levi says about his sister? You know what a liar he is," I retorted at the same time I heaved the bale onto the fork of the Bobcat.

"It can't all be lies. And besides, it doesn't really matter whether it's true or not, does it? If Rose spends time with those two, then she's going to get a reputation for herself, and not the kind I think you're wanting." Jacob climbed into the Bobcat and roared the engine to life. Before he drove away, he shouted over the rumbling, "You better think about warning her."

I stood in the open doorway of the barn watching Jacob roll toward the back feed lots. Shoot, but my big brother was right. I'd thought the same thing when I'd seen Rose spending most of the day in close company with the rambunctious girls.

But what could I do about it?

Rose was stubborn. Here she'd gone and made some new friends in a completely foreign place, and I was going to tell her not to hang around with them? I didn't think so.

At this point I reckoned it was best just to leave well enough alone. After all, how much mischief could she get into with the other girls if she only saw them on Sundays for church and the singings?

"How is your day going, son?" Father's voice boomed behind me, giving me a good jolt. The big man was always sneaking up like that. I turned to see his beaming face and decided not to say anything to burst his fine mood.

"All right, I guess," I mumbled, turning my attention to the tall, dark bay gelding in the nearest stall. Oscar was on loan to us from the Weaver family until I could purchase a new buggy horse for myself. My chest still felt tight when I remembered the night that my horse, Rumor, was killed in the buggy wreck that had nearly taken my own life. There was no question of replacing him, because that was never happening. I'd been there beside his dam's body the night he'd been born eight years earlier, and we'd basically grown up together, sharing a special friendship that few men experienced with their horses. No, another horse wouldn't be taking Rumor's place, but I was sure I could find a suitable horse to get the job done.

After putting the halter on Oscar, I led him into the aisleway and cross-tied him. Seeing a small bloody tear on his neck, I grimaced. I knew where that came from—the demon colt.

Father seemed determined to hang around pestering me. Instead of leaving me alone, he walked up to Oscar's side and probed the cut with his fingers.

"Did that black-and-white colt do this?" Father asked with disbelief.

"None other," I replied while applying a gob of ointment to the wound.

"He's a spitfire," he said, stroking Oscar's chest.

"Ahh, I reckon he'll settle down once he's cut."

"When are you planning to have it done?"

"Actually, I was thinking about waiting a while to see how he looks when he fills out some more. I mean, he's fairly well bred and all…" I trailed off uncertainly.

"Not a bad idea to wait a time. But if I were you, I'd put the little sucker in the small paddock by his self before he hurts one of our carriage horses."

"Good idea, Father."

That was his prompt to leave, but he continued to linger, leaning against the door frame. Looking out and away from me, Father asked, "How do you think Rose is handling her new situation?"

"I'd say she's doing just fine." I paused from the currying

of the dark fur to stare at Father's back. "She's determined to make this work."

"Oh, I don't doubt her determination." He paused, before saying in a quiet voice, "But it will be difficult business for her."

"What are you saying?"

He turned to me with a strange light in his brown eyes. "Son, I know and understand your optimism about Rose becoming one of us and the two of you joining together, but you should hold yourself prepared if it doesn't work out as you intend it."

"Do you know something?" I left the horse to move closer to him. I still believe he was willing to help me reach my goals.

"No. Nothing you should be worrying about at this juncture. But I still wonder myself whether Rose will hold true." He leveled a firm stare on me. "And, if she doesn't, will you be able to let her go?"

I couldn't help but remember the story about his own questionable relationship with a rebellious Amish girl during his youth. He'd turned his back on her, but it was for the best when he'd found true love and a life with Mother. In time, the other girl ran away, abandoning her own husband and child. Father seemed to think that my situation with Rose was similar, but it wasn't. Rose was not the girl from his past…and I wasn't my father.

"I'll do what I must," I said without hesitation. I could have done without two pep talks in one afternoon.

"Right, then—you be watching yourself and how you behave around Rose this evening at the singing. You're both being watched, you know."

It was sound advice. "Yes, Father. I will."

As Father was turning to leave, I rushed to him, capturing his shoulder. "Oh, I almost forgot, Timmy and Matt want to go for a night ride later this evening. Will that be all right with you and Mother?" I didn't see any reason for him to say no, but ever since my first encounter with Rose, I hadn't given my folks much reason to trust me.

Father probed my eyes with his for a very long second before saying, "I see no reason why you shouldn't go along, but again, Noah, you have to be disciplined with yourself. You must take extra care now with your activities while your courtship is being considered."

"Yes, sir, I understand."

"And be careful on that leg. You're healing up nicely and you don't want to set yourself back. I can only imagine what them doctors in the big city would say if they knew you were out riding a horse before you got the brace off…."

He chuckled, then sobered quickly and said, "And, son—" Father had made it only a few feet from the barn door when he stopped again "—please, no racing in the fields with Matthew along. You remember his broken collarbone the last time you all went for an outing and that bulked-up mare bucked him off? I can't afford to have him out of work for any length of time with you not back yet. So keep that in mind."

I couldn't help but snicker to myself picturing Matthew's soft body trying to keep his seat on that mare of his. He was definitely over-horsed. But father's advice was well placed and not much trouble for me to keep. I was just looking forward to an evening out with the guys for a change. Since I couldn't be hidden away somewhere kissing my sweet Rose, I might as well be doing something to keep my mind off the fact.

Seeing Rose once again tucked in between Suzanna and Miranda at the dinner table was troubling. I was going to have to talk to Sarah about the situation. Rose and my sister were good buddies, anyway; it shouldn't be much of a problem for Sarah to keep Rose by her side.

I only half listened to Timmy and Matt trying to talk Edwin into going with us on the ride. I knew they'd be unsuccessful. The kid was a dope, never wanting to do much of anything. It was to a point that I didn't even bother asking him anymore.

My attention was locked on my gorgeous girlfriend. Even dressed in our Plain clothes, she still had a sexy thing going on that none of the other girls possessed. The long stray curl that escaped her cap was especially enticing, and I couldn't help but imagine that hair wrapped around my finger.

Women had it so much easier than we did. I knew Rose wanted me, but I doubted that her body was on fire every time she looked my way. As a matter of fact, my girl had the unnerving ability to ignore me quite well when she was supposed to. And right now as we were finishing the last bites of supper off the plates, she was doing just that—ignoring me. I watched her talking to the other girls as if she'd known them forever. I wouldn't admit it to anyone else, but I was right jealous of those girls for having Rose's full attention.

I had to talk to her that evening, if only a few words. I needed to see those beautiful blue eyes fluttering at me.

As the girls finished clearing the tables, I slowly rose, following the guys out the door. I glanced back, and catching Rose's sweet smile for a second was enough to make me feel a tad better.

As we made our way out to the nets set up behind the house, I looked over my shoulder several times to be sure that Rose was following. She was and with her new bodyguards in tow. Yes, I definitely needed to get word to her that she shouldn't be hanging around with the two of them—and soon.

The evening was getting right chilly now that the sun was settled low in the sky. It was the perfect weather for playing a game of ball, though. I wasn't exactly showing off, but I felt a lot of pent-up energy that I really wanted to direct at Rose. Being unable to, I attacked the volleyball instead.

My chance finally came when Rose sat down cross-legged on the grass beside our game. Either she was tired of playing herself, or she was hoping I'd join her. Miranda was the only other person with her, and the two girls were huddled closely together, talking. I waited for the girl to get up and leave, worrying that she'd sit there beside Rose for the rest of the game.

With darkness nearly upon us, I knew I didn't have much time.

Sarah joined Rose at the same time Miranda went back to the net. Taking the opportunity, I looked around carefully. Not seeing any adult's weary eyes on me, I sat myself down strategically on the other side of my sister. I would have given anything at that moment to have been close to Rose, but I wasn't taking any chances.

Rose eyed me happily, and my heart raced. Wasting no time, I leaned over Sarah's lap, not caring what she heard. "Sweetheart, how are you doing tonight?"

"Much better now that you're within a few feet of me." She smiled sweetly.

Rose was smart, though. She only eyed me for a few seconds before she returned her attention on the game.

Good girl, Rose.

"How does your little butt feel after the ordeal this morning?"

Rose half smiled at me in that seductive way that only she could do. "I'm feeling okay. But, I don't believe I've ever sat still for so long." Then she lost the flirty look and said, "Well, maybe when I took the ACT, but those chairs were much more comfortable."

I didn't have a clue what she was talking about, but knowing we might run out of time, I said, "Hey, you need to listen to me. You shouldn't be hanging around Suzanna and Miranda so much."

Her eyes rounded, and she said, "Huh?"

"Just trust me on this one, all right?" I tried not to sound as if I was pleading, but I probably did, anyway. The way Rose's face went from surprise to irritation sent a chill through me.

I did believe she's going to do what she wanted.

Before I got to say more to her, a half dozen girls were plopping down all around us, sending me quickly on my way.

The last look I received from Rose was a frown. She was thinking, which meant trouble for sure. Why couldn't she just take my advice and be done with it? Deep down, I knew that Rose's headstrong personality was one of the things that I both hated and loved about her. Things were always exciting with her, that's for sure.

But what would I do if she continued to hang around with the girls that others in the community believed were rebels?

"You ready to get the horses?" Timothy asked excitedly by my ear. He'd placed his hand on my shoulder and Matt was close behind him.

I was glad to have a diversion that night—I needed my friends to help me keep my mind off of Rose and everything else.

5

Rose

Sitting on the edge of the seat, I leaned forward relishing the cool wind on my face. It was about the most fun I'd had in ages. Suzanna had her horse, Wynn, stretched out, the mare trotting fluidly across the pavement. The *clip-clop clip-clop* was thunderous and glorious at the same time. Riding in an open buggy for the first time was better than the best ride at an amusement park.

This part of being Amish was awesome.

Miranda pressed into my side on the front bench as one hand braced behind me and the other one held onto her cap. The darkness was nearly complete, and I searched the sky for the Big Dipper. Finding the constellation quickly, I sighed happily. Maybe this sort of life did suit me.

Suzanna pulled back on the long reins, slowing Wynn to a jog, then a walk at the turn. I was surprised when we left the road we were on. Suzanna must have felt my wonder since she said, "Oh, no worries. We're picking up a friend."

I was usually a go-with-the-flow type of person, but when Suzanna spoke the words I felt instant dread. What was the girl up to?

"Who?" I asked, trying to remain calm.

"You'll see," Suzanna spoke perkily, obviously quite pleased that she had me guessing.

We picked up our pace and sailed into the trot again. The road was quiet, and I *almost* didn't worry about getting hit by a truck. I guess it was something I'd have to deal with for the rest of my life: the *buggy fear factor*.

We whisked past several non-Amish homes before slowing again to a walk. I noticed a girl standing at the end of the drive that we were approaching. I stared at the girl as my peripheral vision caught sight of the small tan-colored double-wide behind her with enough beat-up old vehicles in the yard to make it look like a used car lot.

When the girl saw us approaching, a giant smile lit up her face, and she ran toward us in fairly athletic form. She was not Amish, and I wondered who she was.

"Hey, sisters!" the girl shouted just as she reached the buggy that Suzanna now had stopped. The sweetish sweat smell of the horse mixed with the wet leather drifted back to me as I got a good look at the girl for about a second before she leaped up beside Miranda, wedging me even more tightly between the two girls.

Still smiling brightly, the girl leaned out around Miranda, her shoulder-length strawberry-blond locks brushing Miranda's dress as she held her hand out to me.

"Howdy. I'm Summer Sage."

I was startled by the sudden encounter, but I took a breath and regained my composure.

"Hi, I..."

Before I got anything out, Summer interrupted, "Oh, I already know who *youuu* are—the famous Rose Cameron. The English girl who stole an Amish boy's heart and threw away her cushy existence in the modern world—no offense girls—

to become Ahhmish," Summer squealed, her theatrics rising through the proclamation.

"Summer, you should tone it down a bit, girl, or you're going to scare Rose out of the buggy," Miranda said. She immediately ducked when Summer tossed her backpack into the wagon behind the seat.

Suzanna snapped the reins, and we all went back against the seat roughly.

"Nah, we don't have to worry about Miss Rose. I can tell already that she has spunk."

Summer leaned forward again to wink at me.

I wasn't exactly sure where to go with the comment, so instead, I went with the first thing that had popped into my head upon meeting the other musketeer. "Summer Sage is a really cool name."

It was too dark to tell exactly what color Summer's eyes were, but they were light and I imagined them to be the shade of spring grass. Those eyes beamed back at me from the compliment.

"Well, thank you, Rose. It's about the only good thing I ever got from my mamma."

Suzanna barked out a laugh, but I picked up on some deep feelings underneath the carefree comment.

"Guess you don't get along too well with your mom, huh?" I asked, conscious of the warmth from the girls' sides and the coolness of the air. The sound of Wynn's hooves smacking the pavement made me nearly have to shout to be heard.

"We get on just fine, long as we don't see each other much, which is fine as frog hair by me," Summer said, still leaning forward and outright staring at me.

Did she just say something about frog's hair? What planet did this girl come from?

"You're mom isn't nearly bad as mine, Sum," Miranda cooed, just loud enough to barely be heard.

"Yeah, you're right about that. Yours is one mamma I wouldn't trade for."

Summer didn't say it in a mean way, just a totally honest agreeing sort of way. I glanced at Miranda's face for a sign of anger, but there was none. The mousy Amish girl set her mouth firmly and nodded a few times.

"Hey, now, we're supposed to be having a fun girl's night out. No spoiling it talking about rotten parents," Suzanna ordered just as she turned into her own driveway, way too fast to be safe, but definitely thrillingly. The buggy seemed to tilt on the two left wheels for a few seconds, then right itself. I held on to Suzanna and closed my eyes until it was over.

Wynn slowed to a perky walk, none too bothered by her exertion. The girls were all talking, laughing and joking the entire way up the driveway and into the barnyard. I didn't even need to say a thing, which was perfect, because it gave me a chance to observe the dynamics of the group.

Suzanna was definitely the ringleader, but neither Miranda nor Summer were pushovers. They both seemed to appreciate Suzanna's keen mind and contagious sense of humor.

When Wynn snorted a mass of greenish spray into Summer's face as the girl held the mare in place to be unhitched, Suzanna fell to the ground on her knees laughing. The sound of her shrill yapping was even funnier than the sight of Summer pulling her shirt up to her bra to wipe away the goo.

"You...better...put your...sassy...shirt down, Summer Sage, 'fore you set one of my little brothers on...fire." Suzanna laughed the words out. Even Miranda giggled, but I noticed she was also looking around.

"Why, you hussy, Suzanna, training your stupid horse to do that to me *evvvery* single time," Summer said.

Quickly, Suzanna was up and unsnapping the breeching. I moved over closer to watch her fingers work.

"Yep, you know I'm the best horse trainer in the world if I can do that," Suzanna teased.

Two little boys, maybe eight and ten, appeared out of nowhere. They shouted out a few sentences in German, laughing and pointing at Summer, who stuck her tongue out at them, before they rolled the buggy away from the horse. They backed it under the nearest shed and then disappeared again. I could hear girlish squeals coming from near the house, and looking in that direction I spotted a flurry of dresses. I couldn't remember for sure, but I thought Suzanna had said she was right in the middle of eleven siblings.

"Don't you just hate it when they do that?" Summer was suddenly beside me, and I hadn't even noticed her getting there.

"What?" I asked, feeling a bit stupid not knowing what she was talking about.

"You don't speak it yet, do you?" Summer asked holding my eyes captive.

Realization dawned, "Oh, no, no. I can't understand any of it." I felt as if I'd just discovered my new best friend.

"And yet, there they go, always speaking their secret language around us—and here we are in the middle of cow-paddy America," Summer joked, but I wondered if she really meant it deep down.

I know I had thought about it on more than one occasion. It kind of made you feel as if you were being talked about or something—made a person paranoid.

"Ha, and you're always bragging on honor roll grades and about going off to some fancy college someday. I reckon we're the smarter ones, since we speak two languages," Suzanna said as I helped her carry the slimy-with-sweat harness into the tack room.

I was thinking that if the conversation didn't change quickly, our fun girls' night was going to turn into a brawl. Before I had much time to worry about it, the lack of lighting in the pitch-dark barn caused me to bump my head solidly into a saddle rack.

"Owww!"

"I won't even mention the no-electricity thing, since I'm an honored guest," Summer hooted, walking into the darkness to check out my cry, only for the two of us to bump boob to boob into each other.

"Don't even go there, Summer Sage, or I'll be running you down the road. Are you hurt, Rose?" Suzanna said, feeling for my hand until she found it. She pulled me out into the little bit of moonlight. Pushing on the throbbing bump on my head for a minute, she gave me a clean bill of health and then proceeded to herd me and the others away from the white farmhouse and toward a small square building at the bottom of the hill.

The grass was already damp, and we squished along at a near run until we reached the four-foot landing of a porch, my head only throbbing slightly with the jarring motion. Suzanna threw open the door and fumbled around for a minute until she struck a match and lit the light above the round dining room table.

Summer immediately went to the fridge, showing no shyness at all when she pulled out four cans of pop and handed them out. You'd think she owned the place. Miranda sat down tiredly, and I wondered at her lack of energy while I surveyed the neat little guesthouse. There was a mushy gray sofa and a matching chair on one side of the room and a refrigerator, sink and counter on the other. The table was in the middle, and I guessed that the one door led to a bedroom and the other one to a bathroom. With the stark white walls, the place looked as if it was a glorified hotel room.

"Are we staying in here tonight?" I asked, feeling my excitement mounting.

"Sure are." Suzanna spread out her arms dramatically. "Welcome to my home away from home." Rolling her eyes around the small space, she added, "Or better yet, my freedom pad."

"Seriously, this is your place?"

"Suzanna, you better be honest now, or I'll be telling on you," Miranda said fiercely.

"Shucks, Mira. I can dream, can't I?" Suzanna said, dropping into the chair and popping the tab of her pop at the same time.

"You see, Rose, Suzanna only gets to use the guesthouse when we come over for the night," Summer said as she turned to Suzanna, cocking an eyebrow high. "Didn't you say something about not wanting your brothers turning into raging volcanoes...or something like that?"

Summer giggled and took a swig of her drink.

I opened my can and savored the taste of the sweet, dark caffeinated drink. Thank God for carbonation.

"Yeah, you know it, girl. My mother doesn't want you in the house with your tight jeans and skimpy shirts making my brothers all horny like toads," Suzanna said in a joking but more serious tone than before.

"Hey, I don't wear skimpy shirts." Summer turned to me. "Do you think this shirt is skimpy, Rose?"

Examining the snug, elbow-length red-and-white baseball-type shirt, I honestly could say, no. As a matter of fact, it was a shirt that I'd wear.

"I have to agree with Summer about the shirt, Suzanna. Sorry."

"Course you would. You English girls are going to stick

together—then we won't be able to gang up on Miss Summer Sage no more," Suzanna said with a smile.

"Don't listen to her, Rose—we never gang up on Summer," Miranda said as she got up and began looking through the cupboards.

"Do you have any food in here, Suzanna, or are we expected to eat mothballs?" Miranda asked.

"What do you think this is—a fancy hotel?" Suzanna bounced up, heading for the door. "But I'll go gather up some chow for us, anyways. I'm hungry, too."

Miranda followed Suzanna, but when Summer began to leave her chair, Suzanna noticed and quickly held out her hand. "No, not you, Summer. You stay here with Rose so she's not alone. We don't want my mother getting in a tizzy before midnight." Suzanna laughed, but her eyes were determined and she closed the door swiftly.

"Well, doesn't that just suck?" Summer took a swig of her drink and then crossed her arms over her belly as she leaned back. She was a pretty girl, no denying it, but her beauty seemed to be enhanced by her vibrant personality, making her a true beauty.

"How long have you been hanging around with Suzanna and Miranda?" I asked.

"I've known them since we were little kids. My mamma drives the Amish sometimes. When I was younger, she'd take me into town with her when she made runs."

With Suzanna and Miranda gone, the little house was quieter, but still Summer leaned forward and whispered, "How do you like living like them?"

Could I trust Summer Sage?

My instinct told me, yes, and I decided to go with it. For days I'd felt as if I'd been acting out a never-ending play. I didn't feel Amish. Ella was right—I was a fraud. The only thing that kept me from feeling like a total whack job was Noah. He was my one true link to the Amish world. Maybe having Summer as a friend would help, since she was accepted into the community to some extent without actually being Amish. She would understand things better than my father or brothers would—and she wouldn't be against me being Amish, like they were. With her help, I might be able to make my new life work.

Suzanna and Miranda gave me hope, too. They were more like the girls I used to hang around with back home. As much as I liked Sarah and Katie, it would be near impossible for me to live up to their standards. I felt as if I couldn't let my guard down when I was with them. I worried that I'd say or do something that would give me away—and they'd know that I wasn't the obedient, sweet-natured girl they hoped I was.

"It's a lot harder than I thought it would be—and weirder, too," I admitted.

"I got to give you credit. I know how those caps pinch your skull and how itchy the dresses are. The girls dressed me up for fun a couple of times—and one time I even wore the getup to a school dinner in disguise. Most of the kids figured out fairly quickly who I was, but a lot of the adults never even suspected."

She looked off into space, clearly enjoying the memory.

"But what you're doing is way different. Are you mental or what?" Summer said. Her eyes were suddenly glued on me.

"No, I'm perfectly sane. I'm just...well I'm, ah..."

"In love," Summer drawled out the words with a twinkle in her eyes.

"What exactly have you heard?" I demanded, responding to her mocking tone.

She shook her head sadly, looking at me as if I was about to undergo a head transplant.

"Do you really believe that it's going to last?"

"Course I do, or I wouldn't be here in the first place." I felt obligated to say more. "Noah and I are soul mates. I couldn't live without him." I looked her in the eye, daring her to say something snide. But surprisingly she nodded her head in understanding and leaned back.

"It's going to be rough, though. You know that, don't you?"

"Yeah, I do. But you hang out with them all the time and do fine."

Summer laughed. "I spend a lot of time with Suzanna and Mira, but none of the other Amish pay me any mind at all. Then, whenever I get tired of evenings without radios or DVD players, I just go home." She looked at me with sympathy. "But *you* won't ever get to escape."

"When you put it that way, it makes me want to jump off a bridge." I sighed in a kidding way, but deep down, her words chilled me.

"Hang in there, Rosie, you'll be okay." She glanced at the door, and when she turned back she said conspiratorially, "If you ever need a jailbreak, you call me. I'll take care of you."

I couldn't help but laugh at her. I liked Summer Sage, and I believed that she would help me out in a jam. I was almost disappointed when Suzanna and Miranda came through the door.

Within minutes all the white caps were off and we were happily munching pecan pie and homemade ice cream. Definitely a step up from the Doritos and pretzels I was used to snacking on with my English friends.

Running a brush though Suzanna's whitish-blond hair, I was amazed at how long it was—and Miranda's Rapunzel locks went past her butt.

"So you've never cut your hair?" I asked Suzanna as I finished styling the waves that hung down her shoulder to make her look as if she were a fashion model.

"Nope, never," she said proudly.

"So what are we doing tonight, girls?" Summer asked from her comfy stretched-out position on the couch.

"It must be after midnight, right?" I said, looking at Summer who was the only one of us with the time. She checked her phone and confirmed my guess.

"Yeah, ten minutes past to be exact," Summer said.

Suzanna crawled around me over to Miranda, scooting up beside her on the couch and hugging her from behind. "You ready for an adventure, Mira?"

That feeling of apprehension teased me, but this time I pushed it away quickly. "What do you have in mind?" I asked, the words leaving me slowly.

"I was thinking we could go for a midnight stroll through the woods. What do you think, Summer?"

"Sounds wonderful," Summer said, springing from the chair in a fluid motion. "Let's get out of here."

She was at the door in a heartbeat. We were close behind, but when we crossed the threshold, I squeaked, "Wait. Aren't we going to put our caps back on?"

The feel of my hair loose and free on my shoulders was amazing, but what if someone saw us?

Suzanna smirked. "Don't worry, Rose. If we get caught, our hair will be the least of our problems." She said it in a way that made the hair on my neck stand up.

She wasn't kidding for a change.

Seeing her bare feet, I asked, "What about shoes?"

"Don't need them," Suzanna stated with no room for argument.

"No way—I can't run around in the woods without shoes," I declared, going back in and slipping mine on. When I stepped into the pale moonlight I noticed that Summer already had hers on, and once again, I felt a connection to the girl.

"Smart move, Rose—if we have to run, it's better to be pre-pared," Summer said, patting my back.

"I bet I can outrun you barefoot any day," Suzanna boasted.

"Hopefully, we don't have to test your theory," Summer said, darting out in front us and leading the way down the side of the mowed lawn and into the cover of the trees. I glanced back once at the house to see it dark and quiet. Would Suzanna's parents come out to the guesthouse to check on us in the middle of the night? Remembering all the little kids and the busy church day, I doubted it. Her folks were probably sleeping so soundly nothing short of an explosion would wake them.

I mentally kept my fingers crossed, though, as I followed the three girls ahead of me deeper into the woods. There was a path of sorts that we were following, but it was one of those that was seldom used and would not be noticed by anyone. Under the cover of the trees the air was cool, and the smell of decaying leaves laced with the green foliage of the live ones flooded my senses.

Since I was at the end of the line, the trail was more tram-pled for me than the other girls, but I still had to dodge low branches and hop over fallen ones. It was all quiet except for Miranda's heavy breathing ahead of me and the occasional ex-plicit outburst from Summer or Suzanna when they got wacked by a branch or tripped over a root.

I felt giddy with the feeling of freedom. I was away from the judgmental eyes of the Amish. I could be myself for a change and literally let my hair down. I was in no way completely at ease, knowing that if we were caught, Suzanna and Miranda would probably be punished, but I would be kicked out of the community. I could just imagine Bishop Lambright's "I told you so" speech before he happily sent me packing. And then there was Noah—what would he think about me running through the woods in the middle of the night like a wild druid priestess?

I didn't think the girls would say anything to him, but just in case, I decided that I'd have a talk with them before morning. There was no reason to get Noah all worked up, I convinced myself, just as we left the sort-of-trail to head straight down a hill.

We were blazing a new trail now and the going was slower. Summer stopped several times to hold up a branch for us to slip under. Luckily, we reached the bottom of the hill in a few minutes, and with the force of gravity pushing us, we practically jumped into the grassy clearing.

"Are we having fun yet?" Suzanna said, her voice louder than I wished.

We continued on, trudging through the wet grass behind Suzanna, who seemed to know exactly where she was going. I hustled to keep up. Now that the going was clear, Suzanna wasn't wasting any time heading to wherever her destination was.

"Why don't we bring something with us to prune that trail next time?" Summer directed her question to Suzanna, working hard to keep up with the taller girl's strides.

Suzanna kept on walking but barked out, "Are you kidding? And give my parents a road map to our private place? Nope, we hack through the wood a slightly different way each time so no one's the wiser about the escape route."

Made sense to me, and was more proof of how smart—and diabolical—Suzanna could be. I got some comfort knowing that the girl was seriously trying to keep our butts covered.

"Ah, where exactly are we going?" I couldn't hold the question in another minute.

Summer answered me. "Don't be thinking it's anything

fancy, but we're almost there, so keep your panties on," she said, looping her arm through mine.

Except for Summer humming the, "We're Off to See the Wizard" tune, we traveled the rest of the way in relative silence. There was definitely a spring to everyone's step; we all wanted to get to wherever we were going quickly. Suzanna kept us close to the tree line, for cover I imagined, but at one point we did sprint across the corner of the field at full speed before entering the trees again on the other side. Here, there was a definite trail, and once Suzanna's bare feet touched the path, she slowed.

When we reached an ancient boulder formation, Summer grabbed my hand, tugging me into a run again. The other girls joined us as we left the path, jumping obstacles like gazelles—even in dresses. I was proud of myself. I didn't wipe out once.

There it was.

We all came to an abrupt stop. The old, falling-down log house had definitely seen better days. But the picture of the building nestled away in the woods with the moonlight casting a shadowed light over it was charming—and *oh, so creepy.*

"What do you think, Rose?" Suzanna said, motioning her arm to the house.

"Well, it could use a paint job, but besides that, it's a perfectly secluded getaway," I said, taking the lead up the warped steps to the door with its rusted doorknob. After a glance at Suzanna who nodded enthusiastically, I turned the handle and entered the dark room.

Suzanna passed me and fumbled around for a minute or two before a light suddenly illuminated the space. She held an old lantern in her hand, the glow matching the brightness of her happy face.

Within minutes, Summer and Miranda had a small flame rising in the rock fireplace, which had been used frequently,

if the pile of ashes was any indication. There was an assortment of lawn chairs and turned-over buckets fanned out before
the warm blaze. I quickly sat on one of the more comfortable-
looking canvas chairs as the girls pulled up seats around me.

"This is very cool, Suzanna," I said, complimenting the host-
ess while pushing my shoe around in the dusty dirt that covered the floor. The immaculate cleaning skills of the Amish
had definitely not touched this place.

"Thanks. I came across this old house a few years back
when I was hunting with one of my brothers."

"You hunt?" I hoped my voice didn't sound too judgmental. But I was a PETA person all the way, and the thought of
the slender blond girl in a dress beside me hunting Bambi
was unexpected.

"Yeah, course I hunt. So does Mira," Suzanna stated plainly.

"Why?" The heat from the burning logs flowed over the
front of me, stroking the skin on my arms, making my whole
body feel wonderful. I leaned back in the chair reveling in the
warmth and glad for the rest after the marathon hike through
the countryside.

"What do you mean?" Suzanna asked, sounding truly per-
plexed.

Summer jumped in. "I think what she means is, why do you
go out and kill innocent little woodland creatures when you
can buy hamburgers at the grocery store."

I couldn't tell if she was joking or not.

"Why, you should talk, Miss Summer Sage, bringing down
the biggest buck I'd ever seen last year when you went out
with us to the Chippery property."

I turned to see Summer shrug her shoulders. She looked
down at the floor when she said quietly, "Well, that was a heap
of luck for my first time—but I'll not be doing it again."

"Oh, come on, Summer. Everybody feels a little bad the first time—except my brothers. They really enjoy killing stuff. But I did. You get over it, though," Suzanna said forcefully.

"I don't want to get over it." Summer turned to me. "It was so awful. The one instant the buck was staring right at me, his beautiful face up high and proud, and the next, he was on the ground. He writhed around for a minute or two before he finally stopped moving." She sniffed. "As soon as my finger hit the trigger I regretted it."

"But your mother was proud to have all that meat in her freezer for the winter," Miranda said and then added, "We buy most of our meat from the butcher shop or grocery, but when hunting season arrives, all the kids that are old enough, boys and girls alike, take to the woods. Most of the girls do it for the opportunity to get away from the house."

"Yeah, as long as your shitty brother, Levi, isn't going, right?" I was shocked to hear the words spill from Suzanna's mouth—for more than one reason.

"Levi Zook is your brother?" I searched her face for any resemblance to the evil carrot-top.

"Yes, unfortunately," Miranda said in a whisper. The warmth in the room was pushed back by the Amish girl's mood.

"Wow, I didn't suspect that." Focusing on the jumping flames, I could almost see his malevolent face leering at me from his horse in the cornfield.

Reaching her hand out and placing it on my arm, Miranda said softly, "I'm real sorry about what he did—ratting on you and Noah like that."

"It's not your fault." I patted her hand as if she was a child. Wanting to change the subject that had chilled the room considerably, I said, "So you actually hunt to put food on your dinner table?" The question was directed to Miranda, but Suzanna answered.

"Sure we do. Miranda and I both help with the butchering, too."

"*I did not do that.* Suzanna's daddy did mine in exchange for the head to mount on his wall," Summer said as she wrinkled her nose.

"That's kind of sick," I added before I could stop myself.

"Are you saying my father is sick, because he helped Summer with her kill?" Suzanna was stirred up now.

"No. Sorry, I didn't mean it that way. It's just that I feel bad for the deer, that's all."

"How do you think I feel every time I go into her family room," Summer said, thumbing at Suzanna, "and see my buck's head staring at me with its glass eyes?" She shivered.

"You English girls are so wishy-washy about stuff like that. Then you'll go watch one of those movies where everybody gets shot up. But that isn't sick?"

It was very interesting what analogies these people came up with, prompting me to think about some of my conversations with Noah. I wasn't about to agree with her, but she had shut me up for now.

Not Summer, though. "That's just dumb to compare a movie to killing some poor animal out minding its own business," Summer declared, adding another log to the fire in a spray of sparks.

"So you think killing people is okay, but not animals to eat." Suzanna shot the words back at Summer.

Before Summer got the chance to go another round with the debate, Miranda stood up. With one hand out toward the bickering girls, and one hand to her mouth, she shushed them.

"Did you hear that?" Miranda whispered.

Dead silence filled the room after her words. I craned my neck to listen for any sounds, turning my ear in the direction of the doorway that Suzanna had said led to the stairway.

"Was it coming from up there?" I pointed at the black opening in the wall.

Miranda shook her head, "Outside." She spoke so low that I had to pretty much read her lips to understand her.

The four of us moved closer together until our arms were brushing. Summer reached out, taking my hand into her sweaty ones and holding on tightly.

I was not usually a scaredy-cat sort of person, but at that moment my heart was pounding madly in my chest. The sudden dawning that here we were, four teenage girls out in the middle of the woods in a spooky old broken-down house, sent an adrenaline rush coursing through my veins. My sharpened senses caught the scraping against the outside wall, followed by a wailing sound as if a cat were having its heart carved out. Instantly, our arms all tangled around each other, and I could feel Summer shaking beside me. Her face was pressed against my shoulder.

I was afraid, but I was also pissed off. We were supposed to be having a fun girls' night out, but instead, we'd ended up in low-budget horror movie. I was not going to let whatever was out there ruin my evening—or kill any of us.

I pulled away from Summer about the same time a loud stomping started on the front porch. I took up the long skinny board that was beside the fire in my hand and ran to the doorway. I didn't have to wait more than a second before the door flung open to reveal three dark figures who came crashing into the room. I wasn't sure if the screaming was coming from the intruders or the girls, but either way it was too loud to think. That's when I swung the board as hard as I could manage. The thud of hitting something solidly jolted my arm, causing some pain, but I didn't care about that. The human sob that followed my well-placed blow brought me to my senses.

"Damn it. I've been attacked. I think I'm bleeding."

The voice was mildly familiar.

"Oh, you poor dear," Suzanna cooed to the psychopath, wrapping her arms around him as she led him to the fire. Her voice changed to a shrill yell when she addressed me. "What are you, Rose, one of those Amazon women Summer's always talking about?"

Everything happened rather fast at the point she said my name. Before Suzanna had even finished her sentence, I was being swept up into a bone crushing embrace—*by Noah*.

I knew his arms, his chest and his scent.

I squealed in delight as he picked me off the floor and swung me around, my face buried in his neck. When he stopped, his mouth found mine and the urgency of the kiss left me breathless. This was turning out to be a better night than I could have ever imagined.

"Can't you do that later—I think my skull is broken."

Now I remembered that panic-filled voice; *Volleyball-Boy*.

Noah's mouth left my lips and trailed along my cheek to my ear as he put me down. He breathed out heavily when he smoothed the hair away from my sweaty forehead. Holding my face between his calloused hands, he said, "What are you doing out here? You're supposed to be safe—asleep at the Hershbergers."

Irritation swelled inside of me. "I could ask you the same thing—why would you be sneaking up to a run-down house in the middle of the woods to scare some unsuspecting girls?" I still kept my body pressed against him, not wanting to move away even though I was upset.

Noah's voice was husky and honey combined as he leaned down close to my face, his warm breath heating my nose. "I had no idea you were here—or anyone for that matter—until right before we reached the house." He nodded over at Timothy, who had a crowd babying him, which I could now see included the bashful Matthew Weaver.

"It was Timmy's idea to check out this dump. We were on a night ride when he began pestering us about it. Rose, you have to believe me about this," Noah pleaded.

I did believe him, and I was going to show him I did with a big sloppy kiss when Suzanna jumped to his defense unnecessarily. "He isn't lying, Rose. It was me and Timmy that planned it all out."

Still snug in Noah's arms, I said, "You all knew they were coming, and no one told me about it?" My anger was suddenly redirected.

Summer shouted out, "I didn't know anything. About scared me to death, it did." She was telling the truth. No one could lie with that twang going on.

"No, Summer wasn't in on it—just me and Miranda." She was touching Timothy's head, playing the nurse, when she continued. "We thought it would be the best surprise for you and Noah to see each other, unsuspecting like, out here in the night." She stood up, stepping back with her hands on her hips. "The scaring part was not part of the deal." Suzanna's voice sparked.

"Oh, man, Suzanna. I just thought we'd have some fun with you girls. I didn't mean any harm by it." Timothy held out his hand to Suzanna and my eyes were probably bugging out as she took it, sliding down onto his lap.

Noah laughed, repositioning me under his arm and moving us both toward the group and the light of the fire. "Looks like you're the one who got harmed," Noah said as he leaned over Timothy and, placing his hand on his friend's head, began feeling around.

Noah hadn't released me, putting me uncomfortably close to my victim. I probably should have said I was sorry—but I didn't want to. After all, the jerk had brought it on with his actions.

"Wow, Rose, you have a killer swing," Matthew complimented me as he sat down on a bucket next to Miranda. I thought the chair and bucket were kind of close for a platonic relationship, but the two of them weren't being all touchy-feely like the other couple was. My mind was still reeling that Suzanna and Timothy were an item, and I hadn't even had a clue about it. Combine that surprise with being in Noah's arms, and I was overwhelmed, to say the least.

"You look all right, buddy." Noah pulled the nearest chair to him, and in one fluid motion had me sitting on his lap. "Just don't be sneaking up on my girl again, you hear?"

"Yeah, yeah—I learned my lesson right good." Timothy placed his arms around Suzanna's waist, and she leaned back against him.

"That was really impressive, Rose. The way you got ready at that door so fast, then, *bam,* took him out like that. Weren't you scared?" Summer took the chair beside me and Noah, and I felt a twinge of discomfort since she was the only one without a love interest in the bunch.

Noah's arms tightened around me, and he laid his face against my back. It felt so wonderful that I closed my eyes for a second to revel in the soft fluttering feeling spiraling through me.

"I was just trying to save our butts, taking the offensive, that's all." Then something occurred to me, turning my head to Noah's. "And what are you thinking, riding a horse in your condition?"

In the firelight, his bruising was hardly noticeable. "We were taking it easy. No running or trotting. I even rode old Maisy."

"And your parents know that you're out in the woods riding

a horse?" I said, thinking that the doctors were dead-on right to have kept him in the hospital those extra weeks.

"Of course they do. I'm being extra careful to be good now that we have a real chance to be together." He leaned back and sighed. "And here, I end up with you in my arms and I didn't even arrange it. I think the fates are trying to get me in trouble."

"Are you calling us fates?" Suzanna asked.

"Not exactly—but when did you two get together, anyway?" Noah sounded as amazed as I still felt.

Good question, Noah.

Timothy looked at Suzanna for help, and she said, "It's been about a month now, I reckon. You've been pretty tied up lately, Noah, with your accident and all." Suzanna smirked in my direction, sending a warm heat over my face.

"So when are you going to join the church, then?" Noah asked. He started swirling his fingers along my arm with his one hand while the other held my hand firmly.

"Hey, hey, don't go jumping the gun there, Noah."

"What do you mean?" Noah's hand had stilled on my arm.

Suzanna answered for Timothy, "We aren't jumping into a courtship just yet. You know how we'll be watched as if we're little babies. We won't get to have any more fun."

"You should be thinking about making an honest woman of your girl, Timmy." Noah's voice sound harsh. I took his hand between mine, trying to keep him calm.

"I don't need a courtship to be an honest woman. You're just as bad as the old farts that make up all the rules," Suzanna snipped.

"Really, I think it's nice that they can get to know each other in secret first—then if they decide they don't like each other, they can move on without upsetting the entire community over it," Summer jumped in with her opinion.

"And I'm not sure I want to join the church," Suzanna said.

"Oh, don't go saying that, Susie. We're going to eventually join up and get married like we talked about," Timothy said, in the voice of a man trying to convince a woman to do what he wanted, but not sure whether she actually would or not.

"Nothing's for sure, but since we only have a few more hours until sunup, we'd best get some time alone, or else we'll be making Matthew here turn into a tomato, considering his already red face."

Suzanna giggled as she pulled Timothy up and dragged his still-wobbly body through the dark entrance that led to the stairs.

Were they going to do what I thought they were going to do?

This night had shattered my image of Amish girls. When I looked at Summer, she just shrugged and poked at the logs in the fire with a stick, before picking up another log to toss on it.

"Shouldn't do that, Summer, we want the fire to be out when we leave," Noah advised.

"So it's going to be an all-nighter?" Matthew asked, bringing my attention back to him and Miranda. They were still sitting close, but neither one had moved to touch the other. Maybe they were just childhood friends. I had to admit that if they didn't have anything going on yet, they really should have. They would make a cute couple.

"Let's go outside, Rose. I want to talk to you," Noah whispered hotly into my ear.

The idea of being alone with Noah sent a rush through my veins. *Could we behave ourselves?* In a crazy way, the whole structured dating scene in the community was comforting. If you never had the opportunity to do the wild thing, then there was no need to worry about birth control.

Noah must have felt sure of my answer because he gently rose from the chair, depositing me on the floor. He looped his hand through mine and headed for the door, with more smoothness than you'd expect from a guy with a leg brace on. A quick glance back showed a "go-get-him" kind of smile on Summer's lips. Miranda didn't pay any attention to our exit, just staring into the flames and ignoring everyone.

Noah led me back to the boulders where three horses were standing quietly, tied to trees. I picked out Noah's old mare, and, pulling Noah with me, I made my way to her. Stopping, I reached out and stroked her chestnut neck. She smelled like warm fur and cut grass mixed together, and I couldn't help but lean in closer to breathe in the wonderful scent.

"She's pretty," I said running my hand down the wide blaze on her forehead.

"And slow. But Father insisted that if I went riding, it'd be on her for a while longer." Noah leaned against the mare, watching me.

"Are you hurting at all?"

"Eh, just a little in my leg. It's hard to ride with a brace on. I can't wait to get the damn thing off."

"You know, my dad would go ballistic if he knew that you were out riding horses," I said sternly.

Noah rolled his eyes and then tilted his head, eyeing me in that amused way. "Actually, I've been real good. This is the first time I've been on a horse's back—and what, it's about six weeks now since the accident."

I wanted to keep the conversation going, worried that if we stopped talking we'd end up doing something that I wasn't ready for. "It's really amazing how well you're doing." Reaching up, I lightly ran my hand over his face, saying, "Your bruising is almost gone."

Noah closed his eyes when I touched him, and his mouth opened slightly. I wondered if we could be good and just kiss a little bit. My heart began racing in anticipation, but then he opened his eyes wide, and the fierce intensity in them chased the romantic thoughts away.

"How on earth did you end up out here in that shack with those girls, anyway?" His voice was controlled; he hadn't passed judgment on me—yet.

I shrugged and moved over to the boulders, taking a minute to make myself comfortable against the smooth rock before answering.

"Suzanna invited me to spend the night with her and Miranda. I hadn't met Summer until a few hours ago, and I certainly didn't know about the plans to hike out here in the middle of the night."

I searched his face, which was now directly above me. He had his arm stretched out with one hand bracing himself on the rock near my head. Having him looming over me like that made the butterflies in my belly quadruple. Why did we have to talk at all?

Noah's eyes lingered over my face, making my feelings intensify until he spoke.

"You could've just said no and not gone with them."

My physical rush was tempered by his words. "And why shouldn't I go with my new friends? I never get to spend time with you—and all I do at the Hershbergers is laundry and cleaning." I shoved my finger to his nose. "And see this bandage? I got that after I spent two whole hours trying to sew a seam that pulled apart on Mr. Hershberger's pants while I was washing them. I think I'm more than ready for a night out with the girls."

I crossed my arms and looked out into the dark trees, but his laugh snapped my head back. "You don't have to get all worked up. I was just making a suggestion." He chose then to bend down and place his warm lips on mine. I was stubborn, though, going against my body's desire.

I turned my head so that his lips rested on the sensitive place between my jaw and ear. His breath was hot as he whispered, "You know, I'll give Suzanna credit for being an expert at evading being caught, but what if you girls were found out?" Before I could speak, he put his finger to my lips restraining them. "My sweetheart, you would be immediately sent back to your father, the entire community believing that you were the instigator."

I began to speak again, only to have him rush his words out. "And that would be terrible, of course, but even worse would have been if something else happened to you out here in the woods without me to protect you."

Okay, he made a compelling argument, but I didn't even care any longer because when he'd stopped talking, his mouth found mine and he kissed me with such passion that I couldn't even think.

Noah's hand was braver than before, and I briefly wondered about it, as the fingers that weren't tangled in my hair began to rub up and down my side. Somehow, he lifted me onto the ledge of the boulder without me even remembering it. Before I knew it, I had my legs wrapped around his waist, and he was pressing against me.

My body felt so alive that I thought I'd explode with the sensations. Noah's groan and his mouth working on my collar bone certainly didn't help with the combustible feeling, either.

I didn't care about anything at that moment except having Noah as close to me as possible. My body was taking control of my weak mind, and I didn't have the will to stop it. Noah could do anything he wanted to me, and I would just let him. It was inevitable.

His mouth left my skin, and he pressed his ear against my heart. His breathing was hard and hot. I could feel the heat from his entire body penetrating the thick polyester dress. A dress that I really wished I wasn't wearing at all.

"Oh, Rose—my Rose, I love you so much," he stuttered the words out between breaths with such strong emotion that I felt guilty that I'd become irritated with him at all.

He went on, "I don't take a single step all day without thinking about you—wanting you. And here you are, finally in my arms."

He pulled back, locking his eyes on mine. "I couldn't live without you. I couldn't survive a world with you not in it—so you have to be good, and very, very careful."

I understood what he was saying. But I still felt way deep down, beneath all the raging hormones, that I hadn't done a thing wrong this night.

"I think it was sweet of Suzanna and Timothy to do this for us. I mean, I would do about anything to be with you. Being here together like this is a real gift," I whispered, my words mumbling into his hair.

"I know, sweetheart. But the quicker the bishop and the church allow you to join, then the sooner we'll be officially courting. I thought I was done with all this sneaking around." Noah's hands were braced on either side of me, keeping me in a cocoon of safety.

I looked down coyly at him. "So, you don't want to meet like this again?"

He chuckled, hugging me close. His nose was against my breast, but only for a few seconds before he pulled back enough to look at me again with a sober face.

I knew what was coming.

"Rose, it kills me to be around you and pretend that there is nothing between us. I lay awake every night obsessing about you, and when I do finally fall asleep, you are in my dreams."

He signed deeply. "But we have to do the right thing. It will only be a short time when compared to the rest of our lives."

Before I could respond and beg him a little, a crashing sound through the brush stiffened me. I was surprised when Noah didn't let go of me as Summer, Matthew and Miranda burst into the open space around the boulders.

"We need to get going," Miranda stated flatly.

"What about Timmy and Suzanna?" Noah asked what I was thinking.

Summer came right over and, putting her hands behind her, bounced up onto the boulder beside me and Noah. She obviously wasn't shy about physical contact with people who were hugging.

"They're coming." She grinned brightly. "At least, I think they are."

"Well, they better be, or we'll leave them here," Matthew said as he tightened the girth on his dun-colored horse. She was tossing her head in boredom waiting for the humans.

Noah pulled my head down to his face and said close to my ear, "We'll see each other Wednesday at youth night. It's at the Bontragers' place—you'll like it there."

Really, Noah, I don't care where the party is, as long as you're there. I thought it but didn't say it. Instead, I pressed into his body and let him hold me. I was struggling to keep the tears in, which really ticked me off. There was no reason for me to be on the verge of crying as if I was a baby. It was only a few days away.

Noah rubbed my back and petted my hair. I just let him, not caring what the others thought—although, with my limited vision, I could see Matthew fidgeting with his saddle. Summer just stared ahead ignoring me and Noah. I didn't know what was going on with Miranda.

"You guys wouldn't dare leave without us," Suzanna said as

she slid from the darkness of the trees. She and Timmy were a whole lot quieter than the three stooges had been.

Noah lifted me down from the boulder but didn't make a move to release me. I peeked around him to watch as Suzanna followed Timothy to his horse and then stood quietly while he went through the same routine Matthew had, but much more quickly. Before vaulting smoothly onto his bay horse, he kissed Suzanna solidly on the lips. Matthew was already up and having a time keeping his mare in one place. She continued to paw the ground and snort in irritation.

"You girls are heading back through the woods, right, Suzanna?" Noah directed his voice to her back since she was leaned up against Timothy's leg kissing him again as he bent down from the saddle.

She broke away and backed up a couple of steps. I knew how she felt. It was definitely easier to talk when you were out of touching range from your significant other.

"Of course, don't worry about Rose. I'll get her home safe and sound," Suzanna purred.

Satisfied with her answer, Noah turned back to me and asked, "Do you want us to escort you back?"

I felt a little weak-kneed, but Suzanna broke the moment when she barked out, "We're going in opposite directions, Noah. Really, we're capable of getting home."

Noah looked at me, ignoring Suzanna's outburst.

"We'll be fine. Unless we get attacked by a squirrel, I can practically guarantee it," I said.

I would have loved to be with him longer, but Suzanna was right. There was no point in the boys doubling their time for no good reason. And, if she could tear herself away from her guy, then so could I.

Noah still looked conflicted, which made me feel very good inside. While he focused on a space in the air just above my head, his face scrunched up in concentration, Matthew's horse began to bounce in place uncontrollably.

"Noah, I'm heading out now. This mare'll have me in a tree if I don't," Matthew said, fear peppering his words.

"It's all right, go on, before we have another accident to deal with." I got on my tiptoes and lightly kissed Noah. Just as I was going back down on my heels, he gave me a more serious kiss before he let go of me and went to his horse. Maisy stood quietly for Noah to untie her and mount up. He looked a little stiff swinging his braced leg over the saddle, but all things considered, he did rather well.

"I'll see you Wednesday, Rose," Noah called as he turned Maisy and trotted to catch up with Matthew and Timothy, who were only a few strides ahead. He shouldn't have been trotting, and I was about to yell out to him when Suzanna clamped her arm around my shoulder.

She had a sly smile on her lips as she said, "That was a great surprise, wasn't it?"

I nodded my head, smiling. "Yeah, it was wonderful—very brilliant of you."

"Ha, I can't believe you almost killed my Timmy, though. You are such a brute." Suzanna laughed, heading back through the woods toward the field.

"Hey, is the fire out back there?" I thumbed over my shoulder, speaking to any of them.

"It's all taken care of. Don't worry about it," Summer chimed in, falling in step beside me.

"Suzanna, have you met Timothy out here before?" I asked, stretching my legs to keep up with her longer ones.

"Oh, a couple of times, I reckon," she said, happily marching on.

"You have?" Summer squealed. "Why haven't I heard anything about it?"

Suzanna slowed just enough to turn her head and acknowledge Summer's gaping mouth.

"Ah, Summer, I didn't mean to keep it from you, but it happened so fast. And you've been at the beach with your father for most of the summer."

Summer turned to me saying, "My folks are divorced, and Dad and his girlfriend took me to the beach for a couple of weeks." As an afterthought, she rambled, "It wasn't much fun though—Sandra brought her daughter and we don't get along very well."

"Sorry about that, Summer." I didn't want to be rude, but I was more focused on Suzanna at the moment. "So...like, are you and Timothy behaving yourselves on your secret liaisons?"

Suzanna stopped and appraised me with sharp eyes before answering. "You aren't going to tell anyone, are you?"

"Course not." I was slightly offended that she felt the need to ask.

Miranda and Summer moved in closer, forming a tight football huddle. My heart sped up in anticipation of her answer.

"Timothy and I have been doing it, if that's what you're asking." She spoke without guilt or shame.

I lowered my voice, which was silly since we were in the middle of nowhere, but I couldn't help it. "Aren't you worried about getting pregnant?"

"Heck, no," Suzanna burst out. "We aren't stupid." Then she lowered her voice for a change. "Timmy wears a condom."

"For real?" I said, not even trying to hide the shock from my voice.

My brain couldn't handle the thought of an Amish guy buying condoms—or using them.

"It's no big deal once you get the hang of it." Suzanna continued walking, more leisurely this time. She turned to me, asking, "You aren't a virgin are you?"

Suzanna's voice sounded so sure of herself that I inwardly laughed. *Did I look like a tramp or something?* Wouldn't that be something if I was the only virgin in the group?

"Actually, I've never...had sex," I said quietly.

Suzanna stopped again, grabbing my shoulder tightly. "No way—you and Noah aren't doing it yet?" The look on her face was pure astonishment.

"But the whole community thinks you and Noah have been intimate," Miranda finally said. She was also surprised, her eyes wide with disbelief.

"Why would they think that?" I wasn't shocked to hear there were rumors, but you'd think the Amish kids had better things to concern themselves with.

Suzanna thought for a few seconds. "I don't rightly know." She looked at Miranda who shrugged her shoulders. "Maybe it was something Ella said." She reconsidered. "But the way the two of you were all over each other back there, I thought sure that you'd been messing around with him already."

"Good for you, Rose. There are so few of us left in the world," Summer said, wrapping her arm around me. We continued on our way like that even though it made the going more difficult.

"So you've never done been with a guy before?" I was surprised, but not as much as Suzanna was about me.

"Nope—there aren't any guys around here worthy of me." Summer made a "huh" noise and jutted her chin out. I had to giggle. Suzanna roared with laughter.

"You are so stuck up, Summer," Suzanna said when she'd calmed herself.

"What about you, Mira?" I asked, still joined to Summer's hip.

The woods suddenly became very dark and all too quiet.

It was as if the earth had tipped just enough to shatter the illusion of a good time. Miranda didn't speak—and neither did Suzanna, which was the weird part.

After an uncomfortable minute, I squeezed Summer's arm. We both kind of shrugged at the same time. Obviously, I'd hit an off-limits subject for Miranda.

We trudged on along the edge of the field for a while in silence. The activities of the day and night were finally affecting me. I yawned. What I would have done for a cappuccino right then.

When we turned into the woods in the opposite direction from where we'd come down, I thought I was just confused. I looked around, trying to gauge our whereabouts for the first time, and decided that we were definitely going the wrong way.

"Hey, Suzanna—we should have turned right back there," I informed her.

"We're taking a shortcut. Since it's so late, no one will be on the road." She kept going until I grabbed her arm, holding her back.

"We promised the boys that we were going home through the woods." For the first time I felt resentment that I wasn't the leader of our little group.

"Ah, come on, Rose. This will get us home quicker—and it will be easier going."

She pulled away from me as if there was no room for an argument. Miranda followed Suzanna up the hill like a puppy dog. Summer hung back for just a second.

"It'll be fine. Really, we go this way all the time," Summer reassured me, taking up my hand and tugging me. I had to smile at Summer's strength and decided to go of my own free will. After all, we had to be fairly close to Suzanna's farm, and so far she'd had things orchestrated perfectly—except for me clunking Timothy on the head with a two-by-four.

A few more steps up the incline and we came out onto the narrow country road. I yawned again. It must have been near morning, I thought, checking out the dark sky. Now that we were walking comfortably on the road and I wasn't expending as much energy, I was beginning to get cold. Wrapping my arms around my chest, I moved in closer to the other girls.

"What time is it?" I questioned Summer, who pulled her phone from her pocket.

"Almost four o'clock."

"Wow, I thought it was later than that. You know, it's really strange not having a phone or a watch on me anymore," I said to no one in particular and added, "I never know the exact time."

"That would drive me crazy, it would," Summer said.

"I just kind of feel the time. You know, like when my belly starts to rumble, it's lunch, or in the middle of the afternoon I always get sleepy." As Suzanna was going on about her internal clock stimuli the sound of an engine and headlights on the road told us we weren't alone.

We all moved over single file to the side. Suzanna and Miranda kept on going, but Summer turned around and walked backward to check out the vehicle coming up behind us.

"Does anyone know a big, dark-colored dually truck?" Summer asked the rest of us.

"Oh, you've got to be kidding," I growled in my throat.

Turning around, I saw what I'd feared coming straight for us. Even with the headlights blinding me I could make out the bushy head in the driver's seat.

"Okay girls. Just keep on walking." I grabbed Summer's shoulders and forced her to turn around. My statement had finally woken Suzanna from her moody sleepwalking slumber. Curiosity had a hold of her, and she stopped to look back, completely ignoring me.

"Who is it?" Suzanna peered back as the truck quickly approached. When it was almost alongside us, she shouted, "It's your brother!"

Her excitement instantly bugged me. I'd already had to deal with a lifetime of my friends having crushes on my obnoxious brother.

I wasn't at all surprised when he rolled to a stop and lowered his window. The sound of a reggae song flowed out the window. It was heaven in my ears.

Sam's face was partially shadowed, but there was no mistaking the voice.

"Hello, ladies. Are you enjoying an evening stroll?" Sam put on his most honeyed voice for the female crowd, but I could pick up the buried sarcasm. It was the wee hours of the morning and no time to be out walking. And, without the cap and my hair in tangles around me, I knew he recognized me.

"Get lost, Sam," I snorted, hands tightly crossed on my chest.

"Rose, that isn't nice," Suzanna scolded me.

Sam took the lead and ran with it. "Oh, my little sister is *never* nice to me. No matter how I try to take care of her or watch out for her best interests, she never listens to me," Sam said, feigning sadness.

Then Summer gave her two cents, instantly becoming my best buddy for life. "Of course she doesn't want her brother bossing her round, nosing into stuff that doesn't concern him." She placed her hands on her hips and was standing shoulder to shoulder with me. She'd proven to be perceptive, seeing through my brother's stage act so clearly.

"You're not Amish," Sam said, probably not even realizing how stupid the comment sounded.

"You aren't, either, but you don't see me saying anything about it," Summer shot back.

"I guess Rose has given you an earful, and that's why you're so hostile toward me, huh?"

Summer was quick with her reply, not giving me a chance to defend myself. "No, your sister hasn't even mentioned you to me once. Matter of fact, we just met a few hours ago and we've had better things to talk about."

She was doing really well dealing with Sam. I couldn't have done much better, and I was a pro.

Here's where Sam used his favorite diversion tactic by switching the topic when he didn't have a suitable comeback line. "You girls need a ride?"

At the same time me and Summer said no, loudly, Suzanna said yes, more loudly.

I turned to Suzanna, noticing when I did that Miranda was staring at the pavement, not involved in the discussion in the least. She'd been quiet since our chat about sex. Why would my question about her virginity have affected her so much?

"We got to be close to your place, Suzanna, so let's walk," I said as I passed her with Summer close behind me.

"Oh, come on, it's still a little ways and I'm tuckered out," she said a little more loudly to my back. "You're being foolish, Rose. Just because you're mad at him doesn't mean it's fair to make us all suffer."

By the end, her voice held a pleading sound and I slowed, saying, "All right."

"You're too easy," Summer mumbled next to me. I wondered why she hated my brother so much already. I had the excuse of being harassed by the ignoramus for almost seventeen years—what was hers?

Summer, Suzanna and Miranda squeezed into the backseat, and I took my usual shotgun position. The faint smell of perfume lingered in the cab of the truck.

"Were you out with the girlfriend tonight?" I couldn't help the rudeness in my voice. It just came naturally when I talked to Sam.

"Her name is Amber. And yes, we went to dinner and a movie," Sam said pleasantly.

I was sure the last thing he wanted to be talking about in front of a truck full of girls was his girlfriend, so I plunged relentlessly on, "Must have been a *late* movie."

Sam coughed a little, and I could tell he was restraining himself with guests in attendance.

Ha, I might have gotten the last word in for a change.

"So how are you enjoying the whole dress-and-cap thing?" He smirked over at me. "You look awfully stylish tonight."

My mouth opened, but Suzanna beat me to the air space. "Turn right up here. And just go a little ways 'cause we'll walk the last bit." Suzanna was still using the "in awe" voice. When I heard girls do that around my brother, I wanted to vomit.

Sam did as he was told, stopping at an acceptable spot in the road and putting the truck into park. Then he stretched his arm along the top of the seat and turned around. "I've seen you at school, haven't I?" Sam said as he stared at Summer.

The question twirled me around in my seat. Summer's pretty face was absent of any emotion, except the corner of her mouth, which was scrunched up as if she'd bitten into a tart apple.

"I wouldn't have expected a superstud jock like you to notice a country bumpkin like me." Summer's voice had a reined-in seething tone to it, making me quickly look at Sam, who had his brow furrowed. His part-time brain was obviously working hard to remember something.

Summer began tapping my seat. She wanted to escape and

couldn't unless I got out and pushed my seat forward. At warp speed I had her freed and found myself standing on the road with Suzanna.

Summer and Miranda turned, cutting into the vast yard leading to Suzanna's farm and the cozy little girl pad.

Suzanna stepped forward to the window and said, "Gee, thanks for the ride." Then she turned and ran to catch the other girls.

Sam hollered out the window, "No problem."

I should have just turned and fled with the others, but I felt a weird twinge of homesickness. Sparring with Sam had been a taste of home, and I suddenly wanted more of it. Not really the bantering, but the homey part.

"How's it going—are they treating you okay?" Sam said placidly enough.

I rested my arms in the window and told him, "Yeah, they've all been great."

"What the hell are you doing out here in the middle of the night, anyway?"

It was a logical question, but my defense mechanisms went on high alert. "You aren't going to say anything to Dad about it, are you?"

"No. I wouldn't do that. But, haven't you learned your lesson about being out on the roadway at night?" he said seriously. I ignored him.

"These girls work so hard all the time. Every once in a while they get the chance to be kids. That's all we were doing tonight—being kids."

I was shifting my weight to leave when he said, "I'm sure that redhead isn't breaking any nails slaving away in the laundry room. What was her problem, anyway?"

Leave it to Sam to turn everything personal. "Maybe she's

just having a bad night—or maybe you've finally met a girl who's immune to your charms."

With that I pivoted and ran away from the truck at track-star speed. I didn't want to get too deep into a conversation with Sam. He was Dad's spy, and the less that Dad knew about what was going on, the better. If he was aware that I was running around the countryside in the middle of the night, he'd be there at sunrise to pick me up.

Sam had better keep his big mouth shut.

My thoughts were confused as I flew across the dark yard. Part of my brain was thinking about Noah and his warm mouth, and the other part was thinking about Dad, Sam and Justin—and how I missed them—even Sam. I hadn't really thought about how important they all were to me until they were absent from my life. Taking a deep breath to hold the emotions in, I figured it would probably get better with time. At least I hoped it would.

Turning the corner of the little guesthouse, I skidded to a stop, nearly fainting.

Suzanna was standing on the little porch landing in the moonlight with her hands on her hips. Summer had her arm around Miranda, whose head rested on Summer's shoulder.

And there—just a few feet away—was Levi Zook.

Levi's eyes snapped to me. He was still as creepy as before. His bright orange hair flared out from under a black knit cap that was too warm for the September weather. His black eyes, too small for his face, stared at me from head to toe. Levi's mouth twitched in pleasure, as if he was seeing me naked. A cold sweat rose to the surface of my skin.

I couldn't help folding my arms around me tightly. The vibe emitting from the guy was downright scary. There was something seriously wrong with him, and my brain was trying to assess the danger we were in at the same time that I was attempting to puzzle out what he was doing there. I quickly judged him to be alone, which loosened my heart a bit.

"Well, look who's been out gallivanting in the middle of the night." He took a step closer, but I held my ground. If he got too close I was going to kick him so hard in what little balls he had he'd be castrated for sure.

"So, was it you that got these girls out running when they should have been sleeping like good girls in their beds?" he sneered.

"It wasn't Rose's idea," Suzanna snapped in a loud whisper. She was in a tricky situation. She couldn't wake her parents to get rid of Levi; she'd have to do it on her own—and quietly.

Levi's voice came out slippery and quickly. "Oh, I can only guess what Bishop Lambright's going to do to you, Rose, when he finds out."

Surprising me, it was Miranda's voice that rang out. "You aren't going to say a thing to the bishop about this, Levi."

Miranda's head was up now, and I searched for any resemblance to the devil spawn standing menacingly near me. Besides both being skinny, I just couldn't see any.

Levi took several seconds to process what his sister had said before he turned and covered the few steps back to the porch. Both Suzanna and Summer moved in front of Miranda, blocking her from Levi's wrath. My mind was swimming with possibilities.

"What did you just say, sissy?"

Miranda replied in a strong voice, "You heard me."

Levi leaned into the porch with his hands on the little railing as if he was ready to vault over it. "How are ya going to keep me from talking?"

I heard Miranda's intake of breath. This was difficult for her and not because she'd been caught doing something wrong, either. Her relationship with Levi was nothing like the combative dynamic with my brother. Levi really was menacing, whereas when it came right down to it, Sam was a pushover.

Miranda squeezed through Suzanna and Summer and bent down to Levi's face. She was way too close to him, and I instinctively took a step forward, my heart pounding in my ears.

"You say so much as a word about this to anyone, even Nathaniel, and I'll start talking about your own secrets." She had been whispering, but now her voice lowered and I strained to hear. "And it won't hurt me at all. I already got sent away once and you know what? I liked it better than being here around you—and your paws."

Levi backed away from Miranda as if she had struck him physically, his mouth open, his face wide. He stood there for a minute just staring at his sister, unsure what to do or say; then he did find his voice.

"We'll talk about this later." He turned and jogged down into the woods, near the place where we'd entered what felt like an eternity ago now.

I rushed to the porch and without much thought grabbed Miranda and pulled her against me. Her head went down into my hair, and she began to weep. It wasn't a little cry, either, but a full-blown sob.

Summer got the door, and Suzanna helped me shuffle Miranda into the tight quarters. When the door shut behind us, we quickly took Miranda to the sofa, sitting down with her. Surprisingly, she continued to stay glued to me. I let her cry herself out against me while Suzanna sat on her other side stroking Miranda's long hair. Summer was cross-legged on the chair in front of us. She stared at the wall with a thoughtful look on her face.

I noticed the plates with the remnants of our pecan pie still cluttering the small table and Summer's and my bags lying on the floor where we'd dropped them hours before. I was seeing the stuff, but my mind was only half registering everything. Instead, I was processing what I'd just heard.

I could see only one conclusion, and inwardly, I prayed it wasn't true.

Finally, after I don't know how long, Miranda spoke.

"I'm sorry, Rose—but I don't think he'll tell." She sniffed, and Suzanna brought her a paper towel. Miranda sat up wiping the wetness from her face.

"Don't you worry about me, but...but, what about you?" I paused, searching for the softest words, and realizing there was no way to put it mildly. "Has Levi ever done anything to you?"

My eyes caught Suzanna, and my suspicion was confirmed. She already knew.

Miranda let out a big sigh and looked me straight in the eye. Summer had crawled across the floor and was resting her head on my knee, and I absently touched her hair, twirling the reddish locks between my fingers. We were all so close that Miranda could afford to whisper, and that's what she did.

"Not anymore he doesn't. Well, it's been a while, anyway." She gathered herself by looking at Suzanna, who nodded her head in encouragement. "It started when I was nine or so. He's three years older than me, so I'd listen to him. He started making me do things I didn't want to do...and then he'd do stuff." The tears started flowing again, and I rubbed her back. I hoped she didn't give any details, because I was already boiling inside and I didn't think I could sit there and listen. I'd be out the door hunting the scumbag down myself.

"It was terrible. So—awful—went on for about four years and then he stopped. Just like that he never came around me anymore. But still, sometimes he looks at me in a way that makes me worry all over again." She was trembling.

Summer blurted out, "Why didn't you tell anyone?"

"He's my older brother. Why would anyone believe me over him? Whenever I did try to say anything that would give Ma a clue, she'd get so angry with me."

Miranda glanced back at me. "That's why I went away to live at a house run by the Mennonites—a place where troubled teens find their way back to God." Her voice was quiet, but the words were resentful.

"How long have you been away?" I asked, still rubbing her back.

"I guess it's been six months. I was only allowed to return because I promised all sorts of stuff. I didn't really want to come back, but I missed my little brothers—" she looked at Suzanna "—and my friends."

"And you never told anyone at the Mennonite house about Levi?" I asked, trying to get the most filled-out picture I could.

"No. What was the point? He wasn't bothering me anymore—and I didn't think any good would come of them knowing," she said calmly, and I could see the practical Amish mind at work.

A few minutes later Suzanna and Miranda had gone into the only bedroom to sleep. Before Miranda had left, she thanked me for giving her a reason to stand up to Levi for the first time in her life. I couldn't help the tears that streamed down my cheeks at her words.

I stretched out beside Summer on the sofa, which we'd opened up into a narrow bed. My face felt dirty, and my hair was a snarly mess. I usually hated going to sleep, even for an hour, which was about what we had before daybreak, without getting cleaned up and pouring on the moisturizer.

But for once, I didn't care about my nightly routine. My entire image of the Amish world was crashing down around me. I wanted it to stop. I wished I could go back to that day when I first ate dinner at the Millers' and was so shamelessly trying to get Noah's attention. Those were better days—much easier.

I could tell that Summer was still awake. Her breathing was erratic, and she tossed and turned beside me. I didn't feel like talking and I guess neither did she. But I must admit I was sure glad I had a new friend who didn't have to live by the tight regulations that everyone else did.

Staring at the ceiling, I wondered what I should do about Levi. It wasn't really a question of doing something; that was a done deal. It was figuring out the best way to go about stringing him up by the neck, without giving Miranda more trouble— or getting my butt kicked out of the community in the process.

Just as the first spray of buttery light came through the window, I finally closed my eyes, unconsciousness welcoming me into its black embrace.

I found no peace in my dreams, being ever followed by a shadow—one with a pale face and bright red hair.

6

Sam

Staring down at the few drops of milk left in my cereal bowl, I clutched the side of my head. Damn, I hated having to get up early after a late night. It wouldn't have been such a big deal if I'd fallen asleep when my head hit the pillow, but no such luck. I'd tossed around for another couple of hours trying to figure out why the redhead had seemed familiar to me.

And why she'd been so damn rude.

The only thing I'd done was chauffeur her butt up the road a mile, and instead of a little gratitude, the chick became my sister's bulldog. Hell, if the girl looked like a dog, I wouldn't have cared less about her nasty personality, but that wasn't the case. She was actually really pretty—in a country sort of way.

Suddenly it hit me. I leaned back and shouted out an *"Aha!"*

"What?" Justin looked at me with confusion.

"I just remembered where I saw that hot little redhead before." I was so pleased with myself I couldn't help grinning from ear to ear. Jumping up, I carried my bowl to the sink and dumped it in. I was pretty sure it was Justin's day to do the dishes, so I wasn't worrying about it. I had more important places to be.

"A redhead—I thought you were dating a blonde," Justin said.

"Hurry up, kid. We're wasting time," I said as Dad walked in through the back door. He looked fairly run-down from his all-night shift at the hospital.

"What's going on, Sam? It's only seven—you have plenty of time to get Justin and yourself to school," Dad said as he deposited his briefcase on the table and headed for the refrigerator. He pulled out the orange juice, and I handed him a glass, feeling especially generous all of a sudden.

"Ah, there's this girl—a very uptight little woman, actually—who I just figured out something about. And I'm looking forward to talking to her today." Actually, I was almost giddy with the thought of seeing her again, even though I didn't know what her name was—yet.

"Sam, really, you spend way too much time focused on girls." Dad took a swig and tried to give me a "superior adult" look.

I laughed. "Yeah, you're one to talk. How many times have you been out with Tina this week?" I looked over at Justin who shrugged. He wasn't moving fast enough for me, either. I crossed the room, swatting him on the head to get him up from the chair.

"Maybe three—or is it four times?" I finished, looking smugly back at Dad.

He seemed tired and for an instant I regretted saying it. "That's none of your concern. And, as I recall, Tina's made a couple of dinners for us here and did the laundry once, so you shouldn't be complaining."

"When does she become our stepmom?" Justin asked innocently, reminding me of Rose. He took more after her with his quiet, subtle ways of stabbing a knife into a person. Me, I liked to be up-front and attack head-on.

Dad found his sense of humor. "You'll be the first to know, Justin." He messed up the kid's hair and then returned to staring at me. "When did you meet this new love interest?"

Okay, Dad was playing my game, trying to divert attention

away from his own issues. Fair enough, except I couldn't really tell him I'd met the girl on the road in the middle of the night. That wouldn't make a good impression. And then there was the whole Rose being with her and all. I thought for a few seconds and answered as honestly as I could without selling Rose out.

"Met last night—it was no big deal. I don't think she's even my type, really." I grabbed my backpack and keys and headed for the door. "I'll be waiting two minutes, Justin. If you're not in the truck by then, you're riding the bus today."

That got Justin sprinting into the hallway.

"Bye, Dad," I said just as the door was closing. I didn't want to give him any time to question me. He might be a doctor, but he would have made a decent lawyer, too.

Squeezing through the crowded hallway, I couldn't think about much except the redhead. It bugged me, too. I had encounters with pretty girls every day and had never gotten a headache over it before. Maybe it was the fact that she was quite literally the first girl that I'd ever encountered who wasn't instantly enamored with my good looks and charming personality. Sure, some girls didn't get all worked up in my presence, but this chick was actually hostile toward me...making her all the more intriguing. I wouldn't be able to get a good night's sleep until I figured her out and won her over.

Somehow I knew I'd find her somewhere in the junior hallway—and so that was my destination. A small group of the varsity football players greeted me and attempted to slow me for a chat, but I brushed them off. Then several girls in succession went out of their way to get my attention, only aggravating me. I didn't have much time before my English class, and I needed to get this conversation out of the way, so I could get on with my life.

She wasn't hard to spot. Reddish-blond hair like that was not very common, especially if it wasn't out of a bottle, and I was fairly certain this chick's wasn't. I slowed, not wanting to startle her. My heart started to pound with nervousness, making me both angry and totally bewildered. I hadn't felt this way since I'd had a crush on Madison Tully in sixth grade.

Just as I reached her and was hesitating, she turned, and in her hurry to get wherever she was going, she smacked right into me.

Bouncing off, she first looked surprised that I was in her space, and then she glared at me.

"What do you want?" she seethed, hugging her books to her chest.

I felt more confident now that I understood her attitude toward me, and I smiled nicely.

"I just wanted to explain to you about that little incident that happened last week."

Her green eyes narrowed, and she waited. I couldn't help but notice that those eyes went very well with her hair. Even though we were crammed in the middle of the hustle of dozens of kids, I felt as if I were alone with the girl in our own bubble. The girl's intensity was interesting, strumming some chord way down deep inside me.

And, I didn't even know her name.

Skipping ahead, I offered my hand and said, "I don't believe we've been properly introduced. I'm Sam Cameron."

She looked at my hand as if it was a dead rat, not even deigning to take it. I let my hand drop to my side. I had to admit, the fact that she wouldn't touch me made me feel like crap.

"I know who you are," she said without telling me who the hell she was.

At this point, the normal thing to have said was, "It's nice to meet you, my name is blankety-blank," but of course, I wasn't so lucky. I was quickly getting sick of her difficult nature.

"Why do you even care?" She tilted her head, her voice softening maybe a little bit.

I took my chance. "Hey, I'm sorry about what Shaun said to you."

The scene ran through my head for the hundredth time: me, Shaun and several of the other guys charging through the hall to get to practice. When we'd turned the corner, Shaun had bowled this little redhead over. We'd been in a hurry; if we were late to practice again, our play time at the next game was going to be docked. As we'd hurried past the girl, she'd gotten up and I'd only seen the back of her head as she'd begun walking away. I'd commented to Shaun about it, hesitating in the hallway. He'd just laughed, saying out loud something to the tune of "the girl is just a country bumpkin and doesn't deserve my time."

Yeah, I should have gone back, apologized and made sure she was okay, but I didn't. I was in too big of a hurry. Now, as I gazed at the little redhead, a girl who was becoming increasingly prettier by the minute, I was paying the price.

Her face began to brighten as if a light in her brain had just turned on. "So, you're feeling guilty about your buddy's bad behavior. Is that it?"

The twist to her voice said she was mocking me. It was not the response I was hoping for.

"Hey, I just wanted you to know that I was in a rush that day. I'm not a jerk like Shaun."

The hallway was emptying, and I realized I was going to be late to my class. I didn't care, though. For some insane reason I didn't want to break contact with the girl. But she didn't have that qualm. When she noticed that we were almost alone, she brushed by me without speaking.

"Hey, you never did tell me your name," I shouted after her, not caring what the few slackers around us thought.

My heart skipped when she slowed and began moving

backward for a few strides. She called back to me, "Summer—Summer Sage."

She smiled and disappeared around the corner.

I mulled the name as I made my way to class—*Summer Sage*—a very cool name for a very cool girl. And, the fact that she was friends with my runaway sister was just icing on the cake.

7

Rose

I yawned as I dumped the half cup of sugar over the grapes in the quart jar. It was an easy job, but given the sixty or more jars crowded on the counter waiting for sugar, it was also a tedious one. Ruth was at the stovetop, her head hovering over the giant steaming pot when she called me over.

"Rose, come here and I'll show you how to safely remove the jars."

I stifled another yawn, putting my measuring cup down. I hadn't recovered physically from the wild night a few days before. It was Wednesday now, and I was still dragging. Of course, waking at five o'clock every morning to get the laundry and other chores done early enough that I'd still have time to do my schoolwork and keep Dad happy wasn't helping my sleep-deprived situation, either. If I was really Amish, I'd have been done with education in the eighth grade and, like the other girls my age, I'd have more time to do the grueling workload.

Wiping the sweat from my forehead, I joined Ruth at the canning jars. Just the place I didn't want to be, closer to the rolling heat.

Ruth handed me the thingamajig to lift the jars out, which

I did, setting them onto the towel that was spread out on the table. After they'd been removed from the churning water, I added replacement jars, starting the process all over. A crescendo of pops sparked through the air, startling me.

Ruth must have noticed. "When the top of a can pops, it means it's sealed properly." She pressed her finger down on one that had already popped and then picked up my finger and did the same with mine. "See, you test them this way. If they are firm, then they're fine."

I went to touch another one, and she stopped me. "No, don't start pressing them now. Sometimes it takes a while and you will only disrupt the process."

"Oh," I mumbled, surveying the work that still needed to be done. "We have quite a bit of grape juice here, don't you think?"

"In the end, I hope to put up about a hundred quarts. I'm doing extra this year for Emy. She doesn't need to be working over a hot stove in her condition."

The mention of Emilene brought the picture of the gigantically bloated woman I'd met the day before to mind. She'd come over for dinner with her husband and ten kids. The poor thing was having some major swelling problems with her pregnancy.

The husband, Jeremiah, was a useless log as far as the kids were concerned. I'd been stressed out just watching Emy waddle around filling her littlest kids' plates with food. I'd attempted to help, but the kids had seemed to sense I was an oddity and avoided me. The language barrier with the children hadn't helped, either.

"When did you say Emy was due?" I asked as I continued with my sugar-topping job.

"Only about two weeks, but I doubt she'll go that long with

all the difficulties she's having this time." Ruth began adding the water to the jars that I had ready for her.

The afternoon sun was shining in the windows and mixing with the saunalike conditions in the kitchen to make the room unbearably hot. I'd have to change into a fresh dress before the youth gathering since the one I had on was sticking to me in too many places to count.

I smiled, thinking about how strange my thought patterns were nowadays. The figureless dresses were still hideous, but I was *almost* getting used to them. I didn't like my hair in a bun, though, and I reached up to tuck some loose strands back into the cap. Ruth wasn't as strict about my hair being in perfectly tidy condition as Mrs. Miller was, so I got away with not coiling it so tight. Still, it was the worst part about being an Amish woman, I decided—and the laundry.

I missed the boring days when I had nothing much to do except lounge on my bed listening to music. I missed my favorite bands and TV shows, but not as much as I imagined I would—probably because the days were so full of stuff to do. I didn't have any time to lament about what I'd given up to be Amish—and to be with Noah.

Thinking about Noah stirred up all sorts of excitement in my body, remembering how he'd kissed and touched me the last time we'd been together. My mind was so sure of my decision when he was close by. The doubts only crept in when he was away from me.

And then there was the whole business with Miranda and her disgusting brother, Levi. When I wasn't obsessing about Noah, I was replaying the part of the night when Levi had shown up uninvited.

I still hadn't decided what to do about him yet.

And I wasn't so sure I should tell Noah about the situation. First of all, I'd be betraying the oath of secrecy that Miranda had made me and Summer swear to in the morning before the four of us had gone our separate ways.

Yet I was certain that if I thought enough about it, I could come up with a way to make Levi pay for what he'd done to his sister without breaking my promise.

"You look mighty deep in thought, Rose." Ruth stopped her work on the canning assembly line to stare at me.

What should I tell her? Nothing, but maybe she could help me make my decision without learning anything.

"I was wondering about the punishment system in the community." I continued to work, acting as nonchalant as possible.

"The only thing you need to know, my girl, is that if you do wrong, you'll be leaving us right quick," Ruth said firmly.

"I know that. I was just thinking about the other kids." I paused, searching her face for understanding, but she was going to make me spit it out. "What happens to them if they disobey the Ordnung that you've been telling me about?"

Ruth sighed a little, and I could tell she deemed my question worth answering. She wiped her hands on her apron and said, "That depends on what they did."

"Uh, well, what if a courting couple were caught kissing?" I threw out the first thing that came to mind.

Ruth laughed. "Usually, something like that would be taken care of by the parents. Unless the kissing was getting out of hand—then the ministers and bishop would get involved."

Now we were getting somewhere. "Hypothetically, of course, what would the Elders do if a couple did the deed?" I was almost embarrassed taking to Ruth about sex, but she did have ten of her own kids. Surely she was an expert about it.

Ruth's face darkened a shade, and her voice came out harsh. "You and Noah haven't crossed into that territory, have you?"

"No, no. This isn't about me at all. I promise. I just was wondering about what kind of punishment happened to the young people in the community that do things that are considered really bad. You know, like having sex, or drinking and smoking, that sort of stuff."

Ruth's face softened a bit, and she seemed to resign herself to a cultural lesson for me. "First off, not all Amish communities are run the same way. The Forest Grove Church is only about eight miles away, and they follow a very different Ordnung than we do here in Meadowview. When the teens there reach the age of sixteen, they practice *rumspringa*."

Seeing my eyes widen at the word, she chuckled before continuing. "Sometimes I forget just how ignorant you are about our ways. You have to forgive me when I make assumptions about your knowledge. What that word means is that the young people are given the freedom to run around and be wild before accepting the church—sometimes being wild means driving a car or drinking alcohol. Many of those young men begin smoking over there also."

"Amish people smoke?" I was too dumbfounded to keep my mouth shut.

"Not in our community they don't, but elsewhere, the men are allowed to do it in private. A nasty habit if you ask me. But getting back to what we were originally talking about, the youth here in Meadowview are held to a more Godly approach to life, and our church will not tolerate such behavior. If a couple were participating in sinful touching, they would have to go before the church to answer to their wrongful ways."

"You mean they'd have to tell the entire church on Sunday what they did and that's the punishment?"

Definitely horrible, but still better than the torture devices I was imagining.

"Abram would announce the couple's sins to the congregation while the young woman and man sat before the people.

Then they would suffer some amount of shunning. And that varies, depending on the actual level of sin and disobedience."

She waited for more questions as I rolled the information around in my head before I bombarded her. Certainly, Noah and I would have to behave ourselves, or at least not get caught, to avoid such an embarrassing situation. Now I knew that I could *never* bring Levi's abuse of his sister to any adult in the church. The last thing Miranda needed was all the dirty details broadcast by Bishop Lambright to the entire community.

"What exactly happens when a person is shunned?" I'd heard the word before, and just the sound of it sent chills up my arms. Dad had given his own idea of the meaning, but what I was really interested in was the truth from an expert like Ruth.

"Not all churches or families handle a shunning exactly the same way. Basically, though, when a person is shunned they are not allowed to mingle or take a meal with the members of the church for the period of the shunning."

"So if a person were shunned for life, then they couldn't hang around with their family?"

Here's what Noah was so afraid of.

"Oh, some Amish people keep a bit of a relationship up with shunned people, but it is always limited."

Ruth must have seen my disapproval, because she jumped to a defensive position quickly. "Rose, this is difficult for Englishers to understand, but shunning those church members who have chosen a different path than our way is how we preserve our traditions and our whole way of life."

Hearing little Hope barking on the porch, both of us turned our heads to the window. The light shining from a car alerted me that Dad had arrived. Pushing the conversation to the back of my mind, I untied my apron and tossed it on the chair by the table.

Before I ran out of the house, I stopped to smile at Ruth sheepishly. Knowing my dad was here had taken me momentarily out of my Amish character. Ruth eyed me sternly for a second before she nodded at the door, allowing me to be on my way. I grabbed up my notebook of schoolwork that sat on the counter and bolted through the doorway, slowing only long enough to grab Hope as I headed down the porch steps.

The perfectly warm September breeze danced along my skin while I hurried toward Dad's waiting SUV. He barely had gotten out of the vehicle when I crashed into him. He hugged me and Hope tightly, not saying a word.

The sunbeams on my face, Hope squiggling in my arms and Dad's aftershave smell in my nose made me feel as if I'd woken from a crazy dream. It was hard to believe that it had only been a couple of weeks since I'd left him and my brothers to become Amish.

He pulled back grinning down at me. "Do you have your assignments done for me, Rosie?"

Since I was continuing with my schooling on my own under Dad's supervision, I had specific schoolwork to complete each week. The arrangement had made me feel more at ease with the move since I'd be seeing Dad on a weekly basis, but I suddenly worried that he'd take the papers and flee.

"Ah, yeah, but I have questions about some of it."

"Is there a place where we can go over the materials?" Dad asked in a conspiratorial voice.

There was no way I was taking him in the house.

I thought for a minute and decided on the picnic table in the backyard.

Once we were seated, Dad took a few minutes to briefly look over my work. He answered a made-up question I had before folding his arms in front of him and saying, "Looks as if you have a pretty good handle on this learning-at-home business. Are they giving you the time you need to do this comfortably?"

"Yeah, Ruth is pretty good about it. But I do have to get up earlier than I like in order to get it all done," I said, trying to sound upbeat, but whenever my mind drifted to the five o'clock battery-operated alarm going off, my mood soured.

"So you're becoming an early bird, eh?" he teased me.

"No. You know me better than that. What about you, how are things going at the house?"

"Well, let's see. Both Sam and Justin like their new schools. Justin has already made a couple of gamer friends. He had them over the other night. And, Sam is...well, the usual Sam. He's chasing after a new girl right now—some redhead."

A redhead—the lights blinked on in my head.

Dad couldn't possibly mean Summer. Sam only met her a few nights ago...and they didn't get along.

"What's the name of this new girl?" I needed to make sure my Casanova brother wasn't stalking my new best friend.

"I don't have a clue. I guess if it gets serious, he'll fill us in about her," Dad said.

"And how's Tina doing?" I might as well get the question over with. A teeny, tiny part of me hoped they'd broken up in the two weeks that I'd been away.

"She's doing well. As a matter of fact, she'd like to cook a dinner that you could join us for. You're welcome to bring Noah, too." Dad sounded hopeful. Unfortunately, he didn't get the whole Amish dating rules thing. And since I wasn't even officially dating Noah, dinner was a negative. I had to be care-ful that Dad didn't find out that we weren't even a couple yet.

Somehow, I didn't think he'd appreciate the information.

I fished around in my skull for an excuse to decline the offer. "I'd love to do that, but...ah...not for a while yet." Seeing the look of disappointment flash across Dad's face, I added quickly, "I mean I've only been here with the Hershbergers for a short time...." I trailed off, not enjoying Dad's hurt face.

He steadied himself, and I could tell he wanted to say more, but he was biting his tongue back. Tina already had him trained well.

Abruptly, he stood, only taking the time to bend down and scratch Hope's head before saying, "I have to be at the hospital this evening, and I want to make sure Sam and Justin have dinner."

Nice going, Dad. Trying to send me on a guilt trip, huh?

"You're leaving already?" I controlled my voice.

"Yes, Rose. You said yourself that you need to focus on your new life. I'll let you get back to it." He came around the side of the picnic table and gave me a brief hug.

I picked up Hope, holding her tightly against my chest as I followed Dad through the yard. He only acknowledged me again when he was seated in his car.

"I'll be back next week to drop off your grades and pick up your new assignments. You take care. And be good."

With that, my Dad, the guy who'd treated me as if I were a princess since I was a day old, turned around and left me standing there alone. My chest felt like it was about to explode. A tear trickled out of one of my eyes, and I quickly wiped it away.

Dad was playing the psychological game very well. He'd managed to reduce me to a bundle of homesick blubbering foolishness. But what my poor dad didn't understand was that even though I missed him and my brothers, those feelings didn't compare to the overwhelming love I felt for Noah.

Sucking in a deep breath, I turned and walked to the house. Yes, I would be sad being separated from my family, but I couldn't survive being away from Noah.

8

Noah

I mouthed the words to the song, making a good show of it for everyone. My mind was on other things, though, and I couldn't keep my eyes from straying to Rose's beautiful face. She was actually singing this hymn since it was in English, and I could make out her sweet voice above the others. Maybe it was that I was listening more closely for her, but then I caught the thoughtful look on Abram's face as he watched Rose, and realized it wasn't just my infatuation. Rose really had a nice voice. And the bishop noticed—which was probably a good thing.

All around, it had been an excellent day. I was feeling great physically, about the same as I had felt before the accident. And the brilliant smile on Rose's face as she rode Lady up the driveway alongside my sister proved that asking Sarah to invite Rose to ride horseback to the youth gathering was a very good idea indeed.

Seeing Rose so delighted to be astride her horse again was only part of the reason that I orchestrated the ride. I wanted her to spend more time with my sister than she did with the rebel girls. Rose would only get into trouble if she continued to hang out with them. Sarah, on the other hand, was a good girl and would direct Rose on the proper course for a woman in our community. The Plain people would think more favorably of Rose if she stayed close to my sister. It worried me that any of the Elders would see Rose spending so much time with Suzanna and Miranda.

Eyeing Abram again, I sighed. He usually didn't show up for the youth gatherings, but tonight was different. He was here because of Rose—he was checking things out for himself.

He could spy on her as much as he wanted. Unless he had been wandering in the woods late at night, he had nothing on her. I trusted our little group to keep the surprise get-together a secret. Everyone had their own incentives not to talk about it, and they were all pretty stealthy with their sneaking around.

I tried to erase the thoughts of that night, because it got me all fired up inside. The feel of Rose in my arms was better than ever before. And that was hard for me to believe. Each time I touched her, I experienced more desire; just a glance from my sweetheart made the blood pump heavily through my veins. I didn't know if I could rein myself in again if I found myself completely alone with her. All reason went out the door when she was in my embrace. And even though I knew that we had to be especially careful until Rose was allowed to join the church, I still imagined future secret meetings with her, times when I might not stop kissing her.

The song ended, pulling me back from memories of the dark woods. Everyone passed the books to the end of the table in a flurry of movement before they bolted to their feet, leaving the Zooks' garage.

Watching the young people flee the building, I couldn't help but think about the following week's church service—it was at the Weavers' place. I glanced down at Ella, who turned away quickly when our eyes met, making me shiver at the thought.

So far, Ella hadn't started anything, but that could change at any moment. My driver, Mr. Denton, had warned me one day when he was talking about his ex-wife—something about hell not having the same fury as a pissed-off woman.

Watching Ella slither away, I had to agree with Mr. Denton. I'd have to watch out for her in a big way.

My eyes quickly found Rose at the back of the crowd, heading at a more relaxed speed toward the doorway. Annoyingly, I saw that Suzanna and Miranda were flanking her. Sarah was in the mix, too, but there was something about the way the girls were walking that made me think that Rose was bonding more strongly with the two rebels than with my sister. All my careful planning had failed.

Rose, sensing my mind on her, turned to grace me with a smile just before she left the stuffy building for the cooler evening air outside. The cloud cover promised rain later in the night, and I hoped I could get home and have the horse turned out before it started.

"So, Noah, how are things going with your converted English girlfriend?" Levi said in a friendly voice that dripped insincerity.

Was he pushing my buttons to cause a scene or was he just that stupid?

I appraised Levi's pale face before answering him. "It's none of your concern."

"Oh, I disagree about that," Levi said, licking his lips with a snakelike flick, "especially since she's been hanging around my little sister. Mira might pick up bad habits from an English girl who's pretending to be Amish."

I knew he was trying to bait me, but it was still hard not to punch him. Levi Zook had a good butt whooping coming, and I was going to be the one to deliver it.

But not right now.

"Hey, Noah, are you coming?" Timmy asked, suddenly standing on the other side of the table.

"Oh, yeah." I squinted my eyes a little and stared at Levi, who didn't turn away. "It's been nice talking to you," I said in as friendly a tone as I could muster.

A minute later when Timmy and I were walking through the yard, I finally let out the breath I'd been holding in.

"Levi giving you trouble again?" Timmy asked, slowing his speed so that we could talk if I wanted to.

"He's bound and determined to ruin Rose's chances of being accepted into the church—and I don't know what to do about it."

It felt good to get it off my chest.

"Why don't you tell your Da about it? He's a minister, and that way he'll know what Levi's up to before he even does it," Timmy suggested in a low voice.

We stopped, and unconsciously my gaze found Rose. She was already playing ball with her group of friends. I watched her help Maretta up after the clumsy girl fell trying to get the ball.

"I'll do anything to protect Rose. Levi is not going to ruin this for us, I promise you that," I said with more anger than I wanted.

"I know what you're saying and I'll do what I can to help you out, but really, you should talk to an adult about it, before it's too late."

I really wanted to discuss it with Rose before the gathering was over. But the chances of me getting that opportunity were slim at best. Maybe Suzanna could deliver a message to her. I was working it all out in my head when I saw Mr. Hershberger coming up the driveway at a speed that was way too fast for the old guy and his older mare.

Timmy and I both watched James park the buggy close to

the house. The man jumped down with more agility than most fellows half his age and entered the house. Before long, several of the girls were coming up the hill, and Rose was among them.

Just as James came out the door with Libby Zook close on his heels, Rose made it to the porch. I was too far away to hear a thing, but the conversation was animated with both James's and Rose's hands flying around. A few seconds later, Rose took off for the barns at a run.

I started in her direction, but Timmy's hand stopped me. "Hey, don't go doing something stupid." His eyes locked on mine and I knew he was right.

Instead, I went to the house with Timmy beside me. I tried to restrain my speed, walking casually.

Before I got there, I met up with Rachel. "What's going on?" I asked my sister.

She kept moving toward the nets, pausing only long enough to say, "Emilene Yoder is having her babies."

Relief washed over me. I'd had visions of something bad having to do with Rose. Timmy gripped my shoulder with a supportive shake. He'd also been imagining the worst.

It all made sense now. Libby was one of the community midwives, so of course she'd be needed for the birth.

The clops on the driveway brought my head back up. Rose had been quick. She was already behind James's buggy, pacing her Arabian at a slow canter to the driving horse's full trot. Watching Rose go brought an instant depression over me. I wouldn't get to see her again until Sunday.

And Levi could stir up a whole heap of trouble by then.

9

Rose

I sat in the hard wooden chair in the corner of the room wondering what I was doing there. The adrenaline rush of leaving the gathering in such a hurry had left me breathless for a while. Then there was the gallop to the Hershbergers' barn and the award-winning unsaddling job to turn around and jump into Mr. Hershberger's buggy. Now, as I brought my hand to my mouth to cover the yawn, sleepiness made my head heavy.

I glanced at Mrs. Zook who fluttered around Emilene, trying not to bump into the other midwife in the room, a middle-aged English woman who had her long brown hair pulled back into a ponytail. I said a silent thank-you to the universe that the non-Amish woman was there for the event. Her name was Bridgett, and she had an intelligent and calm aura about her that bode well for any emergency that might come up. She was also friendly, which was more than I could say for Mrs. Zook.

Miranda favored her mother in looks, but that's where the similarities ended. When I had hopped into the buggy, Mrs. Zook had purposely turned the other way and ignored me. It had been the first time that an Amish person had been so blatantly rude to me, other than her evil son and Ella Weaver, of course.

"Rose, be a dear, and open that window behind you," Ruth said as she plumped the pillows at Emilene's back.

I did as I was asked, happy for the breeze. The powder-blue room was stuffy with all the bodies moving around. There was Ruth, Bridgett and Mrs. Zook, along with the two sisters-in-law, who looked so much alike I couldn't keep them straight.

I had found the one place where I could stay out of the way and hopefully be forgotten about. I didn't want to see a woman I hardly knew give birth. It wasn't normal for someone my age to be in the room for such a thing, and I figured that I would probably have psychological issues to deal with afterward.

And where was the doctor? It didn't seem safe, especially with Emilene resembling one of those balloon people that floated around in the skies above car dealerships.

Emilene started moaning again. I watched as her mom held her hand, soothing her with words until the contraction passed. Sighing, I turned away from the pain and searched out the window. It was black as ink now, and although I couldn't see the rain, I could hear the pitter-pat of sprinkles on the tin roof. It had been hours since I had first taken my position on the uncomfortable chair.

Staring at the blackness, I listened to the women's quiet murmurs. Sometimes they spoke in German, but often they spoke English for Bridgett's sake. It was all about making Emilene more comfortable, or how the delivery was progressing.

At the moment, Ruth and Bridgett were discussing the point when they would abandon the attempt of an at-home delivery and take Emy to the hospital. Ruth said the driver was waiting outside if needed.

If they took a vote right then, and I was registered to place a ballot, I'd go for the hospital idea. Poor woman could have her epidural and give birth in style. And I could get back to my bed more quickly.

Being a doctor's daughter, I wasn't exactly ignorant of what was going on. Everything that was being said made sense to me. I just wasn't into the whole scene. My mind kept wandering to Noah, wondering what he was doing; or even worse, I'd start to obsess about Miranda. Having Mrs. Zook in the room and witnessing firsthand what a B she was, I felt doubly sorry for her daughter.

I'd always had a very open relationship with my mom. I could talk to her about anything and she'd listen patiently. Then she'd get a game plan in order and help me solve whatever problem I had at the time. Now that she was gone, I realized that she'd been the best mom a girl could have.

I breathed deep, attempting to erase the sadness that suddenly sprouted within me before a tear dropped.

"Would you mind filling this with more ice?" Bridgett had leaned down to me while I was far away in my mind, and her sudden appearance startled me.

She smiled and squeezed my shoulder when she handed me the plastic cup. The smell of peppermint wafted off of her. The pleasant scent perked me up a bit, and I stretched as I stood.

I tried not to look at Emilene as another wail came from her, this time even louder. It wasn't difficult with the women forming a tightly knit wall around her. Hurrying from the room, I guessed my way back to the kitchen.

I kept my eyes downcast as I made my way past the four men sitting at the kitchen table, only to flash a smile at Mr. Hershberger when he raised his fingers from the table to acknowledge me. They were drinking coffee around a platter piled high with sandwich halves. The men were relaxed, not appearing very concerned about the painful cries coming from the bedroom—especially the most wrinkly one, who had his head resting on his propped-up hand with his eyes closed and his mouth gaping.

While I scooped the ice chips into the cup, I turned my head to watch the father-to-be biting into a sandwich. I grimaced, thinking about how easy men had it. Here was the daddy munching on a snack while his wife was suffering through another childbirth. A swarm of children of varying ages were playing nearby on the floor while a gray-haired woman sat in the corner on a comfortable-looking rocking chair with a toddler in her arms.

Shifting my gaze back to Emilene's husband, I growled inwardly. It certainly wasn't fair.

As the drone of the children's voices faded behind me, I walked back to the birthing room, glad that no one had attempted to talk to me on my trip to get the ice chips. I really wasn't in the mood for conversing at that point. Stepping through the doorway, I almost turned around.

Emilene was sitting up and pushing.

It was inevitable; I was going to see not one, but two babies being born.

Bridgett counted while Emilene pushed with all her might, her face bulging and turning a darker shade of pink with each number spoken. After ten babies, I was expecting these to just fall out, but that wasn't the case—they didn't want to come out into the big bad world that easily.

I stood to the side of the bed, peeking around the other women as Emilene strained. After several more minutes passed, I became increasingly nervous. With my heart tapping quickly against my chest, I moved up beside Bridgett and placed the ice chips on the nightstand.

"Isn't this taking a little long for her eleventh time?" I whispered to her.

She gazed over at me, and I could read worry on her face.

"She really wants to have these babies in the home, but—" she looked back down at Emilene "—I fear she may need a doctor's attention."

"My Dad's a doctor. He lives only a few miles away—if you want, I can call him and check if he's home." Seeing the confusion playing across her features, I added, "I'm not Amish. Well, at least not yet. It's a long story."

"Who's your dad?" I had her full attention now.

"David Cameron. He works at Meadowview Regional."

"Oh, my goodness, girl, why didn't you tell me this earlier?" She quickly pulled her cell phone from her pocket and handed it to me. "Go ahead and call him. We'll see what comes of it before we make a decision," she said.

I caught Ruth watching me as I left the room. Surely she wouldn't mind me getting my dad involved if it helped her daughter out. It was hard to find a quiet place in the house, so I resorted to the porch. The raindrops on the roof were actually quieter than the kids inside.

"This is David Cameron," Dad answered all serious-like. He wouldn't have recognized the number. I was enjoying the fact that he would be surprised.

"Hey, Dad, it's me."

"Are you all right?" His voice had gone from calm and collected to on edge in an instant—served him right for being so mean earlier.

"I'm fine. It's just that there's this woman who's here about to give birth to twins. They're her eleventh and twelfth if you can imagine that, and she's having some problems."

Dad quickly processed the information, answering me immediately, "She should go to the hospital right now."

"She doesn't want to. And she has a couple of midwives here, one isn't Amish. Her name is Bridgett."

"You must mean Bridgett Langly. She's qualified to deliver the babies," Dad reassured me.

"She's the one who asked me to call you. She wants you to come over here and help out, if you're not too busy." I probably shouldn't have added the sarcasm at the end because I knew firsthand what a busy guy he really was.

"She's in luck, then. I'm almost home. Where are you at? I'll head straight there."

I told Dad the directions and returned the phone to Bridgett. She was thrilled to hear that the awesome Dr. Cameron was coming to help her out. Even Ruth patted me on the back, thanking me for making the call.

When Dad arrived moments later, the room was quickly emptied of most of the people. I shouted an inner *Go Dad* for taking charge of the overly herdlike women. The only people left in the room were Ruth, Bridgett, Dad, of course Emilene and *me*.

I had tried to make a clean getaway when the other women were dismissed, but Dad wanted me nearby to help. When I attempted to argue with him, he gave me a stern look that said if I spoke another word I'd be spanked. He then said something about wanting someone available to call the hospital if needed and I was overly qualified for that job. Even with Ruth so thoroughly distracted with her own child's predicament, she still managed to smirk at my thorough take-down by Dad.

Old people always stuck together.

I had to admit, I felt much better now that Dad was here, and I could tell that Bridgett and Ruth felt the same way. Mrs. Zook, not so much—she took an obvious disliking to Dad when he asked her to leave the room saying that he had everyone he needed. Her frown at me when she made her exit spoke volumes.

That had been about ten minutes earlier, and in that amount

of time Dad had given Emilene an examination and had her pushing all over again. I don't know if Dad actually did anything specific to get those babies moving or if just having a doctor in the room tilted the earth enough to get the job done, but with her second push this time, baby boy number one was out.

I drifted closer to the baby as Bridgett bundled it and handed it to Ruth. Ruth beamed at me, and I found myself staring down at the pinkish little human in awe. It was hard to believe that a moment ago he was inside his mom's belly, and now he was out here with us.

The second baby was being difficult, and Emilene moaned that she couldn't push anymore. Promptly and totally unexpectedly, Ruth handed me baby number one to rush to her daughter's side.

I held the baby as if it were a grenade, trying not to move a muscle. *What was Ruth thinking, giving the baby to me?* I'd never held someone this young before. I sucked my breath in, hoping that someone would take the baby quickly. If not, I was going to look for one of those identical sisters-in-law.

Emilene's crying felt like a slap in the face, and I looked up to see her exhausted, blotchy cheeks wet with tears. Strands of her gray-streaked hair had escaped the bun, and they hung about her in a tangled mess. Her blue eyes were bloodshot and squinted in pain above dark circles that resembled black thumbprints. Even with one baby out, her body was still grotesquely bloated. At that moment, my heart skipped, and I felt incredibly sorry for her. But despite my sympathy for the woman, if she didn't start secretly using birth control after all this, I would lose any pity for her. I couldn't even fathom suffering through eleven times of this torture.

Dad talked to Emilene encouragingly while he pressed his hand down above the bulge in her belly. The sight of him pushing like that freaked me out, and I chose then to focus on the baby in my arms. It was straining my arms to hold him away from my body, so I brought him in close. Luckily, he was sleeping, and the way he was burrito-wrapped he wasn't going anywhere.

The baby cry snapped my head back up. Dad was cutting the cord while Ruth held a second tiny boy.

Within minutes I was relieved of my bundle, and Emilene was cuddling her two baby boys. She wasn't crying now. Instead, she beamed out from under the new sheets that Bridgett had covered her with. With total efficiency, Bridgett and Ruth had the bloodied cloths hidden in a laundry basket and the room tidied of any evidence of the messy event that had just taken place.

I was still in a daze as the family members—all twenty or so of them—began to file into the room to check out the newest arrivals. Dad had a look on his face that clearly said *who the hell opened the floodgates,* but he kept his composure, instructing Bridgett and Ruth to get Emilene and the babies to the hospital as soon as possible to be thoroughly examined. He offered to call an ambulance, but as usual, Emilene wanted to take the more difficult path, opting to be driven to the hospital in the old Suburban parked outside.

As Dad was leaving, he took my hand and pulled me out of the throng of people. Even with the clothes on, I still felt like an intruder. If I had closed my eyes, the strange language darting around the room would have made me think that I was in a foreign land.

I let Dad pull me through the house, glad to get away from the crowd—and the unintelligible language. When we were out on the porch again, Dad finally looked at me. He shook his head. "I don't get why you're subjecting yourself to this." He pointed to the front door. "That woman should have been in the hospital to begin with. She's just lucky that there weren't any serious complications. Her stubbornness is indicative of her society's unwillingness to evolve."

I tried to hide the smile that was starting to form on my lips. "That's quite a mouthful, Dad."

"I'm serious, Rosie. Don't make light of this situation." He grabbed the hair above his forehead and tugged on it in frustration. "Aren't you getting tired of this fiasco—aren't you ready to come home?"

Dad's voice was stressed and tired. His face was pained. I hated doing this to him, but what choice did I have? If I went home with him, I'd never be with Noah again. I couldn't give up my love.

"I'm sorry, Dad. I can't right now. You promised me you'd give me time to decide, and it hasn't been long enough." I pleaded a little, using the twang in my voice that always got me what I wanted from Dad.

Then he had to go and say something that brought tears to my eyes.

"After delivering those babies, it's hard not to remember the day you were born. Your mother was so happy to have a little girl of her own. I only wonder what she'd think about all this, what she'd do about it."

He pulled me into his arms and hugged me longer and tighter than he had when he'd left in a huff. This time, he seemed too tired to be angry.

When he released me, he went to his car without another word. With a spirit that was heavy from many thoughts and emotions, I watched him drive away. Being around Dad always disrupted my resolve to become Amish. He made me feel guilty and homesick at the same time. I couldn't deal with those feelings and the craziness Noah incited in me. I couldn't handle it all.

The decision came to me. I'd have to limit Dad's visits, because he was only making matters worse.

After Dad left I thought my day was close to being over. I was looking forward to crawling into bed and pulling the thick homemade quilt up under my chin. It was about eleven-thirty and I was ready to head back to the Hershbergers. It would have been glorious to get into a car and drive the few miles home in a couple of minutes, park and walk to the door—but not for us.

I was dreading the long ride, the rocking to and fro up the road, and then the time we'd have to spend unhitching the horse, grooming and putting her out in the pasture.

In retrospect, the buggy ride home would have been welcomed compared to where I actually ended up: wedged in between Ruth and one of the sisters-in-law in the backseat of the Suburban. Since I was Ruth's *new daughter,* tradition or something mandated that I go along to the hospital to get the mother and children settled in. Bridgett followed in her sporty little Mustang, and I wished so hard that I'd been allowed to ride with her that my head began to pound with the strain of it.

I wandered around the hospital like a zombie, following the Amish women here and there until Emilene and babies were finally given a clean bill of health. They would be staying until the next day because of protocol. I suspected that was all right, now that Emilene had the bragging rights of having all twelve of her children at home. The hospital was a whole lot quieter than her house was. She might actually get to take a nap.

Being in the hospital again made a rush of emotions surge through me, remembering when I'd been there the last time— and nearly lost Noah. It was a good thing I was too tired to dwell much on the feelings. Just as we were finally going to make our exit, I nearly ran into Tina coming off the elevator.

Her face registered shock for an instant when she recognized my face, but she recovered quickly, introducing herself to Ruth and the sisters-in-law in a perky voice. How she managed the bright eyes in the middle of the night was beyond me.

"I didn't know you worked nights, Tina," I said, making conversation, but really wanting to get out of there.

"I do about once a month so that I can touch base with the nighttime employees." She rushed through the words, obviously wanting to get on to more interesting topics.

Tina picked up my hands and pulled me a little way from the other women, who continued to stand there staring at us.

"How are you doing, Rose?" She lowered her voice and tilted her head. "Are you okay living with them so far?"

I couldn't say much while I was being spied on. But I did like Tina and wished I could talk to her about Levi and Miranda. *She'd know what to do.* Unfortunately, her solution to the problem would probably involve the cops. I needed a much more subtle approach to hanging Levi Zook.

"I'm doing fine. Maybe sometime I'll come over and have dinner with you and Dad."

I hoped that would satisfy her curiosity for the moment.

I knew I'd succeeded when she gushed, "Oh, you're welcome anytime. Just call me or your dad. Do you still have my number?"

"Yes, I do. Thanks."

"Rose, come along." Ruth was over the Englishers' reunion.

I hugged Tina in a quick motion and joined the women. As I went through the automated doors behind Ruth, I couldn't help but turn and wave at Tina. She stood watching me leave.

Seeing Tina made me feel guiltier still. After all, she was the one who practically guaranteed Dad that I'd be running home for freedom after a few weeks of living the disciplined Amish lifestyle. My three weeks were almost up, and I wasn't running anywhere.

I wondered what that revelation would do to her relationship with Dad.

Minutes later when I thought my meeting with my bed had almost arrived, we pulled into the Walmart parking lot. I was beyond upset by that point, bordering on hysterical when I questioned Ruth.

"Why are we doing this now? It's the middle of the night," I said, my voice rising with each word.

Ruth, who was still looking fairly awake for an elderly woman, focused on me with hard eyes. "Don't you go using that disrespectful tone that you give to your father with me— I'll not be having any of it, young lady. We're going to take advantage of hiring a driver and being in town to pick up a few items that we need." She got out of the vehicle and was talking to the air by that time. "You'll learn soon enough that drivers are expensive and we are thrifty people with our money."

I dragged behind the three women as we made a complete circuit of the store, even stopping for a few minutes in the sporting goods department to buy ammo for one of the sisters-in-law's husbands. It was nearing hunting season, after all, she explained.

I barely listened to her. I didn't care about hunting season, or laundry detergent. Even the blue baby onesies were causing my vision to blur. I just wanted to get out of there.

About the time we were almost checked out and I was placing the bags in the cart, I noticed several teenage girls gawking at us. It dawned on me that it was the first time I'd been out in public dressed as an Amish person. It was strange how all the events of the past couple of weeks, in addition to the hard work I was unaccustomed to, had made me forget about what I was wearing. Sometimes, I found myself freaked out to touch my head and discover the cap. But other than those startling moments I hadn't really thought much about the strangeness of my attire—until now.

One of the girls, a tall brunette, actually had the nerve to point at me, giggling.

That must have been my cracking point. Without even knowing how I got there, I found myself face-to-face with the girl in a heartbeat.

"Do you have some kind of a problem?" I snarled.

Miss-Pointy-Finger was so shocked that her mouth gaped open and was unable to speak.

The plump girl on the left said to the brunette, "Let's go, McKenzie."

But I wasn't done with her yet. I took a step closer, well into the girl's personal space. "Didn't your mother ever teach you that it's rude to point at someone who's different than you?"

Still the girl was silent.

For good measure, I said, "And besides, a girl who's wearing an outdated jacket and ugly shoes is in no position to mock anyone else."

"Rose!" Ruth's voice was close enough that I knew she'd heard me.

The four girls turned and hightailed it toward the door, leaving me alone with my satisfaction and my unhappy chaperone.

Sighing, I turned around slowly and faced Ruth.

"Sorry about that. I just don't know how you deal with being stared at like that," I said.

Her face wasn't as upset as I was expecting. As a matter of fact, she had a little twinkle going on behind her glasses.

She took a deep breath and blew it out. "It gets easier with time—you'll become accustomed to it to the point that it won't bother you any longer."

"Good job, Rose," whispered sister-in-law number one as she passed by me heading for the exit.

"Try to restrain yourself in the future," Ruth said with a slight smile on her lips, choosing to ignore the other woman's comment. She put her arm around me, and together we walked out of the store.

The whole turn-the-other-cheek thing was fine for some people, but as for me, I planned to educate any of the inhabitants of this town who stared at Amish people as if they were freaks.

10

Noah

I got back to the farm earlier than I'd planned since there was no point hanging around the youth gathering after Rose had left. The sky was still the soft grayish color of late evening, and I hurried to get Oscar unhitched and put out before darkness and the rain arrived. It was always easier to work in the barn with some natural light. That was one thing I envied the Englishers of—barn lights.

Father approached just as I latched the gate shut. He held a shovel in his hands, and I guessed he'd been helping Mother with her new rock garden. The dirt on his trousers confirmed my suspicions.

"Did you get those rocks put in?" I stopped to ask.

"Most of them, but now your mother wants to extend the garden to the oak tree." He shook his head in disgust. "Don't reckon the woman will ever be content with the yard."

I couldn't help but laugh. Would Rose have me doing the same kind of drudgery? I highly doubted it. Somehow I couldn't picture Rose gardening—despite her name.

"You're back early from the gathering. Is anything amiss?" Father asked leisurely, but I knew he was concerned. I wouldn't be surprised if he kept records of all my movements.

"Nope—Emilene Yoder is having her babies."

Father looked confused. "And, that affected you coming home early, how?"

"Ruth must have wanted Rose to be there for it," I said.

Father's eyes widened. "Do you think that was a good idea? She's an English girl who's probably never seen such a thing." He started scratching his beard in thought. "Why, after all that, she might not want to have one of her own babes."

My father worried too much about everything. Whether Rose was traumatized about seeing childbirth hadn't even crossed my mind.

"I don't think that will be a problem with Rose, Father. She's not the fainting type of girl."

"Well, that's good to know." Father smiled.

Before he had the chance to leave, I burst out, "But there is something I wanted to talk to you about."

Father was pleased. He enjoyed being an adviser, and to show how interested he was in what I was going to say, he motioned me into the shadows of the barn where we sat on the couple of hay bales that were purposely left in the hallway for such occasions.

"It's about Levi Zook." I shook my head, getting worked up just thinking about the guy.

I made sure that Father was all ears and, seeing his mouth in a grim line, realized he wasn't surprised by the direction the conversation was going. "He's been showing an inappropriate amount of interest in Rose."

Father's voice crackled when he asked, "Has he done something to her?"

"No, not yet, anyway, but I fear that he might bother her… or at the very least try to get her into trouble."

"This is preciscly the reason I don't agree with the way Abram is handling the matter." Father stood up and walked across the hall and back. "If Rose joined the church and you two were courting, then Levi would be forced to leave her alone."

Father's pacing continued, and his voice rose. When Father was worked up, it wasn't a pretty sight. "Rose is such an attractive girl that I wouldn't be surprised if all kinds of difficulties arose with the young men of the community. Right now many are holding back, waiting to see whether she'll be accepted—and if you'll ask for her in courtship." Father eyed me firmly before saying, "Mark my words, son, if Rose is left unhitched in the community, Levi will be the least of your problems."

No, Levi is my biggest fear. I kept the thought to myself, though. After all, Father didn't know the kid the way I did— and he hadn't been there in the field on the stormy day when Levi had asked me to share Rose with him. Levi was sick in the head, and his infatuation with Rose worried me more than if all the other boys in the community combined were pining over her.

Even without Father's awareness of the Levi situation, his position was aligned with my own. He was speaking in my best interest, so I didn't talk him down.

"What do we do about it, Father?"

Father let out a deep breath and looked out the barn door. The rain had started to drop from the sky, increasing to a steady fall within seconds. He raised his voice to be heard over the sound of the rain tapping on the barn roof.

"Son, you best tell Abram yourself what you fear from Levi." He spoke somberly, but he also sounded determined.

"When will I have the opportunity to do that?" I asked, knowing full well that getting the time of day from the bishop was easier said than done.

"Right now is as good a time as any," Father said.

It was then that I heard the clops on the driveway. My heart raced as I jumped up from the hay and stood beside Father, peering into the rainy night. Sure enough, there was a well-lit buggy heading up the driveway.

"What is he doing here?"

"Hmm, seems that there's some sort of trouble with certain young'uns in the community. Abram called a secret meeting to be held."

"Where?"

"Right here in the barn," Father said, looking at me. It was nearly too dark to see his features, let alone his eyes. Leave it to Bishop Lambright to have an emergency meeting in the darkness of our barn on a rainy night.

My heart stalled, thinking about the other night, and how we could be the young'uns Father was talking about, only he didn't know it yet.

"Do you know who he's passing judgment on?"

Father must have picked up on my anxiousness, because he laughed and let me off the hook quickly. "Have a guilty conscience, do you? No worries, though, the young people we will be discussing aren't in your crowd."

Relief flooded through me. "Will the other ministers be coming?"

Seeing more buggy lights on the road answered the question for me.

"I reckon you'll have a few minutes of Abram's undivided attention before the rest have arrived," Father said, slapping me on the back. He seated himself on the hay bale in the darkness.

Now was my chance, and I silently prayed that I didn't mess it up.

11

Rose

My hands were killing me, but the cramp in my left leg felt even worse. Sighing, I stopped scrubbing and stared down the empty roadway. Never in a million years had I imagined myself spending an afternoon this way. It seemed as if I'd been at it all day long, but in actuality, I'd only spent three hours cleaning the white vinyl-covered fencing.

I tilted my face into the warm sunshine and relaxed for a moment, figuring that there was no way I'd get the entire project done before dark, anyway. There was still a good fifty feet to go before I reached the corner, and I was already making plans to squeeze the rest of the work in the following morning. After I did the laundry and cleaned the kitchen, I might be able to rush through my assignments in time to finish the fence job and still make it to Emilene's to help her prepare dinner for her entire brood.

Sighing more loudly this time, I rolled my eyes and shook my head in frustration. The noise got Hope up from her shady place under the tree. She came to me and flopped against my leg. I reached down and scratched the top of her fluffy spotted head, suddenly feeling a wave of anxiety hit me. There was no way I'd be able to do everything. The fence would just have to wait until the weekend—and Ruth would have to deal with it. Helping Emilene with her new babies, Jacob and Joshua, was a priority. That poor woman needed an army of teenage girls by her side.

The sound of the approaching car snapped my head in the direction of the road. My heart skipped a beat, and I jumped up, waving at the dark gray SUV. Dad stopped beside the fence, and I shimmied over the still-dirty rails to lean into the passenger window. Justin's beaming face erased all my earlier worries.

"What are you doing?" Dad asked, his voice raised in agitation.

I shrugged and said, "I'm cleaning the fence."

Justin laughed at the same time that Dad snorted.

"You've got to be kidding. Why on earth are you doing such a thing? Have they run out of floor for you to sweep?" Dad said with sarcasm lacing his words.

I understood what he meant, but I wasn't going to let him know it. The last thing that I needed was for my father to think that I couldn't hack it as an Amish girl. He'd be setting a place for me at his dinner table that night.

"We're holding church here in a month, and Ruth and James want to get the place all fixed up." I paused, glancing back at the grass-stained white rails. "And that includes the fencing...."

I stopped talking abruptly, knowing how dumb it sounded.

"Really, Rose, I don't understand why you're so willing to work like a mule for these people, when I have to twist your arm to do the dishes at the house," Dad said as he took off his sunglasses. He stared at me with narrowed blue eyes.

"Are you ready to come home yet? Have you finally had enough of this nonsense?" He spoke with a quiet yet determined voice.

I couldn't look him in the eye. Dad still believed that I'd be running home in a few days. If he knew the truth, that I had every intention of staying Amish to be with Noah, he wouldn't be as calm and cool as he was now. Dad had a temper that he kept hidden from the rest of the world. I cringed inwardly, thinking about how he'd react when he realized that he'd lost the gamble he'd made.

Hearing the pounding clops on the pavement, I was glad for the opportunity to look away. I watched Marcus Bontrager's wife, Ivy, whisk by at a fast clip. Her hand shot out the window for an instant when she passed, and I raised mine to return the wave.

"I'm doing fine, Dad. And, remember, you promised to give me time," I said in an upbeat manner. I didn't miss the way Justin lightly shook his head before thudding it back on the seat.

Dad breathed out angrily, and said, "I don't have patience for this nonsense today. John Daniels went back to Canada this morning. His elderly mother's in intensive care and isn't expected to make it to the weekend. We're already short one ER doctor, and I don't know when he'll return. I've been working extra shifts as it is and now this."

He put the sunglasses back on and said, "I need to get back to the hospital. Sorry, I won't have time to go over the assignments with you right now."

The first bubbles of elation that washed over me were immediately mixed with feelings of irritation. I struggled to keep my face free of emotion. His crazy work schedule and new girlfriend were the only reasons he was leaving me alone. I knew that I'd been lucky so far. But then why did I feel the heat of anger toward Dad that he was blowing me off once again?

"My folders are on the counter in the kitchen. Ruth is at the house—you can go up there and get them, but I need to keep working on the fence," I said with a cautious voice.

Before Dad answered, Justin was out the door and standing beside me. "I'll stay with Rose while you get her stuff."

"All right, then. I'll be back in a few minutes." Dad eased back on to the road, and I turned to my little brother. He was kneeling in the grass, petting Hope. The big puppy was wiggling with happiness at seeing my brother.

"So, how are things at home?" I asked as I bent down to pick up the scrub brush, trying to ignore the sting of pain from Dad being too busy to give me much thought nowadays.

Justin jumped up and grabbed it out of my hand. He said, "Let me do that. You can take a break for a little longer."

I settled cross-legged into the thick grass and watched him dab the brush into the bucket filled with soapy water and begin scrubbing.

"It's been pretty boring. Dad's at the hospital most of the time. When he's not working, he's with Tina. Since you're not there to do the chores anymore, Sam forces me to do most of 'em." He paused from the work to roll his eyes at me. "He threatens to make me ride the bus if I don't do what he says."

I couldn't help grinning. Some things never changed.

"Maybe you'll have a growth spurt this winter and finally be able to stand up to him." I smiled wistfully, wishing I could be there when it happened.

Justin sighed and dropped the brush into the bucket. I raised my eyebrow questioningly and felt suddenly uncomfortable when I saw the tense expression on his face. I didn't want to hear what he was about to say.

"When are you coming home? It really sucks being at the house alone all the time. It seems that Dad and Sam only sleep there anymore."

I groaned and moved closer to Justin. "I didn't know. I'm so sorry."

Justin pointed at the fence. "Is Noah really worth doing all this crap?"

The sound of desperation in Justin's voice kept me from being angry with him. He was still a kid, and I hadn't thought about how my absence would affect him. Now, on top of everything else that was on my mind, I could add major guilt about what I was doing to my little brother. But the idea of walking away from Noah to return home was unimaginable. I actually shivered when the thought crossed my mind. Even though the workload frustrated me and I missed my family, I could never leave Noah.

When I met Justin's eyes, he must have recognized the firm set of my face. The frown that had formed on his mouth just a second ago quickly changed to a thin line. His eyes lifted to look right at me as he said, "You don't care about us anymore at all, do you? The only thing in the world that matters to you is Noah."

Shaking my head, I said, "No, that's not true. I miss you guys, I really do, but what's between Noah and me is the real deal." Seeing Justin's eyes narrow reminded me of Dad, and I suddenly realized that he wouldn't blindly support my decision any longer. Justin might not be in my face the way Sam and Dad were, but he was on their side nonetheless.

I took a step forward, placing my hands on his shoulders as I said, "You don't understand how love feels, Justin. You've never experienced it before."

Justin took a jarring step backward, flinging my hands away with the action.

"That's where you're wrong. I know what love is. I loved Mom...and I love Dad and Sam...and you, too." He took a deep breath and said, "You might win this game that you're playing with Dad, but you'll regret it someday."

I began to open my mouth, but no words would come out. The feeling of shock numbed my insides as I stared at my brother, wondering when the heck he'd become so formidable.

I barely even heard Dad's car roll to a stop beside us. Justin was around the car and inside it a second later.

"Hopefully, I won't be in such a hurry the next time I stop by," Dad said with a clipped voice.

His little trip up the driveway hadn't lightened his mood at all.

"I'm sure you won't," I lied.

I stepped up to the car and bent down to let Dad kiss me on the cheek.

Dad sighed before saying, "Don't work too hard out here in the sun. Do you have a bottle of water?"

I nodded.

"Bye, Rose," Dad said. He sat for a couple of long seconds staring at me. I held my breath but didn't look away. The look on Dad's face told me that he was battling with himself about what to do. When he finally turned his head and pulled away, I breathed again.

Lady rolling in the tall grass caught my eye, and I watched her stand back up and shake her body. She'd been hanging around the lower pasture all afternoon, keeping me in her sights. The desperate longing to go for a ride struck me, and I had to look away. It would be a miracle if I got to ride her anytime soon. I was too busy now to do such a thing.

The press of depression that I had little time for fun anymore wasn't my main concern, though. The fact that Justin hadn't said goodbye to me and that he'd ignored me when I tried to make eye contact with him was a bigger issue. I'd lost an ally...and maybe the entire relationship with my little brother. A hollow feeling developed in my chest, and the sunshine couldn't stop the feeling of trepidation from sweeping through me.

It was just a matter of time until Dad came for me.

12

Sam

I reached the sidelines a few steps ahead of Hunter. After we poured some water from the cooler into cups, we took a seat on the bottom bleachers. While the breeze cooled the sweat on my skin and the grunts and hits of the other players on the field rang through the air, I took a breath and glanced at Hunter. He was staring at the grass, seemingly lost in his own thoughts.

I quickly weighed the pros and cons in my head, and took the chance. "Hey, do you know a little redhead named Summer Sage?" I asked in a loud whisper.

Hunter looked up at me. It was fascinating to watch the haze disappear from his eyes as they became focused on what I'd said.

"Yeah, sure I do." He ran his hands through his hair and said, "She's a junior, right?"

I nodded my head and forged on, "Do you know her personally?"

Hunter's expression changed from mild interest to a sharper, more intense look, when he smiled and said, "I never really spoke to her, I guess. She hangs out with the country kids and keeps mostly to herself from what I've seen." His smile deepened and he leaned in closer. "She's cute, but I thought you and Amber had it going on."

Just hearing the name Amber soured my mood. The girl was becoming a thorn in my backside. Her never-ending text messages and phone calls were driving me crazy. And the fact that Hunter had immediately assumed that I was after Summer made me regret even bringing the subject up.

"I'm just curious about her, that's all. She's hanging out with my sister," I said with a shrug.

Hunter's eyes brightened instantly, and he sat up straighter. "How's Rose doing? You don't talk about her much."

"It's kind of a sore subject in my household," I said, taking a sip of the cold water. "I'm surprised that she hasn't come home already. Wearing those ugly dresses and caps on her head every day—it's as if she's been possessed by an alien or something."

Quietly, Hunter said, "She's probably just confused. Probably since your mom died, she's been searching for something to fill the hole. Unfortunately, she picked a guy from a backward culture to do it."

Hunter placed his hand on my shoulder, and I glanced up to see a pained face.

"I'm so sorry, man. I really screwed things up that night at the party. I never meant to scare her like that—I wasn't myself."

"Yeah, you've told me that before," I said, wishing he hadn't brought it up again.

A minute of silence passed and I thought he was finished speaking when he said, "I'm never touching any kind of alcohol again."

When I tore my gaze from the action on the field, I looked at Hunter questioningly, wondering what the hell he was talking about.

"My dad used to have a drinking problem. He's all right now, but I remember how he'd treat Mom when he was drunk. It wasn't pretty. I vowed to myself to never do the same thing, but then I acted that way with Rose."

Holding my breath, I studied my new friend's profile. His face was tight with regret. When he looked back at me, it was only for a second, before he dropped his gaze to the ground.

"You have no idea how much I hate myself for what I did to Rose. The worst part is that I've gone and chased away such a sweet girl."

"Ah, don't be so hard on yourself. Believe me, Rose isn't sweet at all," I said as an image of my sister with her hand on her hips and her eyes shooting fire rose before me.

Hunter snorted, "No, you're wrong about that, Sam—dead wrong."

The warning look that Hunter shot me made me catch my breath. Even after everything that had happened that night and the fact that Rose was delusional and living a lie in the Amish community, the guy sitting beside me was still smitten with her.

My mind rolled the information around for a minute until a smile spread my lips. Maybe Hunter still had a chance to win my sister away from the arrogant Noah Miller, after all.

When the coach shouted, "Cameron, Braxton, you're up," I jogged with Hunter onto the field.

My mind was only half on the practice, though. I glanced at Hunter and thought, *Here's hoping, anyway.*

13

Rose

Trying to re-coil my hair in the bouncing buggy was not an easy task. Holding the bobby pins between my lips, I worked quickly with my fingers. By the time Mr. Hershberger pulled to a stop at the intersection, I had the pins in and my cap on.

Quickly I forgot about my hair. Looking out the window at the bright golden-and-red leaves on the passing trees, my heart sped up. The sun was just making its appearance, and light sprayed wrapped the countryside in autumn coziness.

I loved this time of the year, when the crisp days arrived and the wind picked up. Of course, the hard breeze made it colder, especially early in the day when the dew was still wet in the grass. I buttoned up my new corduroy jacket, thinking how lucky I'd been to find it.

Controlling the smile that threatened to take over my mouth, I thought about how Ruth had patiently taken me to three different Amish stores before we found exactly the right one on a Walmart clearance rack. She'd only reluctantly agreed to browse through the big store's assortment and was surprised that we found a jacket that was acceptable to her and stylish enough for my picky tastes.

I'd discovered that Amish women did have some freedom

when it came to their appearance. I was allowed to pick cloth for my dresses in an assortment of colors that were reasonable, although the patterns for the dresses were fairly limited.

I was especially proud of myself as I smoothed out the bright turquoise material of the dress I was wearing. *I'd actually sewn the thing myself.* Well, with quite a bit of help from Ruth, but still, I'd contributed in a major way.

It was hard to believe that it was October. On a Saturday like this, if I hadn't left my family to become Amish, I'd probably be getting ready for an afternoon of sitting in front of the TV watching college football and pigging out on pizza and chips.

I still missed Dad and my brothers, but the fact that they were keeping their distance was probably for the best. I felt a deep sense of contentment that each day I made it through, I was getting closer to my goal of being with Noah.

It had been more difficult than I'd ever imagined, though. In the many weeks since our meeting in the woods, the only contact we'd had was on Sundays or at the youth ball games. Being so close to him, without being allowed to talk to him alone, had been almost unbearable.

Somehow I'd managed to survive, and amazingly, I hadn't gotten into any trouble yet. The work at the Hershbergers' place kept me so busy that, when I wasn't doing laundry, canning or baking, I was grateful to be sleeping. Ruth was constantly praising my efforts, which made me stronger, and I had to admit that I'd learned a lot from the old woman. I figured if the end of the civilized world came, and mankind had to resort to living off the land, I'd be up to the challenge.

Breathing in the warm fruit smells of the fried pies, I leaned back and relaxed. The entire buggy was filled with the scents of apple, raspberry and cherry all mixed up with sugar and dough. Even though I'd eaten three of the donut-size pastries fresh out of the oven for breakfast, my mouth still watered.

The pies were the reason we'd gotten up earlier than usual—to make a hundred of them for the benefit auction that was being held at the Weavers'. Ruth had said everything from horses and farm machinery to antiques and dinnerware would be there. All the stuff was donated from local people and the money raised was going to build an addition onto the crowded schoolhouse.

My heart thumped harder thinking that I might actually get the chance to talk to Noah, and maybe even sneak in a kiss. I'd been planning all kinds of scenes in my head since I'd learned about the auction that Ruth had said was always bursting at the seams with people. Surely, Noah and I wouldn't be noticed if we snuck off for a few minutes.

"Rose, did you enjoy making them pies this morning?" Mr. Hershberger asked conversationally. He'd been gradually warming up to the idea of having a strange English girl living in his house. I guess I wasn't all that strange anymore.

I leaned in between Ruth and her husband. "Yeah, it was kind of fun—especially the sampling part."

He laughed. "I must say, if my taste buds are any sign, you did a good job baking this morning."

I beamed at the compliment. "Thanks."

Ruth chimed in, "Yes, Rose, without your help, we wouldn't be able to contribute so many to the cause today." She turned to look at me, her face wide and friendly. "I do believe that you've made an excellent adjustment to our Plain ways."

My breath caught in my throat, and I sniffed. I'd thought at the beginning that Mr. and Mrs. Hershberger were just a means to an end. But, after the weeks I'd spent living with them and working beside Ruth, they'd become important to me—as if they were really family. Ruth could never replace my fun Aunt Debbie, or my Grandma who lived in Florida or the other one in Wisconsin, but she'd filled a spot that needed filling.

Ruth went on to say, "You can check in with me regularly, Rose, but I believe that we'll have enough help at the food tables today."

My spirit soared, and I had to restrain my voice from sounding too excited. I didn't want her getting suspicious, after all. "So...I can just hang out with the other girls, then?"

"A few of those girls might be working, you know," Ruth said, dampening my mood just a tad.

"Ah, just try to enjoy it, Rose. You've earned a day of fun." Mr. Hershberger actually winked at me before he pushed his black hat lower on his head and focused on the roadway that was now congested with a mix of buggies and cars.

I sat impatiently on the edge of the seat as Mr. Hershberger maneuvered Dolly through the traffic. It was strange seeing the cars, pickup trucks and buggies lined up together waiting for a parking space.

The sun beamed down on the tawny field that was dappled with loaded wagons. I spotted one wagon which appeared to have only old-fashioned washing machines on it, and I cringed at the sight of it.

Looking from left to right I watched all the people walking up the hill to where the action was taking place. This event was definitely larger than the schoolhouse benefit dinner. There were as many English people wandering around the wagons as there were Amish.

As if the smell of the pies wasn't enough, now the scent of grilling meat invaded my senses. The thrumming of the auctioneer's voice carried through the air as we made our way past the field where the vehicles were turning in. Throw in the people milling about with the smells and sounds, and there was quite an air of festivity.

Mr. Hershberger stopped beside a metal barn that had been turned into a makeshift restaurant. That's where the wonderful smells were coming from, and I gladly jumped out of the buggy with our box of pies. After Ruth stepped down, Mr. Hershberger clucked Dolly back into movement, heading to the barns.

I followed Ruth into the throng of women who were working to set up their wares, saying "hi" to someone almost every step of the way. I'd been around long enough to have met most of the females in the community, from the itty-bitty ones to the ancient matriarchs.

Maretta appeared and, without asking, grasped the side of my box.

"Looks as if it'll be a pretty day for the sale." She bubbled with excitement.

"Sure does," I answered, and then lowering my voice, I asked, "Have you seen Noah yet?"

Maretta did a quick glance around and whispered back, "Saw him taking his buggy down to the barn a few minutes ago, I did." She smiled, happy that she had important news for me.

My thought pattern immediately switched gears to wondering how quickly I could dump the pies off and get to the barns.

"Did you make those pies on your own, Rose?" Rebecca came up behind me, squeezing my shoulders. I was sure that if the front of my body hadn't been blocked by the box, she'd have been hugging my guts out the way she usually did— *thank you, box.*

"I can't take credit for them, but I did help."

"She's being modest. She did a lot more than just help," Ruth said as she squeezed by me, motioning to an empty space on one of the tables.

"Ruth has been telling us all kinds of positive things about you." Rebecca put her arm around me when I set the box down. "And don't you go thinking that people haven't been noticing…'cause they have."

She smiled warmly, and I got the distinct feeling that she was trying to get a point across, but I didn't want to let the excitement in until I knew for sure that I'd be allowed to join the church. It'd been about seven weeks now, and I was more than ready to officially be Noah's girl.

Rebecca and Ruth wandered away with the other women, but Maretta stayed behind to help me arrange the pies neatly on the table. As we worked, Suzanna snuck up from behind and poked me in the back with her long finger.

"Oww!"

"You need to be more observant than that." Suzanna grinned. The blonde girl was absolutely glowing. She grabbed my arms and pulled me close to whisper into my ear. "I got news for you."

"What?" I had an inkling the news was about Timothy.

"Not here." She clutched my hand and pulled me toward the door.

"But I should help Maretta with the pies," I said, looking over my shoulder.

Suzanna stopped just long enough to say to Maretta, "You got it covered, right?"

The easy-going girl nodded her head vigorously, still smiling. So I let Suzanna drag me through the women and out the door into the sunlight.

Suzanna didn't turn in the direction of the barns as I'd hoped, instead leading me into the crowd of people walking to the wagons. I searched for Noah in the sea of faces while I listened to Suzanna, who whispered loudly as we crept along with everyone else.

"I've made a decision," Suzanna announced, finally releasing my hand.

When she didn't say anything further, I interrupted my mission to find Noah and looked at her.

"And..." I prompted.

She breathed out, "I'm joining the church."

I felt mixed emotions at hearing these words. I was happy that she'd be able to be with Timothy, but I was also miffed that in order for her to be with the guy she loved, she had to join a religious institution.

And I was in the same predicament.

Since she glowed beside me, I tried to sound thrilled for her. "Oh, that's great. When will it take place?"

We'd reached a wagon piled high with all kinds of garden tools. My brain registered that I'd never seen so many rakes in one place, even at Lowes.

"I'm hoping in a few Sundays. Now that I've made up my mind, I want to get it over with, but they'll be some classes to suffer through with the bishop first."

"What kind of classes?" I asked, slowing my forward movement to stare at her.

Suzanna shrugged and continued walking. "Bishop Lambright will drill into our heads the oaths that we're making to the church and the Ordnung rules. That way we won't be able to declare ignorance in the future."

She seemed to have gone all distracted on me for a few minutes, not saying anything and pretending to look at the stuff on the wagons. I examined a couple of sets of dishes and then unbuttoned my jacket as the sun rose in the sky. The fact that I was even looking at the ceramic things showed I'd changed a lot since I'd moved in with the Amish.

"You know—" Suzanna had my attention again with her squirrelly tone "—you might be allowed to join at the same time as me and Timmy."

I put the yellow cup down with the others and stared at her. "Are you serious?"

"I don't know, but I reckon there will be several others doing it that day." She paused and had a faraway look when she said, "I've talked to Miranda about it. Matthew's already in the church, and I think he really likes her, but she hasn't given me an answer yet." She lowered her voice even more. "I don't know if she'll ever join."

She'd said the last part worriedly, and I thought how strange it was the way minds could be redirected. It wasn't that long ago that Suzanna hadn't wanted to join the church herself. The desire to mate was definitely a motivator. No wonder membership was up.

Ella Weaver passed by, openly giving me a dirty look. I repaid her with my own scrunched-up version of an alien face. If that was the worst the jealous girl could dish out, then I was safe.

"It's Miranda's choice." Just as the words were out of my lips, the hair went up on my neck and a chill rippled along my arms. When I shifted my eyes, they landed immediately on the cold black ones belonging to Levi Zook.

He stared shamelessly at me with a crooked smirk frozen on his mouth. Nathaniel was beside him inspecting a chain saw.

Suzanna must have seen where I was looking, because she seethed, "I hate him."

I glanced back at her breaking contact with the carrot head who'd gone from being just a prick in my mind to a real sicko in such a short period of time.

"I know what you mean."

I hadn't forgotten about Levi. As a matter of fact, I thought about him quite often, but I hadn't come up with any ideas on how to bring him down—*until now*. When I glanced back at Levi to see him still looking at me, the trickling of a plan began to grow in my head.

When Summer bounded up to us, her reddish hair shining on her shoulders in the sunlight, the idea came together. I knew that I could do it with her help.

"Hey, wuz up?" Summer said in a high-pitched voice. Clearly, she was happy to see us.

"Where've you been? I haven't seen you in a long while," Suzanna asked.

Summer slid in between us as we made our way back toward the food barn. We were going against the wave of humanity, and the three of us squeezed in tighter, refusing to separate.

"Oh, I've been tied up with schoolwork and Mamma's been too busy to take me anywhere it seems," Summer replied. I eyed her 60s-style jean jacket, wanting one just like it badly. I might be able to put up with wearing frumpy dresses, but I didn't think that I'd ever get over the inability to make a statement with my clothes again.

I bumped into Summer in a friendly way, saying, "Like your jacket."

She looked down at it. "Gee, thanks—yours is nice, too." She winked at me. "Hipper than Suzanna's for sure."

"Summer Sage, I don't know why I even bother with you," Suzanna said with mock anger.

"Cuz, ya love me," Summer said, throwing her arm around Suzanna's shoulder.

Suzanna snorted and then laughed loudly just at the moment we entered the building.

We stopped by the fried pies, and to my delight there were only about half of them left on the table. Maretta had moved down to the sandwiches, and Sarah was now in charge of the baked goods.

"Hey, Rose. Noah's been looking for you," Sarah said before she was ambushed by a customer.

"Wonder where he is. I've been looking all over for him," I muttered.

"Why would you want to hang around with him when you have us?" Summer giggled, elbowing Suzanna in the ribs.

"Only you would ask such a stupid question," Suzanna said. But she didn't get to hear Summer's follow-up, since her mom called her over to the serving line.

Summer said, "Ha-ha," and then stepped in back of me.

Suzanna stuck her tongue out at Summer who was peeking out from behind me.

"See you later, Rose," Suzanna said, purposely ignoring her other friend who was hiding against my back.

As I watched Suzanna drag herself to her job, I was seriously contemplating going to help her and the other girls, but Summer grabbed my arm and threatened, "Don't you even think about it. I need some company."

Yeah, and actually, I need you, too, Summer.

We bought ourselves each a hot sandwich and a cola and proceeded to the picnic tables set up outside in the trampled grass.

While we ate I looked around for Noah—and Levi. But I couldn't find either of them. As Summer munched on her sandwich, between chews she said, "Your brother is stalking me."

That got my attention.

When I looked back at Summer she had a smug tilt to her lips that made me believe her.

"Are you kidding me?"

"He hunts me down in the halls every day to say hello and ask how I'm doing," Summer said.

"And what do you say?" My brain was now being pulled in several directions, but Sam's interest in my friend was definitely worth my concentration.

"I ignore him for the most part."

Summer took a swig from her bottle and set it down a bit harder than was necessary.

"Why, don't you like him?"

"Ha, he has this attitude. As if he's a gift to the female population of the school and I should be going all goo-goo eyed over him."

I considered her attitude for a minute and decided that she must like Sam a little bit, otherwise she wouldn't get so torn up about his popularity with the girls. God help her, though, if she did fall for him.

"Usually, the girls are chasing Sam, not the other way around." I caught her eyes as she squinted in the light. "Maybe he's really into you. I mean, it's not like Sam to go out of his way to talk to a girl, unless he's interested."

"His girlfriend keeps him pretty busy, I'd say." Summer definitely had a hint of anger in the tone of her voice. I laughed out loud. "That's exactly what I called Amber in my head when I met her. Sam's still with her?"

"I don't know for sure. Sometimes they're together and he ignores me, other times, when he's free of her and his football buddies, he shows up, acting all friendly." She seemed to be considering what she'd just said, weighing the possibilities.

"I'll only give you this advice once and whether you take it is up to you, but you should watch out for Sam—he'll break your heart," I said softly and honestly. I didn't want to see Summer go down the road of the dozen girls before her.

"Maybe he'll be the one with the broken heart," she quipped, catching me totally by surprise.

While she finished off her sandwich, I reappraised her. She

was pretty, colorful—and unique. She might just be the one to tromp all over Sam's soul for a change. But I didn't want the responsibility if it backfired on her.

"You've been warned." I sighed.

She just smiled back at me with an evil spread to her lips, making me think again that Summer would be the one to help me nail Levi's skinny ass to the wall.

I leaned over the rough wood of the table and whispered, "Do you have your phone on you?"

"Yeah, course I do."

Summer was curious about the change of subject, and she leaned in closer to hear what I had to say.

I quickly told her what I had in mind, watching her expression go from rapt interest with big green eyes to worry when she began chewing on her bottom lip.

It was a crazy plan, and one that probably wouldn't amount to anything, but it was better than nothing. And, even though I trusted Suzanna fully, I didn't feel comfortable bringing her into the situation. The last thing the Amish girl needed was to have to deal with the fallout. On the other hand, I believed that Summer was up to the challenge.

I sat, barely breathing, while I watched the redheaded girl stare at the boards of the table top for several long seconds. When her eyes rose, her mouth was set in a grim line of determination. My belly suddenly rocked with nervousness when she nodded slowly.

She was with me.

When I finally did spot Noah, he was beside his dad and Jacob, eyeing some hulking plow thing. He kept looking up and searching around, making the pleasant butterflies push the queasiness I was feeling aside. He was looking for me.

I ducked behind the tent flap and let out a strong breath.

As much as I longed to walk over to Noah and have his hot eyes on me, I hardened my heart with another breath and a slight shake of my body. It was good that he was busy—the last thing I needed was for him to ruin my plan. The success of which depended an enormous amount on how I believed Levi would act if given the opportunity to be alone with me. Hopefully, if I was right, within the hour I'd have a weapon to hold against Levi—one that would keep him forever away from Miranda and off my case, too.

Maybe I was dead wrong, but I highly doubted it.

What I was doing wasn't exactly entrapment. It was more like giving a jerk a situation to show his true and nasty colors.

As I made my way around the wagons, nodding my head and smiling at several ladies who acknowledged me, my heart began to drum faster and my legs felt jellylike. I thought I had things worked out in my mind, but I was still a nervous wreck.

When I saw the source of my inner conflict I slowed, preparing myself. Before I made it to my position, Emilene strolled up, catching me off guard. She was holding one of the babies while Jeremiah followed with the other one.

"Hi, Emy, how are the boys enjoying their first big outing?" I said, stopping to peek under the little blue blanket covering Emilene's bundle. I had to admit the squirming little guy was cute. In all our visits to the Yoders' to help with the cooking and laundry after the birth I'd discovered that babies were okay—especially now that I knew how to hold one.

Seeing the pleading look on Jeremiah's face, I was on alert that he was getting ready to dump his bundle on me.

"I believe they're enjoying it. Joshua here hasn't woken at all, but Jacob has been a bit fussy."

Before Jeremiah got his chance to skip out of his parental duties, I said, "I better go help with the food. They're probably missing me."

I hightailed it past them.

The encounter had interrupted my preparation, and now that I was almost on top of Levi I had to think quickly.

I took a breath and smoothed the blue material at the front of my dress flat. Picturing Miranda in my head, I looked up at Levi. Only this time, instead of the scowl that usually accompanied my face when I met his eyes, I swallowed and kept my face neutral. Knowing I had only one chance, I held his gaze for several seconds longer than any girl would before passing closely by him.

My heart was attacking my rib cage, and sweat cooled the skin under my dress. I had a brief moment of, *Oh, my God what am I doing,* before I peeked over my shoulder.

It worked. Levi was following at a discreet distance. I continued past the women selling their goodies. The smells and jovial sounds coming from the building seemed as if they were a world away, I was so intent on my mission.

I walked past the first barn I came to, the big one where all the horses were lined up in tie stalls. Then I passed the second smaller barn where a few cows had their heads hanging over the gate. By that point there were only a few meandering guys whom I guessed were being nosey about the Weavers' farm.

I turned into the old tobacco barn. As my eyes adjusted to the dark interior I was satisfied to see that it looked exactly as I'd expected: a few rusty pieces of machinery stored on one side and some round bales on the other. There were several chickens pecking around in the dirt, giving me something to focus on while I waited for Levi to arrive.

My legs were steady and my head clear when he walked through the opening, a smile twitching his thin lips. His expression made my stomach crawl, but I stood my ground and watched him carefully.

He approached confidently, before pausing at one of the

bales, pulling out a long blade of yellowish grass. He broke it and popped one piece into the side of his mouth, dropping the other half. I watched it fall to the ground, a hen hurrying to the place where it landed.

Anxiously, I lifted my head again. Levi was directly in front of me, close enough that I could smell the sweat on his shirt.

"So, what are ya doing out here, Rose?" He drawled out the words in a low voice.

Oh, yeah, the jerk was working hard to sound all nice and friendly, but I knew better.

"It's really none of your business," I snapped.

His eyes narrowed, and judging from the even thinner line his lips became, his temper was heating up.

"It's not a good idea for a girl that looks like you to be wandering off by yourself. You should be thanking me for coming down here to check in with ya."

He stretched his arm out to the post beside me, partially hemming me in.

When I went to move away, he snaked his hand out and grabbed my wrist. He was faster than I thought he'd be and even though this was what I wanted, I wasn't expecting it to happen quite so quickly.

"Let go of me," I growled, trying to yank my arm away.

"Why should I? After all, you gladly give your kisses away to the likes of Noah Miller. Why not spread yourself around a little bit?"

He got a hold of my other arm, and I started to struggle with him in earnest. The last thing I wanted was him to really touch his mouth to mine—or worse.

"Stop your struggling, you little whore, so I can give you what you deserve." He pulled me in more tightly, and I was vaguely aware of the dust around our feet rising up and the chickens scurrying out of the way as we struggled.

"Please, Levi, don't do this. Let go." I writhed against him. I hadn't planned that his spindly body would be so strong or that I wouldn't be able to get away.

"Go ahead and beg me to stop. I like that...." His voice broke mid-sentence, and in a blink he was smashing to the ground.

My mind only had a second to register that Noah was on top of Levi, hitting him.

Summer stepped out from behind a bale of hay. Catching her eyes, we simultaneously nodded at our success. A second later we were scrambling into action, pulling at Noah's arms and shoulders before he messed up my plan in a really bad way. After all, I'd been anticipating that Summer would be the one to join me in battle against Levi if it was needed, not Noah. And, although the sight of Noah attacking Levi sent a thrill through me, I was also suddenly terrified at how it would all play out.

After a moment of tugging, Summer and I managed to pry Noah away from his punching bag. He breathed madly between the two of us, his gaze still locked on his victim.

Levi was resilient, though, and even with his left eye already swelling shut and blood running freely down his face, he managed to spit in our direction.

Noah tried to break from our grip to attack Levi again, and I almost shouted, but I kept my voice at a steady hiss, still not wanting to bring attention to us.

"Noah, stop. Please, come on."

I managed to get his face between my hands, and when our eyes met, his arms came around me and he squeezed me tightly into his body.

"Did he hurt you? Tell me what he did." Noah pulled back enough to search my face, demanding an answer.

I hadn't expected Noah to become part of our scheme and with only a moment to think about it, I decided that he could never know about Miranda, which meant my plan would have to extend to him. I didn't want to lie to him, but I wouldn't break Miranda's confidence. And I didn't know exactly how Noah would take it if he knew that I had baited Levi even a little bit.

All in all, it was best that Noah was kept in the dark on this one.

I eyed Summer and could tell she was with me one hundred percent. Something about the set of her jaw and the glint in her eyes told me I could trust her. Summer and I would be the only two people in the world who would know the whole truth.

I touched Noah's face with my fingertips. "I'm okay, Noah. He didn't get the chance to do anything, because of you."

"How touching. But you just wait 'til everyone hears about this and sees my face." Levi was up, although he was standing awkwardly. He pointed to Noah. "You'll be punished by the church for sure 'bout this and you—" his finger pointed in my direction "—will never be accepted into our community."

Noah began to go for Levi again, and I threw my arms around his waist to stop him.

"Noah, stop," I said, throwing all my weight into holding his body back.

My hands calmed Noah, and he spoke to Levi with pure loathing in his voice, "Do you really think that our people will be okay with you trying to rape a girl?"

Levi managed a half smile with his swollen face. "The story they're gonna get from me is that little whore enticed me down here to seduce me. And do you think Abram is gonna believe an English girl, over me, a church member?" he snarled, "I don't think so."

He turned and limped as fast as his injured body would take him by us and out the doorway.

At that point I was feeling a crazy adrenaline rush along

with the shock of Noah's arrival. My mind was quickly running through all the possible scenarios and preparing for them all. Having the incident being brought out into the open was definitely not part of the plan. But maybe Noah bursting in to save the day might play out even better in the end.

Noah put his hands to his face, rubbing in frustration, and cried out, "God, this is terrible. He's right, damn it. No one will believe us."

That's when Summer finally spoke, her performance proving that she could be a Hollywood star someday. I relaxed a bit, knowing she could handle the situation.

"They have to believe, Noah, because I have proof."

She held up her phone to Noah's face.

"What..." I shushed him while Summer played the video for Noah to see. It started at the point that Levi asked what I was doing in the barn and ended at the beginning of the fight.

Noah looked between me and Summer in confusion. "I don't understand. Why were you here in this old barn, Summer?"

Summer had told me that she took a drama class as a freshman, and from what I saw now, it definitely paid off. She looked at me hesitantly and then spilled the beans, her voice believably reluctant.

"Uh, well, you see, I came down here to meet Rose so that she could use my phone." She jumped in front of me and raised her voice, "I'm sorry, Rose, but it was going to come out in the open, anyway."

I huffed a little and turned away from her, feigning anger.

"Rose, tell me why you would sneak back here to use her phone—who where you going to call?"

I looked him in the eye and lied. I hated lying to him, but I had to think about the bigger picture, I couldn't falter now.

I shook my head and said, "I wanted to talk to Amanda.

It's been so long and I missed her, that's all. I didn't think it would be a big deal."

When Noah looked up at the rafters, not wanting to make eye contact with me, I went on, "I certainly wasn't expecting Levi to follow me here, and...and..."

That got him. A blink later I was in his arms, just where I wanted to be. I peeked past his arm at Summer, who was leaning against the hay, frowning slightly.

And that's how Bishop Lambright and Amos Miller found us.

14

Noah

I stared at Rose, who sat beside Summer on the couch. She was twirling the string of her cap around her finger, only to let it go, over and over again. I spared a glance at Summer, who was chewing on her pinky nail while she stared out the window into the fading evening light.

The last few families that had stayed until late in the afternoon to help clean up the Weavers' farm were gone now—along with Levi Zook, who'd left hours ago. Even the Weaver family had evacuated the premises, except for Mervin, who right now was arguing with Father in the other room. Mervin had taken it upon himself to be Levi's defender since Levi's own father didn't want to press the issue. William Zook knew his own son and wasn't nearly as upset as Libby Zook had been when Levi showed up in the middle of the auction bleeding and bruised.

Abram was in there listening to both sides, probably thinking about which biblical quotes he could use. I thought Marcus Bontrager was still there, but his silence made me wonder. And of course, James Hershberger would have remained. But I hadn't heard him speak in a while, either.

And then there was Martha Lambright, who sat on the floral chair beside the couch. She was reading from a Bible, only occasionally looking up to smile at one of us. The woman gave me the creeps with all her friendliness.

No one could be that nice all the time.

The voices rose again, and Martha's eyes caught mine for a second. Luckily for Rose and Summer, the words were in our language so they hadn't a clue what was going on. I, on the other hand, didn't have that luxury.

Father was making his point that if Rose had been granted the request of joining the church months ago, none of this would have happened, while Mervin was arguing that Rose was not fit to walk the Amish life. James had tried to inter-cede earlier about Rose, but he couldn't get much in between Father and Mervin going at it. I hadn't heard Marcus say a thing, but I had spotted him earlier. I reckoned he was doing his usual thing of not putting his neck out for anybody.

Besides twirling the string, Rose was unusually calm. For me, the worst part of our house arrest was sitting for hours with nothing to do but look at the walls. Summer had it a little better, since she at least had her phone to play with.

Rose had kept busy early on by working her way through the few hunting magazines lying around. I smiled, remem-bering how she'd wrinkled her nose in disgust at the pictures.

She was so precious to me, but still, I couldn't rid my mind of the nagging feeling that there was more going on with Rose than what she told me. It didn't make any sense that she'd risk everything to sneak away from the auction to meet Summer in a barn to secretly call her city friend. It stirred all kinds of questions in my mind.

Was Rose doing other things behind my back because she felt like it?

I knew it would not be an easy go with her. She hadn't been raised in our ways and she was used to always getting what she wanted, either through her cuteness or her intelligence. We were so close to having her accepted into the church, Father had told me so, and now…now it might be over—and all because of a cell phone.

The heavy thuds coming closer brought all four of our heads up in a flash and our bodies followed suit. Abram entered first, followed by Father, then James and Marcus walking together. Mervin brought up the rear, his bright blue eyes flashing.

Abram faced Summer, who shrank back a little against Rose. Rose put her hand up against Summer's back to brace the redheaded girl. The two girls looked completely different, one with the dress and cap, the other wearing tight jeans and a jacket made of the same material.

But looks were deceiving in this instance—they were both Englishers.

"Let me see the video you have, young lady." Abram spoke almost harshly to Summer.

She pulled the phone out and began to hand it to the bishop, but Rose stopped her and said, "You'll need to start it for him."

"Oh, yeah," Summer said. She pressed a few places and slid her fingers along the screen.

She held up the phone close to his face.

Martha had risen from her seat and was now peeking around Abram to view the video for herself. I watched as both of their eyes lit up in surprise, either from the technology or Levi's words and actions. By the end, Abram was shaking his head and pulling his beard.

"A disgrace, that boy is," Abram said, pushing his wife, whose face was as pale as vanilla ice cream, in the direction of her former seat. The bishop ordered Summer to show the video to each of the other men, with Mervin being the last to view it. By the time Mervin sat down, he'd clearly changed his mind on the matter.

Abram motioned for Rose and Summer to return to the couch. A minute later he pulled the kitchen chair that Marcus had brought to him up close to their knees. The girls looked more confident now that the ministers had seen with their own eyes what had happened.

Marcus sat on the chair closest to me, and Father remained standing, pretending to search out the window. There was still tension in the air, and I knew that we were just beginning.

"Your mother drives Amish, doesn't she?" Abram asked Summer.

"Yes, but I don't see…" Summer's voice was clear and collected as she began, only to be cut off by the bishop right quick.

"It doesn't matter whether you understand my questions—just that you answer them," he said, leaning back into the chair and sighing. He definitely wasn't used to dealing with English girls.

He continued to grill Summer.

"And you occasionally spend time with the young women of our community?"

"Ah, yes, sometimes." Summer wasn't giving more information than she had to.

"Which girls?" Abram asked.

I didn't know if Abram picked up on it or not, but the girl was beginning to seem amused, her lips pressed together, although she was trying hard to contain it.

Abram grew impatient, and he motioned in quick hand jerks for her to continue.

"Which girls?" She repeated the question to herself and glanced at Rose before saying, "Well, I've been real busy lately, and I don't guess I've been around anyone recently."

Abram's words grew louder with his irritation. "When you

do come around here, girl, who do you spend time with? Please just answer me."

She stalled, not wanting to speak, but I saw Rose poke softly at Summer's thigh to get the girl talking.

"Usually, Suzanna and Miranda, but I've hung out with Sarah, too—and, of course, Rose." She smiled, probably trying to throw the bishop off the trail.

"And why were you in that lower barn today?" Abram's voice was low and steady again.

Maybe even he realized that he'd get further with honey than vinegar with these girls.

As if it were a rehearsed speech, Summer said, "Well, you see, I met up with Rose at the wagons and she told me all about how she loved being Amish and all, but that she missed talking to one of her old girlfriends. A girl named Amanda. Well, Rose was wondering how she was doing and how the school year was going for her…"

Here, Abram began flapping his hand again to encourage Summer to get to the point.

"…and stuff like that. So, I suggested that Rose use my phone to give her friend a call, but Rose didn't want to. She was afraid that she'd be going against your rules, and she *did not* want to do that."

Abram had it with Summer, and his tone showed it. "Yes, I understand all that, but, why…why were you in that barn?"

Summer became more animated, saying, "Oh, it was my idea that we go find a place where she could make the call in private. The little barn at the back of the property was the perfect place."

"To sneak off and get into trouble," Mervin threw in unexpectedly.

"That will be enough, Mervin," Abram told the other man as if he were talking to a child.

Mervin's red face and tight lip indicated that he wasn't happy about the rebuff.

Abram went on talking to Summer. "Now let me get this straight. You went down to the barn to meet Rose so that she could use your phone to make a call, is that correct?"

"Yep," Summer nodded.

"And, at some point, before Rose had the chance to use your phone, Levi showed up?"

"Uh-huh."

"And you were hiding behind a bale of hay and decided to videotape your friend being harassed, instead of going to her aid?" Abram said in a quiet, but very confident voice.

Summer's face faltered for a second, then she recovered. "Well, it was a total shock 'n' all, but…well, I never did like Levi Zook. He always gave me the jitters, staring at me when I'd be visiting with Miranda…and I was kind of afraid of him."

She glanced at Rose who looked away—Summer was on her own with this one.

"Honest, I would've helped her out if Noah hadn't shown up." She paused to gauge where Abram's mindset was. She must have realized she hadn't convinced him, so she blurted out, "It's just what English kids like me do nowadays, we videotape stuff that happens. You know…things that are really interesting, like car wrecks, catfights…a kid being picked on…."

Summer would have rattled on forever if the bishop's hand hadn't come out to silence her.

Headlights shone through the window as a vehicle pulled into the driveway, and Abram said to Summer, "Is that your ride?"

"Yeah, probably my mom's here," she replied.

Abram breathed deeply and said, "Young lady, you will need to take a break from your visits with the girls in our community."

"But…" Summer's face dropped, and I felt sorry for her.

Abram cut her off again. "Our young people have enough to deal with, without the type of temptations that an English girl like you brings to the table."

"For how long?" Summer asked. Her voice was deflated.

Before Abram could answer, Martha cleared her voice and said, "Since this is the child's first offense, and she's never been a problem before, maybe you could find it in your heart, Abram, to be lenient with her."

I was shocked that Martha had spoken. The other three men in the room were also staring at the bishop's wife, disbelieving looks on their faces.

Abram glanced from Martha to Summer and then back to Martha, who smiled at him in one of those wifely "do what I ask or I'm going to make your life miserable" kind of ways.

Abram was a pain in the backside most of the time, but he was a smart man.

He said to Summer, "Two months will be sufficient—this time."

Summer's phone went off, making everyone jump, except for Rose, who was still overly subdued despite everything going on.

Summer glanced at the screen and announced to the room, "My mom wants me to hurry."

"All right, you're dismissed," Abram said to Summer, although she was already rising to leave.

As she walked by I heard her mumble, "Mom won't be happy about this."

I wondered if anyone else heard.

Everyone's attention turned now to Rose.

She waited patiently, her hands folded on her lap, as if she didn't have a care in the world. The picture was completely out of character for a girl who was one of the most anxious people I knew.

"Now…what do we do about you?" Abram said thoughtfully, staring at Rose.

"I think you ought to be more concerned with Levi than with me," she said, sitting up straighter. "What kind of punishment is he going to get?"

My father joined the conversation.

"Yes, Abram, the girl is right. What are your plans for Levi?" he asked.

Abram sighed, sinking back in his chair. At that moment he seemed as old as he was for a change.

"Obviously, Levi's actions were terrible—he will be dealt with accordingly." His eyes met Father's. "Don't worry on that account."

Mervin's voice shot though the room. "But this girl was with our community on the trial basis of her being well behaved—and she's caused this ruckus with her actions."

Martha, with a disapproving frown, said to Mervin, "Don't you go accusing this poor girl of starting it up with Levi. That video clearly showed that she was the victim of Levi's disgusting appetites."

"That's not what I'm saying, Martha. If she were where she was supposed to be, nothing would have happened."

"There's no excuse in the world for Levi to have behaved the way he did with this girl, or any other one," she said with finality, leaving no room for an argument.

"You still aren't getting my point, Martha." Mervin settled back into his side of the sofa, resigned to let the woman win if his weaker voice were any indication.

"It seems that we have two matters here that are separate and not connected," Abram said as he stood up and took his preaching stance. "First, Levi was completely in the wrong, and it worries me to think that if the redheaded English girl hadn't taped the incident, we might have been inclined to believe Levi's rapt denials. But as it worked out, modern technology was beneficial to us and we were given a window into the truth." He paused to look everyone in the eye before he went on to say, "And Levi will face the consequences of his actions toward this girl." He pointed to Rose, and I wondered if he'd forgotten her name.

"The second issue is that Rose disobeyed our rules by attempting to use a cell phone in secret." He stopped to think and smoothed down his white beard. "Honestly, such an indiscretion by any of the youth in our community, especially the first time, would not be a serious matter." The bishop looked with resolve directly at Mervin as he finished his thought. "So it would be unfair to Rose to treat her more severely, because she was not born into our ways."

I swiveled in my seat to see Mervin's reaction. He frowned but held his tongue.

Father spoke, "So this incident will not be held against Rose?"

Abram shook his head and answered, "It's not as if she went out and purchased a phone for her own use. I think it is up to James to punish her as he sees fit for this violation."

James had remained quiet the entire time, sitting in a chair in the corner. I'd forgotten about him. But now he had something to say, and he said it with surety.

"I wasn't the happiest fellow in the community when I learned that an English girl was joining our family—and all because she fancied one of our handsome young bucks." He smiled at Rose and continued. "But I have discovered over the past two months that this young lady is a hard worker. She's proven to be dedicated, polite and resourceful. Above all else, she has impressed me with her willingness to listen and learn." He nodded his head and faced Abram. "I believe Rose would make a fine addition to our church and I request that she's allowed to join with the others in a couple of weeks."

Rose's eyes bugged out, and her mouth opened—*finally, some reaction from her.* My own heart beat heavily in my chest.

We were almost there, almost together.

Mervin stood up and said loudly, "But she hasn't even had time for all the training. And then there's the matter of her boots."

James snorted, showing some fire in his blood. I wondered myself what the hell Mervin was talking about—*boots?*

Rose had the look of opening her mouth to speak, but Martha, seeing that Rose was getting worked up, rescued my girl by explaining, "You see, Rose, it was brought to our attention by one of the young women in our community—" her eyes had strayed just long enough to Mervin that I knew it must be Ella "—that you wear special boots when riding your horse, boots that normally wouldn't be allowed for us." Martha sounded almost apologetic.

Rose couldn't hold it in any longer. She blurted out a "Huh?" with a confused face.

Abram must have been itching to get out of there, because his impatience was spilling over again. "The boots you wear—the boots. They're unacceptable—much too flashy for our girls."

"But, they're just old brown lace-ups," Rose argued. I wished that I could move invisibly and place my hand over her mouth.

"Again, it doesn't matter what you think, young lady, as long as you obey," Abram said. The man's frustration was obvious.

To my relief, Rose held her tongue.

It seemed that at this sign of obedience from Rose, the

bishop had made his decision. He said to the other adults in the room, "James Hershberger is an honorable and wise man. If he believes that this young woman is ready to join our people, then I will support him. After all, I've been keeping an extra close eye on her, and she has, for the most part, behaved admirably." He eyed Rose seriously before continuing. "The fact that the girl is still among us after two months of living our ways shows that she has the type of resiliency that might make her a good woman in the eyes of the Lord."

For dramatic effect, Abram spread his arms and asked the room, "Who are we to keep a person who is so determined and has proven herself fit for our Plain ways from reaching that goal?"

The question seemed to settle over the room. Glancing at Rose, I could see that she, like me, was holding her breath.

Father said, "I support James's request wholeheartedly." But he was still stoic, not celebrating just yet.

Marcus's voice came out more firmly than I expected when he said, "I accept this girl into our church." He looked relieved that he'd spoken and gotten it over with.

We all turned to Mervin, who coughed out, "So be it, then."

My gut was on fire. *Rose had done it.* Somehow, my little English girl had worked her charms on the ministers. Except for Mervin, who—because of Ella—no amount of charm would have swayed.

I focused my sight on Rose, and my heart hammered loudly enough for everyone to hear. She smiled softly, almost shyly at me.

"I guess it's official, then. Rose, you'll be one of us now," Martha said, crossing the room and embracing Rose tightly.

Rose's eyes met mine briefly, and my blood slowed. Her mouth could lie, but those beautiful eyes couldn't.

She was terrified.

15

Rose

I closed my eyes, thinking back to a trip we took to Walt Disney World a few years earlier. Life had been easier then—and very different. Mom had been healthy and full of energy, going on all the rides with me, Sam and Justin. Dad didn't enjoy the amusement park attractions, so she'd always been the one on the roller coasters, screaming with her hands up.

It was funny to think that I hadn't even known that Noah existed back then. I certainly had never given a thought that there were people in the middle of the country who lived their lives as if they were stuck in a time warp. Buggies, caps and three-hour church services hadn't even occurred to me in those days.

Everything had changed.

Listening to Bishop Lambright drone on and on, my mind had completely fogged over. The soft press of Suzanna and Miranda's bodies on either side of me was the only thing that told me that I wasn't dreaming. Yes, I really was sitting in a small room, adjacent to the schoolhouse, receiving my final lecture from the bishop.

The classes that I'd attended the previous weeks had been pretty much the same. Bishop Lambright had spent hours ce-

menting into each of our skulls the ways of the Amish people, which were governed by the community's Ordnung. He'd
taken special care to impart onto us the seriousness of the
vows we were taking to the Amish church.

Now here I was, within an hour of becoming officially an
Amish woman. I'd agreed to obey a doctrine that I didn't understand, and to be honest, really didn't believe in. I felt as if
I was a fraud. And to make matters worse, the seriousness of
what I was about to do had been weighing heavily on me for
several days. I'd barely been able to keep food in my queasy
belly, and, at the moment, I wasn't feeling any better. Butterflies raced around inside of me in a chaotic frenzy, and I
rubbed my sweaty palms together in an attempt to erase the
wetness.

Lifting my head, I glanced around to see how the others
were holding up. Timothy looked calm and resigned. He was
leaning back in his chair, staring into thin air with his eyes
glazed over. John, who sat to his left, had his head resting on
the palms of his hands. Occasionally he tapped his fingers,
but otherwise he appeared resolute. Joshua, on the other hand,
sat slouched with his feet fidgeting to the point of annoyance.
When Josh's gaze rose, he quickly looked away when he saw
me watching him. The kid was always a nervous wreck, and if
I paid too much attention to him, I'd absorb his constant agitation, making me even more uptight than usual.

Suzanna must have felt it, too. She placed her steady hand
on my knee and squeezed. Her reassuring touch made me
feel a little better, if not more confused. The rambunctious
girl whom I'd gone running through the woods with the first
week that I was with the Amish was still in there—as I could
tell from her sparkling eyes—but that girl was now hidden
most of the time. Ever since Suzanna had announced that she
would join the church, she was a changed person. I'd watched

in disbelief as she began to spend more time with the other women on Sundays. She was careful not to be seen talking to Timothy by his buggy on Sunday mornings or at the nets after the singings. Somehow, she'd managed to control her barking laughter, which now seldom erupted from her mouth. If it did, she'd quickly bring herself under control after glancing around worriedly.

Even though Suzanna appeared to have had her body snatched by an alien, Miranda was the one who'd shocked me the most. When she'd told me that she was joining the church, I'd felt a mixture of happiness for her that she'd chosen to be with Matthew and utter disgust that she'd given in so easily. She was the one whom I'd thought would hold out longer, be the quiet warrior that I'd imagined that she was.

Miranda's behavior hadn't changed as dramatically as Suzanna's had, though. She'd always been as silent as a church mouse, blending in with her surroundings. I shifted my eyes and studied her next. She sat perfectly straight and still. Her eyes were fixed on a point on the opposite wall, and I followed the path of her gaze to see the cross on the wall.

Maybe of us all, Miranda was the only one who was joining up for reasons other than to begin courting. The thought sobered me.

The bishop stopped before me, and jarring me to attention, he asked, "And what does humility mean to you, Rose?"

I had to quickly process his words and wake myself up at the same time. Everyone was staring at me, including Amos Miller and the other ministers who were seated in the corner.

Clearing my throat, I looked back at Bishop Lambright and said, "To be modest...and accept that you're not perfect."

The bishop smiled slightly and slowly nodded his head. "That's close enough." He paused and looked at each of the boys and girls in turn before he said, "Always remember that being humble is our way."

He motioned for us to stand. The boys took their places behind the ministers, and Maretta led the girls to the end of the line. I managed to stand, but my legs were shaky. I took a gulp of air as a thousand thoughts shot through my mind. Images of Dad, Sam and Justin loomed in front of me. The distant sound of remembered music haunted my ears, and I saw myself dancing, rising up into a pirouette and then leaping across the dance floor. The rumble of a car's engine coming to life as I turned the key, making my heart race in excitement, along with flashes of my former friends and the places we used to hang out at clouded my vision. It was all about to be lost forever. As I crossed through the doorway into the large room, I heard the somber voices of the entire congregation as they sang a hymn. I crowded in closer to Suzanna's back, trying not to look at the expectant faces that turned to watch as we walked past. Before I took my seat on the bench, I glanced over my shoulder. My breath caught in my throat when I spotted Noah.

In the instant that our eyes met, he smiled, calming my heart and mind.

When he was within reach, there was only one way to go— only one way that I wanted to go. My desire to spend my life with the young Amish man with whom I'd fallen in love months ago was stronger than all the worry and doubts combined. To be with Noah was worth leaving my world and joining his. As long as he was with me, I could survive anything.

A sense of surety filled me that hadn't been there before, and I was breathing easily again.

When the bishop began speaking, it was in the Amish language. The entire scene was like a fog in my mind, and the only solid being was Noah. I could feel his dark eyes on my back, and that sensation kept me from bolting out the door.

There was a murmur of voices behind me before the bishop began moving down our line. As he went, he poured the water in the ladle onto the heads of each of the boys. Seeing Suzanna remove her cap, I followed suit, along with Miranda. When the cold water trickled through my hair to touch my scalp, I swallowed hard.

The bishop's words were distant and foreign, but the feel of the water was all too real.

My heart skipped and a cool sweat broke out on my skin.

I thought to myself, *What have I done?*

My eyes snapped open when I felt the jab in my side. I was back in the metal-sided building, sitting on the rock-hard bench between Suzanna and Miranda. I blinked a few times, seeing that the service was over. I must have zoned out completely.

I rose from the bench slowly, my body feeling as numb as my mind. I couldn't help thinking how *not happy* Dad would be to learn that I'd joined the "cult," as he so eloquently had put it. The fact that I'd kind of fibbed to Mr. Miller when I'd told him that Dad was okay with it was on my mind, too. At some point it would probably come back to bite me on the butt. For now, though, I had to go with the flow—I had no choice.

"I'm so happy for you, Rose." Rebecca gave me her usual bear hug with Sarah and Rachel smiling brightly on either side of her.

"Thanks," I murmured.

Then it was Ruth's turn to congratulate me, with a more reserved squeeze, but her eyes were misty.

Sarah sidled up alongside me, politely pushing the adults

away. "You didn't understand the announcement, did you?" she said, grinning from ear to ear.

"Ah, I didn't understand any of it, except the part where the bishop sprinkled the water on my head," I replied, suddenly bothered with myself for not picking up any of the Amish language by that time.

She leaned in close to my face after grasping my fingers and said excitedly but still in a whisper, "Abram announced that you and Noah are a courting couple."

"Really?" After my mouth dropped, I closed it again quickly.

"Yeah," Sarah confirmed. That's when I noticed Noah standing a few people behind her, with a smile rising on his handsome face.

I smiled back, momentarily forgetting the turmoil of the past few hours. Right there was the reason for everything. My love for Noah and willingness to do whatever it took to be with him couldn't be a bad thing.

Noah waited patiently behind several of the women who went out of their way to tell me how pleased they were to have me as a member of their community. I was half distracted watching Noah out of the corner of my eye, but I tried not to be rude, thanking each woman in turn.

Was Noah really going to talk to me?

I'd become accustomed to the silent treatment, having to rely on my instincts and his flirty looks to know that he still wanted me. Now that I was a member of the church and our courtship was announced to the congregation, were things going to be different?

Seeing Noah stroll casually toward me, my heart skipped and my tummy got tight. Just before he arrived, Katie stepped in front of him. She gave me a quick hug and said, "Now we're going to be sisters." She chatted with me for a minute longer, and while she talked, through the sea of beards and caps, I caught sight of a furious stare—Ella Weaver. When our gazes touched, she spun away in a flash.

Until Noah and I were officially married, that girl would continue to give me trouble—I just knew it.

When Katie moved on, Noah wasn't taking any more chances of me being caught by someone else. He stepped forward until he was only a few inches away.

Before he spoke his eyes swept over me. The mischievous smile that sprang to his face told me he liked what he saw, even though it was packaged in a figure-hiding hunter-green dress.

"Hey there, beautiful," he said softly, sending a pleasant warmth through me.

"Hi, yourself." I fidgeted in place, not sure what I should do or say. I felt as if all the eyes in the building were on us, but when I glanced around, they weren't—just my paranoid mind working overtime.

"I'm very proud of you," Noah continued in a quiet tone as his hands fidgeted in front of him. He was nervous, too. Or maybe he was just itching to grab me and start kissing, the way I wanted him to do.

"Why?" I asked, kind of already knowing the answer.

His eyes flicked up as if he was flabbergasted with me.

"Because you did it—you kept your head on straight and survived the last couple of months. Now we're finally together."

"Aw, this doesn't exactly feel like we're together," I chided, but underneath it all, I was frustrated.

"It'll get better. I promise." His eyes held mine, not letting go, and the tingle of anticipation ran over my skin.

Yeah, everything was all right.

Just as I was about to leave, Miranda pulled me back. Her face told me she wanted to talk. We waited as a stampede of young people evacuated the Bontragers' building.

When all the kids were gone and only a few middle-aged women and old men hung about, Miranda stepped closer.

In a coarse whisper, she said, "Do you know what happened to Levi?"

The mention of his name sent a chill through me, and the evening light seemed to dim. I hated thinking about the guy, let alone talking about him. Now that he was in trouble with the Amish authority, I hoped that life would be easier for Miranda.

Things sure hadn't worked out the way I'd originally planned, but possibly it was all for the better. If I'd threatened Levi with the video, he probably would have tackled me and Summer for the evidence. I'd underestimated just how violent he was. Noah bursting in on the scene had ended up saving the day, and now the Elders knew firsthand what a creep Levi was. Hopefully, that bit of knowledge protected Miranda from her brother's manipulations forever.

"I knew he was going to get punished, but I haven't heard a thing," I whispered back to her.

Miranda surveyed the room and then brought her dark eyes—almost the same black as her evil brother's—back to mine. "He's been sent away."

"Where to?" I asked as my heart pattered faster. I had secretly worried about what the psycho would do to me when he got his Get-of-Jail-Card.

"To the same place I went to." She paused to glance around again. "Da and Ma argued about it late into that first night. But in the end, Da won out and Levi made the trip when the sun came up the next morning."

"How long will he be there?" It had worked out better than I ever could have dreamed. I breathed easier, my heart calming.

"Don't know for sure, but I reckon it'll be for a long while." Her voice became freer as she spoke.

I thought Miranda seemed happy, but since I didn't know her well, I wanted to make sure that everything that Summer and I had done had served its purpose.

"And how do you feel about that?" I said the words slowly.

Miranda took my hands between her cool ones, her deep eyes widening. "Oh, Rose, thank you." I began to correct her, but she shook her head, "I don't want to know the details, but I'll always owe you one for getting Levi out of my life. Even now, if he does come home someday, everyone won't believe him so surely—and it's all because of you."

A quiet thrill spread through me. I'd wanted to help Miranda and give Levi some justice, and it seemed that I got a package deal. The happy look on Miranda's sunny face was well worth the risk. Somehow, I'd have to get a message to Summer. She needed to know that her sacrifice wasn't in vain.

"I'm glad that you're okay now," I told Miranda, hoping deep down that she could get over whatever crap her sick brother had done.

"Oh, I'm more than okay. And you remember, if you ever need help, I'm there for you."

I nodded my head once, fearing a release of tears was imminent. Miranda motioned to the door, and we walked out into the chilled autumn air. The wind had picked up, and leaves were sprinkling down from the maple trees along the drive. I held my face up into the brisk air, enjoying the static energy around me.

Before we reached the nets and all the dark-clad bodies around them, a voice behind me nearly made me jump out of my skin.

"Are you ready to go?" Noah asked.

I turned to see him grinning broadly at me.

I'm sure I stopped breathing altogether. "Are you kidding me?" I squealed.

"Shh, don't get too excited or they'll send a chaperone with us." Without touching me, Noah put his hand behind me and pushed the air into my back to get me moving.

I glanced at Miranda, who smiled and said, "Have a good time." Then she turned and jogged across the yard in springy strides. She was going to be all right.

A gust of air threatened to take off the black bonnet that covered my cap, and I held it on with one hand while I clutched the front of my coat closed with the other.

Noah was walking in long, ground-covering strides, eager to get to his horse and buggy. I had to nearly run to keep up, and I managed just fine thanks to the adrenaline pumping through my veins.

Noah already had Oscar hitched up and ready to go. All he had to do was untie the horse from the rail. Before I climbed in, he hurried back and held out his hand to help me. I was shocked and looked around to see if anyone was paying any attention to us.

"It's all right." Noah's voice sounded different, as if he was all grown up and feeling sure of himself. Sam used that tone sometimes, and it always bugged me, because it didn't seem totally honest. But with Noah, it sounded extremely sexy.

The touch of his warm hand sent tingles into my fingers, and amazingly even that little contact made my whole belly warm. *Whose insane idea was it to allow us to be alone together?* I wondered as I seated myself beside Noah for the first time since he'd dropped me off at the Hershbergers' months ago.

He snapped the reins and sent the buggy over the driveway faster than I was used to. Mr. Hershberger took his dear sweet time when he was driving. Noah's urgency to get away from the community—and be alone with me—was thick in the crisp air.

I studied the side of his face as we journeyed along the road at an extended trot, the clip-clops of the horse's hooves striking the air as loud as gunshots. His chin and cheeks held some stubble that I hadn't noticed earlier, and the stiff hairs fascinated me.

"Now, don't you go doing that." Noah smiled, meeting my gaze for a second before turning back to the road.

"I'm not doing anything," I defended myself playfully.

"Looking at me all sexylike, that's what."

He was flirting with me, and I loved it.

"Where exactly are we going?" I asked, putting my hand on his thigh to really throw him off.

He sighed in acceptance, and I grinned to myself. I had him just where I wanted.

"We're going to your place to hang out." Too fast for me to know it was coming, his hand was free of the reins and holding mine. He brought it to his lips and kissed it gently, and slowly, as if he was savoring every moment.

"What are we going to do there?" I purred, wanting him to feel the same crazy stirrings inside that I did.

Noah slowed the buggy to make the turn, leaving my hand alone for just an instant before he had it back resting warmly in his.

"We need to talk about how this is going to go so we don't get into trouble." He sounded more serious, the adult voice creeping in. I didn't know if it was the words or the tone that prickled me.

"More rules?" I sighed dramatically.

"Don't go getting all moody on me. It's just that there are some things we're going to have to be careful not to do."

When he saw me roll my eyes, he asked, "Didn't Ruth talk to you about this courting business?"

Actually she had. I knew what he was about to tell me, and

I wasn't a happy camper that he was really going to try to live up to the ridiculous standards that the Amish tried to enforce. It was no wonder that when they finally did get hitched they were popping out babies left and right.

Noah had waited long enough, and squeezing my hand tightly, he asked again, "Well?"

I stared ahead, focusing on a tumble of leaves making their frenzied way across the road.

"She said that we were a hands-off courting community."

"Yes, that's right. And do you understand what that means?" Noah coaxed, loosening his grip on my poor hand.

I looked back at him and couldn't keep the pitch out of my voice. "You've got to be kidding—right?"

Infuriatingly, he laughed at me, kissing my hand with an open mouth that sent the warm fuzzies through me once again. I would probably faint straight away if he kissed me on more delicate parts of my body.

"Don't worry—I don't intend to go months without touching you. You can be sure of that."

I felt lighter and happier at once.

The feeling didn't last long when he went on to say, "But we have to be extra careful around others in the community. Do you know why?"

I thought it was a dumb question, but I didn't say so. "Ah, so we don't get into trouble and have our courtship rescinded."

"I don't know about that last word, but we aren't only being careful to avoid punishment." Noah took his eyes off the road longer than I would have liked to make a definite point. "If we're really good, then my parents and the Hershbergers will allow us more freedom together, which is what we want—right?"

We were almost to the driveway, and I became very brave.

"Of course—but just how strict are you going to be?" I pushed into him with the side of my body and kissed his neck.

I didn't get the reaction I was hoping for when he groaned in an angry way.

"What?" I asked, worried that the gorgeous man beside me was becoming a prude.

He sighed loudly. "It's your brother behind us."

"No way." I swiveled on the seat to search out the little window in the back. I could see the green truck—and Sam's bushy head.

"Darn, he has awful timing," I mumbled.

"He's following us up to your house. I wonder what he wants," he growled.

My doubts at the morning's ceremony hit me again and nervousness took hold of my body. Sam could read me like an open book—how was I going to keep it from him that it was official now?

I was Amish.

Noah didn't say another word as he drove the horse back to the barn. He continued to watch his side-view mirror, though, frowning the entire time.

Sam stayed as close as our shadow until we were parked. Noah was so disturbed about the appearance of my brother that he jumped down and began unhitching the horse, leaving me to make my own way down. He had forgotten me, but before I crept completely out of the buggy, he came back and held my hand as my first foot hit the gravel. Once I was out he went back to the horse, maybe hoping that if he ignored Sam, my brother would disappear.

"How's it going, little sister?" Sam strolled up and made himself comfortable, leaning against the buggy. The smirk on his face as his eyes swept over my dress bugged the crap out of me, but I ignored his about-to-laugh look and appraised him.

He was wearing a sweatshirt that I hadn't seen before with his school's logo on it—a blue roaring panther. He also had on new Reeboks. God, I was jealous.

I crossed my arms in front of me, preparing to do battle.

"Wonderful—how about you?"

I pretended to be interested, but deep down, I was curious about Sam. Especially after what Summer had said about him. Had he finally met his match?

"Oh, pretty good. I'm starting on both the offense as a receiver and defense as a linebacker." He shrugged.

"Really—you're playing both?" I was slightly shocked. Sam had always played defense because of his hulking size, but he could run fast, and I knew he wanted to catch the ball. Where would he find the stamina to play most of the game?

"It's a small school. They needed another receiver after two of the first-string guys got mono." He was talking to me but staring at Noah, who was all but ignoring him. I would have bet Noah was listening to every word, though.

"Is mono going around?" The longer I kept up the casual conversation, the less likely he'd ask about the legalities of my Amish existence.

"Hah. Not to me. I'm being extra careful, but I know four kids with it right now."

"How's Amber?" I stalled some more.

He laughed. "I broke up with her last Friday." He brought his eyes back to me, suddenly very focused. "You see, I met this other girl I like. Only the chick won't give me the time of day."

Since Noah had taken the horse into the barn, Sam and I were alone. Glancing toward the dark opening of the barn's doorway, happiness spread through me. Noah must have been planning to stay awhile—I only wished that my dumb brother wasn't here.

Taking my cap off, I leaned against the buggy. Maybe if I

wasn't freaking Sam out with my outfit, he'd stop looking as if he was going to choke on his own laughter.

"She hasn't succumbed to your prowess yet, huh?" I couldn't help but snicker. It really was funny how baffled he seemed.

"I thought you might be able to help me with that." He smiled brilliantly, forgetting that I was immune to his charms.

"What can I do?" I asked.

"It's that redhead that you hang with—Summer Sage." He said it as if that bit of information filled me in on the big picture.

"Soooo—" Maybe I was being childish, but I wanted to see how far he was willing to go to get with Summer. That girl had proven to be an A-lister and I wasn't going to allow Sam to bring her down.

"Look, I haven't asked you for a favor in a long time...."

Before he could go on, I cut him off. "Yeah, I think the last time you asked me for one, I introduced you to Madison, and you dated her for two weeks and then dumped her after you had her convinced that you loved her." I spit out the words, hands on my hips.

"Hey, that's not the way it happened at all. And besides, I've already met Summer—and talked to her a little bit. What harm could it do if you just put in a nice word for me?" Sam had left his reclining position and was getting in my face.

"It could do a lot of harm if you treat her the way you treat all the other girls unfortunate enough to become your victims."

Sam got his pleading voice going, and I started to think that what Summer had said about Sam being the one to get hurt might be prophetic. I hadn't seen my brother this worked up over a girl since—never.

"It's not like that this time. I think Summer's really interesting. She's different than all the other girls—it's as if she doesn't give a shit about what anyone thinks. And, for the first time in my life, the girl isn't chasing after me. I'd like to get to know her, that's all." He put on a puppy dog look, and I caved when he actually said, *"Please."*

"Oh, okay, I'll see what I can do, but I'm not making any promises—Summer has a mind all her own."

His smile reminded me of a self-satisfied cat, and I instantly regretted helping him out. Ugh, Sam was as bad as me in terms of always getting his way.

Swiftly changing the subject, he said, "So, have you been enjoying all this...stuff?" He spread his arms out and looked seriously at me.

"Yes, I have. If I do you a good turn, then you owe me one."

Now he looked concerned. "What do you mean?"

"Just leave me be and let me live my new life. That's all I ask." I lowered my volume, hoping Noah wouldn't hear. He might not like what came out of Sam's mouth, and I figured Sam was more likely to talk quietly if I did.

The wind had settled, and the sun was close to disappearing. I figured it was around seven o'clock, and I was anxious to spend some time with Noah before he had to turn around and leave. I looked pleadingly at Sam, betting he wouldn't want to risk me taking back my promise. Or better yet, pushing Summer to leave Sam, as I already had.

"You're nuts. And I'm not the only one who thinks so."

"Really?" It wasn't surprising. If I wasn't living my life, I'd think I was crazy, too.

"Dad is just biding his time regarding this whole thing. If he weren't so busy at the hospital and with Tina, you'd be home already."

My hackles went up. "He promised to let me decide," I seethed.

He leaned back again on the buggy, all relaxed now that he *thought* he'd gotten his way.

But that could change in a heartbeat.

"Yeah, and he'll keep his promise, but he's upset that you don't ever come over to the house even though he's invited you several times. Hell, if he didn't come here to get your school-work and bring Justin with him, you'd never see either one of them." He caught my gaze and held it. "Is that what you want—never to see Dad and your brothers again?"

Maybe I could do without you, but then softening, thought, but Dad and Justin were another story altogether.

"Sam, try to understand this. It's hard for me to be around you guys right now. I'm still getting used to my new life, and you all make me feel...well..."

Sam finished for me with his own words. "Out of place, homesick, guilty."

I stood up straighter. "Hey, you asked me to help you out. Getting on my nerves is not going to serve you well, Sam."

"Yeah, I know." He pulled away from the buggy and gave me a quick hug, totally surprising me. "Just don't forget about us, okay?"

He turned to leave and paused, saying, "You can back out of this nonsense anytime. Nothing is set in stone."

His eyes swept over me once more, and this time he didn't control his laughter. His loud chuckles floated back to me as he climbed into his truck and left without another glance at me.

Watching him go, I felt a swirl of conflicting emotions. Sam hadn't pissed me off as much as he usually did. In fact, he acted fairly amicable, but having him around was like seeing Dad or Justin. It was too upsetting; it stirred up my inner doubt.

That was the thing I hated the most—not being sure whether I was doing the right thing.

"Don't listen to him." Noah was behind me, so close I could feel his body heat.

I turned and quickly placed the cap back onto my head.

When my hands were free he grasped them. "You were spying."

I already knew he was, so it didn't really matter.

"You're everything to me, and we've finally reached the point where we can be together. I'm not going to let your damn brother mess things up for us." He didn't cuss very often, so I knew he was feeling insecure.

I reached up and brought his face down to mine and kissed him softly, carefully. His lips worked on mine more tenderly then they ever had, and I guessed that maybe because we were finally kissing as a real Amish couple he didn't feel the nervousness as he had before. His tongue slipped into my mouth. At the same time his mouth was busy exploring, his hand moved up and down my back, rhythmically, wonderfully.

Noah's mouth opened wider, and his tongue became hungrier. I pressed into him, pushing my breasts against him.

About the time my mind was thinking some very X-rated things, Noah pulled back and wiped his mouth.

"Shoot, stop that. James and Ruth could be watching from the window." He was out of breath and breathing too fast at the same time. Maybe his body was more of a wreck than mine, after all.

I didn't like that he was blaming me for the inferno blazing between us. I looked at the darkened house and saw only two rooms with dim light showing through the windows. One was the kitchen and the other the Hershbergers' bedroom. They usually went to sleep around dark, so it wouldn't be a stretch to believe that they were already in bed reading their Bibles.

I took a step back and said, "Gee, maybe you should head on home before I tempt you into doing something you'll regret later."

Before I got away, his hand locked on my arm, and he breathed out. "Don't be difficult, Rose." He stepped in closer,

"It's just that you drive me crazy when you're in my arms. It's as if all my brain activity stops and all I want to do is..."

"What?" I whispered to him.

"More than anything I want to make love to you."

His words didn't shock me, but the turmoil he clearly felt about his perfectly normal longings did. Noah really wanted to be good—and if he had his way, I might actually be a virgin on my wedding night.

"I want you to make love to me."

"That's the problem. Neither one of us has the sense to hold back. But we have to. We can't lose what we've won. We have to control ourselves."

Again, his doom-and-gloom attitude amused me, and I giggled a little, causing him to frown deeply. The darkness was complete, and I was chilly now that he wasn't crushing me against his body. "So what do you want to do now?"

"Let's go to the house and hang out on the couch." He took my hand and pulled me along. His voice became loose again, and I snuggled under his arm. "It's been so long since we talked, really talked. I have so many things to tell you—"

Noah rambled on, and I only half listened to him. I was obsessing about how long the whole courtship thing would be. And...I was wondering if Noah was becoming so addicted to me that he might change his mind about becoming English someday.

The secret wish that I'd had for so long came to life in my mind...and for the first time I thought it might be a real possibility.

16

Sam

"Hey, Hunter, why don't you ride home with Shaun?" I suggested, but at that moment I wouldn't have taken no for an answer.

"Sure, what's up?" Hunter asked, hesitating on the sidewalk beside the parking lot.

"Nothing," I mumbled. "See you tomorrow." I split away from him and the other guys, speeding to a slow jog back up the sidewalk.

Damn it, I was feeling nervous, and I didn't enjoy the strange sensation at all.

The cloudy day had fit my mood, until the moment when I'd spotted her sitting under the tree in front of the school where kids usually got picked up. The sun wasn't shining now, but the day sure did seem brighter.

The cool breeze tugged at my hair, still wet from the after-practice shower, but I felt warm with anticipation. I slowed, crossing over the grass, watching her reddish-blond hair flutter around her shoulders. She was alone, and considering school had been let out two hours ago, I felt sure that something was up.

I thought I'd have a few more steps to collect myself and decide what to say when she turned and looked straight at me. Seeing the roll of her eyes and the way she dropped her head to her phone after seeing me approach did not help my confidence level.

She was wearing a red-and-brown plaid jacket that had a line of fake fur around the hood. I focused on the way her hair mixed in and contrasted with the tannish fluff as I cleared my throat.

"Ah, miss your ride?" I asked in a friendly way.

"Why do you care?" she snapped, not looking at me.

Okay, I'd had about enough of her ruthless meanness toward me. I'd never done a thing to the girl.

"What is up your butt?" I lost all sense of nicety, letting her have it.

Then she did look up, and her green eyes glinted like emeralds. I decided in that second that I had to make her my girl. And once I made up my mind about something, I *always* followed through.

Looking me straight in the eye, Summer said, "My mom was supposed to pick me up hours ago, but she got called on an Amish run and now she expects me to wait around here until six."

It was turning into a brilliant day.

"So you need a ride?"

"You offering?" she said, subtle hostility still in the air.

I couldn't help but smile. It was so perfect. "Yeah, I'll take you wherever you want to go."

"Anywhere at all—like a beach in Florida, or maybe New York City?" Now she was flirting. I could tell for sure with her softer voice and tilted head.

I didn't even have to think about it. *"Anywhere."*

She jumped up and brushed the leaves from her butt before she began walking toward the parking lot. I caught her in two strides, falling in beside her.

"You get off easy because I only want to go home today." She glanced up at me, and hotness spread through my veins. I'd experienced the sensation before, but not from just a second of eye contact.

We walked in silence to my truck, which she must have remembered since she walked right to it. I jumped in front of her, and after unlocking the passenger side door, I held it open for her.

"Hah, are you playing some game at being a gentleman?"

"No, actually, I am a gentleman," I said, shutting the door quickly behind her before she had a chance to change her mind.

Climbing in, I decided to go out on a limb since she was behaving a little more civilly. I turned my gaze to her and asked, "Want to get something to eat?"

"Don't have any money," she said, staring right back at me.

"Hey, that's no problem at all. I'll treat." I wanted her to say yes so bad it was making my chest ache.

Summer narrowed her eyes at me and said, "Why would you do that?"

Was she that bleak-minded? It wasn't difficult to figure out my intentions. Hell, I liked the girl—she should know that.

I decided to take an honest approach, and I shrugged, saying, "I'm hungry. I always get a bite to eat after practice, and I wouldn't feel right eating in front of you."

"It won't bother me in the least," she said, still keeping my eyes captive.

If I read Summer right, she wanted me to chase her down like a wolf on his prey. She wanted me to work for her attentions. And for the first time in my life, I was willing to do just that.

Starting up the engine I flicked on the music and said, "I'll get you some food—you can eat it or leave it. It's up to you."

Pulling onto the roadway, I felt better than I had in days. My last conversation with Rose had been on my mind, and seeing

Summer daily in the hallways at school but having her avoid me as if I was the plague had put me in a stormy mood. Now, she was sitting beside me in my truck, the scent of vanilla coming off her.

Damn, she smelled good.

She reached over and began skimming through the radio's channels. She settled on a song that was not the sort of stuf I thought she'd listen to. "You like that Mumford and Sons?" I asked, nodding to the radio.

"Sure do."

I was going to have to work a lot harder to get this girl to talk. Something I was definitely not used to. Girls were usually talking machines, and the fact that this one wasn't vocalizing much intrigued me all the more.

Strategizing, I decided on Sonic. We could eat some decent food and still be in the privacy of the truck. And I could keep on smelling her.

"This okay?"

"Yep."

"You don't talk much, do you?" I parked, turning all my attention to the lovely girl beside me.

"I do when I got something to say."

Guessing that Summer wasn't going to be too forthcoming on what she wanted to eat, I asked for two orders of cheeseburgers, fries and chocolate milk shakes.

Settling back in the seat, I leaned toward Summer a bit. I didn't want her jumping out of the cab—or worse yet, punching me in the nose.

"I'm a vegetarian," she said, calmly staring me down again.

My mind hardly had time to digest her words. *Really?*

Then she burst out laughing. Hell, I thought she was beautiful when she looked miserable; now she was irresistible.

"No, silly, I was just kidding you." She paused and shifted her weight, facing me. "Do you ever see Rose anymore?"

"Not very often—I did get to talk to her for a few minutes on Sunday, though."

Seeing Summer's rosy face filled with curiosity, I suddenly felt completely at ease, and I wanted to talk, get things off my chest.

"It's crazy, this whole thing with her joining the Amish. I don't know what Dad or she was thinking," I said.

"Why did your Dad let her do it?" She was resting her chin on her hand, which was relaxed on the back of the seat. She looked warm and inviting, and I kind of lost track of the conversation.

"Huh?"

"*Your Dad,* why did he let Rose join up with them?" she said with an amused tilt to her voice.

"Did you know that our mom died a couple of years ago?"

When she nodded her head and her face went all sad on me, I had to turn away.

"Well, I think Dad is just confused about how to do things now. He's a doctor, so he's superbusy, and then there's his new girlfriend messing with his mind."

I glanced at Summer, and she waited quietly, expecting more, so I went on. "The relationship between Rose and Noah was very intense right off the bat. Since they couldn't be together, I think it made matters worse. I don't understand how Rose can live that backward lifestyle for months—it makes no sense."

Summer said softly, "Love can make people do all kinds of crazy things."

I caught her eyes, and some kind of connection sprang to life. It was as if I'd just opened my eyes for the first time.

The knock on the window jolted me back to the world, and I rolled it down, taking the food and paying the woman. I made sure to give her a tip, respecting anyone who would do such a sucky job.

I passed the food over to Summer and was enormously pleased to see her scarfing her food down like a hungry animal. I liked a girl with an appetite—and one who would not waste my money on her meal.

We ate for a minute, just chewing and swallowing. I was thinking that a burger had never tasted so good.

Summer wiped the juices off her lips, and taking me off guard, she said, "You know—I'm banished from the Amish community for two whole months." She watched my reaction, and I suddenly felt as if maybe we were on the same side of whatever game Rose was playing.

"What for?" I was angry for her, feeling almost as if a slight against the girl sitting beside me was one against me.

"It's a long story, but basically it involved a cell phone." She rolled her eyes slightly.

"Who has the authority to tell you something like that?"

I was beginning to think maybe Rose was being held against her will. Otherwise, how else could she put up with such bullshit?

"The bishop told me—and my mamma isn't too happy about it, either." She bit into her hamburger with more vigor.

I filed what she said away in my mind and then asked, "Do you think Rose is really happy with the way things are?"

Summer looked up into space, thinking about it, before answering me. "I don't know, really. When I've hung out with her, she seemed upbeat, not complaining much about the Amish. Really, I don't know how she's doing it. I've dressed up in Suzanna's frocks for fun, and it's awful. And, let me tell you, keeping your hair up beneath one of those caps all day is torturous."

"That's the thing that boggles me. Rose is a *lot* like you. She hates being told what to do, and she loves her freedom. So what the hell is with her?" I said."It's all about love. Rose and Noah have it bad. Guess we'll have to wait and see if it's enough to keep them together."

I drove extra slow on the way home, trying to stretch out every second with Summer. I'd never enjoyed being around a girl as much as I did with her. Once she let go of her bulldog mentality, she was bubbly and sweet. And behind that country talk, she was smart.

I was disappointed when she pointed out her double-wide house, and I pulled in, turning the engine off.

She controlled a grin as she looked at me quizzically, probably wondering why I'd cut the engine when she was supposed to be getting out and going on her merry way.

My eyes briefly surveyed Summer's home. She lived a pretty blue-collar existence as far as I could tell; the cheap-looking porch jutting out from the front door and the damaged trampoline and old junk cars as landscape said her mom wasn't overly concerned with appearances.

And, in the course of a few seconds, I'd counted four scary-looking pit mixes slinking around. The fact that they weren't barking signaled to me that they were used to company—and I didn't like that thought at all. My heart racing, I realized that I didn't want to leave Summer there. I wanted to bring her home with me. What the fuck was wrong with me?

When I finally turned to her, I was struck with how much she needed me—even though she didn't know it yet.

"Well...uh, thanks for the ride—and dinner, too." She opened the door, about to leave me, but I wasn't ready for her to go yet.

I reached out and grasped her arm, pulling her back in. "Wait. Ah, I was wondering if you'd like me to pick you up in the morning. You're not really out of the way or anything."

I waited, not breathing.

"Hmm, I don't know, Sam. My mamma might not like that." She was thinking about it, though, which was a start.

I let go of her, feeling that she wasn't about to leap away, and took my phone out.

"Why don't you ask your mom and I'll call you about it later."

It was better that I got her number, rather than the other way around. She might never call me back.

She smiled. "Okay."

She told me her number, and I was extra careful, not wanting to get it wrong. Then she did slip out the door. I hated that I didn't have another reason to stop her. The cool air sneaked into the cab before she got the door shut, making her exit even more dramatic in my mind.

I watched her walk slowly to the house, the dogs lacing around her legs. She took her time to pat each one. I got the impression that she was in no hurry to enter her little redneck abode, either.

As I drove away I was satisfied that I was well on my way to making Summer my girlfriend. I also couldn't help but smile when I remembered how sweet it sounded when she said my name.

17

Noah

I paused, balancing on the balls of my feet while I looked out from the scaffolding. My leg was still sore, but I had the brace off and that's all that mattered. I loved these warm autumn afternoons when the mornings were crisp, but by noon, the sun was up high, blazing in the sky, forcing me to shed the jacket.

Wiping the sweat from my forehead with the handkerchief, I wondered where Rose was. When I'd called her the day before to invite her to the frolic that was being held by the community to fix up the house that Jacob and Katie were moving into I could hear her excitement clearly, even on the phone. I smiled, thinking about how the past few weeks had gone. Our Sunday evening courting had seemed to settle Rose and had also given us the opportunity to learn more about each other. The other times that we'd been together, we'd always been on edge and in a hurry. Now, every week we had several hours of alone time to talk and even get a little of the touching in that we weren't supposed to be doing.

Even up here surrounded by the sound of hammering and the voices of a dozen other Amish men, I still blushed, thinking about Rose's soft and willing body. Shaking my head, I tried to fling the images from my mind so I could focus on what I was doing.

"Are you feeling all right, son?"

Father was working beside me. I think he mistook the pleasurable feelings I was experiencing for pain.

"Never better," I answered honestly.

Father took a swig from his bottle of water, and said, "Courting Rose has suited you well, hasn't it?" I glanced at Father and saw a knowing smile on his lips.

Father had discussed at length all the feelings that I'd be experiencing now that I was spending more time with Rose. He had warned me that God had reserved the pleasures of a woman for the wedding bed, and I'd best remember it. He'd also told me that if I were to cross the line with Rose before we'd said our marriage vows to the Church, I would be defiling her.

I didn't quite see the last part the way he did. After all, if I was the only man who claimed her, then I certainly couldn't defile her for myself.

"Yes, Father." I looked at him, and for some reason I wanted to talk to him about Rose...and things. "I love her more each day and..."

I sighed, not knowing how much I should say, but deciding that I was a grown man now, I hoped Father would treat me as such. "I'm finding it more difficult to...stay chaste. I feel as if she belongs to me, that we're already committed to one another." I breathed out, glad to have spoken my heart to Father.

Father nodded and looked off toward the field, where dried-up cornstalks were bristling against each other in the stiff breeze. "I remember well how it was with your Ma and me. I could barely keep my hands off her. Remember it like it was yesterday, I do."

"How did you restrain yourself?"

He shook his head and laughed. "When it got too bad, we moved our wedding date up a month." Then he became serious again. "Have you and Rose talked about the marriage yet?" He almost hesitated when he said it, and I wondered what his worry was.

His question poked me a bit. I'd tried to pin Rose down on the day that we'd take our vows, but she kept avoiding the conversation altogether. She'd also been complaining a lot lately about the work she had to do at the Hershbergers. I was seriously worried that she was getting ready to bolt.

"I don't know if Rose is ready for marriage so soon." I spoke low, not wanting the men who were working on a nearby section of the roof to hear.

Father nodded slowly, thinking he understood what was going on but missing the point entirely.

"You must be patient with her, son. Some women take a while to open up to the idea of a physical relationship with a man. Women are not made like us. They don't find the pleasure in the bed that we do. But, Rose is very young, only seventeen, right?"

I nodded. "Within a few months, she'll be itching to marry you. Besides, you hardly have enough money set aside to start a family proper anyhow."

"You're right."

Father went back to work, and so did I, only I was so immersed in my thoughts about Rose that I wasn't accomplishing much quickly. Father was so off about Rose. The problem with my girl was that she wanted me as badly as I wanted her. And I didn't believe that Rose wouldn't enjoy the act of lovemaking. She had given every indication that that part of marriage would suit her just fine. What put my stomach in knots was worrying that she would drag the courtship on to a point that I couldn't resist her any longer.

Jacob's loud voice brought me back to the frolic. "Noah, look who's arrived."

Jacob pointed to the buggy coming up the driveway. I could see James and Ruth clearly, and I caught a glimpse of Rose in the backseat.

I climbed down the ladder, saying, "I guess it's time for a break, guys."

"You've worked harder than you ought, still recovering and all. Why don't you take the afternoon off and spend some time with Rose." Jacob patted me on the back as he scooted up the ladder taking my place beside Father.

Father said, "Ah, don't know if that's such a good idea, Jacob." He winked down at me, and Jacob looked confused.

"Did I miss something?" Jacob asked.

"No, Jacob. Get back to work and don't be sparing your thoughts for me. Only a week to go and you'll have a bride of your own to move into this glorified shack with."

Several of the men laughed as I walked away, Father's voice being the loudest.

I leaned against the oak tree beside the walkway while Rose went with Ruth to take a couple of casseroles into the kitchen for the workers' supper. I knew Rose wouldn't keep me waiting long—the excited smile she'd flashed at me as she passed by had told me that much.

When she did come out the door minutes later, Katie was beside her, and I got the feeling that they were talking about Jacob and Katie's wedding. Maybe some of Katie's enthusiasm would wear off on Rose. I hoped so, anyway.

A few steps before they reached me, Katie smiled and veered off to the front of the house. *Thank you, Katie.* I grinned to myself, pleased with how intelligent my soon-to-be sister-in-law was.

Rose looked beautiful, as usual, in a sky-blue dress, a few

stray strands of her wonderful rich brown hair swirling around her face. I ached inside to reach out and pull her into my arms, but I behaved myself and smiled instead, nodding for her to join me as we walked into the backyard. I'd already scoped the lay of the land while I was waiting and had picked out at good site for a private conversation.

We walked in silence, I slowing my long legs so she could keep up easily, but it was difficult since all I wanted to do was rush her to the secluded grassy spot alongside the trickling creek.

When we finally arrived, I took my jacket off and laid it down for her to sit on, which she did, dropping down in a very unladylike movement. I glanced around to make sure that everyone was gathered on the front and far side of the house before settling down a few inches from her. I didn't think we'd get in any trouble, as long as we kept our hands to ourselves.

"This was a great idea," Rose said in a hushed tone, tilting her chin up sideways in an inviting gesture.

I looked down at the measly flow of water for a second to get my head on straight again. Would she always have the ability to turn my brain off with a glance?

Risking the look back, I said, "I wish you wouldn't do that to me."

"What?" she asked innocently. I knew full well she was aware of her charms.

"Be a good girl. Bishop Lambright is probably peeking around the corner of the house."

I grinned when Rose swiveled, searching for spies.

She turned back to me with a small frown on her lips. "I thought that since we're officially courting, they'd lighten up."

"In some ways they do, and in other ways, they pay more attention." I leaned in a little closer, but still a safe distance.

I watched her pouty mouth tighten in concentration, and I wondered what she was thinking about.

"So what were you and Katie talking about?" I ventured.

"She's excited about the wedding next week." Rose stretched out her legs and leaned back, raising her face to the sunlight. "She was apologizing for not asking me to be one of the servers. Seems that she had everyone picked at about the time I went to live with the Hershbergers." She paused, looking back at me, and went on, "I think it had a lot to do with her dad—and her sister."

"Yeah, you're probably right. But this way, you can experience the entire wedding without having to work half the day."

She sighed. "I don't care about it. But do you think Ella is always going to have it in for me?"

I thought for a few seconds and answered honestly. "Yes, but the longer you're with us, the less likely that she can cause trouble."

"So you think she still can?"

"No, not really—maybe you can try to be friends with her," I suggested, not surprised by her response.

She snorted and said, "No way. Sorry, you know I love you, but I'm not going to work at mending the fences with that girl."

"I understand," I said, itching to take her hand into mine, but looking around again, deciding against it. There were too many people around.

"So how long will this take today?" she asked, looking back at the driveway as another buggy arrived.

"Reckon we'll go 'til dark since we got so many men to work today."

"And…this is called a frolic?" She laughed when I nodded and said, "When I hear that word I picture people dancing in a flowery meadow."

"You know better now, don't you?" I said—just listening to her voice made my stomach go tight.

The warm sun soaking into my skin and the sound of rustling leaves in the trees relaxed me and made me brave. "Have you thought anymore about a springtime wedding?" I asked quietly.

Rose stared off into the fields, not looking at me as she answered. "I think we're kind of young still."

I swayed closer to her and said in a whisper, "So, how long do you want to wait?"

She turned back to me and smiled, nearly taking my breath away. "Not forever. Let's enjoy ourselves for a while first."

"That didn't come close to answering my question." I was becoming frustrated with her.

She sighed. "How about after I'm eighteen?"

"You're only turning seventeen in a month." I continued to stare at her. "That's a long time to wait for us to be together."

"But we are together," she said quietly.

"You know what I mean. It's going to get harder and harder to be around each other without…you know, sleeping together." I tried to hold her eyes, but she looked in the direction of the house again.

"And you would never think of doing it before we're married, right?" She kept her eyes away from me.

At that moment, I didn't care if anyone saw; I took her hand and held it low to the ground. "You know how I feel about it. I want to do this the right way. If we're going to spend the rest of our lives together, anyway, what does it matter if we marry in a few months or in a year?" I desperately wanted to convince her, but I felt her pulling away and it scared the hell out of me.

She turned back, studying me for a few seconds before she

asked, "What do you think about all the rules we'll have to live by?"

I wasn't expecting that and didn't exactly understand where she was heading. "What are you talking about?" I hoped the edginess I was feeling didn't make it to my voice.

She sighed deeply and began lightly trailing her finger over my wrist. The feeling was amazing, partially distracting me from her words but unfortunately, not entirely.

"I've been thinking about how we'll never be able to walk down the street holding hands…or…dance together."

My chest tightened, and worry began to seep through me. "Are you having second thoughts about being Amish? 'Cause it's a little late now."

Quickly she moved in closer to me and said, "No, that's not what I mean. It's just that, life is so much more difficult than it has to be for us." She rolled her eyes at the same time she huffed a breath of air out her mouth. "Just the other day, after I'd spent three hours doing the laundry, I managed to rip my maroon dress in the ringer. It took me another hour to repair the damage. And, I miss wearing my riding boots…." Her eyes settled on me, and after a few seconds of silence, she said in a whisper, "Don't you ever question this Ordnung thing?"

"You took a vow to follow the Ordnung of our community. You agreed to our faith and beliefs. Now you're questioning it?" I was becoming angry with her, even though a part of me understood how she felt.

"Sorry—I didn't mean to stir things up. I just wanted to talk about it, that's all." She pulled her hand away and wiped the back of it against her nose and sniffed.

Losing her grasp sent me into a tailspin. More than anything in the world I wanted Rose, and the thought, even the smallest hint, that she'd not remain Amish and spend the rest of her life with me made me so afraid. Without thinking, I

226 Karen Ann Hopkins

covered the inches to her and put my lips against hers. The sigh that came from her mouth into mine erased the fear and replaced it with a boiling desire.

My mouth moved on hers in perfect rhythm, our tongues playing a game meant only for us. As long as I had her captive in my arms I didn't worry about her leaving me. I knew that she couldn't, because she was as obsessed with me as I was with her.

But the moment was shattered when our lips separated an inch and my eyes opened. Not too far away, behind Rose's cap, I saw the last person I wanted to see. She was standing partially hidden behind the house—watching us.

It was Ella Weaver, and judging from her wide eyes and frowning lips, I knew the ax was about to fall.

18

Rose

Walking up the pebbly driveway behind Ruth, I clenched the top of my coat to keep the icy wind out of the space where there was no button to hold the material together. I glanced up at the overcast sky that was placing a gray curtain over the world and thought that it was a crappy day to have a wedding. I made a mental note to *not* schedule my wedding during the middle of November in Ohio.

Approaching the building where the ceremony was to be held, I saw a hundred or so men already gathered in front of the entrance. They stood like statues—their flapping coats and the lift of their beards in the wind was the only movement in the group. There were no balloons or decorations marking the event. No flowers were displayed in the Weavers' church building, either. I knew before I even reached the dim interior that the same benches would be set up, the only big difference being the six chairs that were lining the front for the wedding party.

I'd been given the opportunity to thoroughly check things out the day before when I'd volunteered to help get the Weavers' place in tip-top shape for the event. I'd worked mostly on scrubbing the benches and sweeping the floors, but I'd also

made my way to the smaller white building near the house
that was usually a garden shop where the Weavers sold ceramic lawn ornaments. The country store had been turned
into a reception hall. Not the kind of place that I was used
to for an after-wedding dinner, but I had to admit, a suitable
space for a gathering.

Katie's favorite color was the dark rose shade of burgundy,
and that was the hue she used to decorate the dozen long
lines of tables that were set up. Every ten feet or so there was
a flower arrangement of white roses adorning the tables, and
before each seat was a votive with a white ribbon tied around
it. Interestingly, the names of the bride and groom, the date
of their wedding and the Bible verse, "The Greatest of These
Is Love, 1 Cor.13:13," were engraved on the little candles and
also the napkins that were placed on the dinner plates.

The wedding party table had more flair, with a lace cloth
resting on top of the burgundy one. The extra-large flower
display held pure white roses mixed in with red ones that
didn't match the tablecloths perfectly but still blended well
enough. The three-layer cake was displayed in the center, and
the ivory-colored roses that decorated its edges were perfect
enough to be real flowers. There were only six chairs placed
on the one side of the table, reserved for Katie and Jacob and
their attendants.

The vision of the reception building disappeared when Ruth
and I finally reached the greeting line. I felt the gazes of the
men on me, and when I searched around, a dozen pairs of eyes
shifted quickly. Even though there were many new faces in the
crowd, I got the feeling that they knew about me and my story.

One of the Weaver cousins wasn't shy about the gossip,
either; just the day before, she'd asked me bluntly how I was
surviving the Plain life. I'd opted to just smile and mumble
"great" and had kept on with my scrubbing.

As I looked around at the sea of dark-clad people, I felt as if I was more of an outsider than I ever had been before. The complete lack of voices, with only the whistle of the sharp wind blowing as sound, caused my heart to drum faster. I'd realized over the past few months that when the Amish people were alone or in small groups, they seemed more normal to me, more approachable in a way, but it was the total opposite on church days. When the whole community came together, there was the oppressive feeling of being watched that affected everyone present, from the oldest right down to the smallest toddlers. They all changed, completely losing any personality that would set them apart on any other day of the week. Worry would spread through me like a flood on such occasions. Today was worse—everyone was even more reserved and cautious than usual. The creepiness of it tightened my insides and made me shiver.

Ruth stopped in front of me, and I huddled against her, letting her plump figure shield me from some of the weather. I only peeked around her sheltering body to catch a glimpse of Katie and Jacob sitting on white plastic lawn chairs, along with their attendants in front of the building. The early winter wind was gusting right into their faces, but they still nodded and smiled at the well-wishers as they passed.

I knew that beneath Katie's black coat was a navy blue bridal dress. She'd been able to choose any shade of blue she wanted for herself and her attendants on the special day, but blue was the only color allowed in this community for a wedding. The idea of the bride wearing blue was bizarre enough, but the fact that the dresses were exactly the same as the church ones except for the white aprons, was even more disheartening. How could a girl feel beautiful on her special day in a frumpy dress? I knew I was being shallow, but no matter how hard I tried, I couldn't lose the negativity over the lack of dress options. My spirits had dipped even further when Sarah had told me weeks before that there would be no bridesmaids in colorful dresses or guys in snappy tuxes. No cute little Amish flower girls, either.

Sighing, I swallowed hard, trying to relax my throat, which had suddenly tightened. I'd learned months ago that if I thought too much about the differences between Noah's world and mine, I would become a nervous mess. The unwanted doubts were the worst in the dark of night. Sometimes they'd pester me for hours while I'd toss and turn, desperately wanting to fall asleep. I'd learned that the best way for me to get by was to do as little thinking as possible. Up until this day, it had worked pretty well. Whenever the thoughts would creep into my mind, making the prickly anxiety rise within me, I'd focus my attention on Noah, and that's what I did now.

He was sitting beside Katie, and I sucked in a quick breath at how handsome he looked in his black coat with a bit of the aqua-blue shirt visible. He appeared older than his eighteen years and very serious. Seeing Noah's uptight expression made me frown, and I hid my mouth in the collar of my jacket as I turned to see the other attendants.

My vision darkened significantly when my gaze settled on the wicked witch of the west. Even though Ella's navy blue dress whipped around her legs and the wind blew the strings of her cap wildly around her face, she still sat as if she was a queen at the head of her court—her fake smile stretching her mouth wide. Her doe eyes stalled briefly on me, but true to her unemotional-in-front-of-an-audience ways, she completely ignored me and kept on smiling.

I wanted to kick her in the shin when the time came to walk by her for what she'd done to me and Noah. Running straight to the bishop to report that she'd seen us kissing by the creek had been a rotten thing to do, even for her. Katie agreed with me, taking up against her sister. But it hadn't mattered. We'd broken the law, kissing in broad daylight and only yards away from half the congregation.

I still didn't have a clue what Noah had been thinking when he'd hijacked my mouth so suddenly. It was puzzling since he was the one who was always on my butt about being careful.

Because of Ella's big mouth, Noah and I were now serving a punishment of three subsequent Sundays in a row without courting. That meant no phone calls, dinners or chaperoned visits—nothing. Ruth thought the bishop was being lenient on us, but I certainly didn't agree with her—we'd only been kissing. The one satisfaction I had from the whole scene was that Ella had gotten to see me and Noah all over each other.

As I huddled behind the others waiting in line, the cold pierced through my black coat, feeling like a million tiny pins pricking my skin. I shifted from foot to foot wishing everyone else would feel my pain and get moving.

I didn't risk another glance at Ella, not wanting to become angry. Instead, I checked out the guy sitting next to her. Rebecca had told me that Jacob was having a childhood friend and cousin named Lester as his other attendant. Looking at the man sitting beside Ella, I could see the resemblance to the rest of the Miller clan. He even had the same thick dark hair, laced with golden highlights.

The girl beside Noah was another cousin, only this one from the Weaver side. I thought her name was Christine. She was average-looking, with a wide nose, dull eyes and no distinguishing characteristics that would make me remember her the next day.

Jacob's mouth was pinched in the tight smile of a man who didn't seem to be enjoying himself one bit. That didn't surprise me—guys usually weren't into the wedding ceremony itself—

they were too busy looking forward to the honeymoon. Heat warmed my face for a few seconds at the thought.

We inched closer to the wedding party, and I couldn't help feeling sorry for Katie that the day was so dreary and the vibes so solemn. Taking another glance over my shoulder at the view of the rolling tilled earth and the steely sky, my mood soured once again. I wished that the tiredness that had a hold on my spirit would let go. Today was supposed to be a happy occasion.

Minutes later, when we finally reached the bride and groom, Ruth said a few words in German that I, of course, didn't understand, but I smiled and nodded at those seated as we drifted by—except for Ella whom I narrowed my eyes at, only to be repaid with the same smile she was offering everyone else.

I doubly hated her for her inhuman composure in all situations.

When I faced Noah, I was unsure what to do, but he smiled at me and then winked before I left him. The wink was enough to lift my spirit a little and soothe my temper toward Ella.

Noah still loved me, and that was all that was important.

Once free of our greeting duties, Ruth made a beeline into the building, and I said a silent hurray for her. She took us about midway down the benches, and there we made ourselves as comfortable as possible. Rebecca was seated in the front row of seats directly behind the wedding party seats, along with Sarah, Rachel, little Naomi and Grandma Miller who'd come in from Pennsylvania with Grandpa a few days earlier. They were lucky enough to be sitting on chairs similar to the ones that the wedding group were seated on outside. There were also a number of women around them that I didn't recognize. I was intrigued to see that the chairs set up for the family members were coed. Several men and all the Miller boys were already there mixed right in with the women.

Not so for the rest of us. Our side, which was the left, was packed full of women, while on the far benches a few of the older men, who had too much sense to stand around outside in the nasty weather, were making themselves at home.

I sat listening to the murmurs and conversations of the women around me. Ruth was chatting away with another elderly lady on her other side and ignoring me completely, which suited me just fine since I was taking deep breaths, trying to stop the spasms of shivers that kept rocking my body.

Just about the time I'd stopped trembling and was getting bored with the waiting, Suzanna slid in beside me. Amazingly, she was wearing the exact same turquoise blue that I had on.

I fanned my dress out for her to see, and she laughed. "Are you copying me, Rose?"

"Guess I could say the same to you," I told her as I lightly bumped into her shoulder.

"I just came from the kitchen where all the servers are working like mad to finish the meal." She rubbed her hands together vigorously for warmth. The inside of the building had several gas heaters operating, but they didn't do much for the large space.

I was already nearly drooling at the thought of all the food I was going to get to eat in a few hours, and Suzanna's update made my tummy clench in anticipation.

"So what's on the menu?" I asked.

Suzanna looked at me funny, and then she said, "I keep forgetting that you've never been to one of our weddings before." She smiled to herself and said, "We almost always have chicken for the main course. And it's specially cooked and seasoned to taste so yummy. They'll be the mashed potatoes, green beans, coleslaw, salad, bread and a slew of pies," she said.

I got to thinking in a different direction, and asked, "Will Noah have to eat dinner with the wedding party?"

"Yeah, reckon so," Suzanna said. Her face lit up, and she went on to say, "But even if he didn't, you two aren't allowed around each other for a couple of weeks, right?"

I felt deflated and mumbled, "Uh-huh. It's not fair."

Suzanna's voice changed, and I turned to her when she said, "Yeah, I know."

"What?" I said, hearing the anger within the words.

She turned her bright blue eyes on me and leaned in closer. "You and Noah not being able to keep your paws off each other has caused trouble for all the courting youth."

"Why, what do you mean?" I put my ear closer to her face. As I listened to her, I watched the building filling up with the not-so-festive-looking people.

"The bishop and ministers have clamped down on everyone, because of the little make-out show you two did behind Jacob and Katie's house. We've been told that we aren't allowed to go off a little ways from the group and sit together at the singings no more. And, the guys have to head home on Sundays by eleven now." Suzanna's face tightened with irritation.

"Why would you be punished when it was me and Noah messing around?"

Suzanna leveled a hard look on me. "It got the grown-ups thinking, it did."

I didn't know what to say. The ridiculous overbearing attitude of the community's leaders wasn't my problem, but still, wanting to smooth things over, I said, "I'm sorry. It wasn't as if we planned to get caught."

She glanced at me and said, "It's all right, but you need to be more careful in the future, or we won't be spending any time at all with our boyfriends."

Suzanna handed me a program, as they were being passed

down our row. The cover had a picture of a bundle of roses with the caption, "Love never fails, 1 Corinthians 13:7-8"

When I flipped it open, I was thrilled to see English writing. The hymns were in both languages, but the rest was good old-fashioned American.

I shouted an internal yay, and began reading. Skipping over the songs and sermon, I stopped at the marriage vows section. After reading them, I decided that they were fairly simplistic. Both husband and wife agreeing that the Lord had ordained the relationship, and to care for the other if they became sick. The last vow was promising each other that they would love and not separate from each other until God separated them through death.

I was surprised that there wasn't an entire paragraph dedicated to the wife obeying the husband.

"What do you think so far, Rose?" Ruth asked me quietly.

Looking around, I saw that the room was full, and the cold wind that had been blowing in the front sliding door had ceased when the heavy wooden frame was pulled shut.

"It seems the same as an ordinary church day so far, except for the extra people," I told her.

"Our weddings aren't a fancy affair, but the dinner afterward is always pleasurable," Ruth said, before turning back to her buddy on the other side.

The droning sound of the murmurs of hundreds of people, the scraping of the benches on the cement floor and the press of the wind against the building combined to make a gentle buzz in my ears.

I was still cold, but it wasn't as bad as before. Suzanna sat silently beside me, and I wondered what was going through her mind. Was she making plans in her head for her own wedding day?

Before I caught on, the entire congregation began to sing.

The Amish were singing in German, but I was able to follow along in the program.

> *Now then, cheer up, you Church of God,*
> *Holy and pure,*
> *In these later times,*
> *You who are chosen unto a bridegroom*
> *Called Jesus Christ,*
> *Do prepare yourself for Him.*
> *Lay your adornments, for He comes soon,*
> *Therefore prepare the wedding garment,*
> *For He will certainly have the wedding,*
> *Now, allowing you to be parted from Him eternally.*

The second song began, and it was in the same level tempo as the first one. I pretended to sing along but spent most of the time studying the people around me.

Everyone was bundled up in dark coats, their pale faces looking down at the programs speaking out the words of the song with no spirit. The women stuck out the most with their large black bonnets covering the little white caps on their heads. My mouth twitched when it occurred to me that they all looked like Goth Quakers.

The wedding party still hadn't made their appearance, and I squeezed closer to Suzanna and interrupted her singing. "Where are Jacob and Katie?"

"They're in the council room with the bishop and ministers getting talked to about the sacredness of marriage and the seriousness of the vows they're making. They'll be here soon," she said, then went back to her singing.

A little blip in the back of my mind registered again how Suzanna was different now that she was courting Timothy. It was almost as if some of her soul had been sucked out of her. It made me wonder—was that happening to me?

After the third song, the door opened a couple of feet and Jacob and Katie walked through, followed by their attendants and the ministers. Bishop Lambright was the last in, and he was the one who closed the door. The air settled again into cold silence.

The wedding party seated themselves in the chairs, while the ministers took their places on a long bench that faced the congregation. I could only see the back of Noah's head, which frustrated me, but I was happy that Ella sat several seats away from him.

Amos went to the front and spoke in his language for a half an hour or so. I watched him amble in front of the crowd, wondering what he was saying. Suzanna stayed focused on the first sermon, while Ruth kept her attention on the wrapped-up bundle on her lap.

I hadn't a clue when the baby had arrived. I just turned around to see him there sleeping soundly. I knew it was Joshua because of the name embroidered in cursive on the blue blanket that protected him.

I was happy that little Josh was there to give me some entertainment, and I cooed and stared at him—until Ruth got the wild hair to hand him over to me. I actually leaned away, shaking my head, but probably thinking that any young woman would love to hold a baby, she shoved him at me.

He was adorable and smelled really nice, like fabric sheets. Still, sitting in the middle of a bunch of stone-silent, not-so-humorous people, I tingled with the fear that he would begin fussing.

Since I was so focused on the baby, I hadn't noticed the change of guard. Now Marcus Bontrager was center stage. He was reading scriptures from the Bible, and I wasn't benefiting at all from his foreign words so I continued to give my attention to the baby, who had woken Suzanna from her trance. She was now fidgeting with the blanket around his face and making silent O's to him.

I should have received an award for making it all the way to the sermon before having to pass Joshua back off to Ruth.

Once the baby began making hunger gurgles, Ruth quickly unloaded the baby to Emilene, who shuffled out the door with him. She was probably going into the house to nurse him. When she left, one of the sisters-in-law followed her out the door holding a similar bundle that must have been little Jacob.

For the next hour or so Bishop Lambright talked, and talked...*and talked*. I found myself thinking about the bones in my butt that I never even knew existed before joining the Amish. The three-hour-long services hadn't gotten any easier for me; if anything, my stamina seemed to be faltering sooner.

After nearly an hour or so of the bishop's foreign ramblings, all the servers came parading into the building single file—the group of thirty-plus young people filed into the vacant seats behind the family, freakishly quiet for such a large group. The guys and girls sat together in this instance, every other person an opposite sex. That part interested me, but I didn't perk up significantly until there was a pause when Jacob and Katie rose from their seats and stood before the bishop. They faced each other, and I sat up straighter, peering around the bonnets in front of me to see.

The bishop would say a few words, and either Katie or Jacob would each in turn answer with what I assumed was a yes or "I do." The whole exchange of vows only lasted a few minutes, and I thought to myself that all the boring hoopla at the beginning should be eliminated entirely.

A depressing heaviness brought my shoulder down, and I sighed at the sight of Katie. She held no flowers and wore no special adornments. She was a beautiful girl, and I imagined her in a long, flowing white gown, her hair raised high in an elaborate bun with sparkling jewels holding the strands in place.

Closing my eyes, I envisioned a brightly lit church with sunflowers and ribbons lining each side of the aisle. There were bridesmaids waiting at the front of the pews dressed in jade-green knee-length dresses. Each girl, and there were several of them, held a bouquet of wildflowers, the purple-and-gold blooms blending together to create individual warm glows in their hands. The flower girl stood closest to the radiant bride, peeking out from behind the wedding gown. The little girl's dress was a mirror image of the bride's gown, except for the green sash around her waist and the puffed-out shorter skirt.

The groom in the vision turned to look back, and I saw him clearly: *it was Noah*. My wedding—the vision was what I'd fantasized my own dream wedding would be like since the time I was ten years old.

Popping my eyes open, the harsh grayness of the room and the darkness of everyone in attendance shocked my eyes. It was as if someone had dimmed the lights, and I searched the faces to see the joyous happiness that I imagined every wedding guest should hold.

They didn't look unhappy, but the whole event was so reserved that it didn't feel as if a wedding was taking place. *And this is what my wedding will be like.* My heart sank another notch as the next song began. Wrapped up in my selfish longings, I didn't attempt to sing this time.

A wedding day was supposed to be extra-special for a girl—and now that anticipation was gone for me.

My positive-thinking mind tried to push the darkness away by sending me thoughts of Noah and his arms around me, protecting me and holding me close. It was okay to give up a normal wedding to be with the guy you loved. I just had to keep reminding myself of that.

When the service finally ended, the wedding party filed out first, followed by the close family members. The servers and then the rest of us left the building last. Everyone was orderly and quiet, and I fell into the line with the rest of them, remaining silent.

The quiet, distant emotions of the entire crowd seemed to lift instantly as each person crossed the threshold into the cold, crisp air. Even my heart felt lighter as the wind smacked me in the face, chasing away the grogginess that I'd felt for the previous couple of hours.

Suzanna left me to join her family, and I stayed close to Ruth as we met up with James and left the building. I gazed up at the sky and was thankful to see shards of sunlight slicing through the clouds and landing on the farm. I figured it was a good omen to have the sun make an appearance on the wedding day, and I was glad for Katie and Jacob that it graced the ceremony.

It was still freezing, though, and I hugged my jacket tightly around me as we headed to the reception building. The short distance took longer to cover than it should have, because of Ruth's conversations with the many women we bumped into on the short walk. Ruth introduced me to each woman in a proud mamma way, calling me her new daughter. I had to admit that everyone was friendly, making me feel more at home.

When we entered the reception hall, the warm air and delicious smells slammed into me, and I couldn't help but smile. This was more like it, I thought, when I saw the people in the room displaying more liveliness than they had all morning. The air that had felt cold and bleak earlier was pushed aside to be replaced with the aura of goodwill. The feeling seeped into my skin, erasing the lingering melancholy.

I continued in Ruth's shadow as we moved around the room, until we found the section of one of the long tables with our names at the place settings. It was nice to sit in a chair, and I sipped my water as my eyes darted around the room, taking in the more boisterous side of the Amish.

When most of the people were seated, my gaze rested on Noah. He'd been waiting for me to look his way, and when I did, he flashed me the biggest smile; it lit up his whole face, sending an explosion of spastic butterflies careening through my belly.

Would it always be like that when he looked at me?

I smiled back, lifting my water glass to him. His smile turned to a mischievous grin as he raised his to mine. I caught Ella's smile turn to a tight frown for an instant when she saw Noah's and my interchange. Surely, if she complained about us toasting each other, we wouldn't get in trouble. But then, doubt crept in, and I reluctantly turned away from Noah to avoid any problems.

I spotted Suzanna sitting with her family a table away, and she smiled when she saw me looking. Maretta grinned happily when she met my eyes, and Miranda, who sat almost directly across from me at the next table, also smiled warmly and winked before continuing her conversation with the woman at her side.

The Millers were seated along with the Weaver family at the table closest to the wedding party. Isaac waved to me when my eyes passed over him, and I returned the gesture. Noah's little brothers had accepted me into their fold, but I found it difficult to be around them since they reminded me of Justin, which made me feel guilty.

Very quickly for such a large group, there were servers appearing with trays of food. I was lucky to have Sarah working at our table, and she spared a second to bend down and ask me how I enjoyed the ceremony. There was a spritz of sarcasm, and I knew she was teasing me. I told her I survived it, and she laughed as she placed a plump piece of white meat on my plate.

Then a procession of servers arrived with mashed potatoes, followed by creamed corn, salads and bread. I was careful not to touch my food, knowing that there would be a moment of silence before we could dig in. The workers did their jobs well, and in less than ten minutes everyone had full plates. The bishop led the silent prayer before releasing us to stuff ourselves.

I was in my own little world, eating my scrumptious food and trying not to look at Noah, when Ruth nudged me. The women across from my seat had asked me a question, but I'd missed it.

"Excuse me?" I stammered.

"Ruth tells me that you are new to the Amish. Are you settling into their ways?" the woman said in a smooth voice.

Before answering, I quickly ran my eyes over her. I noticed for the first time that she was dressed differently than the other woman; she had a very small lacy cloth on the top of her head that rested against her bun. Amazingly, her dress was bright and yellow. I guessed her to be in her thirties, and the two little girls on the chairs beside her to be maybe six and ten. They were also wearing plain but bright yellow dresses.

I found my voice, "I'm doing well, thank you."

My interest was pricked, but the sharp way the woman stared at me made me feel a little vulnerable. I instinctively didn't want to give up too much information.

"I'm Cynthia Webber. And these are my daughters, Lilith and Shannon." She motioned over to the wedding party table, saying, "Katie and I are first cousins."

"It's nice to meet you." I reached across the table, and she quickly took my hand and gave it a light shake.

I couldn't keep my curiosity down, and before Ruth could start talking about something else, I popped out, "If you don't mind me asking, are you Amish?"

She laughed a little, but not in a mean way, and said, "No, I'm Mennonite. But I was born Amish."

Cynthia's slender, hawkish face waited for my response.

"How did that happen?" I blurted out.

"Really, Rose..." Ruth began to chastise me, but Cynthia was quick and interrupted.

"It's perfectly fine with me for the girl to ask some questions. I'd imagine she has many of them skipping around in that pretty head of hers."

Yes, I did, but something about the woman's overly helpful demeanor made me decide to hold back next time.

"You see, before I joined my community's church, I decided that the Amish life didn't suit me well. I went to live with an aunt who was Mennonite. I met my husband there." She nodded at the nice-looking blond man on the other side of the youngest girl. "And the rest is history."

"And your family was okay with that?" I couldn't help but feel astonished.

"Not at first they weren't, but since I hadn't officially joined the church yet, they didn't shun me." When she said the word shun, she glanced over at Ruth, and I felt the air tingle with discomfort. That word seemed to be the Amish equivalent to an offensive word.

Ruth jumped in at that point and changed the subject, to what I didn't know, because she was speaking her indecipherable language.

Cynthia's eyes met mine, and I knew that she wanted to

talk further; why I couldn't say, but she definitely had things on her mind.

As the conversation turned into the foreign language, I zoned the voices out and munched on my fat slice of home-made bread. Now that my eyes knew what to look for, I surveyed the room for other Mennonite people.

Sure enough, there was another family wearing the same little cloths on their heads and sporting green dresses that looked as if they came out of a Goodwill store from the six-ties. I also noticed several groups of Amish people who were dressed differently than the Amish from my community. They were wearing larger black bonnets, and the fronts of their dresses had white triangles of material attached to them. There were even a few English people sequestered in the corner that I hadn't noticed before.

By the time I was done doing the CIA thing, the pies had arrived. I picked a piece of chocolate mousse and a slice of lemon off of the tray. Cynthia's daughters' eyes widened when they saw me shoveling two slices onto my plate, but I didn't care. This was the best part of the day, and I was going to enjoy it to the fullest.

Before I'd finished the last bit of the chocolate, the back of my neck heated, and I knew without looking that Noah was watching me. I tried to resist turning, but within seconds I did look, and his gaze sent shivers through me. I must have blushed because Cynthia had noticed, and she was talking to me again.

"Is that your boyfriend?" she pointed her strong chin to-ward Noah.

This time I looked at Ruth, who nodded that it was okay for me to speak. Really, the idea that I gave a flip about what Ruth thought proved that I liked the old woman and valued her opinion.

"Yeah, that's my guy."

She smiled, but the spread of her lips did not reach her eyes, and I wondered why she was so interested in my life, anyway.

As the wedding guests finished their meals, they stood in line to give Jacob and Katie their congratulations. Ruth hung back, enjoying her talk with the woman to her right. Mr. Hershberger was deep in conversation with the woman's husband, and I began to reach for the last wedge of bread in the basket when the squeeze of my shoulder made me forget about it.

"Hey, do you want to go see the wedding gifts?" Miranda whispered in my ear.

Oh, God, thank you, I said in my mind at the opportunity to do something other than listen to old people speak a language I didn't understand.

When I softly poked Ruth's mushy side and asked her if I could go, she tilted her head and looked for Noah first before she said, "Don't be getting into any mischief, Rose. Spending any time with Noah is still off-limits."

A prickling of anger shot through me, but I controlled the feelings and nodded obediently. Before I was away from the table, I caught Cynthia's gaze on me again, and I looked quickly away, not wanting to deal with whatever problem she had.

I did spare a glance at Noah before I walked through the door, but he was speaking intently with an Amish guy who appeared a few years older than him. I didn't recognize the man and figured he was another one of the dozens of cousins. I felt jealousy surge through me that the man had Noah's undivided attention.

We were hardly through the door when Suzanna joined us, falling in on my other side. The sun was buttery in the afternoon sky, but the clouds seemed reluctant to leave entirely.

The sprinkles of light were deceiving as the wind still pushed the crisp air steadily against me.

I started to wonder about the brilliance of heading down to the tent that housed the tables full of presents for the bride and groom. I could see the canvas popping in and out from the wind and knew that the interior would be downright cold.

Still, I was happy to get away from all the strange people in the crowded building and followed the girls down the hill with more energy than I'd felt all day.

When we went through the flaps that were tied open with thick cords of rope, it took only a second for me to realize that we weren't alone in the tent. Just beyond the tables that were piled high with mounds of presents were four teenage guys who looked Amish but were different. My mind quickly decided that they were with one of the groups of overdressed Amish I saw in the reception building. Their hats sat higher on their heads and their jackets appeared shorter. But their appearances weren't the thing that set them aside from my Amish the most.

With shock, I watched as the one boy took a drag from a cigarette.

Instead of beelining it straight out of there, Miranda moved toward the boys with purpose. My head snapped to Suzanna, who shrugged and hid the weak smile on her lips with her hand.

Oh, no, I was going to get into trouble again, I thought as we passed the colorfully wrapped presents. The sight of a chain saw with a bow caught the attention of my disturbed brain. That was not a wedding gift I'd ever heard of before.

We stopped a few steps from the little guy group and the smell of tobacco drifted through the air to me. It wasn't a smell I liked, and I wrinkled my nose.

Miranda began talking to the guys in German, and by the

way the conversation was going, they all seemed to be well acquainted. The boy I'd first noticed smoking moved closer to Miranda, and my mind registered that she leaned in to him.

Oh, crap. This is growing worse by the minute.

Suddenly the words were English, and I took a good look at the guys who were now addressing me. They were all smoking, which showed they were an equally ignorant bunch. Two of them looked enough alike to be brothers, both with longer, messier hair than I was used to seeing on Amish guys' heads. One of them was blond with light eyes, and the other was darker, and he didn't raise his head to the three of us at all.

"Yeah, I like being Amish," I answered the question coming from the blond guy.

I didn't appreciate the way they were looking at me. I just wanted to get out of there, and I decided that this was my opportunity to take a stand against peer pressure and save my butt from further punishment. Even though these guys seemed comfortable with their cigarettes hanging out of their mouths, I knew Bishop Lambright would have a conniption if he learned that we were hanging with rebels like them. Not to mention what Noah would say.

"You girls want a sip of something sweet?" The blond one pulled a small bottle of Jack Daniels halfway from his oversized stash pocket.

They had booze?

Moving forward, I grabbed Miranda's arm.

"We have to go now," I said rudely, pulling Miranda up beside me. Suzanna joined us, moving as swiftly as I was.

I could hear the boys laugh behind us and say something I couldn't understand, which caused Suzanna to return their comment over her shoulder without slowing down. Miranda was moving freely with me, but I wasn't going to give her the opportunity to change her mind, so I kept my hand clenched tightly on her arm.

Once outside, I sighed heavily and asked Miranda, "What was that all about?"

Miranda looked everywhere but at my face. Then she began walking slowly back up the hill. Her silence held for a few more steps, and then she said, "Levi used to hang out with those guys sometimes. Jordan was always nice to me, so I thought I'd go say hi to him. I didn't want to go alone."

Instead of going back into the reception building, Miranda veered to the left, taking us to the buggy shed. Once we were out of the bitter wind, she leaned against the inside wall. She obviously wanted to talk, but didn't know how to get started.

I turned to Suzanna and snapped, "Did you know what she was up to?"

"Yeah...I thought it would be fun to talk to some other guys for a change," Suzanna said, not meeting my gaze.

I had to close my mouth that had dropped open. "But what about Timothy?"

Her head bolted up, and she said firmly, "It isn't like that at all. I was just supporting Miranda...." She thrust both her hands toward the other girl. "She finally found a guy she likes. Unfortunately, he's from the Rocky Ridge community. But, hey, for Mira to have any interest in a guy after all the stuff with Levi is an improvement."

Okay, that made sense. I crossed over to Miranda, stepping over the shafts of the two buggies parked in the shed.

"Do you really like that guy?"

She shrugged, and when her eyes reached mine I knew that she didn't at all.

"What about Matthew? I kind of got the impression that you were sweet on him. Now that you're a member of the church, you two can begin courting." I said it quietly and slowly, not wanting to upset her with the wrong words.

She stared off into space, saying, "I do like him, but I don't think I'm good enough for him."

What she said stung my mind. I felt a renewed fury toward Levi, hoping that he never came back.

I closed the distance and took her hands in mine. "Now you listen to me, Miranda. You are absolutely worthy of Matthew. And I can tell by the way he looks at you that he has a huge crush. He's just too shy to do anything about it," I said, putting my arm around her.

She leaned her head on my shoulder and whispered so low that I wasn't sure if Suzanna could hear her. "It's just that I'm not a clean person and he'll know." She pulled away and frantically searched my eyes. "He'll know, everybody will know."

I understood. Thinking through all my late-night conversations with Amanda and Brittany in the course of a few heartbeats, I looked into Miranda's dark eyes that seemed even more startling against her pale white skin than usual. When I started speaking I felt pretty confident that what I was saying was true.

"You're wrong about that. If you keep it a secret, he won't ever be the wiser. Levi will never talk, and Suzanna, Summer and I will go to our graves with it. You need to forget about the past and move on. Be happy, Miranda. You deserve it."

"You know this for sure?" Miranda was loosening up a bit, and I started to relax.

"Yes—especially an inexperienced guy like Matthew. He'll never know," I said confidently.

She began nodding her head and then wiped a tear from her eye. Standing up straighter, she gave me a hug. When she released me, she said, "You saved me again. I'm going to owe you a bunch of favors, you know."

"Just being my friend is enough." Seeing her doubt, I said, "I mean it. Now, come on, let's get back to the party. Maybe there's some pie left."

Miranda giggled, and Suzanna said, "Good Lord, you eat like a horse."

I could hardly argue with her about it, so I didn't. We hiked across the yard in silence, not needing any more words between us—our shoulders occasionally brushing at our close proximity was enough for all of us.

The front of the reception building was crowded with people, and Suzanna took the lead squeezing through the bodies to reach the door. Before I made it through the opening behind Miranda, a light grasp on my arm pulled me up.

I turned to see Cynthia staring at me. Most of her banana-yellow dress was covered by a dark coat, and she was alone.

"Do you need something?" I asked, trying not to sound too bothered.

She pulled me to the side, away from the press of the crowd. I willingly followed her, believing that with so many people nearby, she wouldn't do anything drastic.

And I was intrigued, in a dark way.

"Rose, I just wanted to share some advice that might help you get through this experience easier. You see, when I told you earlier that my family let me leave, it wasn't as simple as all that." She sighed and shivered, and I didn't know if it was the cutting air or the memories that affected her body. "My family didn't speak to me for seven years. Not until Shannon was born. The Amish are very stubborn people, and they will completely turn away from children who go astray. It wasn't as bad for me since I wasn't breaking an oath to the community by becoming Mennonite, but still, my family put me through hell because of my decision."

I studied her keen features and asked, "Why are you telling me all this?"

"Because I get accurate feelings about people, and meeting you, I can say with almost certainty that you won't make it as an Amish woman." She said it kindly, but that didn't matter to me. It was the words that bit me.

"That's where you're wrong. Guess your fortune-telling days are over," I said.

"I'm trying to help you—that's all. You should be aware that there are alternatives for you and your boyfriend if you find that you can't handle the Plain life."

Alternatives were something I needed an abundance of. I nodded and listened carefully to the strange woman.

"We Mennonites share many of the values that the Amish do, such as the simpler lifestyle and strong sense of faith in the Lord, but we are allowed to drive cars and use electricity. There are also New Order Amish who use more technology and aren't as restrictive. There are options for you if it doesn't work out in the Meadowview community."

Her face sparked as if she'd just thought of something, and she said, "And if your Amish boy isn't willing to compromise, he might not be worth sacrificing your own life for."

With that, she smiled and walked away. I watched after her until she was enveloped into the crowd of dark-clad people.

My brain was frozen from her last sentence. Was this woman some kind of sign from the universe that I was making a terrible mistake with my life? Had she been sent to guide me onto the right path?

I couldn't even feel the cold any longer; my body was on fire with doubt and confusion—until I saw him. Noah had stepped through the door and was searching for me, his head moving back and forth in quick motions.

When he saw me, our invisible string jumped alive, and the ice in my mind thawed.

Cynthia was wrong...she had to be.

19

Noah

I stared at the clear night sky, picking out the Big Dipper. It was comforting to see the faraway bright lights that were always there, unchanging.

The door opened behind me, and I spared a glance just long enough to see that it was Father and not Rose joining me. She must have been still working with the other girls to clean the dishes from her birthday dinner, I thought with an irritated sigh. Rose was seventeen now and closer to the day that I'd make her my wife, but I wasn't as peaceful in the knowledge as I'd imagined I'd be on this day.

"Son, why are you out here in the chill night air?" Father asked, placing his hands on the railing and leaning into them.

"I was just thinking," I replied, not looking at him.

"It seemed that Rose was quite taken with your gifts. What do you think?"

I remembered for some seconds, recalling her shocked face when Jacob and I had carried the plush tan recliner into the living room for her. She'd had about the same reaction to the mantel clock at first—before she'd laughed. An inside joke, she'd told me, but I could tell that the Amish idea of suitable gifts for a woman soon to be married might not be the same as an English girl would expect.

"Sometimes, I feel that—" I struggled for the words "—that Rose is Amish, and I don't even think about her English past. But then there are other moments when she seems so different from us."

"And…?" Father questioned softly.

I finally faced him, saying, "Like tonight. I gave her gifts that any Amish woman would have been thrilled with, but even though Rose smiled and acted excited, I don't think she really was."

"You might be reading more into this than need be." Father repositioned himself so that he was leaning back on the railing with his arms crossing his chest. "All women have their moody days. I'd think you would already know that from your sisters."

"This isn't about hormones. My gifts for Rose were for our home together. I'm afraid that she's having a hard time accepting that in a year's time, she'll be a married woman," I said reluctantly, not wanting to admit to Father that Rose might be having second thoughts.

"You need to talk to her about your concerns, and you need to be patient with her. I understand that you might be ready for married life, but if Rose isn't just yet, then you'll need to give her more time." Father nodded toward the door and said, "Why don't you take her home before James and Ruth head out? That will give you a little extra alone time to talk."

"That's a good idea."

Father held his hand up and warned, "You be minding yourself, though. You just got past the punishment, and I reckon you don't want to lose any more time with your girl."

I understood what he meant, and I nodded. I'd not intended

to kiss Rose the way I had at the frolic, but then when I was around her, all my good intentions went out the window.

Rose cuddled in under my arm and said in a shivering voice, "It's really cold out tonight."

At that moment I wished that I had her in a comfortable car with the hot air blasting, but that wasn't our way—or hers now. Glancing down at the top of her bonnet, I pulled her in even closer, wanting to shield her from the chilled night air.

I'd planned to wait until we were at the Hershbergers' before I brought the subject up, but I found I couldn't wait that long.

"Did you have a nice birthday?" I asked quietly, with a roughness to my voice I didn't want.

"Yeah, of course I did. Why?"

I dove right in. "You seem a little off this evening. Is there something wrong?"

She was silent for a minute before finally answering me. "The party was so nice that your family put on for me… and I'm really touched about it, and the presents you gave me were…overwhelming." She paused as if searching her thoughts, before going on to say in a firmer voice, "But I missed my dad and brothers."

I was taken aback by her words. It hadn't even occurred to me that Rose would still be upset about her family not being invited to the celebration.

"I explained the reason to you already. Until we're married, the less time you spend around them, the better. They'll only try to change your mind, convince you that you're making a mistake. You don't need to deal with that kind of turmoil." I tried to sound sympathetic, but the vision of a leering Sam popped into my head, and I didn't feel so kind.

"Yeah, but it's not right for me to stay away from them on my birthday. It's just crazy."

Before I had a chance to respond, she started up again with more agitation in her voice. "And you know what? If I keep avoiding them, my dad is going to freak out and then there's no telling what he'll do."

She sat up straight and pulled away from the warmth of my body.

"Your father promised to let you decide, and you have. He was okay with it when you joined the church. Why would he do something now?"

Something changed in her posture, a sort of drawing into herself, and immediately my inner alarm bells went off.

"Uh, it wasn't exactly like that, Noah," she whispered. Her hands were clenched in fear on her lap.

"What are you talking about, Rose? You asked him to allow you to take the vows, right?" The sinking feeling was already in the pit of my stomach, and I knew the answer before she uttered a word. Damn.

"I'm sorry. I'm so, so sorry. But I never talked to him about it. I was afraid that he'd say no and take me home… I *knew* he'd say no," she cried out.

I parked the buggy beside James's barn and focused my mind as quickly as I could. Rose had lied to my parents then, too. They'd probably understand the situation and be supportive of her going against her own father to join our church, but they might be compelled to discuss it with him, anyway. They wouldn't want the deceit on their consciences.

Deep down, I wasn't surprised at all. I just hadn't questioned her about it until now because I didn't want to face the truth. I'd always known that getting Dr. Cameron to allow his daughter to take the serious step of being baptized into an Amish church was the biggest obstacle to Rose and me finally being together. I was as much to blame for the deceit as Rose was.

I looked at Rose, who was staring at me with wide, frightened eyes. My first and only instinct was to protect her at any cost, and I grabbed her hands and said, "Listen, we *cannot* mention this to my parents or to anyone else in the community, even Suzanna. No one must learn that you took the vows to the church without getting permission from your father."

She sniffed. "Why?"

"Because if my parents knew, or anybody else, they'd tell your family about it. Once your father found out what you'd done, he'd take you away. I'm sure of it."

I pulled her into my arms and kissed the side of her face, breathing in warm flowers. It was amazing that she could smell like warm flowers, even when frost was in the air.

She whimpered, "I'm sorry."

"It'll be all right. We'll keep as silent as a cat guarding her kittens about it—the longer that you're with us, the less likely that your father will come for you. It's already been over three months, and he hasn't done a thing about it, so maybe he's accepting your decision."

She buried her head in my coat and I held her as if I would never let her go. I hoped that what I'd told her was true—but I feared that her father and Sam hadn't changed their minds about anything.

20

Sam

Damn. It really sucked playing the spy for Dad. I tried to keep my eyes locked on the red minivan as I maneuvered through traffic on the increasingly slippery road. The blue pickup that passed in front of me momentarily broke my eye contact with the van. *Shit.* I couldn't lose it now. I accelerated and managed to get enough speed to inch past the car. Not really enough room for my dually to *politely* get back in front of it in the heavy traffic, but hell, I was on a mission.

Gunning the engine, I made it back into a spot where I could see the white bonnets bobbing around in the van. Good. I was still with them. The rain mix that had been falling all day had picked that moment to change over to snow, and the large puffy shapes were dotting the windshield in ever increasing intensity.

It was just dumb luck that I'd spotted the minivan filled with Amish women drive by as I was pulling out of the school parking lot. A little Mario Andretti driving and I managed to catch up to them. I knew the chances of one of those goofy caps being on my sister's head were pretty slim, but I'd take the gamble. It was worth it. I guess.

The minivan got into the right turning lane, and I backed off a bit, not wanting to be noticed by Rose if she was in the vehicle. I followed it into the Walmart parking lot.

"What are you doing? We're supposed to be at Bradley's house in twenty minutes," Hunter asked with an edge to his voice.

I glanced over at him briefly. "Quiet. I'm trying to think," I said, ignoring his aggravated grunt.

From what I could see, the lady driving the minivan was, oh, probably in her forties with short reddish hair. I'd seen the woman driving the Amish around town in her van but hadn't taken much notice of her before now. She didn't work too hard for a parking spot close to the store, instead pulling the van into the first space she came to at the back of the lot. I found a space in the next row, about four cars away. I positioned my truck facing the back of the van but not in an obvious location where I'd be seen. I was pretty good at this secret agent crap, I decided, as I cut the engine and waited for the occupants of the van to file out.

No. The first two weren't her. But it was damn near impossible to tell with them all dressed the same. They were all sporting larger black caps that seemed to be fitted over the white ones, which made seeing their faces even more difficult. The only difference I could register in my head was the varying shades of blue skirts the girls wore, whipping out in the wind below the black coats. *That was it.*

How could Rose dress that way—and all for a guy?

I couldn't help chuckling when I got a good look at the last girl slipping out of the van. It was Rose—must have been my lucky day. I patiently waited, watching the small group head for the store's entrance. Funny, she actually moved differently than the other three girls and two older women she was with. Rose had a more confident stride, her back straight, looking around the parking lot as if she was purposefully searching for someone.

Maybe this chance encounter was serendipitous, after all.

"Are you following Rose?" Hunter asked quietly, as if it was a big secret.

When I swiveled around, I could see that he was doing the same thing as me; staring at the Amish women as they made their way to the store.

"Yeah. Got a problem with it?"

"Heck, no, I've been dying to see her again," Hunter said, still stalking my sister with his eyes.

I breathed out a deep sigh. If Hunter had been more charming with my sister months ago, she wouldn't be in the situation she was in now. Yet, as I studied Hunter's wide-set eyes and the determined set to his jaw, I admitted to myself that there was still a chance that he could woo Rose away from Mr. Suspenders.

"Look, I've got to talk to my sister, but we have to be careful about this. I don't want to freak her out or anything." As an afterthought, I added, "Or get her into trouble with those people."

"Maybe if they got mad at her, they'd kick her out of their club. Then she'd have to come back to the real world, and get on with her life," Hunter suggested.

He had a point. Sometimes I forgot that Hunter was a pretty smart guy. He took all the same accelerated classes I took, and got mostly A's. The dumb jock thing was just a facade. He actually had a brain in his pro-athlete body.

As I grasped the door handle, I said, "Yeah, and you'll be waiting for her in the *real world,* right?"

"Maybe," was all Hunter said as he jumped out of the truck and met me on my side.

I didn't like how nervous I was getting. I was going to talk to my sister, not face a firing squad, I told myself. The flakes of snow were changing back to rain again, splashing my face and head as they came down with more force. *What a miserable day.*

The weather had definitely soured my mood, and having to deal with Rose's bizarre form of rebellion was putting a hard edge on my emotions as I walked through the automated doors along-side Hunter. I tried to soften my face a bit, so I wouldn't scare the old lady greeting the customers in the doorway. When she looked my way, I rewarded her with a big smile. The way she smiled back, warmly, as if she were a proud grandma, I knew I'd won her over.

Now onto business. I hesitated only a second before head-ing to the grocery aisles. Hunter slunk along beside me silently. Maybe he was nervous about the encounter, too? He hadn't been around Rose since the night of the wreck. Serve him right if he was getting all worked up. I admired that he'd cleaned up his act since the ill-fated party that seemed forever ago, but it would take a hell of a lot to erase his actions in Rose's eyes. Even though I was usually optimistic about things, I doubted if he could pull this off.

Glancing down the rows from left to right, I spotted a few of the Amish women pushing a cart down the bread aisle. Nope. Rose wasn't with them. I continued my search, hoping I'd catch her alone.

After several minutes and exhausting the grocery section, Hunter and I headed over to the beauty stuff. Hunter suggested it, and it was a good bet she'd be there. When I finally found her, she was staring at some bottles of lotion, looking pretty bored. The girl standing with her looked to be Noah's sister. Couldn't remember her name, but I think she was the older one.

"Hey, sis, did they let you out of the house today?" From the look on her face, it was probably not the best thing to have said to her straight off. Her eyes threw daggers at me.

She breathed in deep, and when she exhaled, a growling sound came with it.

"I see you're still a jerk, huh, Sam?" Her voice was colder than the weather outside.

Hunter almost laughed but swallowed the sound, a little too late, because now Rose's icy glare was directed at him.

Clearing his throat, Hunter said, "Hey, Rose. It's good to see you."

"Sorry, I can't say the same," she replied rudely.

Man, she was in a fouler mood than I was. Before it got into a shouting match, I altered my voice and said as nicely as I could manage, "I want to talk to you, Rose, just for minute."

The Amish girl piped up. "I think we better get going."

Rose shot her friend an irritated look. After chewing on her lip for a few seconds, she glanced from me back to the Amish chick.

"Sarah, I want to talk to Sam alone. Okay?" Her voice was amicable to an untrained ear. But to me, I knew what she was really saying was *you better get the heck out of my way and let me do what I want.*

Sarah stepped closer to Rose and whispered, just loud enough that I could hear, "Are you sure?"

"Yep, I'll catch up with you at the van," Rose said smoothly, with no room for an argument.

Sarah sighed but did what Rose said, walking away. Smart girl.

Rose then glanced around with nervous energy. "We need to go somewhere more private."

Her voice carried a kind of vulnerable twang to it. A sound I hadn't heard coming from her mouth since she was ten. Shucks. Brotherly protectiveness began invading my senses.

"Let's go to my truck," I suggested.

She shook her head. "No. I can't do that." After another bird-like look around, she said, "Just follow me."

Before Hunter had the chance to shift his weight, Rose held her hand out, narrowing her eyes at him. "Not you."

For a brief second, a look of hurt flickered across Hunter's face. I shook my head in sympathy for the guy. Falling for my sister was going to cause him a lot of heartache.

"Go on to the truck, Hunter. I'll be there in a few," I told him.

Hunter started to turn, hesitated and moved toward Rose in a blur. He got pretty damn close to her, and even though I could tell she wanted to step back, she held her ground, only swaying her upper body a bit.

"Look, Rose, I'm really sorry about everything that happened that night." He paused, with a deeply drawn breath, and then said, "I hope whenever your life gets straightened out, we can be friends." Hunter waited for her to respond, but when it was obvious she wasn't going to say anything, he left us, moving briskly away.

"That was kind of harsh."

"Why? I didn't say any of the things I was thinking," she mumbled as she headed to the back of the store.

She was clueless. "Sometimes not saying anything is even worse than chewing someone out," I informed her.

"Oh, are you a relationship counselor now?" she asked sarcastically, turning right past the shoes and then left along the aisle at the back of the store. I had to hustle to keep up with her feverish stride. She finally stopped by the shelves filled with green bags of cat food. Dozens of smiling tabbies' faces stared at me.

She turned to face me. After another quick search around her, she said, "What do you want?"

I'd had my little speech memorized in my head for weeks, but now, seeing my sister in the flesh, dressed in the ridiculous clothes, I could only laugh at her. That didn't go over well.

Wham. She smacked me across the chest.

"I don't have time for your comedy show." She looked behind

her and then over my shoulder, before saying in a frustrated hiss, "I don't have much time at all, so if you have something to say, out with it already."

I got myself under control, but damn, it was going to be difficult to have a serious conversation with her dressed like that. "Okay. Okay. I'm sorry. You got to understand, you look strange to me." Rose folded her arms across her chest, popping one hip up while she waited for me to continue. She was still not happy with me. And, she didn't seem to understand at all.

"You know, Dad and Justin, Aunt Debbie, they were all really upset that you didn't come see us for your birthday."

Number one thing was off my chest.

She sniffed. Avoiding my eyes, she said, "Yeah, I'm sure they were."

"Well, what about it? Aren't you allowed to be around your family anymore?"

Rose shifted uneasily, not answering me. Her being without words told me something was definitely up.

"Come on. What's going on in your little Amish world?" Seeing her lips tighten, I surged on with my interrogation. "Are you happy with all the rules? Are you enjoying the fact that you have no freedom at all?" Still there was no response from her. "Is Noah really worth it?"

That got her. She locked her blue eyes on me and whispered, "Yes, he's worth it." She sighed, then leaned back against the cat food and blew out hard, angrily. "But it's been more difficult than I ever imagined."

"Have they been mean to you?"

She shook her head. "No...not really. They are *very* controlling. You wouldn't believe the half of it." She stopped to check the vicinity again, then she rolled on. "I can't even wear my lace-up boots when I ride." She said it as if was the worst thing in the world.

I shrugged. "Why not?"

She said fiercely, "Because the Elders think they're too flashy. Can you imagine, my old, dingy, brown boots *flashy*? And that's just the beginning of it. I can't even wear a watch!" she nearly shrieked, although quietly.

"Then why don't you get out of there?"

"I love Noah, that's why."

"So you're going to live this way, miserable, for the rest of your life?"

"Well, it's not all bad. The Millers and the Hershbergers are so nice to me. And I've made some friends."

"You didn't answer my question. Are you going to continue with this craziness or what?" I was becoming irritated with her, and it probably showed in my voice, although I was trying to sound amicable.

She pushed away from the bags and got up close, invading my personal space. When she was close enough that she must have felt that no one sneaking up on her would hear, she breathed out, "I think Noah might go English."

I couldn't help but feel exasperated with her. "Oh, come on, Rose, we've been through this before." When I saw her hopeful eyes, I asked, "Why? Has something changed with him?"

"No, not exactly, but I think he might be coming around to my side." She said it a little sheepishly, and I suddenly felt sorry for nature boy.

"So, your plans all along were to convert Noah—and not really stay Amish yourself? Is that it?"

"No, Sam. I'll stay Amish if that's what it takes to be with Noah." She looked dramatically horrified at my question.

"You're not convincing me. And, besides, how much time are you going to waste on this endeavor? The holidays are in a couple of weeks. Are you planning to shun your family for Christmas?"

Number two thing was now off my chest.

I leveled a hard look at her, but I thought that I was being pretty mild. She needed some sense shaken into her.

"Oh, I don't know. I really want to see you all for the holidays, but Ruth and James have a lot of family to visit. And, there is *so* much work that needs to be done."

Then she rambled on for a few minutes, something about Mrs. Hershberger's daughter having twins, and having to do the laundry for her, scrubbing a fence by hand and making two hundred whoopee pies for some event. I tuned it all out. None of it mattered in the least.

Really, my sis was losing her freaking mind.

I interrupted her. "Look, Dad wants to see you for Christmas, and that's the end of it. So you better work it out."

"Yeah, I'll do the best I can," she muttered, staring off into space as if she were some kind of zombie.

"We're all going to Cincinnati to stay at Aunt Debbie's for the holidays. Think about it, Rose—you can hang out with Amanda and Brittany, and go shopping at the mall with Aunt Debbie for the last-minute sales. You'd have a blast."

"Oh, I don't think I'll be allowed to go away for that long."

"Why don't you just bring Noah with you?"

I thought it was the perfect solution, but then she rolled her eyes and spat out, "No way will they let him do that. He'd have to have an Amish adult chaperone along, and that would be just terrible—as if his folks would even allow him to leave town during Christmastime, anyway," she said with a pout.

Before I had a chance to respond, a couple of Amish women appeared at the end of the aisle. At that moment, they reminded me of a pair of harpies that just found lunch.

"Rose. Come with us now, we must go," the older, gray-haired lady said. I figured she was the infamous Mrs. Hershberger. She was a little chubby, but still managed to be sharp-faced. Other than that, there wasn't anything really distinguishable about her.

"Coming." Rose gave me a fake smile, before whirling around to join the women. When she met up with them, both women put a hand on either of her shoulders and guided her away and out of my sight.

What a mess Rose was in. It was obvious she wasn't enjoying being Amish, and it was just a matter of time before her house of cards collapsed. Still, I had the nagging feeling that the fool girl might do something insane, like marry Noah, before she got her head on straight.

If I had anything to do with it, that wasn't going to happen. I'd tell Dad about my encounter with Rose when I got home, and I'd encourage him to go ahead with the family crisis intervention plan he'd been talking about. That's what he called it, but what Dad really meant to do was to kidnap Rose from the Amish and force her to live in Cincinnati with Aunt Debbie and Uncle Jason. This charade had gone on long enough. We'd all figured she'd only last a few weeks at most with the strict disciplinary lifestyle of these people. But, to all our amazement, especially Tina's, she'd proven she had a pretty tough constitution. Four months was enough, though.

I suddenly remembered a discussion I'd had with Summer weeks ago, and after a few seconds of thought, a plan began to sprout. Someday, Rose would thank me for it.

I slowly walked through the store, not paying any attention to the people passing by me. I was too absorbed in thought.

Dad needed to take action—the sooner the better.

I sat at the table waiting for Dad. I figured any minute he'd come surging through the doorway. I had a million thoughts swirling in my mind—I was on the verge of a major headache.

Mostly, I was focused on getting Rose out of her delusion, but images of a certain redhead kept making appearances, too.

The fact that our relationship hadn't gotten past niceties in the hallways at school was killing me. She wouldn't let me pick her up in the mornings, and every night after practice she was already gone. She'd laughed when I'd asked her to the movies, and when I would spot her in the sea of students, she'd actually turn around and head the other way after making eye contact. We had lunch at the same time, but she stayed in the far corner of the room with a few other country girls. What the hell was wrong with her?

Before I had the opportunity to ponder the question further, Dad swept into the kitchen with a gust of cold air following him. He shut the door quickly and headed for the fridge to get his usual glass of milk.

"How was your day?" he asked, filling his glass to the rim.

I wasted no time with small talk, needing to get it out so I could forget about it. "I saw Rose at Walmart." My words had effectively gotten his full attention.

"How is she? Did you ask her why she didn't come by for her birthday?" Dad said, instantly annoyed.

"I don't think she's ever coming home. She seems to have taken to this Amish thing just fine, and she has her sights on a wedding in the near future." I threw in the last bit to really stir him up, which it did.

"Damn it. I should never have listened to Tina about this. Sure, a normal, weak-willed girl wouldn't have lasted a week with those crazies, but our Rose is stronger—and more stubborn—than that."

Dad pulled out the chair beside me and leaned back. He stared at the ceiling for a few seconds, then wiped his eyes vigorously with the hand not holding the glass.

"Listen, I've been thinking about what you and Aunt Debbie

have been planning..." Seeing Dad's eyes narrow, I remembered that I'd eavesdropped on his telephone conversations to know that bit of info. "Sorry, Dad, you talk kind of loud—and I heard you say something about taking Rose back. Have you got any ideas how to go about it?" I asked, guessing already that he didn't have anything near as developed as what I had planned.

"I don't know. Tina has advised me that it would be traumatic for Rose and everyone else if there is a large crowd around, but I can't easily go onto the Hershbergers' or the Millers' properties, either, and do it without causing major problems with the neighbors." He looked up and squinted at me with a suspicious face and said, "Do you have something in mind, Sam?"

I smiled at him, knowing that in a couple of minutes he'd be impressed. "Actually, I have it all figured out already...and you won't have to worry about making a scene in the neighborhood—and we'll get Rose back."

Dad leaned in, focused on me completely as I talked. He nodded several times and asked questions or made points here and there. By the time the discussion was over, he looked a whole lot more relaxed.

"That might actually work, Sam. But you're sure that you can arrange the timing of it all?"

"I'm sure."

"Then, the only part of this business I see a problem with is the letter," Dad mused out loud just as Justin walked into the kitchen.

Dad looked at me, and I nodded my head toward my unsuspecting little brother, who just so happened to have a very similar writing style to Rose's flowery doodles. The whole artsy thing had bypassed me entirely to pop up in both my younger siblings.

Dad's eyes widened in understanding, and for a second I wondered whether he was so desperate to get Rose back that he'd bring Justin into the chaos and deception.

I didn't have long to guess, though, when Dad said, "Justin, come on over here. I have something very important that I need to talk to you about—something that I need your help with."

21

Rose

It was wonderful to sit beside the woodstove, sipping creamy hot chocolate with the sound of Summer's giggles sparking the air. The perky redhead was wearing a hunter-green sweater that set her eyes off brightly, and I couldn't help but wish that I had something similar in blue.

No way was that possible now.

"If you saw your brother's confused face each time I blew him off, you'd laugh till your head popped off. It's classic, it is." She blew on her hot drink and eyed me with uncontrolled mirth.

Some weird sibling protection instinct snarled in me, and before I could pull it back, out of my mouth sprang the words, *"Why do you hate him so much?"*

She set her mug down on the table and stretched her arms over her head, reminding me of a fluffy house cat that had just woken from a nap.

Tilting her head slightly, she said, "I don't hate him."

"You certainly act like you do, taking pleasure in hurting him and all," I scoffed.

"Hey, are you changing sides here or what? Don't forget

that you were the one who warned me about Mr. Casanova."
She still had a twitch to her lips, but she was calming down.

"Yeah, I know, but seriously, Sam has been running after you longer than he has any other girl I know of. Maybe you should give him a chance."

Why I said something that stupid, I had no clue.

She picked up her mug and took a little slurp only to grimace when the heat hit her tongue. She said, "Hmm, I just might do that. But Sam had to earn my attention the old-fashioned way before I gave in."

I envied Summer that she could be so blasé about her feelings for a guy. I certainly couldn't have just blown Noah off for months. Was Summer a more independent-natured person than myself, or was the instant chemistry that Noah and I shared too much for either of us to have played games?

"So, do you still like being Amish and all?" Summer asked in a serious voice, with no mocking undertone.

I had to think before I replied. There were things I liked about my new existence; like the camaraderie of the women— and being around the horses—but I was always questioning whether I'd be Amish if it weren't for Noah. The answer was always a resounding *no*.

The laundry, mending and cleaning was ridiculous. The rules bugged the crap out of me, and my lack of knowledge about the language didn't help, either. It was strange that I'd coped as well as I had—must have been the power of love.

I looked around the kitchen to make sure Ruth hadn't snuck in. Far as I knew she was doing some extra cleaning in the building that we'd be hosting church in that Sunday. It didn't need it or I'd be out there helping her. I'd already gone over the space with a fine-toothed comb—almost literally. The idea of having church at our place for the next couple of weeks was daunting, to say the least.

Lowering my voice, I was honest with Summer. "I don't know. Sometimes, when I'm with Noah, everything is fine with the world. But other times, it's like waking up in a nightmare."

A look of concern spread over her face, and I was instantly glad she'd stopped by for a visit.

"Gosh, Rose, that sucks. Do you think you're going to stay Amish?"

"The alternative would be to leave Noah, and I'll never do that," I said, scooting my chair a little farther back from the stove to avoid melting.

"See, that's where you and I are different. If I fell in love, I'd give my life for my guy, but not my soul," she said cryptically.

"What are you saying?" The fact that Summer was getting all philosophical had me suddenly on edge.

She gazed at me with steady eyes and said, "That if you give up your spirit, who you really are, for a guy, you won't have much left to love him with."

Before I had the opportunity to chew on her deep words, Ruth walked in, bringing the cold air in with her body. The few seconds of chilly breeze felt nice in the blazing warm kitchen.

"How would you girls like to go to town for some last-minute church shopping?" Ruth asked as she poured herself a glass of water.

"I didn't think we were going until tomorrow," I said.

"Well, that was the plan, but Summer's mom just called and asked if we wanted to share a trip to the store." She glanced sympathetically at Summer, before saying, "Seems that the woman is a little short on cash this week and couldn't afford the gas on her own. It works out to everyone's benefit if we go, since we'll save on the taxi charge and Tonya will have her gas money."

I had a funny feeling creep through me, and I asked Summer in a whisper, "Didn't you say that your mom was upset about your shunning from the community for two months?"

Summer nodded her head, her face puckered up in thought as she mumbled, "Uh-huh."

"Isn't that kind of weird that she'd be calling Ruth, then?" Part of my brain registered that it wasn't any of my concern, but still...

"Sure is. But then, my mom is stranger than a purple 'possum. Reckon she's over it now that the time's up. Looks like you finally get to meet her," Summer said, rising from the chair.

Pulling on my own boring winter attire, I couldn't help but feel unsettled about the out-of-the-blue call from Summer's mom.

Tonya turned out to be an older version of Summer as far as looks were concerned. Her hair was the bright strawberry color that Summer was so lucky to have, but streaked with gray here and there. Instead of green eyes like her daughter, she had dark hazel ones that could also be called pretty.

She was friendly enough, chatting away with Ruth as if they were old pals. Summer rolled her eyes and leaned over to me in the backseat to say, "Mom's putting it on awful thick for some reason."

I tried to get rid of the goose bumps that popped up on my arms at her words.

We drove past Walmart and headed to the other side of town where the extreme discount grocery store was. Ruth liked to shop there, saying that the Superstore overwhelmed her. "Too much to look at there," she'd say every time we made a trip to the little bit of civilization known as Meadowview. Lucky for me, though, we usually shared our rides with the Millers or the sisters-in-law, so a stop at the big store was inevitable.

Pulling into the parking lot, I noticed how quiet this part of town was, and I thought that it was just a matter of time before this ma-and-pop business closed down.

Tonya said that she was staying in the car, had some paperwork to do, and I briefly thought that it was odd that this particular woman would need to do that sort of thing as I slid out of the car behind Summer.

I was in more of a hurry than Summer was to get into the warmth of the store, and I looped my arm through hers to get her leisurely butt moving. Ruth was already to the entrance when a tug-of-war ensued between me and Summer as she slowed, lifting her face to the sky to catch with her tongue the soft fat snowflakes that began fluttering down.

One minute everything was quiet and tranquil, and the next all hell broke out. From the corner of my eye I saw the police cruiser pull up beside us, and I heard Summer ask, "What do you reckon the Po-Po want?"

I didn't have time to answer her or react when the door flew open and out stepped the cop who oozed a "by the book" personality with his middle-aged clean-cut face. There were several reasons a cop might want to talk to us, all of which were racing through my frantic mind, but seeing Dad come out the backseat told me everything I needed to know.

I pulled away from Summer, noting her shocked face that I was actually going to attempt a run from the officer, but I didn't make it but a few feet before the cop had my arms held down at my sides. A second later he passed me off to Dad who took no chances, keeping the vice grip engaged.

This cannot be happening. I shrieked, "You promised to let me decide."

Dad didn't say a word; his face was fixed in grimness, and I figured that his doctor's ability to defuse a situation by remaining calm was kicking in. I struggled in his hold, though, not making it easy for him.

Summer, bless her heart, jumped right into the action and grabbed hold of me as if she was going to keep my dad—and the officer—from taking me away.

"Hey, this isn't right. You can't go nabbing people like this," Summer shouted.

The officer took a more offensive position and pried Summer away from me at about the same minute her mom arrived on the scene.

Tonya said, "Come on, Summer, this ain't none of your concern."

Summer yelled back, her redheaded temper blasting, "This is my concern, 'cause Rose is my friend."

"Trust me, Summer. This is for Rose's best. She should be with her kin instead of working like a dog's slave for them Amish," she said, putting her hand out toward Summer, only to have it batted away by her daughter.

"So you're somehow in on all this?" Summer spread her arms out, motioning to the cops and my dad. "How did you even meet up with Mr. Cameron?"

"It was her brother who came by the other day, just after you got on the bus, and talked to me about it." Her voice softened a bit, as if she hadn't been expecting her daughter's violent outburst about the situation. "Honestly, Summer, you got it all wrong on this one—Rose needs to go back to her home."

Summer didn't seem to be listening to her mom. Instead, she said to me in a defeated voice, "Sorry about what Mamma did. And, if my hunch is correct, I wouldn't be forgiving Sam anytime soon. I know I won't be."

The finality of it all clouded over me. Summer stepped back closer to her mom, but she didn't look at her.

Dad whispered in my ear, "Come on, Rose. You need to behave like the grown-up young woman you so want to be." The slightly begging tilt to his voice sobered me a bit. It wasn't as if he could put me on house arrest. I'd be able to sneak off anytime I wanted.

"It's all right, Summer. Please tell Suzanna and Miranda that I hope to talk to them soon." Dad loosened his hold and pointed at the backseat of the cop's car.

Just when I was resigned to my fate and about to move my limbs into the vehicle, Ruth appeared beside the car and asked the officer directly, "What in heaven's name is going on here?"

The officer finally got his chance to play good cop. He tipped his hat to the old woman and drawled out, "Sorry about the confusion, ma'am, but this gentleman here is the young lady's father, and since she is still a minor, he has every right to bring her home. I'm just here to make sure it goes smoothly."

"Dr. Cameron, why have you changed your mind, then?" Ruth asked with a fluttering voice.

Uh-oh, here it comes.

"My apologies, Mrs. Hershberger, for the suddenness of taking Rose home, but I felt there was no other way to do this that wouldn't be problematic." He sighed. "Really, my original intentions were for Rose to experience your lifestyle for a few weeks, and then on her own, choose to come home. I've been patient, but I feel that almost four months of this nonsense is quite enough."

"Nonsense—I'd hardly call your daughter's choice to live the Plain life and take vows in our church 'nonsense.'" Her mouth tightened, and her eyes narrowed, showing her displeasure with Dad.

"Vows?" Dad turned to me, and I shrugged, looking away. What could he do—spank me?

Dad breezed on, "It doesn't matter what she might have promised to your church. She is still a minor and can't make serious decisions about her future without my consent." Dad was still using his friendly doctor voice, and I wondered how long it would hold out.

The officer said, "Doctor Cameron, I think we ought to get going."

He probably had donuts to get to, I thought darkly.

Since I couldn't control being yanked away from the Amish, the least I could do was make it easier for Ruth—and Noah, who I knew would freak out when he heard.

I said to Ruth, "Don't worry. I need to talk to Dad about all this stuff and...sort of, like, figure things out. I'll be back soon."

Dad began to nudge me closer to the cruiser, but I turned back to Ruth and said, "Please tell Noah that I'll call him soon, so he doesn't worry."

Ruth nodded, and if I didn't know the tough old woman better, I'd think she was tearing up over me.

Before I bent into the backseat, I sprang back up and yelled to Summer, "I'll call you—and thanks for being such a good friend."

I didn't hear a reply, because in the next instant I was ushered into the car by Dad, who had the door slammed right behind me. Officer Whatever climbed in and pulled out of the parking lot while I steadied myself against the back of the leather seat and peered out the window. Tonya was heading back to her car, but Ruth and Summer were still standing on the wet pavement watching me drive away from their lives.

Dad didn't even bother trying to talk to me, which was good for him, because I wouldn't have even obliged him with a grunt. I stared out the window, watching the businesses and stores of town gradually disappear to be replaced by farmhouses and lonely, empty crop fields.

Deep down, I'd known all along that Dad wouldn't allow me to be away indefinitely. I'd been mentally preparing myself for this kind of scenario, although I hadn't envisioned a cop in the mix, or standing in a freezing parking lot. Poor Noah—this would hit him like a freight train. He had no warning or preparation. What would he do when he found out? Would he come and try to rescue me as if I was a damsel trapped in the top room of a tower?

Or would he begin to reconsider what he was willing to do to be with me...and become English?

After I stepped from the cruiser, the officer leaned out the window and said to me, "You're a very lucky young lady to have such a caring father." He raised his hand up. "Good luck to you."

I didn't respond. As far as I was concerned he might be speaking the truth, but he was still the enemy—one of the people tearing me away from Noah.

Dad put his hand on my shoulder as we reached the door, but I shrugged it off, snarling, "Don't even try to be nice to me now."

The dazed feeling that had hung over me on the drive home was disappearing, anger taking its place. Dad could have talked to me before hiring out Sam to do his dirty work. I hoped Dad's reflexes were sharp, because I didn't know what I was going to do to my big brother when I saw him.

I was almost to the top of the stairs to my old room when Dad had the audacity to say, "We need to talk. Now, Rose."

"Ha. Try and make me."

I kept going until he said, "There's someone here to see you."

My brain burst with the picture of Noah, and I turned and trotted back down the stairs. Dad stood at the doorway, which led into the family room, and said softly, "Just keep an open mind."

That startled me, but before I had time to react, the door was open and I was shoved through by Dad.

My peripheral vision caught the impression of Sam sitting on the couch beside Justin and Tina with her legs pulled up beneath her on the cushy recliner. But I didn't look at them or even acknowledge that they were there. My eyes were locked on the person sitting directly across from me on the love seat.

Seeing her face, so much like a younger version of Mom, made the tears explode from my eyes.

Aunt Debbie had me in a bear hug without me even realizing either one of us had crossed the room.

"It's okay," she soothed, "everything will work out fine."

I couldn't talk. The seepage from both my eyes and nose were making it impossible. I certainly didn't understand my meltdown, either. Seeing my only aunt never brought on this kind of rain shower before. Smelling her familiar tangy perfume and hearing the voice that had read stories to me when I had still been wearing pigtails, I couldn't help but feel emotional.

The hugging thing went on for a minute or two more until obnoxious Sam said, "If she doesn't stop soon, Dad, she'll end up like that green lady with the big nose in *The Wizard of Oz*."

Then he said the line with the voice, and I pulled away from Aunt Debbie.

"I'm melting, oh, my, I'm melting."

I pointed my finger at him and seethed, "You aren't my brother anymore."

"I don't think a verbal proclamation can undo the genetic stuff," he said, smirking.

I was going for him when Aunt Debbie held me back, and Dad jumped in between us.

"Sam, shut up," Dad said, which closed my traitorous brother's mouth.

"Let's sit down over here, Rose, and talk this whole thing out." Aunt Debbie pulled me back to the couch that she'd vacated earlier, as far away from Sam as she could take me without leaving the room.

Tina asked me, "Would you like something to drink?"

"No, I'm fine," I said, my voice trembling.

Dad took a seat on the lone chair, and then everyone in the room stared at me. All but Justin looked worried or nervous; he just smiled in his dorky, just-entering-puberty way.

I had had enough of the silence. "That was a pretty crappy thing to do to me, Dad," I said, trying not to sound hysterical.

Dad exhaled and dove right in, "I never dreamed that you would actually stay with those people—or take vows of membership to their church. I was hoping that you would..."

I broke in, heat flaring in my soul, "Yeah, yeah, you already made it clear that you thought I'd come running home in no time at all. But I proved you all wrong, didn't I?" I glared at Tina, angry with her for not being able to control Dad. She took it in stride and shrugged.

Aunt Debbie joined in to rescue Dad. "Your father is worried about you. You have to understand that the decisions you make right now, as a young adult, will affect the rest of your life." She began toying with my hair the way she always did, and it felt good, calming me down.

"I love Noah, Aunt Debbie—you guys kidnapping me won't change that fact."

"You were not kidnapped," Dad injected.

"Oh, pulling up in a cop car at the discount grocery store and nabbing me isn't kidnapping?" I said.

Aunt Debbie took over the conversation before Dad flipped out. "I agree that the method of extracting you from the Amish was extreme, but you're here now with us, talking, so it worked." Before I opened my mouth, she took a breath and went on, "What do you think about coming to live in Cincinnati with me and your Uncle Jason?"

The words didn't even have a chance to solidify in the air, when I burst out, "No way. I'm not leaving Noah."

My mind was panicking. Could they force me to go? Would they?

Dad said, "You have no choice in the matter, you're going."

"That's not exactly what your dad means."

"No, Tina. Don't go sugarcoating this. She needs to hear how it's going to be. We tried it your way and it didn't work—so now I'm laying down the law," Dad said sharply, his blue eyes glistening like ice.

I was so pissed that I jumped off the couch and informed him loudly, "You can't make me do anything. I'm almost an adult, and unless you put a leash on me—which as far as I know is still illegal in the U.S.—I'll go running back to Noah the first time your backs are turned."

I didn't really want to include Aunt Debbie in my meanness, but it was war now.

Dad leaned back and looked to Aunt Debbie. She nodded but remained silent. The look that passed between them terrified me. It meant an allied front.

"Here's what's going to happen, so listen carefully. You are heading to Cincinnati this afternoon with your Aunt Debbie. Justin is taking off from school early for Christmas break, and he'll be going, too. I'll sign you up for classes at Fairfield High beginning with the new semester. You will have the opportunity to continue your dance classes, and I've arranged for you to work part-time at Dr. Jerrod's vet clinic. He's a good friend of mine, and he's doing me a favor on this."

Here he took a breath before continuing. My mind was numbing with his words. "You will not have access to a cell phone for some time, and I've already discussed the importance of you not contacting the Amish with your close friends and their families in Cincinnati. No one there will be enabling you to come back here, so don't even try it. Sam, Tina and I will be there for Christmas...and I intend to sell this place in the New Year and move back to the city."

I couldn't digest his words properly. *Did he just say that he was moving?* He was willing to do all that just to keep me away from Noah?

"What about Lady and Hope?" I asked, knotting the first kink in his plans. I would have to go back to get them—he wouldn't force me to leave them, I was sure of that.

"Already taken care of," Sam said, snapping my head toward him and his arrogant tone.

"What do you mean?" I breathed.

"While you were being kidnapped—" Dad snorted at Sam's statement, but Sam continued. "Sorry, Dad, but facts are facts. Justin and I snuck over to the Hershbergers' and collected your animals up. Dad borrowed a trailer just for the occasion."

"Lady and Hope are here?" My mind was whirling as Justin bounced off the couch and ran out for a minute, only to return with the growing puppy in his arms. He was struggling to carry the big ball of fluff until she leaped from his hands and ran to me. I let her climb onto my lap as I sat back down, running my hands through her thick fur. A tear fell from my eye, and I sniffed in the tears that were threatening to overwhelm me.

"Lady's in the barn. I gave her some hay and a bucket of water, but you should check on her before you leave," Sam said quietly, without his normal rudeness.

Anticipating my next question, Dad said, "Sam and I will take care of her this week and we'll bring the mare with us when we come for the holiday. Her old stall is waiting for her at J & D."

"This is going to give you a chance to experience all the things you've been missing living in that backward society. You'll have all your old friends, your dog, your horse...and your family. It's only right that since you spent all that time with those people that you now give us one more chance to change your mind about your future," Aunt Debbie said, moving her hand from my hair to my back. Her voice was soft and coaxing.

But I wasn't fooled, and I wouldn't be coerced.

I glanced around at my family. Justin had the decency to turn away when our eyes met, probably embarrassed. Sam looked quietly smug. Tina smiled encouragingly, and as much as I wanted to hate her for taking Mom's place, I just didn't have that fight left in me. She really was nice, and that was all there was to it.

Then there was Dad with his confident face—but I could tell he was still insecure from the way his foot was fidgeting. Aunt Debbie was her usual happy and optimistic self, sitting straight up and ready to take on the world. In her mind everything would be fine if we all sat around a table and talked our problems out. But, I had a surprise for my liberal-minded aunt—some things couldn't be negotiated, like my life with Noah.

I grabbed on to what she said and turned the tables on her and Dad. "So you're saying that if I stay in Cincinnati and do the whole suburbia teen thing, that you'll accept whatever choice I make in the end?"

Dad answered quickly. "Not so fast. We aren't talking about a few weeks here. You're going to live in your Aunt's house, and then mine when I've found a new place, until you reach the age of eighteen."

That was a whole, horrible year away.

I couldn't be separated from Noah for that amount of time; I'd die for sure. But what choice did I have but to go along with the charade and hope that in a few months, my family would loosen the leash on me and I'd have the opportunity to meet up with Noah? If they thought I was going along with it all, they'd eventually let their guard down.

And then I'd be gone—plain and simple.

I looked Dad in the eyes, and holding his gaze, I asked, "Will you support my decision when I turn eighteen?"

Dad looked at Tina, and she nodded to him. He said, "I will, Rosie. If a year from now you want to come back to live here as an Amish woman, I won't try to stop you. All I ask is that you give your old life a fighting chance—and you stay away from Noah until you're of age."

I guess I could give the English lifestyle a go again, after all. I certainly wouldn't miss doing laundry the early twentieth-century way, but there was no way in hell that I was going to go an entire year without Noah—not happening.

Putting on my best actor face, I nodded and let Dad pull me into a hug. His Old Spice cologne was a familiar tickle in my nose. I almost felt sorry him.

Dad was in for a rude awakening.

22

Noah

I paced back and forth in the kitchen, trying to absorb what Ruth had said. Rose had been taken away by her father and the police. She was gone.

"What did the officer say again, Ruth?" Father asked, and I paused in stride to hear the story again.

"He was friendly enough about it, said that Dr. Cameron had rights over his minor child or something to that effect." Ruth sat with her hands tightly gripping the table.

"And you said Tonya was in on it?" I asked, barely controlling my voice level.

"Oh, most certainly. She admitted it to Summer, who seemed totally in the dark." She sighed in a huff. "Can you imagine her calling me to share a trip into town, and then she does this— What is wrong with the woman?"

"She was probably still angered about Abram telling her daughter that the girl couldn't come around for two months," Father put in. He scratched his beard and looked thoughtful.

"All this doesn't matter. We have to get Rose back," I spoke out, resting my hands on the table as I looked at Ruth, James, Father and Mother in turn. "What are we going to do?"

Mother said softly, "Son, I don't know if there is much we can do."

"Ach, Rebecca, the girl is of an age that she should be allowed to make up her own mind on the matter," Father said, frustration rising in his voice.

"The doctor is her father. He has authority over her until she's eighteen," Mother said.

"I am not waiting a year to have her back. I'm going to get her right now." I started for the door, but Father had my arm in a hurry, holding me.

"Let me go." I tried to twist away, but although I was big and strong, Father had amazing strength.

"We need to think this through before we take action. If Doctor Cameron has the law on his side, then getting Rose back will be more complicated."

The knock at the door turned all our heads. Ruth quickly scuttled over, opening it. Abram and Martha Lambright were standing there, both with worried frowns.

"What's this I hear that Rose has been forcibly taken from us?" Abram's voice boomed into the Hershbergers' kitchen.

It took several minutes for Ruth to relate the story again and to answer the questions that Abram and Martha popped out to her during the telling.

By the time she was finished, only the women were seated. The men were ready for action.

"The thing that I don't understand is that Rose told us that her father was accepting of her choice." Abram stared at me with his intimidating eyes and asked, "Did she deceive us, Noah?"

I ran my hand through my hair, not sure what to say. I didn't want to get Rose into trouble, but the truth was the truth and it would leak out eventually.

"It's not exactly that she lied. She wanted to join our community and live our ways—and she knew her father wouldn't consent. She was hoping he'd have a change of heart in time."

"You knew about this?" Abram asked pointedly.

"Not until recently. And what could we have done about it after she had already taken the vows? She is a member of our community now, right?" I was getting emotional, and I didn't want to. I sucked it all in and breathed out slowly to calm myself.

Abram smoothed out his beard, thinking. The silence hung in the air for a minute or two before he spoke again. "Rose is definitely a member of our church, yes. That's not an issue here. But the point I feel is important to make is that our children finish school in the eighth grade. They spend the next several years working around their households and farms or within the community. A girl of seventeen for all intents and purposes would be considered a woman to us, and therefore of an age to make her own decisions…and be married."

Abram focused on me and asked, "Are you ready to take Rose as your wife, Noah?"

Without thought, I said, "Yes, I'd marry her tomorrow if she'd have me."

"You aren't ready to start a family so soon," Father said.

Mother jumped in. "We'd help out if the marriage needed to be moved up. They could live with us for a year or so until Noah had his finances in order."

"You'd be welcome to stay in our bunkhouse, Noah," James offered.

Abram looked around the room and said, "All right, then, so we're in agreement that Noah could marry Rose sooner than intended if the issue arises?"

I felt better having the bishop on board. As strict and difficult as the man could be, he would be an excellent ally to have in a fight.

Father asked Abram, "Do you have a course to take?"

"Yes, I do. My driver is parked outside. We'll go to the Cameron house together to speak with the doctor. I do believe the sooner we leave, the better."

Everyone got hustling around, picking up their coats and black bonnets. There was nervousness in the air that you could almost get a hold of, and it must have shown on my face, because Martha came up behind me and patted my back, whispering, "It will all work out in the end. Have faith in the Lord. He will bring you and Rose together again if it be His will."

I didn't like the *"if it be His will"* part. I would get Rose back even if God was against it.

The snow fell harder now, coating the ground like a fluffy white blanket. It would've been a beautiful evening if it hadn't been for the fact that Rose was being kept from me. I felt better talking to her father with my little army, but still, deep down, I had a feeling that it wouldn't matter who I brought along. Doctor Cameron was a stubborn and proud man. He would not let Rose go so easily.

And then, what would I do if he didn't give her back to me?

Thoughts raced through my mind as we walked up the stone path toward the old wooden door, our feet crunching in the snow. Father had already warned me to let Abram do the talking, so I hung back, allowing the man to reach the door first and begin knocking. Lights were on in the house, so I knew they were there, but no one rushed to answer the door. The thought then occurred to me that maybe Doctor Cameron wouldn't even talk to us.

He had to answer the door; I had to see Rose.

When the door finally creaked, David held it only partially open, blocking the way with his body.

"Can I help you?" David asked politely, as if he didn't know why we were there.

Abram cleared his throat and said, "Doctor Cameron, I'm Bishop Abram Lambright. We met a while back at a singing."

"Yes, I remember." David's voice was becoming curt.

"May we come in? There's a matter that needs to be discussed." Abram was composed and friendly, obviously not expecting the English man's reaction.

Ignoring Abram's request, David said, "No, there isn't anything that we need to discuss." David found me in the crowd and stared at me when he said, "Rose will no longer be a part of your community."

I couldn't stand there any longer and moved forward before Father's hand could grasp me. When I was beside Abram and close enough to the door to feel the warmth in the house pushing out, I said, "I want to talk to Rose."

"Sorry, but she's not here." He suddenly reminded me of Sam; I saw the resemblance of father and son.

"We'll wait for her." If I had to sit in the snow all night I would.

David smiled. "You obviously don't understand. Rose left for Cincinnati with her aunt this afternoon. She won't be back."

The words echoed in my head painfully. Abram put his hand on my shoulder and told David, "I am sorry about the disruption to your life, but these two young people love each other, and Rose made oaths to our church that won't disappear just because you sent her away."

"She was in no state of mind to make the decisions she's made in the past few months. Her relationship with Noah was a mistake, and she sees that now." David pulled out a small envelope from the inside pocket of his jacket and thrust it toward me.

I saw my name written on the front, and I stood frozen, too afraid to take it.

Abram pinched the envelope between two of his fingers, and once David was free of it, he said, "I want you to respect Rose's wishes, Noah, and don't try to contact her in the future. You all have a good night," he said, shutting the door abruptly.

Abram took my hand and put the envelope in it. "You need to read it."

My heart slowed, and the world seemed out of focus as I opened it and read.

Noah,
Please forgive me for telling you this in a letter. I know it's cowardly, but I couldn't face you in person. I miss my old life—my family and friends. All the work that's expected of me as an Amish woman is too much. I'm tired of doing laundry the old-fashioned way, scrubbing fences by hand and cleaning every inch of the Hershbergers' house to perfection. I'm not even allowed to wear my old riding boots in your world. I can't stay Amish, it's not for me. Please leave me alone and go on with your life without me.
Rose

The words cut deep into my heart, almost killing me it seemed as I stood clutching the letter, the script blurring before my eyes.

"What does it say, son?" Father was beside me, and I handed the note to him. I was hardly aware of him skimming it over and passing it around to the others.

"Is this Rose's handwriting?" Martha asked.

I thought about the times I'd seen her writing, and I looked back at the paper, my eyes coming into focus. As much as the sudden burst of hope I experienced made me want to believe that Rose had not written the letter, studying the intricate swirls and dots told me the hard truth.

I looked at Martha's face, which was full of optimism, and said, "It's hers."

Ruth said, "If you ask me, it doesn't sound like something Rose would say."

Then Mother chirped, "And she wouldn't leave without saying goodbye to the other girls, and all of us."

I didn't know what to say. A part of me wanted to defend Rose and say that she'd been forced to write the letter, forced to go back to the city. But, I knew that she'd been putting the wedding off, not even wanting to discuss our future plans. She'd complained about the exact same chores to me. Maybe she'd hated being Amish all along and was just searching for an opportunity to get away?

We stood there, the seven of us, huddled in a circle on the Cameron's walkway in the snow and cold. The fluffy flakes were becoming larger and catching on Father's beard, making it look as gray as Abram's. I didn't want to leave, hoping that David would open the door and tell us that it was all some kind of a sick joke—that Rose was in the house waiting for me.

But I knew that wasn't going to happen.

Abram's hand gripped my shoulder tightly, and my mind was so black that I hardly heard him when he said, "God is all powerful, Noah. You need to pray to Him for guidance and strength. There is reason in all He does. You must have faith."

His words were empty to my ears.

How could I live without Rose?

23

Sam

I pushed through the bodies with deliberate purpose—to get the hell out of Dodge and to catch the little redhead. She was walking quickly by herself to the buses. I had to reach her before she put one of her cute suede boots onto the step. I went into a run, darting through the cattlelike teenagers. Damn, I wasn't used to the frenzied scene in front of the school when the classes let out for the day. I was supposed to be in the locker room getting dressed for a workout, but here I was, running down the object of my obsession as if I were a lion taking down a gazelle.

I reached her just before she climbed onto the bus, and snaking my arm out, I got a hold of her shoulder and pulled her back.

A little out of breath from the mad run and nerves, I panted, "Hey, I want to talk to you."

Her pretty eyes, which were like warm spring grass, narrowed. She spat, "What for? Do you want to dig up some more information for your schemes?"

I was expecting her reaction to be less than amicable, so I wasn't ruffled when I said, "We need to discuss this. You've got it all wrong."

Seeing her about to blow me off and get on the bus, her body just beginning to pivot and the angry eyes of the old dude driver on me, I whispered in desperation, "I have news from Rose for you. Don't you want to know how your buddy is doing?"

I'm not a praying type of guy, but I said a silent prayer at that instant that the fool girl would be intrigued enough to listen to me.

A flurry of emotion passed over her conflicted face before she finally relented, saying, "What about Rose?"

I looked around at all the scrambling kids scurrying to their buses, hoping she'd get the hint, before I said, "We can't talk here. Let's go to my truck."

"No way—you talk here, now and quick or you lose your chance." She crossed her arms over her jacket, tilting her body slightly so that the icy wind didn't catch her in the face.

Okay, it wasn't the most suitable place to talk a girl into forgiving a guy, but I'd make the best of it.

"I was doing Rose a favor by helping my dad to get her out that Amish craziness." Seeing that her puckered expression didn't change at all, I barreled on. "Look, Rose is having a great time in Cincinnati. She's been shopping with my aunt and hanging out with her old friends and my little brother. She wanted a way out—she needed it. You know yourself that she didn't have any business joining up with that nonsense."

The crowd was thinning, but I hardly even noticed, I was so intent on the beautiful girl looking up at me with utter hatred in her eyes.

"You are the worst kind of person, Sam—*a traitor.* You sold out your own sister because you didn't like what she wanted to do with her life. She wasn't hurting herself. I thought this was what we fought those stupid British people for, to have the freedom to live our lives the way we see fit. You are a prejudiced pig—and you better stay away from me from now on. I'm not interested!"

Her words were like a slap to the face. Damn it to hell, I'd really done myself in this time. By doing what I had to do to wake my brainwashed sister and hopefully bring some normalcy to our family once again, I had thrown away my chances with the only girl that I'd ever really liked.

Standing there on the sidewalk in the whipping air, I watched the buses leave in a long, orange train.

And the only person who could get me out of this pinch was the one person on the planet who'd probably rather cut out her own eyeballs than help me.

24

Rose

I must admit, I'd missed people-watching at the mall. Taking a sip of my cola, my eyes wandered over the food court, checking out everything from one girl's hip hairdo, to the tattoos running down the arm of an otherwise nerdy-looking guy.

Snapping me out of my transfixion was Amanda's irritated voice. "Really, Rose, you're like a zombie to hang out with now."

Letting my gaze settle on the gorgeous blonde sitting across the table from me, I snorted. "Hey, I was perfectly happy to stay locked up in the house, but noooo, you had to drag me out on this boring 'adventure.'"

Amanda's head tilted, and a spark flashed across her features, deepening the frown on her face. I'd definitely pissed her off, but I didn't really care much. After all, she was just one of my jailers now—another person who wouldn't let me use their phone to contact Noah.

"I would've thought that living with the mild country people would have taken you down a notch. Instead, you're a bigger bitch than ever."

I was so numb that her words hardly registered. When I lifted my eyes to her glinting ones, Amanda blasted on, "You are pathetic. You've got family members, *and friends,* who love you, and are all going out of their way to please you, keep you occupied, and all you do is whine and moan like a spoiled baby." Tough love coming from Amanda was *not* a good thing. During the three weeks that I'd been back to convenience-land, she'd listened to me, cried with me and cussed at my family with me.

I guess she was over it all now and just wanted to move on and get back to normal.

One of my favorite songs began to play in Amanda's purse, and she quickly answered her cell. She abruptly rose and left the table to have the secret conversation away from my ears. I briefly wondered who she was talking to and then dismissed the phone call entirely, not really caring.

Honestly, I didn't care about much these days. I'd barely spoken to Aunt Debbie and Uncle Jason during the holidays, and it was impossible to settle down with Dad and Sam hanging around, pretending that all was right with the world. And they thought the *Amish* were crazy.

In just a few days I'd be back to my old high school, walking the halls and sitting at proper desks with qualified teachers looking over my shoulder. To say that my mind wasn't ready for it was an understatement.

I couldn't believe that Christmas and New Year's had passed and I still hadn't heard from Noah. But of course, was I stupid? If I couldn't get a call into him, how the heck would he get a hold of me? He didn't know my aunt's phone number or address, and all the letters I'd tried to get out so far had been intercepted by my aunt who seemed to have an agreement with the postal service.

Still, when I'd lain awake in the dark each night staring out the window at the stars, I'd imagined all kinds of scenarios where Noah would track me down in the suburbs and rescue me as if we were in a fairy tale.

What was Noah thinking? My sudden disappearance must have crushed him. I knew that Ruth was torn up about it, and I was sure the Miller family would feel the same way. The picture of Suzanna's mischievous face beside Miranda's wispy one materialized, blocking out the bright lights of the food court for a moment, and I got a little choked up. I knew I'd miss Noah horribly, but I wasn't banking on my weepy feelings about the rest of the Amish people to whom I'd become close.

And then there was Summer. Besides Noah, I probably missed her the most.

Seeing that Amanda was still distracted with her animated phone call, my mind started to wake up, and I judged the distance to the pay phone outside the restrooms. I wouldn't have much time to make a call, that was for sure, but Summer would have her phone on her and she'd definitely answer it. I looked at the slender blue watch wrapped around my wrist, realizing that I'd learned to appreciate the small convenience immensely.

It was almost five, a good time to get a hold of my red-headed friend.

With a speeding heart, I stood up and casually made my way through the tables to the trash cans. Once I'd dumped the contents of my tray, I glanced back at Amanda to verify that she was still occupied.

She was gone.

Popping from behind me came her voice, which I noticed was more pleasant than when she'd left the table.

"Hey, girl, guess what?"

Her over-perkiness immediately put me in defensive mode. "What now?"

"Sam just pulled into the parking lot with Heath and some other buddy of his that he brought from Meadowview," she said happily.

Whether her good mood was because she was hooking up with her main squeeze or she had some diabolical plan arranged with Sam was anybody's guess.

"And that's supposed to be a good thing?" I demanded. Irritation washed over me—for the first time in weeks I had the opportunity to use a phone, and Sam showed up to ruin my chance.

"Yeah, it'll be fun for us all to hang out together. Just like old times," Amanda said, ignoring me and searching the entry doors.

I knew when they walked into the building it would be hard to miss them. High school football players were like that; they commanded attention when they went out in public.

"What about Brittany? Maybe you should call her if you're interested in a reunion," I suggested.

Usually Amanda and Brittany were inseparable, so when Amanda said, "No," like a bullet out of a shotgun, I became doubly suspicious.

She went on to cover her tracks by saying, "Aw, she's babysitting her niece tonight, so there's no reason to even invite her. It would just bum her out."

A minute later I understood Amanda's pushy behavior. Strolling in through the glass doors was Sam. On one side of the Benedict Arnold was the tall, good-looking Heath, and on the other side was the equally tall Hunter Braxton.

What was he doing here?

Catching his very happy smile to see me, I realized that he'd probably come all the way to Cincinnati with Sam just to piss me off. Hadn't Sam already learned not to play matchmaker with me?

Before I could escape, the athletes had reached us, and a second later Amanda was nestled under Heath's arm.

Before any of them could say a word, I blurted out, "You

should have called Brittany." I jerked my thumb toward Hunter. "They would be perfect together."

Amanda's eyes widened, but before she could produce a comeback, her boyfriend swatted me on the shoulder in a friendly way that almost put me off balance. "Hey, it's good to see you, kiddo—it's been a while."

"Oh, shut up." I was not going to act like everything was perfect, because it definitely wasn't. They were all keeping me from my Noah—and my life.

The guys had the good sense not to say a word, all shuffling around on their feet uncomfortably, but Amanda didn't have that qualm. "You are out of line, Rose...."

Before Amanda got too many words out, Heath jumped in and said, "Come on, I want to go look at those sneaks." He tugged Amanda away from me.

"Some things never change. Honey drips from your mouth, Rose," Sam said sarcastically as he waited for me to follow his partners in crime.

I hadn't talked to him in the weeks since I'd been exiled to the city. I knew it bugged him more than me barking out catchy comebacks, so I turned and stalked along behind Heath and Amanda, who both would turn at intervals to check if I was still with them. And I thought the Amish were single-minded.

When the happy couple turned into the athletic shoe store, I made a beeline for the bench centered in the middle of the marble-floored hallway. Sam followed on my heels, squeezing in beside me to make room for Hunter.

Sam's voice was overly nonchalant when he said, "So...have you talked to Summer lately?"

That did it.

I rounded on him and let my fury fly. "I would have talked to her a bunch of times by now, but wait a minute, let me think.

Oh, yeah, I'm on phone arrest. I can't touch them, talk on them or even look at them. So how the hell would I have talked to the girl that you're stalking?"

He actually looked confused for a second. He even pushed his fingers into his bushy mess of hair to scratch his head.

"Oh, yeah" was all he managed before Heath called from the store's doorway.

"Hey, Sam, come check these out." Heath was holding up a pair of hideous giant black-and-orange sneakers.

"Just a sec." Sam glanced at me with the look of a guy deciding whether he needed to drag me into the store to keep an eye on me—or if he'd get away with not making a scene and leaving me sitting on the bench.

Hunter must have been thinking the same thing, because he said, "Hey, bro, if she makes a run for it, I'll catch her."

My head darted toward Hunter, but he didn't look at me. He should have been afraid to, because I was ready to knock him out.

Sam glanced between the two of us and, after nodding to himself, took the few steps needed to enter the store.

Hunter's voice lowered to a whisper. "Hey, you can use my phone."

It took a second to register what he'd said. I turned and *really* looked at him and was surprised to see an anxious, yet serious expression on his face.

"Really—you'd do that for me?" I glanced into the store just in time to see the posse heading straight for us.

"No way now," I mumbled, slouching down on the bench in defeat.

Amanda eased down next to me and squeezed my knee. She was trying to patch things up, and I would have been more than willing to be buddy-buddy again if she'd just lighten up and let me use her damn phone.

What I heard Hunter say next nearly dropped me on the floor.

"Rose and I are going to check out the sporting goods store. She likes to ski, too, so we're going to see if any of the gear is on sale." His voice sounded so believable and casual that for an instant I got heated until it reached my dumb brain that he was setting up a rendezvous for me to use his phone.

Sam frowned a bit and was about to say something, but I'd never know what, because Amanda piped up first. "Oh, that's a cool idea. You two go check it out. Heath didn't eat a bite tonight, so we're heading back to the food court." She paused and looked straight at me for a second. "Meet up with us there when you're ready. Okay?"

Heath wasn't shocked and went with the flow. I doubted he was hungry at all. Sam just looked conflicted, as if his brain was trying to wake up.

I didn't give my oaf of a brother the opportunity to figure it out. "Will do— See you guys later."

I turned swiftly and headed in the direction of the store we were supposed to be going to. I did enjoy skiing, but the slopes were the furthest thing from my mind.

Hunter fell in easily beside me, matching my stride comfortably. I glanced up at him, and when he caught me spying, he smiled tentatively for a second before focusing on the oncoming traffic. I still fidgeted inwardly that he had his own agenda, and I might end up in worse shape by trusting him, but there was something about the way he had offered his cell to me and then so easily lied for my benefit that made me want to trust him. I needed any and all allies I could get at this crisis point in my life.

We walked through the mall, moving together to avoid mowing down any patrons, and I couldn't help but sneak a peek at Hunter every few stores. His dark blondish hair hung loosely on his head, all the strands flowing to the right side. He was tall and athletically built, like Sam and Noah. But he was more slender than they were, moving like a tawny mountain lion stalking his territory.

When he glanced down at me, I quickly looked away.

"I've wanted to tell you for a long time how sorry I am for the way I treated you that night at the party. I was drunk...and way out of line." He paused, looking away briefly to turn his head back to me with searching eyes. "I hope you can forgive me. I don't touch the stuff anymore—quit that very same night."

I struggled to keep from rolling my eyes. The guy didn't give up easily. But I was fairly certain that if I told him that I'd rather jump into a bathtub filled with snakes than forgive him, he'd turn around and leave with his cell phone. It was nice of him to accept responsibility for being a jerk, but honestly, I didn't care much either way. I just wanted the phone.

Sucking in a breath and avoiding his gaze, I breathed out, "It's all right, really. I'm over it. We're okay."

He was silent for a minute, but I noticed out of the corner of my eye that he held a slight smile on his lips. When he spoke again, I was surprised by the change of subject.

"Have you ever skied?" Hunter asked as we turned into the sporting goods store.

I was distracted for a few seconds by the fake waterfall surrounded by plaster boulders, a prize eight-point buck poking out from the plastic foliage and the black bear rearing back on its hind legs to angrily greet us.

Tearing my eyes away from the store decorations, I answered, "I love to ski."

Hunter slowed and grasped my arm, saying excitedly, "Hey, do you want to go to Perfect North Slopes with me next weekend? I usually take my snowboard, but I'm going to check out the skis here and maybe upgrade from my old ones."

It was more information than I needed or wanted. But still, the fact that he was the only person around at the moment willing to help me out did sink into my anti-Hunter brain, making my voice come out sweet. "Maybe...I'll have to check it out with my aunt first."

His mouth rounded for a second, then widened into a broad smile. His hand still rested warmly on my arm, and I glanced down to remind him about it, but he left it there. I fought within myself about what I should do about his show of familiarity. I didn't want to ruin my chances at getting an escape driver lined up—but leading the guy on was a no-no also.

He pulled out his phone, making me forget his hand. As I went to grab it, he lifted it up to a height that I'd have to stretch for it.

Irritation swatted at my skin while I stared at the phone. Although, Hunter's hand had lowered a fraction, I'd still have a difficult time making a grab for it.

He took a breath and opened his mouth to speak. I cussed in my head several times before he found his words.

"You know, I've wished for a long time that you and I could be friends, get past everything that went down last year. I really do like you and want you to be happy." He paused, and I heard the *but* coming before it passed his lips. "But, maybe you shouldn't go jumping back into the Amish lifestyle so quick. I mean, you need to give everyone else a chance to change your mind about it before you do anything drastic. You're an amazing girl. I'm sure you don't want to live with that kind of regret. For your own peace of mind, you should be absolutely certain that becoming Amish is what you want."

It was as if the edges of my hostility were instantly smoothed, becoming softer. The words floated around in the air, and even though there was a steady stream of people dividing around us, I felt very much alone with Hunter in that busy doorway. His wide-spaced greenish eyes were flecked with brown, and they stared at me intensely.

He was right. I should be absolutely certain that it was worth it to become Amish to be with Noah. I knew firsthand now what I'd be giving up if I left my world for his. But it wasn't so much what he said that affected me—it's what he didn't say. Hunter didn't tell me it was wrong or stupid to become Amish. He simply said that I should make sure that it's what I really wanted before I did it. He believed that it was my choice.

Flustered, I looked off into the camo clothing, my eyes landing on a heavy brown coat adorned with leaves, and said, "Oh, don't you go cramming advice down my throat, too."

He laughed. "You're safe with me. Really, I'm not going to judge you or tell you what to do. I just want your friendship— that's all."

He handed me the phone, brushing his thumb over my hand before he turned away, blending into the crowd.

The phone was cool in my hand. As my heart sparked into a frenzy, I made my way into the arctic clothing department and hid close to an overflowing rack of puffed-out ski jackets. Then I dialed Noah's number.

Ring, ring, ring, ring—I waited through the trills, my heart slowing with each one. No one was home; or maybe they were all shut up in their warm house and couldn't hear the loudly ringing bell coming from the shed. Either way, I wasn't going to get to talk to Noah.

I finally disconnected, feeling that I was somehow giving up on Noah by shutting the phone off. I closed my eyes, picturing his face, the creases at the corners of his warm brown eyes were stretching as he smiled at me, his full lips lifting into a grin that promised a hot kiss.

Opening my eyes, I sighed, my body feeling weak from disappointment. But even in my gloomy mood, I still had a glint of hope as I dialed again.

I perked up, taking a quick intake of breath when Summer answered.

"Hello?" Summer said. She sounded so cautious it made me laugh into the phone.

I controlled my giddiness and squealed, "Summer, it's me. I finally got a chance to call you."

"Oh, my God...where *are* you?"

Summer's voice was music to my ears, and the life came back to my limbs as I said, "I'm still in Cincinnati, but I'm working on a plan to get back to Meadowview." I looked around for Hunter, and seeing the coast was clear, I lowered my voice further and told her, "You see, there's this guy, Hunter, a friend of Sam's, who might help me." Then I stopped again, and not being able to wait any longer, I asked her, "Have you heard anything about Noah—anything at all?"

The dead silence from Summer's end stalled my heart.

"Summer?" I whispered, fear gripping my insides.

Her voice was reluctant when she finally spoke. "Yeah, I ran into him at the Diner a couple of weeks ago. He...he said that it was over between you two. Something about you not being Amish material. He was really rude, and after barely a minute talking to me, he bolted, saying he had better things to do than waste his time on someone like me."

Summer's voice had quieted, and I could tell that her feelings were hurt, but I couldn't find it in myself to care. I was so wrapped up in what she said that I couldn't even properly process the information.

"There must have been some kind of mistake. You must have gotten it all wrong...." I insisted.

I'm not Amish material...

The words bounced around in my head, instantly causing

a throbbing pain. Hadn't I done enough loads of laundry or mended enough of Mr. Hershberger's pants for Noah?

"I'm so sorry. I don't know what got his britches into such a wad, but I'm not lying to you. That's what he said. Then he just stomped away."

I couldn't talk; the tears were streaming down my face, and my voice was stuck in my tightened throat. I didn't want to cry, but I knew I wouldn't be able to stop.

After a minute of saying nothing, Summer ventured, "Rose, are you still there? Are you okay? Rose?"

I sniffed it in. "Yeah, I'm here. Listen—don't tell anyone I called you."

"What about Suzanna and Miranda? They've been going crazy worrying about you, same as me," Summer said with confusion in her voice.

The last thing in the world I needed was for it to get back to Noah that I was pining away for him. Hot air clutched my lungs, and I said, "You can tell them that I'm fine...that I'm happy here in Cincinnati."

"But...?"

I didn't let Summer say any more.

"I can't talk now. I'll call you again soon." As she started to protest, I ran over her words, saying, "I promise," and I hung up.

Pressing the phone to my chest, the tears flowed freely and soon I couldn't see two feet in front of my face. *Why would Noah abandon me?* I knew he loved me—wasn't it enough for him? Maybe he'd decided that I wasn't worth the trouble, or maybe he was ticked off that I'd lied to him and his parents about Dad giving me the go-ahead to join the church.

Whatever the reason...he didn't want me anymore.

"Rose, what's wrong?" Hunter's voice was in front of me, but I couldn't see him through the mess of liquid in my eyes.

He came closer, putting his hands on my shoulders and giving me a gentle shake. "What happened? Are you okay?"

His voice was worried, and the sound of it made me cry harder. The fact that I was at the mall with him instead of cuddled up on the Hershbergers' couch with Noah shook me to the core, and even though I tried to cut the theatrics, I couldn't.

Somehow, in the few seconds that Hunter had gotten a hold of me, he'd managed to pull me into a tight embrace. My face was against his chest, the musky cologne beneath his shirt invading my senses, while his hands softly rubbed my back up and down. The alarm bells went off in my clouded mind, but I didn't pull away or snap at the guy for hugging me.

I needed someone to comfort me.

And for once, I didn't have to worry about being caught.

25

Noah

The sun that warmed my face was also melting the snow on the rooftop of the Schrocks' barn. The drips that were present earlier when I'd gone through the door for Sunday service had turned into a steady stream of drops that splattered the ground like a mini rainstorm.

The pause in the winter weather had lifted my spirits a tad, and I relaxed on the bench, listening to Timothy and Suzanna babble about nothing in particular. Occasionally, Matthew or Miranda would throw in a few words, but the conversation was dominated by the happy couple.

Closing my eyes, I enjoyed the wisps of warm air that would settle on me each time the breeze let up. I drifted off to near sleep listening to Suzanna chirping about how wonderful it was that Miranda and Matthew had finally gotten together officially. I was happy enough for Matthew, but if truth be told, I was in the frame of mind to warn any guy away from a woman.

They were nothing but trouble.

I was barely paying any mind at all to the others, when Suzanna's words brought my ears to full attention.

"Yeah, Summer told me that she's been talking to Rose a lot lately and that she's doing well."

Miranda said, "I still can't believe that she didn't even come around to say goodbye to us."

I noticed the melancholy wafting around Miranda when she said it, and I suddenly realized that I wasn't the only one who was betrayed by Rose's selfishness. These two girls had been her close friends, and Rose had tossed them away as if they were dirty laundry water.

"What else did Summer say?" I hated asking, but it would be on my mind the rest of the day if I didn't.

Suzanna hesitated for a second before meeting my gaze and saying, "First off, she said that you treated her like she was dirt on the floor, and that she wasn't surprised that Rose had left you."

I narrowed my eyes and shot back, "It wasn't like that at all. I just didn't want to talk to the girl. The less I know about Rose, the better."

"But you're the one asking now," Suzanna retorted, her nostrils flaring with her words.

Before I had the chance to stick up for myself, Timothy helped me out. "That's not what he said, Suzie. He asked what Summer said, nothing about Rose at all."

"Oh, please, of course that's what he meant. Why else would he care what Summer said?" Suzanna was sitting up straighter on the bench, in killer mode.

Timmy must have noticed her attitude. He just shrugged and began staring at the ground. He was turning into a spineless dolt, the same as Jacob had once he'd started courting.

"I was mean to Summer, probably because the feelings were still so raw. I honestly don't care what Rose is doing now." The disbelieving looks from all in attendance forced me to utter, "Really, I don't."

"So, you wouldn't be interested that Rose has been hanging around with the same guy that chased her away from that party last year, causing you to have the wreck?" Suzanna spoke softly, but her words streaked through the air.

I'd been doing a grand job of not thinking about Rose. My anger had given me the strength to deal with the dying feeling that I'd first experienced when I'd realized that Rose had really left me. I'd kept myself busy with the construction crew during the day and doing farm chores until after dark each evening. Everyone was careful not to mention her name around me or say much of anything on the matter.

Hearing that Rose was with that jerk again sank my heart to the pit of my stomach. Images immediately sprang to mind of Rose kissing the guy, hugging him…*and worse.* I brought my hands to my head and rubbed vigorously, trying to rid my mind of the sickening pictures.

"I'm so sorry. I shouldn't have said anything," Suzanna said quietly.

"I would've found out about it eventually" was all I could say. The hole in my heart that I'd managed to keep patched up was gushing fresh blood. It hurt so bad to lose Rose, but to know that she was in another man's arms was torturous.

"Hey, Noah, have you met the Schrocks' cousins who are moving here from Indiana?" Matthew's voice seemed far away, but his random comment caught my attention.

"Yeah, just a little while ago after the service ended. *Why?*" I was suspicious, already clued into the direction he was going.

"Uh, well, the one daughter…what was her name?" Matthew turned to Miranda.

"Constance," Miranda said.

"Yeah, Constance, she's our age and a nice-looking girl." Matthew was blushing at the same time he was making faces at Miranda to diffuse any jealousy that his lackluster attempt at matchmaking might be causing her.

I searched in my head, trying to recall the girl, but was unable to. I hadn't noticed that she was pretty; that is, if she really was.

"Can't say that I remember her," I said to the group.

"This will jar your memory," Suzanna said, nodding her head toward the doorway of the building where the girl had just appeared with Sarah.

And they were heading straight for us.

"This is Constance," Sarah said to Suzanna, ignoring me and the other guys completely.

While Suzanna made small talk with the new girl, I took the opportunity to study her. Anger at Rose gave me the incentive to allow my eyes to wander over the girl from head to toe, carefully and completely.

Matthew was right. The girl was attractive. She had dark reddish-brown hair pulled up neatly into her cap. Her delicate features put me in mind of an old-fashioned doll, and the wide-set brown eyes that glanced at me were docile and friendly. Instantly, I knew that there weren't any burning flames within the girl—and that was what drew me to her. *She was the complete opposite of Rose.* Here was the type of girl that was passive and agreeable—the kind that would follow her husband anywhere. She would be content to take care of the house and children.

I'd been burned by the fire and learned my lesson well. What I needed was a solid, earthy girl like this one to tear my mind away from the past. Constance might just be the one to help me forget about Rose.

Watching Sarah lead Constance away to the house, I said

to the others, "I think I'll hang around here this afternoon to help get things ready for the singing tonight."

Timmy slapped me on the back. "Excellent move—it's good to see you back in the saddle, my friend."

"Hey, and it was my idea," Matthew said proudly. Suzanna and Miranda didn't say a word. They didn't need to. Their narrowed eyes said it all.

26

Rose

I fidgeted while I looked at the snow-topped hills through the smudged glass. My mind was far, far away from the bustle of activity of the skiers getting their gear together behind me.

Why had I agreed to come up here with Hunter? Was I losing my freaking mind?

Hunter had politely pestered me about the skiing trip for two weeks before I'd finally caved and agreed. Perhaps it was because when I'd needed a favor, he'd handed me his cell phone, or maybe it was that he'd told me all the things that I wanted to hear after I'd learned that Noah had turned away from me.

He'd said I was better off without a guy who believed that women should stay home and care for a bunch of kids instead of being out in the world enjoying a career. And he'd said that the garbage-bag dress didn't do much for my attractive figure.

Hunter had seemed to know what to say that night—and he'd somehow managed to make me believe that there was life after Noah. That maybe, just maybe, I was better off without him.

Of course, part of my acceptance of the rupture in my life was that I was so angry that Noah would say that I wasn't Amish material. Hadn't I dried out my hands enough doing the laundry his foolish way? Hadn't I sat up straight enough during those horrendously boring three-hour church services? Hadn't I been obedient enough?

Wrath was the best way to get over a guy, I decided. And I had plenty of that emotion to spare. But despite the bitterness I felt, I still had moments when memories of my life with the Amish would come back to me. The wonderful dessert smells floating through Ruth's kitchen or Suzanna's addictive laugh would send a jolt to my heart occasionally, making it difficult to breathe. I did have some really good times in the community, even though I didn't get to watch TV, listen to music or go to the movies. I'd learned to compensate for the absences in that world by doing other stuff, like running through the woods in the middle of the night with friends—or sneaking in a kiss or two with an overly uptight Amish guy on Sunday evenings.

My heart still ached as if it had been frozen solid and then hit with a sledgehammer. But I ignored the pain, focusing on getting caught up with my classes at school and reestablishing old friendships. I'd also started my part-time job at the vet clinic the week before, and I had to say that it was probably the biggest distraction of all for my wrinkled-up heart.

After all, it was difficult to wallow in self-pity when you were dealing with a beautiful black Lab that had been hit by a car or an elderly Persian with tumors. I was learning that there were more important things going on in the world than my love life.

Turning my head to search out Hunter who had finally reached the counter to rent the skis for me, I wondered what I should do about him.

Originally, the plan was to use him to get back to Meadowview...and Noah. Since that need had vanished, I was left with a little bit of a guilt trip about the guy. He'd definitely proven himself worthy of my friendship, but still, I knew he wanted more than just to be buddies.

He'd insisted that's all he wanted, but the way he'd stare at me when he thought I didn't notice was a dead giveaway.

I figured that the usually confident Hunter Braxton was terrified to make the first move because of our history. *He was waiting for me.* But I wasn't ready for another relationship, and definitely not with him.

Admittedly, Hunter was gorgeous, and I'd found out that he was really polite and chivalrous when he wasn't under the influence of alcohol. He also got excellent grades in school and was planning to go to the University of Kentucky in the fall on a football scholarship to play for the Wildcats.

The guy had it all going on, and, annoyingly, he'd somehow managed to awaken the butterflies in my belly with his longing eyes. It was a dull feeling compared to what I'd experienced with Noah, but then, I didn't expect to ever feel that kind of intensity of emotion again. Heck, I didn't want to.

Who needed guys, anyway? Summer had proven that a girl could be happily single. So could I.

My resolve weakened a bit as Hunter made his way toward me; a sly smile was on his lips as though he'd happily eavesdropped on my thoughts.

"God, it seems like everyone in the tri-state is hitting the slopes today," Hunter groaned, but he didn't lose the wisp of a smile as he sat beside me.

He took the liberty of pulling my leg onto his lap and started to tug off my street boot.

"Hey, I can do that myself," I protested, but weakly. Sometimes it was nice to be treated like a five-year-old—and this was one of those times.

"Just want to make sure these are the right size," he said, putting the ski boot on my foot and clamping it. "How does that feel?" he asked, taking the opportunity to place his hand on my knee, which didn't surprise me in the least.

"Feels fine," I said, noticing the way his hair kept falling into his eyes.

His coy smile broadened, and he said, "I have a surprise for you."

"What?"

He nodded behind me, and I couldn't help the speed that my heart raced to as I turned around.

My eyes searched the busy room for something that I would recognize as a surprise, and it didn't take long to see what Hunter was talking about. My heart exploded in happiness when I spotted Summer's bright smile. I had only a second to catch Sam's silhouette beside her before I jumped up squealing in delight.

"Hey, wait a minute. Let me get that boot off so you can move."

I thrust my leg toward Hunter and let him pull the ski boot off before I slipped my foot into my own boot in a fluid motion. Happiness had the better of me, and I couldn't help squeezing against him in a quick hug of gratitude. My brain registered Hunter's warm response as he curved his body around mine when I'd given him the chance. I pulled out of his grasp quickly and bolted to Summer.

Summer's eyes went wide, and she raced through the crowd to meet me. The full-body hug we gave each other was bone-crushing, and I thought to myself that Summer was very much like me, an all-or-nothing type of girl.

"Are you surprised?" Summer nearly shouted.

"You bet I am. Hunter never breathed a word about it until just now."

"Hey, sis," Sam interrupted. He stood there looking like a forgotten old dog on the porch.

"You were in on this scheme, too?" I asked Sam, mentally wondering if I should give him the heads-up that I'd forgiven him already with a hug. The weeks of separation from my older brother had softened me a bit toward him. Just like Dad and Justin, he'd been trying to protect me from messing up my life. Now I knew that he'd been right about Noah all along.

With my fingers fidgeting at my sides, I mentally deliberated for a few seconds. Remembering Sam's smirking face each time he'd seen me dressed Amish decided it for me. I'd skip the hug and ease him off the hook gradually.

When I glanced to the side, Hunter was beside me, close enough for passersby to assume we were a couple. Funny thing was, Sam had taken up the same possessive stance next to Summer.

"Yeah, actually, it was all my idea," he said, all full of himself.

"Oh, shut up. It might have been your plan, but I'm the one who had to put up with two hours of being trapped in the truck with you to get here," Summer told Sam, with hands on her hips and eyes flashing.

Instead of Sam making a sarcastic comeback, he just smiled and said, "And I'm so happy you graced me with your presence."

Summer was at a loss for words, which was cute, because I didn't think that happened to her often.

I decided that I'd had enough of the guys invading our feminine reunion. While they swatted each other in a friendly greeting, I grabbed Summer's hand and pulled her toward the tables and chairs with the view.

"You guys can start on the slopes without us. We got some serious catching up to do," I said.

"I'm not skiing, anyways," Summer blurted out.

"*At all?*" I couldn't hide my confusion.

Sam filled me in. "She only came up here to see you, Rose. Even though I offered to pay for her rental and give her a private ski lesson, she told me, ah, something to the effect that she'd rather get rolled down the mountainside naked before she'd put those glorified pencils on her feet. You can try to change her mind, though."

Sam was smiling fondly at Summer—again setting off signals in my head. He really did have it bad for her.

"Don't even bother with it, Rose. I meant what I told him." Summer's body and voice were stiffened with resolve.

Strangely, I looked to Hunter for—God knows what—and he said to me, "Don't worry about the rental. Just have a good time with your friend. I want you to have great day." He smiled before he left with Sam to attack the mountainside.

Did he really want me to be happy, or was he just an excellent actor, trying to get me into a compromising situation?

Only time would tell.

"He's yummy," Summer said. "I've always thought so—and he's never been rude to me, either."

I swatted her on the arm and laughed. It was so wonderful to have her there in the flesh.

"Come on. Let's get a hot chocolate and find a seat where we can watch the guys coming down the hill," I said.

Summer mumbled something about not caring to see Sam at all, but she went with me, anyway, for the drinks and then let me pick the seating arrangement.

Sipping from my cup, I studied the girl before me. She was still full of vinegar, telling me all about life back in Meadowview with her colorful country twang going on. I also couldn't help noticing her wide-eyed interest in everything going on around her.

"Is this the first time you've been to a ski resort?"

"Course it is. I've never been able to afford anything like

this before," Summer said as she searched the hillside intently. I knew she'd never admit it, but I would have bet money that she was looking for Sam.

"Why don't you let Sam treat you, then? From what Dad says, he's making pretty good money working part-time at Lowes now."

"No way am I going to let your brother think that I owe him something. I only agreed to come on this trip to see you," Summer said briskly and then dropped her eyes, becoming suddenly mesmerized by the hot liquid in her cup.

I thought for a minute and said, "You know, I wasn't sure before, but now I feel completely safe in saying that Sam has fallen hard for you. Maybe you should give him a chance... he's not that bad."

"What about you and Mr. Sexy out there. Are you two an item yet?" Summer turned the tables.

"No. We're just friends."

"Why? I only saw the guy with you for a minute, and it was obvious that he's madly in love." Summer giggled after she said it. The sound irritated me.

"I don't have feelings for him, that's why."

"Yes, you do. Don't lie to me, Rose."

"What makes you say that?"

"First off, you wouldn't have come up here to spend the day with the guy if you weren't into him. Second, he's gorgeous and sweet-natured, so why the hell not give him a go?"

Summer's eyes narrowed, and she held my gaze.

She had me. I said with defeat in my voice, "Guess for the same reason you won't take a chance on Sam."

"*Why's that?*" Summer's voice lowered, threateningly. She was waiting for some earth-shattering proclamation, but she would be disappointed.

"Because neither one of us want to get hurt." I looked out

the window at the dots of people sailing down the white slopes. Admitting what I knew in my heart all along to Summer made me feel a little better.

She nodded her head in agreement. "Yep, I understand your situation and all—being so bound up with Noah, just to have him turn on you like a copperhead would sour any girl on men. But I don't reckon I know why I feel the way I do."

The fact that she'd mentioned Noah and I wasn't crying was a good thing. Out of everyone in the world I knew, only Summer, and maybe Sam, wasn't going to pussyfoot around his name.

"Have you ever had a boyfriend?" I asked Summer. At one time I would have been expecting her to say dozens, but now I wasn't so sure.

"Oh, I've had a few hand-holding and peck-on-the-cheek sorts of things going on, but never a real boyfriend."

"But you're so pretty and smart and fun to be with. Surely the guys are hitting on you all the time—right?"

She was thoughtful for a minute, and after she took a swig of her drink, she said, "Umm, yeah, guys have come on to me and all, but I guess I don't want to end up like my ma."

"What do you mean?"

Summer's eyes passed over me and settled on the people coming and going at the entranceway. It was obviously a difficult conversation for her, so I waited quietly for her to continue.

"Mama's been married two times and had more boyfriends than I can count on both my hands. She can never seem to find one that'll stick around for long. They come in and promise her the world and then they fly the coop. Maybe I learned from her to be leery of the opposite sex."

That made perfect sense. I suddenly felt better that she'd confided in me. It was easier to solve a problem when you knew what it was.

"Summer, listen to me. Your mom might have had all those bad relationships, because she's the one with the issues, not the guys," I suggested.

"Huh?"

"Seriously, you are not your mom. She's made decisions that affected her relationships, but you don't have to follow in her path."

"That's exactly what I'm doing—not following Mama's lead," Summer protested.

"Right, you shouldn't be dating a bunch of guys just to have a boyfriend around. That would be stupid. But to give a guy like Sam—who's really into you—a chance is something altogether different."

Summer's eyes stared into mine, her jaw set firmly, until a crooked smile crept up the side of her mouth. The look made me sit back, knowing that Summer's bright mind had just thought of something—and that I should be worried.

"Okay, miss Dear Abby." Her smile was definitely wicked now. "I'll give Sam a chance if you give that hunk of sugar out there the opportunity to rub Noah from your mind."

"I don't even think about Noah anymore," I lied.

"Yeah, right."

I sighed, and as if God had just sent me a sign, I spotted Hunter in his green jacket making his way down the advanced slope. I watched him swish and bend to have a perfect run, before turning back to Summer's smirking face.

She and Sam would be perfect together—and it seemed the only way *that* was going to happen was if I turned the tables on her and accepted her proposal. Besides, saying that I would make the effort was very different from actually hooking up with Hunter. I had no intention of dating anyone, but I could put on a little act for Summer's benefit in order to get her to open up to Sam. They'd be happily dating in no time, and

Hunter would be just a memory in my life. Summer would thank me someday for my ruse.

"Okay, *but on one other condition,*" I purred.

Summer exhaled, sitting up straighter. Disbelief peppered her features.

"*What?*" she said hesitantly.

"That you get your butt out there on the bunny hill and let me teach you how to ski."

Summer took a short minute to decide. Her worried look slowly changed into one of anticipation, and she said, "Ooookay. But you better not laugh at me."

I shook my head vigorously. "I promise I won't."

I had my fingers crossed under the table, though.

"Cause if you do, you'll be eating snow. And I keep my promises."

For the first time in forever I felt alive—and free of worry and doubt. I was being a kid again.

And maybe it was worth losing Noah for.

27

Noah

I leaned up against the wall, watching the guys go at it on the makeshift basketball court in the Schrocks' gathering building. Sweat still sealed the shirt I was wearing to my skin from the hour or so that I'd been out there.

Shifting my eyes without moving my head, I kept a watch on Constance, who was hanging out with Sarah and Maretta just a few yards away.

Timmy and Matthew had already left with their girlfriends, and I was deeply satisfied that earlier, when the gang had all been present, Constance had stayed cemented to my sister's side. The new girl didn't show any interest in the two rebel girls, even though they'd tried to prod her for information with false friendliness.

Suzanna and Miranda were solidly on Rose's side, and I doubted that they'd want to hang out with a goody-girl like Constance. And she had shown common sense by picking up on the undercurrent going on.

I'd also been impressed that Constance kept a low profile, smiling and answering in a friendly manner when spoken to, but not going out of her way to bring attention to herself.

Again, I couldn't help but compare this new female to my

fiery ex. And I could easily say that they were completely different. *Thank God.* This time I was doing it right and sticking with a girl who wouldn't break my heart.

I had to get to know the girl better, though, before I asked to court her. Since she wasn't volunteering to flirt with me any, I guessed I'd have to take the lead.

I swallowed some of the nervousness and directed a question to Constance. "How do you like Meadowview so far?"

Since I was looking straight at her, she couldn't mistake that I'd spoken to her.

Her eyes brightened, and she boldly took a step closer to me to be heard over the bouncing of the ball and the shouts of the guys on the court.

"I like it very much."

She answered me in English, but her words were a little strained, letting me know that she was more comfortable talking in our birth language, so I changed over to German and pushed on with the conquest.

"When will you be officially making the move?"

"Father finalized the house deal two days ago. I think we'll begin bringing our belongings here next week. Mother wants to be settled before spring planting."

Constance's voice was soft and very girly. She didn't have that sexy, husky tone that Rose had, but the sound of it was still pleasing. Her lips were shaped like a heart, and at the moment they were tilted up in a grin that made me guess that they would be responsive to a kiss. The direction my thoughts had gone caused a heat to swell in my groin, and I looked away, realizing that maybe Father had been right—possibly, I could be attracted to another girl. At some point during my thoughts, Sarah and Maretta had wandered away, and I found that I was standing alone with Constance. Well, not really alone, as there were more than thirty young people hanging out in various spots either on or around the court, but alone enough to make my stomach tighten.

I plowed on. "So, ah, do you have a boyfriend back in Indiana?"

She looked directly at me in an inviting way that reminded me a little of Ella—but without the craziness attached.

"No, I don't." She smiled shyly after she said it and looked away.

The action did something to my heart, melted it a little, making me feel that this particular girl was special.

"I'm glad to know it," I said, catching her gaze just long enough to see hot pink flush her face.

"I'm Noah, by the way." I couldn't help but laugh a little at the absurdity that we hadn't even been introduced yet, and I was already set on courting the girl.

"I know your name. Sarah told me all about you. I'm Constance."

"I found out your name also." Then a thought occurred to me, and I decided to go with it.

"Did Sarah tell you that I just got out of a relationship that didn't end well?"

Constance looked up quickly, showing me a concerned face before she shied away again.

Rose would have held my gaze until I shifted my eyes.

"Oh, yes, she told me that you dated an Englisher who wanted to be Amish. But she changed her mind about it and left the community," Constance whispered, having the good sense not to blast the conversation out loudly.

I felt relieved that she already knew the story. It was impossible to talk about but something that any girl I got involved with would eventually hear all the sordid details about. I felt more at ease that Constance still held the sweet grin on her blushed face even knowing about my past. That meant I had a chance with her.

Another thought passed through my mind—had Rose ever blushed? I didn't think so.

"Would a nice girl like you be willing to give a guy who'd made such a mess of things a chance?" I asked her quietly, hoping that her answer would be what I expected but still worried that maybe she wasn't interested. If that were the case, my options here in Meadowview were empty.

She looked up and held my gaze for the longest time yet. I could see desire in her wide brown eyes. I knew her answer before she spoke and my insides calmed.

"Yes, I would give you chance, Noah."

"Are you serious? You just today met her." Sarah's mouth was sagging, her eyes bulging.

I clucked Oscar into a road trot on the straightaway before answering her. The warm day had led into a chilly but clear night. The sky was bright with stars, and the road was free of traffic, all in all a perfect way to end a very good day. I felt better that I'd made my decision, freer in my mind somehow.

"Listen to me, after having gone through all that with Rose, I now know exactly what I'm looking for in a wife and partner."

"And what's that?"

"The exact opposite of her," I said. Seeing Sarah's look of incredulity, I went on to say, "Constance is Amish. She thinks like an Amish woman, wants the same things in life that I do. She is pure in her beliefs and thoughts."

"And you don't think that Rose was?" Sarah asked in a way that sounded like an argument, but I didn't let her opinion ruffle me.

"No. She wasn't. Rose pretended to want what I did so that

she could play around with me long enough to decide that she didn't want me." I tried to mask the venom in my voice but probably failed.

"Oh, I don't believe that Rose purposely set out to hurt you. It's just that she couldn't handle living our ways. Do you really blame her so?"

I fired back, "Course I do. I loved her with all my heart, and when she had the opportunity to split, she did just that. I'm sure she's not so pure anymore, dating that football-playing as..." I trailed off, not wanting to offend my sister's ears.

Sarah's voice lowered, and she stared at the passing dark fields. "I'm so sorry that you're hurting and all, but rushing home to ask Father and Mother about a courtship with Constance doesn't seem like the best thing to do."

"Why the hell not?"

Sarah sat silently for a moment, and I worried that maybe my harsh words had angered her. But then she did speak.

"I worry that you're going to hurt Constance in the end."

"What are you talking about? I plan to start courting her and then marry her by the end of this year. She's a few months older than me so we won't have to wait long."

Why was my sister being so difficult about this? Did she want me to stay a bachelor forever?

She whispered something that I couldn't hear over the pounding hooves, forcing me to pull up on the reins. I slowed Oscar to a walk and finally a stop.

I turned back to Sarah and barked, "What did you say?"

My timid little sister met my eyes and said with a fierceness that shocked me, "I think that the love you and Rose share is too strong to ever be over. At some time, you'll want Rose back, and when you do, you won't stop until you have her—even if it destroys Constance."

Her words shook me to the core, raising the bumps on my

arms even though I wasn't cold. But there was some truth to what she said. I would always love Rose, but I was damned determined to make her suffer for what she'd done to me.

And what better way to do it than to marry another?

28

Rose

It had been the best kind of day. The warmth of Hunter's arm pressed against mine as the movie images flashed on the big screen. I wasn't really paying much mind to the show, though; I was thinking about the fun ride I'd had that morning with the other girls at the barn.

The mounted drill team that my trainer, Sandra, had created was amazing. Riding the horses to music at a gallop was a real blast, and I couldn't wait until springtime when we'd have our first intermission performance at the local horse show. Lady enjoyed moving to the beat, and I was surprised at how well she accepted being crammed in tight beside the other horses as we executed the difficult maneuvers.

What I loved the most about it was that it was similar to dancing—only on a horse's back, combining my two favorite activities together. Although my schedule could barely take another activity between my ballet classes and working at the vet clinic, I'd felt that if I could survive until school let out, I'd be in good shape during the summer.

Hunter's laugh rang out beside me. I watched him for several long seconds, once again realizing what an upbeat sort of person he was. He laughed easily and loudly for everything,

not just the movies. I had to admit, as much as I'd tried to ignore his text messages and telephone calls, I'd been drawn into
a closer friendship with him due to his sunny disposition. My
promise to myself to blow Hunter off quickly had been harder
to keep than I'd anticipated, and here I was, sitting beside him
at another movie.

But what was the point? Hunter would be off to college in
the fall, anyway. And then he'd be gone—just like Noah.

I'd tried hard to block him from my mind, but my ex-
boyfriend was never far from my thoughts. The busy days
helped. But those times when I found myself alone, Noah's
face would rear up before me, and even though my anger toward him was still as sharp as a dagger in my heart, I also
longed to kiss him again. My heart sank at the knowledge that
I would never be in his arms again, and tears slipped out of
my eyes at random times. The only reason that I was sane at
all was because of Hunter. He'd saved me from the burning
grief that threatened to consume me.

It had been weeks since our ski trip, and during that time
Hunter had been in constant contact with me, either by phone,
text messaging or Facebook. He'd even made the trip to the
city several times with Sam to visit. He never pushed me physically, which I was grateful for. The relationship had remained
friendly, and I was in no hurry to take it to the next level.

Whenever I'd begin to feel the darkness of depression moving in, Hunter would appear in some form or another to distract me from the sorrow that I kept hidden deep within me.
The time I'd spent with the Amish was fading away, becoming
like a hazy and jumbled dream. A part of me wanted to hold on
to the memories tightly, reliving the moments over and over
again, but the other part desperately wanted to shield myself
from the pain and just forget.

Hunter's touch startled me as he lightly grasped my hand,

pulling it over to his knee and resting it there. I glanced at his face with raised eyebrows, and he smiled before turning his attention back to the movie.

He didn't release my hand, though.

After a minute I began to relax as the heat from his fingertips penetrated my own. I made no attempt to free myself from Hunter's hold, instead drifting my body a little closer to his and leaning into his arm. I could see the corner of his mouth lift into a broader smile and warmth spread throughout me. The feelings made Noah appear in my mind, but I erased the image quickly, hating myself for the lack of control I had over my mind.

Since Summer had started dating Sam, she didn't hang out with Suzanna and Miranda anymore. That saddened me, thinking about the great times we'd all had together, but it also meant that I didn't hear much Amish news through her anymore. Several times I came close to picking up the phone to call Ruth—or even Sarah—but I never did. I was afraid to stir up all the feelings again. Besides, I didn't know if they'd even want to talk to me. Noah sure didn't. Maybe they all hated me, the English girl who couldn't hack it.

I guessed that Sarah was probably dating that guy Edwin by now, and Joshua and Jacob were more than likely sitting up by themselves. Ruth had to do all the work on her own again, and I felt a stab of guilt when I thought about leaving her so abruptly.

Worst of all were my thoughts about Noah. What was he doing with his life without me in it? Had he found a girl to snuggle up with on Sunday nights? *Oh, God, if it were Ella I'd just die.* But then again, it might bug me even more if she were a nice girl whom I couldn't hate.

The credits running on the black screen and the lights coming up woke me from my musings.

"Did you like the movie?" Hunter asked, not letting go of my hand as we walked out of the theater.

I didn't lie to Hunter about things, and I answered truthfully, "Honestly, I don't remember much of it. I was kind of zoned out, thinking about stuff."

Hunter held the door to his new Mustang open for me, and I sank down into it. I smiled slightly, thinking about how proud he was to drive me around in it. Of course, that meant that poor Sam was at the mercy of his old friends for a ride when he came to the city. My dear brother was already upset that he'd missed a weekend with Summer by coming with Hunter to his aunt's house, but appearances were everything in the teenage world. Aunt Debbie would not have taken to the idea of Hunter spending the night at the house with only me as the object of his attention. Somehow, as long as Sam was along, it was all right to Aunt Debbie to allow my potential boyfriend to sleep over—and Sam and Hunter had worked out some secret agreement to make sure Sam made the sacrifice once a month.

It was all kind of weird, but so far it worked out okay. I could only imagine the heart attack Ruth would have if she knew that Hunter was sleeping under the same roof as me, and completely unchaperoned. I'd been a good girl, though. Maybe she'd have been proud of me.

I would never know.

"You've been awful quiet tonight. Is something wrong?"

Hunter's voice was so tight that I felt his fear. He was afraid that I was getting ready to tell him that I only wanted to be friends. I glanced over at his straight profile, his hair hiding his face partially.

I didn't answer him, instead, following the bright passing lights on the business signs with my eyes. How different this world was from the Amish one. I hadn't missed the traffic and the overwhelming amount of civilization in the suburbs. I'd grown quite fond of the dark, quiet country nights.

Unzipping my jacket as the heat blasted from the vents, I reached out and turned the knob and said, "I've just been thinking about how you'll be going away to college in the fall, and I've kind of gotten used to having you around—even if you are a couple of hours away."

"Is that why you've been holding back on me?" he asked.

"Well, really, what's the point of us starting something up if we won't be together in a few months, anyway?" I didn't want to sound depressed, but I was sure I did.

He chuckled a little, catching me off guard before he pulled into an empty parking lot and killed the engine.

Grabbing my hand, he pulled me closer and said, "Hell, I thought this whole time that you just wanted to be friends— that the way I'd acted last year at the party had screwed up my chances of ever having you for myself. Now I find out that you do want me, and you're worried about me not being around."

"Ah, something like that," I muttered, suddenly very aware of how alone we were in the darkened furniture store lot. And the fact that for the first time, I'd kind of given Hunter the green light—to something.

"You listen to me, Rose. It's going to be more than a few months before I leave. And I could always come here and go to Ohio State to be closer to you—the papers aren't signed yet. You'll be heading off to school a year later, and we could make arrangements to be at the same college. Hell, we could get an apartment together."

Hunter was getting way, way too far ahead of himself. But, I couldn't help the moisture that got worked up in my eyes at what he'd said.

"You'd actually change schools to be closer to me?"

"Absolutely."

"Why?"

Words weren't going to work for him. In a swift movement, he had his arms around me and his mouth on mine. I vaguely recalled the last time we'd kissed, when I bit him, and I wondered why I hadn't enjoyed his warm mouth back then— because I sure did now.

Hunter's tongue pushed between my lips in what felt like a desperate attempt to show me how he felt instead of simply telling me. His lips were full and firm; his scent from the musky cologne he wore tickled my senses, and I breathed him in more fully as I opened my mouth to his.

I didn't know how long we were lip-locked in total abandon, but the flash of lights did get our attention.

"Shit," Hunter said as he pulled away from me and lowered the window.

"This is not a make-out destination," the cop said before he asked to see Hunter's driver's license.

I wiped my mouth and zipped up my jacket, suddenly feeling bare naked. The way my heart was pounding, I was surprised the officer didn't call an ambulance. Hunter's kiss was definitely better the second time around and well worth the wait. And strangely, even though he wasn't Noah, I had felt safe and secure in his embrace.

Maybe there was a chance for me to rid Noah from my brain forever.

When we pulled out of the parking lot, and the cop turned in the opposite direction, we both breathed out, bursting into laughter.

"That was some kiss—brought a cop down on us and everything." He laughed again, taking up my hand and squeezing it.

He said with a surety that made me believe him, "Don't worry. I'm not going anywhere. I promise."

★ ★ ★

Lying in the bed that I now considered mine, I stared at the stars on the ceiling. Justin and I'd had some fun sticking the galaxy up there right after Christmas, a present from Sam who seemed to know the right gift for a near suicidal teenage girl after she'd been ripped away from the love of her life.

The stars blinked in and out of my vision, hazing over for some seconds to burst into clear brightness the next when my eyes would focus again.

Was Noah the love of my life or just a first-time crush that the years would erase from memory?

It was more difficult to see his face when I thought about him now, and since I didn't have any pictures of him, it was almost as if he'd never really existed—as if I'd dreamed him up to help me get over my Mom dying, or something psychological like that.

I opened my mind and heart up for the first time in so many weeks and let Noah flow back in. Hugging the pillow close and pulling the covers up over my head, I sniffed, letting the tears flow. *No, I knew the truth.* I could try to fool myself all I wanted, but it wouldn't change reality. I would always love Noah. I'd taken oaths to a community and culture that I wasn't born to in order to be with him.

It had definitely been the real deal. But Noah wasn't willing to leave his world for me, and that stung my heart.

Yet Hunter would change all his well-laid plans to be with me, a girl he wasn't even officially dating, before he'd even received a kiss. Had I been stupid all along? How could I have not seen how into me Hunter was—and that he really was a good guy?

The questions bashed my brain, making it impossible to sleep. I was so confused that my head pounded with the conflicting thoughts.

Was Hunter the one for me?

As if on cue, the soft creak of the door opening stopped my breath and sharpened my senses. I listened as the door scraped over the carpet and then to the quiet steps on the floor coming closer. I knew before I even peeked over the covers that it was Hunter, but seeing him in his sweatpants and T-shirt standing beside my bed sparked my heart into a frenzy of beating.

"What are you doing?"

I was afraid that he'd just majorly messed things up for himself. One kiss and he showed up in my bedroom in the middle of the night—not good.

But when he got down on his knees and peered at me seriously, I wasn't afraid.

"Rose, I just wanted you to know that I have deep feelings for you." He reached out and tenderly smoothed the hair away from my face, and I suddenly didn't want him to leave. I didn't want to have sex, but I didn't want to be alone, either.

I sat up a little and held my arms out to him. "Will you stay a little while and hold me—just until I fall asleep?" I added with a more severe tone, "No funny business."

I couldn't make out his face very well, but I knew he was smiling when he climbed onto the top of the covers, sliding his strong arm under my head and pulling me in tight to his chest with the other.

His warm breath on the side of my face and the flutter of his fingers on my back sent a shock of desire coursing through me. I wondered if he was as bothered as I was, and I thought about finding his lips in the darkness, but I didn't. I knew that if we started kissing, it would be the end of it—we'd go all the way for sure.

As much as I wanted Hunter at that moment, as wonderful as his body draped over mine felt, I knew I wasn't ready for him in that way. Listening to his breathing even out, I thought that, ironically he'd probably beat me to dreamland.

I was relieved that I had on my full body Eeyore pajamas, so that if anyone did find us in the morning, both fully clothed and me wearing something as unsexy as what I had on, they'd know we hadn't been messing around.

I relaxed, reveling in the feel of being held by a strong guy who loved me. If I closed my eyes, I could imagine it was Noah beside me. *But I would try not to do that.* It wasn't fair to Hunter to be thinking such thoughts. It was already bad enough that I didn't tell him that I loved him back. But I couldn't lie to Hunter. I had decided that I'd always be truthful with him. And even though I knew in my heart that someday I could love him, that moment hadn't come yet.

My heart was still calling out another name.

29

Noah

I washed the dirt of the volleyball game from my hands, trying to keep my heart calm. Tonight was the night.

I was confident Constance would say yes; she'd given every indication that she wanted to spend the rest of her life with me. After a few months of courting her, I was sure that she was the right girl for me. Father and Mother were supportive of my decision, which made it even easier.

Drying my hands, I paused to glance in the mirror above the sink. I thought I looked older than before. I guess it was to be expected, though. I'd basically lived one life already. I tried not to let Rose enter my thoughts, but it was impossible to keep her entirely locked out. She'd probably always be there, lurking in the shadows, flashing her bright blue eyes at me and messing with my mind.

I wasn't going to let the memories ruin the good thing I had going with Constance, though. It was the middle of April, and I'd turned nineteen the week before. I was more than ready to begin my adult life. Marrying, having children and farming were what I'd always wanted, and now I was closer to reaching my goals. I couldn't look back and fret over an English girl who never even loved me—a girl who was temporary.

I looked out the window at the buggies that were already leaving the singing, filled with couples who were all too happy to get away from the spying eyes of the adults. The air was warm, despite the cloudy skies, darkening softly with the setting sun that couldn't be seen. As much as I welcomed the warmer weather, it also stirred thoughts in my mind that I'd rather leave locked away. I breathed out hard, suddenly feeling the tightening in my gut that always accompanied a reminder of Rose. I couldn't help but associate the growing heat with her. She sometimes seemed to be made of nothing but heat.

As I watched Matthew snap the long reins, sending his open buggy down the drive with Miranda sitting close beside him on the bench, I couldn't stop myself from wondering what Rose was doing at that very moment, so far away in the big city. Did she ever think about me? I liked to believe so but wasn't sure at all. The connection that we'd shared had vanished, leaving a feeling of disconnect that was like a deep hole inside of me. When I thought about what I'd lost when Rose had left me, the pain was too much for me to bear, and I'd quickly seal her away, busying myself with thoughts of Constance and our life together.

And that's exactly what I did now.

I hurried out of the bathroom, trying to spark my excitement for what I was about to do. I reasoned to myself that within minutes I'd have my girl and we'd be on our way behind the line of buggies—toward a future together as a family. It was a day of celebration, not a time for letting the hard memories of a girl from my past beat me down.

I wouldn't allow Rose to rule my mind. I was over her.

Rounding the corner into the kitchen, a sight caught my attention that slowed me, maybe even worried me for no good reason.

"What are you doing, Ella?"

Ella had been holding an envelope up and studying it intently when I walked in. Since she was in my family's kitchen and had no business snooping through our stuff, the sound of my voice brought her whirling around.

She set the letter down on the counter and smoothed out her dress before answering me in a calm voice. "Oh, I didn't know you were in here—thought you'd be with Constance."

Her voice was laced with fake friendliness, but her eyes were dark with something else.

"Don't matter what I'm doing. This is my house." I watched as her face changed expression, a slight frown easing onto her mouth. Whether it was for real or an act was a mystery to me.

Ella knew she had to say something, so she did. "I was just tidying the counter for your Mother. The little kids came in here and made such a mess today." She smiled coyly back at me again and went on to say, "Is everything going well with Constance? She's such a nice girl—much better suited to you than the other one. What was her name?"

"You know her name." After a quick look around to make sure we were alone, I lowered my voice and said, "And, it's none of your damn business about Constance. You best leave well enough alone."

Ella's eyes widening was the only indication that my words hit the mark.

She walked to the door, only pausing to say over her shoulder, "You have a nice evening."

The encounter rattled my nerves, but I tried to block the weasel from my mind as I headed out myself. I had much more important things going on than to worry about Ella Weaver.

Just before I reached the door, I was tugged back by an invisible string. What had Ella been looking at, anyway?

I crossed the kitchen and grabbed up the envelope. *My heart stopped.* I took a deep breath and held the paper up closer to my eyes. It was the letter to Sarah—from Rose.

Rose's fancy cursive writing and the little drawn flowers in the left-hand corner froze the blood in my veins. Sarah had told me a couple of days ago that she'd received a letter from Rose. She'd said that Ruth, Suzanna and Miranda were also honored with short notes from my ex-girlfriend, thanking them for their helpfulness and friendship in the community. There was a buzz in the church about Rose finally making contact—and the fact that she hadn't even mentioned me once hadn't escaped anyone's notice, either.

I'd washed the information from my mind. It was inevitable that I'd hear about her sooner or later, but the timing was kind of strange with me about to get engaged.

Looking down at the already opened letter, I was tempted to pull out the note and read. *If anyone had the right to do such a thing, it was me.* But to prove to myself that I was really done with Rose and that she wouldn't be chasing me around in my dreams, I let the envelope drop onto the counter.

I only half noticed the return address in the upper corner. Guess she was hoping to be pen pals with my sis.

Unwilled, Rose's beautiful face blocked my vision—I remembered so clearly the soft smile that would play on her lips, and it warmed my insides. I had to forget her, I inwardly screamed. I wouldn't let her destroy my new life.

When I opened the door and stepped out into the moist spring air, the trickle of a thought still played within my head.

Why was Ella so fascinated by the envelope?

Constance cuddled under my arm, and I breathed in the fresh lilac scent of her shampoo. She always smelled nice and fresh, not Rose's sexy smell that would drive a man crazy, but the kind of smell that made me want her without feeling I had to have her.

I never wanted to feel the insanity of that kind of need again.

The creaking of the porch swing distracted me, and Constance's silence didn't help any. I wished she would say something, make it easier for me to work up to asking her, but she was a quiet girl and I couldn't expect her to suddenly be talkative that night.

It wasn't exactly that I needed reassurance, but I wanted a sign that I was doing the right thing. The determination that I'd felt earlier had diminished when I'd neared Constance's home.

Turning, I lowered my face and touched my lips against hers. It was pretty much the same as always; Constance opened her mouth willingly and joined my passion with enthusiasm.

Her kisses were sweet and sufficient to arouse me, but I was always the one who had to initiate the contact. Constance's complacent personality, combined with her fragile, doll-like face and body, were any guy's dream, and I had to reassure myself again that I was lucky if she'd have me.

Constance was not Rose, and a part of me hated that fact—but the rest of me was grateful. This sweet girl beside me wouldn't cause the kind of drama that came with a wild English girl, and staring down into her large dark eyes, I knew I was doing the right thing for once.

"Constance, in the past few months you've become very special to me, and I can't imagine my life without you in it. I love you…and I pray you'll be my wife."

I held my breath, waiting.

But she didn't leave me hanging for long. Constance's face lit up, the inner shine lightening my heart when she breathed softly, "Of course, I'll be your wife. I love you so much."

And for the first time, Constance came to me, pressing her body into mine as she sought my mouth out with hers. Her forwardness awakened a desire in me that had been dormant for so long. I knew I'd made the right choice.

At long last, my heart was content.

30

Sam

Pressing Summer into the couch, I could barely control the heat spreading through my body. She ran her mouth over my neck, stopping to nip me here and there and then move on again.

It had taken a while for Summer to drop her barrier, but now that she had, she was driving me insane. I didn't have much time to dwell on the fact that she was still holding out on me, refusing to let go completely, when her mouth found mine again.

Somehow, she'd managed to get on top of me and was straddling my waist while she kissed me. Her sweet smell of vanilla, combined with the feel of her hair brushing my face, had me so worked up that I could hardly breathe.

Broaching the no-fly zone, I eased my hand up under her shirt and began exploring. The soft moan that erupted from her lips drove me on more confidently as I rolled her on her back and began trailing my tongue over her sensitive jawline. I wanted her to want me—more than anything I wanted this girl to belong to me completely.

"Oh, you're going to make me faint dead away, you are," she groaned, lifting my head so she could kiss me again.

I felt that was a good sign, and I charged through Summer's comfort zone, running my hand under her bra—big mistake.

As if the lights had come on in the middle of the night, Summer snapped out of her friendly state in the blink of an eye.

She grabbed my hand and pulled away at the same time. "Now, what do you think you're doing, Sam Cameron? I didn't give you the go-ahead to start touching my boobs—and with your little brother in the house and all. That's just plain sick."

As frustrated as I was, I couldn't help but chuckle at her choice of words. She was so damn adorable—definitely a girl worth waiting for.

"Justin is off in some faraway fantasy realm slaying dragons on his Xbox. Trust me—we don't have to worry about him." I sat up, reaching for the cola and taking a swig. I hoped the cold liquid would settle my body down. Otherwise I'd need a cold shower.

Summer ignored me for a few minutes, pretending to watch the B horror flick on the TV, but I didn't let up staring at her. Finally, she faced me and crawled back on my lap, taking the can from me and having a drink herself. The little action told me she wasn't pissed, and I was elated just to have her on top of me again.

"I already told you, Sam, I'm not having sex with you for a looooong time. And no amount of your lips, tongue or hands is going to change my mind."

I grinned; couldn't help myself. "Yeah, you did tell me that. But you can't condemn a guy for trying."

I began smoothing her wild hair behind her ears, wondering how long it would take to get her into another make-out session.

"Stop it, Sam. I just remembered something important to tell you."

Her face brightened, and I resisted the urge to kiss her. Instead, I settled back on the couch, holding her snugly on my lap.

"I was going to tell you first thing, but then you got me all distracted." She blushed and said, "Guess what Suzanna told me this morning?"

I had to search my brain—who the hell was Suzanna?

Summer sighed, rolling her eyes. "You know, the Amish girl that I hang out with sometimes. The one who was good buddies with Rose."

I still didn't have a clue.

Summer's face was now flushed from frustration instead of embarrassment. "The blonde girl that you gave a ride to that night when we were walking on the road..."

The girl's face suddenly materialized from memory. "Oh, yeah, I remember now—what about her?"

"Not about her, silly. It's what she told me is the news."

Her face was so excited that I humored her and pretended to be interested.

"Okay, please tell me all about it."

She swatted me a little harder than necessary, saying, "Don't be stupid. This is important. You better listen up." She took a deep breath, and once she was sure I was all ears, she let it out, and said, "Noah is getting married in June."

The news exploded in my head. Summer had finally managed to get my mind off her luscious body.

"That was quick. What the hell, is the guy some kind of polygamist?"

"Huh?" Summer was confused.

"You know, one of those Mormon people who shack up with several wives." The lights still hadn't blinked on in Summer's eyes, so I continued. "Wasn't he going to marry my sister just about four months ago? How could a guy go from a dramatic relationship like that to marrying another girl in such a short time?"

Summer finally got my gist. "He's hooked up with a little china-doll type who has no personality whatsoever. She just smiles and worships the ground Noah walks on. Least, that's what Suzanna says."

I thought for another minute. Having Noah officially off the market was the best news I'd heard in a long time.

"I wish him a long and prosperous marriage—without Rose. Hah."

Summer was twirling the strands of my hair that were at my ears, and I thought we were about to get back to business when she said, "Noah hates Rose now. He'll never forgive her for breaking up with him in a letter. It about killed him."

Her words again cooled my vigor and unfortunately caused a bunch of crazy thoughts to drift into my head.

"How do you know about the letter?" Shit, did Rose know, too?

"Suzanna just told me about it today. Guess the Miller family has finally let the information slip. You know them Amish like to keep their secrets, but stuff always gets out eventually."

Damn it. Not good, not good at all. I must have had some serious agitation on my face, causing Summer to ask, "What's wrong? You look like you just upchucked a frog."

I glanced at her cute face but had to turn away. I hadn't really thought about the Noah situation for weeks. Rose was happily dating Hunter, and he was treating her like the queen she thought she was. Hell, Dad was even seriously thinking about bringing her back to Meadowview now that the suspender-wearing Romeo was out of the picture.

Everything had worked out just the way it was supposed to. Then why did I feel like shit?

Dad and I had worked in Rose's best interest. If we hadn't made our move when we did, Rose would be the one getting married, instead of some brainwashed Amish chick. The letter had been the icing on the cake—the one thing that would keep Noah from tracking Rose down as if she were a bleeding gazelle. He had to believe that Rose didn't want him anymore. That was the only way we'd have success.

"What's going on?" Summer took both her hands on the sides of my face and tugged me until I was staring into her glittering eyes. "You can tell me anything. Really, you can."

Feeling her softness against me and my eyes wandering over her anxious face, I had a moment of clarity. I could trust her.

"Summer, Dad and I did something...something that probably affected Noah's feelings toward Rose."

Her face dropped.

"Go on," she urged quietly, removing her hands from my face but not leaving my lap. I guessed I had a few more minutes of her sitting on me before she was shrieking and heading for the door.

"The day that Dad kidnapped Rose from the parking lot, Noah came by that night with some other people from the community. There was this one old dude with him. I think he was the bishop or someone."

Summer interrupted. "Was he scary-looking?"

"Yeah, I guess so. I didn't have a great view from the corner of the window." I had no clue what difference it made.

"Yep, that's the bishop, then."

Getting back on track, I said, "Dad and I knew that Noah wouldn't let up on Rose unless he thought that she didn't want him anymore."

"What do you mean?"

I sighed in disgust with myself and Dad. "It was a shitty thing to do, but we did it for Rose. It was the only way to get the two of them separated, so she could move on with her life the way it was supposed to be."

Summer's voice held a trace of panic, and I figured she already knew, but she asked, anyway. "What are you saying, Sam? What did you do?"

I locked my eyes on hers. "Justin wrote the letter. Not Rose at all. She doesn't know a thing about it. My kid brother wrote the letter to look like Rose's handwriting under Dad's direction. And mine."

I waited for her wrath to come, but instead, after several uncomfortable seconds, she sighed. "So this means that Rose never dumped Noah, right?"

I nodded.

"And, Noah, thinking that Rose didn't want him, moved on with his life and hooked up with the perfect Amish girl—and Rose, thinking that Noah didn't want her, because of what he told me, landed in Hunter's lap. But Noah only said the things he did to me cause of his hurt feelings that Rose had left him... which she didn't."

Her rambling was a good thing—I think. At least she wasn't yelling at me for being a jackass.

"Sam, you have to talk to Noah, and quickly," Summer pleaded. She leaned into me, nearly jumping out of her skin.

"No—the last thing I want is for him to go hunt her down and drag her back into the nineteenth century with him."

Summer's jaw set, and she pulled back. "You can't just let him go and marry that other girl believing that Rose doesn't love him—because she does. And he loves her, too."

"I sure as hell can. I got what I wanted, and so did Dad and Justin. Rose is back. That's all that matters. I'm not doing anything to mess things up now." Before Summer could attack, I said, "Look, Noah's perfectly happy with this new girl. You said so yourself that she's perfect for him. And I know for a fact that Hunter loves Rose and treats her like she's a Disney princess. And Rose has fallen for him. So what's the big deal?"

Summer's voice rose to such a high level that I worried Justin would be woken from his gamer coma. "The deal is, Mr. Romance-Wrecker, that it's all a lie—a big fat *lie*. How can you go on living your life knowing that you and your Dad cut up true love?"

"Very easily—because I know it was the right thing to do."

Her eyes bulged, and I guessed I was going to have a couple of lonely weeks ahead of me, but I felt fairly certain that our relationship had matured to the point that my little sister's love life wouldn't disrupt it forever.

I began to change my mind when I heard Summer's next words.

"You listen to me, buddy. Either you're going to tell Noah the whole truth, and let destiny have her way...or I'm going to do it for you. The difference between the two options is that if I'm the one that has to get the job done—" she breathed out with deliberation and promise "—then it's over between us. Do you hear me, Sam Cameron? There'll be no more kissing and feeling—nothing. And I keep my promises."

I wouldn't have taken any other girl seriously, but this one I did. Summer's face was set in grim determination. She wasn't kidding.

I either set my sister up for a life of servitude and misery, or I lost the girl of my dreams.

This time the choice was easy.

Sitting in my truck in the Millers' driveway gave me some time to think, weighing down my mood even further. The light drizzle wasn't helping matters, either. It was as if Mother Nature was against me. Plus, I got the creepy feeling that most of the Amish family was peering out from the windows spying on me. It was probably to be expected with the cryptic answer I gave to the little boys who'd come out to see what I wanted.

It wasn't any of their business, anyway.

I wanted to get the conversation over with and go my merry way. Maybe, when the deed was done—and with a little sweet-talking—my girl would come over and hang out with me that night.

The fact that Summer was convinced that my dad was the grim reaper wasn't going to help my life, either. My first priority was getting things patched up myself with her, though. Later, I'd worry about the family dynamics. And there was still Rose to consider.

At least Summer had agreed to put the ball in Noah's court. He could do with the information what he wanted. No need getting Rose riled up for nothing if the dude was going to stay happily engaged to his new squeeze—which was what I believed would happen, anyway.

Summer had a different prediction, but I could only pray that she wasn't right.

The old work truck coming up the driveway got my attention. It was showtime.

Amos and Noah stood in the rain for a minute looking in my direction before Noah broke away, coming toward me alone.

I blew out the air I'd been holding in. I really hadn't wanted to talk to the dad also. Dealing with Noah was quite enough.

Noah opened the passenger door, and without leaning in, he asked, and rather rudely I might add, "What do you want?"

"I need to talk to you."

Noah half laughed. "I'm busy."

I watched the water dripping from the side of his outdated hat. Damn, I was already in a sucky mood, and his arrogance was pressing my last nerve. "It's important."

I could tell he was still ready to bolt, so I added, making a mental deliberation that I wasn't going to beg him, "It's about Rose. You need to hear me out."

Uncertainty flashed across his features, but after looking off into the rainy field for a couple of seconds, he climbed in.

The water belting the outside of the truck obscured the world from view, and within seconds the windows were fogged over from our breath. It was clear that neither one of us was anxious to talk to the other. I must admit, if I were setting up a movie scene, this would be a good one for the final showdown.

"What's so important that you'd hang around in the rain waiting for me to get home from work?" Noah asked with narrowed eyes. It was obvious the guy was good-looking, but I still couldn't fathom what my sister saw in him.

"I came here to give you some information that might change your mind about your wedding. I really hope it doesn't, because from what I hear, you've found yourself a real nice Amish girl to settle down with."

"Just spit out what you came here to say. I don't have time for you and your mind games."

I hesitated. I'd already thought of a million ways I could tell him the truth, but none seemed to elicit the outcome that I wanted. How could I tell him that Rose never dumped him, and *not* have the guy sniffing after her all over again?

"Is Rose okay?" There was a change to his voice, as if his mind had suddenly come alive with possibilities for my visit.

Damn. I could tell by the tone of his voice, he still had feelings for my sister.

"Rose is fine. Actually, she's more than okay. She's been dating a good buddy of mine, and they've become really close."

Noah's voice roughened instantly. "Why is that my concern? Did you come over here to rub Rose's loose relationships in my face?"

"Hey, don't make insinuations about her. First you want to marry my sister, and then several months later you're engaged to some other chick. You should talk, *stud.*"

I tried to control my voice, and I didn't punch him, which showed my patience with the guy. When his hand hit the handle, and he was ready to exit the conversation, I stopped him.

"Wait. Don't leave until you've heard me out." Noah's eyes snapped fire at me. But he stilled his body, waiting. I thought of Summer's sweet face and found the reason to go on.

"Rose didn't write that letter."

Noah's brown eyes widened, and his mouth dropped open. "The handwriting was hers—I know her writing," he said defensively.

I shook my head. "It was Justin's handwriting in the note to you. Dad and I encouraged him to do it. He has that same kind of artsy doodling style that Rose has. He missed Rose as much as Dad and I did, but he was less verbal about it. We told him what to write and he did it, with the extra incentive of finally being allowed to get online for Xbox Live. You were tricked by a thirteen-year-old with an addiction to the game world."

I watched Noah digest the information, his face staring out at the watery world.

"She didn't go to the city on her own?" he asked carefully.

"No, man—Dad forced her to go live with our Aunt Debbie. She sure didn't want to."

After a couple of minutes, his silence began getting on my nerves. It meant that he was thinking hard, which probably didn't bode well for my sister.

In a last-ditch effort to interrupt the inevitable outcome, I said, "Noah, sounds like you got a great thing going with your new woman...and Rose is happy with Hunter. Let it go. The two of you were never meant to be together, anyway. It was just a mistake."

Noah's head snapped at me, his eyes becoming slits. But he didn't say a word. Instead, he grabbed the handle and flung the door open. He jumped out into the storm, slamming the door without a backward glance.

The seat he vacated was still wet from his body, my only clue that the conversation had been real. Clicking on the windshield wipers, I caught one last view of Noah before he entered his house.

There was bound to be some interesting discussion in there tonight. I revved the engine, letting Noah slip away from my mind. After all, I hopefully had a date with my little redhead, and I didn't want to be late.

Only time would tell what kind a blowout would come from my confession. Till then, I wasn't going to lose sleep over it.

31

Rose

I pressed my forehead with my fingertips, trying to force the answers in. *God, I hated trig.* The warm sun shining through the window on to my paper made it even worse. I wanted to be at the stable, riding Lady in the arena on this beautiful spring day.

The past few days of straight rain had given me some serious cabin fever. It figured, the gray skies finally broke up, and I was stuck alone in the house doing homework.

The tangy smell of the daffodils below the window wove together with that of the drying pavement in front of the house to bring on a wave of nostalgia. I loved springtime. Closing my eyes, I let the sound of the birds twittering to each other fill my head.

Just a few more questions and I could climb into my pickup and head to the barn. I couldn't help but smile that I finally had my license—and my own wheels. Opening my eyes up, I gazed through the window at the red truck in the driveway and grinned.

Guess Dad finally did trust me.

Probably the dinner a couple of weeks ago with Hunter had helped with Dad's lightening-up process. The fact that Hunter

was doing pre-med classes and willing to transfer his schol-
arships to play football for the Ohio Bearcats had convinced
Dad of our seriousness as a couple.

Checking my phone, I saw that if I worked quickly I might
even have enough time to hang out with Amanda and Brittany that evening, watch a movie and pig out on junk food.
Since Aunt Debbie and Uncle Jason were away for a couple of
nights at a conference, I'd welcome the company.

It was a shame that Hunter was in Meadowview and on
strict orders from Dad and Aunt Debbie not to come for a visit
this weekend. And way too bad that he was on a mission to
impress everyone in my family with his good manners and
behavior.

I worked the last questions out the best I could and slammed
the book closed. I had the twinge of worry that they were all
screwed up, but the sunshine was calling me and I had to listen. Grabbing my purse and hoodie for later when the sun
went down, I breezed out the front door.

Even with my sunglasses on, I needed to shield my eyes
from the rays. That's when the out-of-place vehicle parked in
the cul-de-sac caught my attention.

Why was an old work truck parked in front of the house?

My heart froze, and a chill went up my arms even though
the warm breeze was caressing them. The vehicle looked just
like the Millers' work truck—and the old guy driving it looked
just like Mr. Denton.

My breathing stopped altogether when I heard the truck
door slam shut, and I saw Noah walk around the front. He
stopped beside the driver's window and leaned in for a few seconds before stepping back and watching the truck drive away.

Then he turned around.

The world went dizzy, and the last thing I felt was the hard,
cold cement of the porch as I crashed down to it.

★ ★ ★

"Rose. Rose. Wake up. Please talk to me—or I'm going to call Mr. Denton to come back and take you to the hospital."

I wouldn't open my eyes.

Oh, my God—my, God. Noah was here, in the suburbs of Cincinnati, cradling my head in his lap—cooing to my limp body as if he gave a damn. What was going on? Maybe I'd hit my head and had a concussion.

I must be dreaming.

I risked it and peeked through my eyelashes for a second before slamming them shut tightly again. He was there—and he'd caught me looking at him.

"Rose, stop acting like a ninny and open your eyes. I just saw you do it, so I know you're awake. Come on..." He fluctuated between pleading and threatening, causing me some major indecision.

When he picked me up like a child, I finally popped my eyes open.

"I can walk just fine, thank you." Who did he think he was, picking me and carrying me around?

"I better carry you in. You might have a fractured skull or something." He was strong enough to easily hold me with one arm and his fully recovered knee, while he pushed the door open with his other hand.

Then he had the nerve to say, "You know, you really should lock the door when you leave. This might not be the inner city, but there sure are a lot of folks around here, and some of them might like to sneak in here and wait for a pretty girl like you to return."

"Put me down—right now."

I squirmed, but he wouldn't drop me. Instead, my movements seem to tighten his grip.

Finally, after making a sweep of the downstairs, he deposited me onto the couch. He sat down beside me, flinging his arm over the back of the seat. Then he let his chocolate-colored eyes wander slowly over every inch of me.

My head was swimming with the impossibility of it all. That Noah was sitting only inches from me on my aunt's couch, over a hundred miles away from where he was supposed to be, had reduced my brain to mush. But that wasn't the terrifying part; the way his eyes traveled over me was. The warm explosion in my belly and the tingles shooting through me could not be denied.

I still wanted Noah like no other—even Hunter.

"What the hell are you doing here?" I wasn't going to let him turn me into a puddle. I wasn't going there again.

Before I could react, he reached out and took a handful of my hair and brought it to his nose. I pulled back, yanking my hair—and it hurt—away from him.

"I'm so pleased that you didn't cut your beautiful hair. I was so worried that you had." His eyes settled onto mine, calm and confident.

He went to touch my face, and I swatted his hand away and stood up. Noah was in sync with me and rose at the same time.

"I'm sorry. I understand that this must be a shock for you to have me showing up out of the blue."

"That's putting it mildly," I said. "What do you want from me? Why did you just get dropped off like...like you were invited?" My brain was frazzled, and my body was attacking me from the inside, wanting to fling itself into Noah's arms.

God, I wanted to melt into him so bad it was killing me.

"Haven't you talked to Sam at all in the last couple of days?"

"No. Sam and I aren't in the habit of chatting on a daily basis. What does he have to do with any of this?" I searched his face for answers, only to see a slight smirk rise up.

"Well, then, this might be a bit of a shock to you. Let's sit back down so that we can talk." He reached out for me, and I jumped away from him and ran.

It was stupid, I know. Maybe back when he'd gotten out of the hospital I could have outrun him, but under normal circumstances, compared to his perfectly muscled construction worker body, I was a slowpoke.

I did manage to clear the stairs and make it to my room before he was on me. I didn't get the door shut, though.

"Stop acting like an infant. This is serious. We need to talk."

He grabbed my body, putting me into a wrestler's hold, and lifted me onto the bed, where he then deposited me.

He sat down facing me, too close for my taste—or safety from myself.

"Rose, clear your mind of all this nonsense and just listen to me. Your brother came by two days ago to talk to me. I guess he had a revelation of conscience or something, because he admitted doing a terrible thing to us."

I stared at him, waiting. I couldn't speak, I could hardly breathe.

"He told me that the letter that your father gave me the night you were taken was a fake. They had forged the thing to make me think that you didn't want me. That you left me on your own free will."

"What letter— They who?" The desperation that had appeared in his eyes scared the crap out of me, but his words, they triggered an understanding of the reason that he hadn't come to my rescue—that they had all abandoned me—it made sense.

"Your father— He had Justin write a letter that basically said that you had decided that the Amish world wasn't right for you. It said that you didn't want me to contact you—that you wanted to move on with your English life."

The tears began to trickle, but I sucked them back in. "My dad did that—he lied to you about me not wanting you?"

"Yeah, and Sam was in on it. That's why I never tried to contact you. I thought you had decided that I was no good for you, that the Amish life was not what you wanted." He took my hands and moved in closer to me. Close enough that I could feel his warm breath on my face.

"Rose, sweetheart, if I had known that you were forced to leave, I would have come for you. Like I did today, I would have hired a driver and come and gotten you, taken you away into hiding somewhere until you turned eighteen."

His eyes were so intense; his hair fell about his head in a beautiful mess. The sight of him caused my heart to thump faster in my chest and liquid warmth to spread out to every inch of my flesh.

My mind suddenly processed that we were completely alone. No chaperones for miles and miles, no one to spy on us—or stop us from doing *anything*.

I had missed his touches and his kisses so much.

"You would have done that for me? Left your family and community to take me away like that?"

His answer was significant in a way that I didn't even understand myself, and I caught my breath until he spoke.

"Darling, I would have gone to the edge of the world to keep you with me. The only reason I gave you up is because I thought that's what you wanted me to do. I believed that you really wanted to go back to your old life, and I wouldn't force you to stay with me if you didn't want to."

The dam of my emotions broke, and my tears flowed freely. "I needed you so badly. I waited for you to come, but you didn't. And then Summer told me what you'd said to her—and I gave up. I gave up on us."

"I'm so sorry. I never stopped loving you. Even though I was angry, I couldn't stop. I tried to convince myself that I didn't have to have you in my life—that I was better off without you, but just under the surface you were always there. Every night I dreamed of you and no other."

Noah's eyes were wet when he crushed me into his chest. I buried my face in his shirt, holding on to him for dear life. I'd dreamed of this moment too many times to count, but I never thought it would happen. His hands on me felt real, but I still wondered in a far corner of my brain if I was imagining it.

He sure felt real when his mouth finally smashed into mine, his tongue urgently spreading my lips and entering my mouth. With unthinking instinct, I responded, pressing against him with my heart full of thankfulness that I was once again in his strong arms.

"God, I've missed you...please let me touch you—*please*," Noah begged as he gently pushed me back.

He didn't need to plead with me. I wanted him—all of him.

My tongue kept up with his, my hands roaming over his body until I freed him from his stupid shirt.

I only caught a glimpse of his muscled chest before his head blocked my view as he bent down to kiss and lick parts of my neck. I didn't need to see his body when my hands were my eyes. While he kissed and probed me with the fierceness of a caged animal finally set free, I rubbed his hard belly with my hands, loving the feel of his strength.

It didn't take long for him to free me of my shirt. When Noah unclasped my bra and pulled it away from me, I sighed. He moved back just enough to look at me, and although I probably should have blushed, I don't think I did.

It felt so comfortable, so right. We belonged together. There was no doubt of that in my mind anymore.

As Noah started on the top button of my jeans, I knew I wouldn't stop him. There was no need to stop now.

The hell with everyone who'd tried to keep us apart—

They had failed.

32

Noah

How could I feel exhausted yet completely awake at the same time? Staring down at Rose's sleeping face; her mouth slightly open, her eyes fluttering from a dream, I was overcome with an incredible love for her. The intenseness of it all squeezed at my insides, almost to the point of pain.

Was love supposed to hurt like this?

I let my eyes travel down lower to where the blanket was slipped back, exposing her bare breast. The sight sent a flash of heat surging through me, and I quickly pulled the cover up, hiding her forbidden body from my view.

I sighed, laying my head on the pillow as images of the night before reared up in my head. I tried to shake the thoughts away, knowing full well that if I didn't change direction right quick, I'd be waking Rose.

I hadn't planned to make love to her, but finally having her in my arms again had completely undone me. I couldn't stop the hurricane of desire that had taken hold of us both.

It would have been impossible.

But now, lying beside my love, with the shimmer of sunshine streaming in through the flowery curtain, I worried about what I'd done. It wasn't just about breaking an oath to the church or God. There was the real possibility that I'd gotten Rose with child.

Glancing at her angelic face, I groaned, shutting my eyes. She wasn't ready for that kind of a responsibility yet. Rose was still in need of babying herself. But I had to make plans just in case.

Father had allowed me to begin keeping my carpentry paychecks a few months back, so I had a few thousand saved up. Not enough to move out straightaway, but enough to build on.

I was lucky that Father had been so generous with me; most of the young men in the community had to wait until they turned twenty or twenty-one to be allowed to save their own earnings. Up until then, we had to give about ninety percent of our paychecks over to our parents. It was a situation that most accepted easily enough until we were ready to settle down with our own wives. Then the prospect of having to wait an extra year to have the money could strain a parent/child relationship.

Maybe I was jumping the gun. I understood the cycle of mating. There was a good chance that Rose wasn't even fertile right now. But, if she was, and all the times we… Ack, she would definitely be pregnant.

My mind started racing again, thinking of the possibilities, until a name popped into my head, causing a totally different kind of pain. *Constance.*

What was I going to do about her?

I'd been so intent on finding and talking to Rose that I had totally forgotten about Constance—the girl I was supposed to marry in just a few months.

I had committed a terrible sin. Even though I knew deep down that I didn't really love Constance, I was willing to enter a marriage with her just to erase Rose from my mind—and hurt my ex-girlfriend.

The little groaning, growl that came from Rose as she stretched and rolled closer to me set off all the bells my body needed to jump from the bed.

I quickly found my pants and pulled them on, not taking any chances of falling from grace yet again.

Feeling a little safer, I sat on the side of the bed, while I put my shirt on. I knew what I had to do now, marry Rose as soon as possible. No more games.

Nothing—or no one—was coming between us ever again.

"What are you doing?" Rose said, tucking the blanket up under her chin, as if she was suddenly shy.

I couldn't help smiling and shaking my head in amusement. She was so sweet. I'd already seen every inch of her—and now she was going to hold out, like a prim and proper girl?

I don't think so…

I bent down and kissed her lips softly, like a butterfly landing on a flower. Just when her mouth began to open and her hands got behind my head, I pulled away laughing.

"Golly, didn't you get enough of that last night?"

She pouted back at me, settling onto her pillow.

"Not really—you know, my aunt and uncle don't get back until tomorrow morning sometime. Which means you and I have a whole day together." She smiled seductively at me, and I almost climbed back into bed.

Instead, I got up and began pacing the small space. I only half noticed the light greens and pinks of the room, even though I focused on the drapes and upholstery, trying desperately not to look at Rose.

"Rose, we need to be talking, *not*…doing other stuff right now."

"Aww."

I risked a serious face in her direction. "I mean it. This is too important to play around with."

She sat up, taking the covers with her, thank God. "What?"

Had she lost some brain cells during our separation? I waved out my hands. "This, us. What we're going to do."

Seeing her retain the flirty look, not really paying me much mind, I rolled on. "I heard you have a new boyfriend. What about him? Huh? Have you been warming him up at night, too?"

I don't know where the words came from, but when I let them fly, a stormy cloud erased all signs of friendliness on Rose's features.

I'd just gone too far.

"If you're too stupid to know that you were the first guy I ever did it with, then it's your problem," Rose shouted.

I crossed the room and grabbed her shoulders, hating the look of hurt I'd put into her beautiful eyes.

"I didn't mean it. I'm sorry. I know it was your first time. Even without the evidence on the sheet, *I'd know it*."

Her eyes were still narrowed, threateningly. "Then why say it?"

"Because I'm jealous, I want you all to myself—like before. I want to marry you and have children with you. But…you might not feel the same way about me anymore."

I searched her face, which had softened, although the look of concentration there scared the hell out of me.

"Rose, will you still be my wife?"

She bubbled with laughter and flung her arms around me, forgetting the blanket. I struggled to hug her and pull the material up around her.

"I never stopped loving you. And, I think I proved that I wanted you several times last night…." My face flushed and I had to look away. "But what about your life? Summer said you were pretty serious about some new Amish girl. What's that all about?"

Her voice held the same jealous tilt that I was sure mine had. We were both in the same boat—neither one of us could stand the idea of the other being with someone else.

Because we weren't supposed to be—God wanted us together.

I breathed out. I had to be honest with Rose from the get-go. No more lies between us.

"It's worse than that. I, uh, well…asked her to marry me." I struggled with the words and then watched her face drop in disbelief.

She tried to shake me away, but I held her firmly. "You've got to understand that I thought you had moved on—and that we weren't ever going to be together."

"But to go out and propose to another girl in just a few months—that's insane," she shrieked, but stopped her struggling to continue staring at me with a gap-mouthed expression.

"It's different for us. You already know that. Us Amish, marry young. We don't shack up and live in sin for years before taking the chance on a relationship."

She set her mouth tight and scrunched her eyes, saying, "So you think it's better to run off and marry a girl you don't really love just to have sex?"

How she managed to turn everything around was beyond me. "It's not like that at all. I was lonely and angry. I was willing to get together with Constance to help me forget about you."

"So, Constance is her name, huh?" The focused wrath that was shooting from her eyes startled me.

I pulled Rose's face only inches from mine and said, "You are the only woman that I have ever loved—or will love—ever. I'll forget about your relationship with the football player, if you can erase mine with Constance from your head."

"But I'm not engaged to Hunter," she shouted.

"Like I said, you English do things different. But at least I didn't marry her."

She quieted for a minute. I was too afraid to say anything that might get her riled again. I really didn't enjoy fighting with her, but the alternative, with her all naked and us alone was something I was trying to avoid.

"Okay, I see where you're coming from. What are you going to do about this chick?"

I gathered my wits and said, "The same thing that you're going to do with your boyfriend. Break up as nicely as possible, *and right away.* I don't want that jerk coming around you any more than you want me spending time with Constance."

"Hunter is not a jerk. He helped me out when I was devastated over you," she said firmly, but with less venom than earlier.

A powerful wave of hatred toward the guy crashed over me. I would not share Rose with anyone.

I said in a low voice that meant business, "I will not tolerate you continuing a friendship with this man. You have a choice to make. It's either me or him."

Something passed over her features that stilled my heart. She had feelings for the guy, I was sure of it. Even though I had proposed to Constance, I had no serious connection to her—other than respecting her for being a good woman.

"Noah, you're the one I love and want to be with. It's just going to be a little difficult telling Hunter. He's going to be shocked, and I don't want to hurt him," she said softly.

"And you don't think that Constance is going to be heartbroken? She's been planning a wedding, for God's sake. Think about what I'm going to have to deal with."

I could see it written on her gorgeous face that she didn't really care much about Constance's feelings. Rose was the love of my life, but she was also not the type of girl to give another female any leeway with her man.

Before she got the chance to answer me, the beep, beep of a car horn made us both jump. I moved to the window and pulled the curtain aside just enough to see the work truck at the curb.

"Who is it?" Rose squeaked as she leaped out of the bed with the blanket wrapped around her as if she were in a cocoon.

When the bell rang, I knew he was already at the door.

"It's Mr. Denton," I said with more calm than I was feeling.

"What arrangements did you make with him?" Rose disappeared into the closet, and I watched her shoot the blanket out. The thought of her bouncing around in there, trying to get her clothes on in a rush, totally distracted me for a few seconds.

"Ah...I told him just to leave me here until...I called him," I stammered out.

Rose's voice came through the closet door at the same time the bell rang again. "Do your parents know you came here?"

"No."

She finally popped out from behind the door with her hands fumbling on her zipper and her face as white as a ghost.

"They're going to kill you." She pinched her hair, pulling it back in anxiety, and said, "And, they're going to hate me forever. I thought... Well, I didn't really think much about it last night, but didn't you have a plan? Some story about going to visit relatives in Iowa or something?"

I crossed the room to her, wanting to soothe the crazed expression from her face. "Indiana, not Iowa—I don't have any kin that I know of in Iowa."

I got her in my arms and held her tightly. She rested her

face against my chest, and I swear I could feel the hammering of her heart through our clothes and skin.

"It's going to be all right. We're together now and that's all that matters." I lifted her chin and looked down at her. I wanted to reassure her that everything would be okay—even though I knew we still had a difficult road ahead of us.

"I'm going to have to go home with Mr. Denton. The poor guy probably rented a room last night—honestly, I forgot all about him. I imagine Dad's been calling the old guy's cell phone all night.

"So here's what we're going to do—just listen to me. I'm going to talk to Father and Mother and tell them what your family did to us. I believe that they will support us getting back together under the circumstances that we were torn apart. I plan to explain things to Constance as soon as possible." I took a breath and continued. "I want you to give me your new cell phone number, and I'll call you tonight. In the meantime, you need to break up with that je…guy right away. All right?"

Rose's little face looked frightened, and I couldn't help myself from bending down and spreading her lips with my own. God, she tasted so good.

The bell ringing again made her mumble into my mouth, "Uh-huh."

I hated leaving her again, but I had issues to resolve at home before we could finally begin our life together.

As I held Rose's body against mine, one thing was for sure, though—I would never allow her to be taken from me again.

33

Rose

I sat on the bed feeling more alone ever before. Flopping over, I buried my face in the pillow, breathing in Noah's scent that lingered on the material.

A smile played on my lips as I thought about the night before. It had been more than perfect. Besides a couple of awkward moments, everything had been just as I'd dreamed it would be—only better.

Sighing, I hugged the pillow, wishing it was Noah. It might be days or even weeks before I saw him again. I missed him already, and he'd only been gone a few minutes. Now that he was back in my life, what would I do without him?

The blissful sensations my body was experiencing could only last so long. Already, angry thoughts were trickling into my mind about Dad and Sam—and Constance. I wasn't sure how to deal with Dad. The fact that he'd actually corrupt my little brother into committing forgery and lying about it was incredible. Obviously, he was serious about me not being Amish.

What would he do when I told him I was marrying Noah? Probably disown me.

Sam was easy. I'd punch him the next time I saw him. Although my anger toward him was not raging the way it was with Dad—at least he'd come through in the end and 'fessed up. I figured Summer had something to do with it.

Scattering my thoughts, I decided I would have to call Summer to tell her about me and Noah. She would probably be upset with me, but then again, I doubted she'd be able to hold out much longer with Sam putting the charm on thick.

Then there was this new Amish girl I hadn't even met. What was Constance like?

Summer had said that she'd heard the girl was pretty, but shy. Since the Amish didn't like broadcasting their wedding dates early, I understood why Summer hadn't heard that news yet. Or maybe if she had, she'd been reluctant to tell me, the good friend that she was.

Constance didn't really much matter as long as Noah dumped her butt in a hurry. Still, it would be pretty uncomfortable at the church gatherings being around her, that's for sure.

Thoughts of dumping brought Hunter to mind. I really didn't want to hurt him. He'd been so patient with me. And there were other things, like the way we related to each other and the fact that we could hang out together without a chaperone. I'd gotten used to going to the movies and concerts with him, doing all the normal stuff that teenagers did with their boyfriends. I could be myself with Hunter, literally let my hair down, and be me.

Not so much with Noah. Did all those things matter when you loved a guy?

I rolled over and stared at the ceiling, sighing to the empty room. *Could a girl love two guys at once?* I knew I loved Noah—with all my heart. But I definitely felt something for Hunter, too; what, I wasn't sure, but something.

Just as I was reaching for the phone to call Summer, hoping that she'd be awake at nine o'clock on a Saturday morning, the phone rang, shocking my heart for a second, until I saw the name—*Hunter*.

I stared at the phone while a battle took place inside of me. Should I answer it or let him leave a message?

The next ring got me, and even though I was slammed with guilt about Noah, I picked it up and said, "Hey."

"Hey, baby, how ya doing?" Hunter's voice was upbeat and fresh, as if it were the spring air pressing against the window.

My voice froze in my throat. At that moment, I knew what I had to do. The love I had for Noah was all-consuming. I couldn't walk away from him if he wanted me.

I had to be with Noah.

Forcing my voice out, I said, "I'm okay. What about you?"

"What's wrong? You sound funny. Are you really all right?" Hunter's tone had changed instantly. I couldn't pretend for long with him—he knew me too well.

"Uh, I'm having a problem...that I need to talk to you about."

I hated this part. It would kill me to do this to him.

"Do you want me come over? I will. I'll leave right now and be there before noon."

Even in my tattered state, I had to smile. He knew that my aunt and uncle were gone for the weekend and that a visit from him was off-limits.

"You know that would be against the law," I said, loosening up a bit.

"I could sneak in and out without anyone the wiser. I wouldn't expect anything—you know—physical, or anything like that. We could just hang out and watch a movie or something. I hate that you're there all alone."

I didn't know if it was the concern in his voice or his words that made me feel as if I were about to cry. He was worried about my virtue—and it was all gone now, given away to another guy.

Hunter pressed. "Well, what do you think?"

"You can't do that, Hunter. I, ah, have Amanda and Brittany coming over, so I won't be alone. Don't worry about me. I'm fine."

"No, there's something up. I can hear it in your voice. You're upset. *Why?*"

I tossed the die in my head and went with it. "Noah came to visit last night."

I popped the words out quickly, before I could change my mind.

There was silence, horrible silence for a minute, and then he said, "What did he want?"

I took a deep breath and plunged in. "Dad and Sam set us up, Hunter. They faked a note, had Justin write it, and said that it was from me. Noah thought that I didn't want to be Amish, that I didn't want him." I rambled on like a mad woman. "That's why he never contacted me or called. That's why he hooked up with the Amish chick and got engaged."

"Does this mean everything has changed for you? Are you going back to him, Rose? Is that what you want?"

Hunter's voice was more combative than I'd expected, making it easier to be tough on him.

"I'm sorry, but I never stopped loving him."

"He's not right for you. You will regret it, if you go back to him. You will be making a huge mistake with your life," Hunter said with a certainty that bugged me. He sounded like Dad or Sam. I was tired of people telling me what was good or bad for my life. It was my life.

"Look, I like you a lot, but I can't deny my feelings for Noah. I can't change that I love him."

I heard him snort into the phone, and when he did speak, anger was drizzled into his words. "When I told you that I loved you, I meant it. I wasn't fooling around, playing games with you. You won't be happy with Noah in the end—that I'm sure of. But if you have to go and ruin your life, I won't stop you, because unfortunately, you need to learn this the hard way. I'll be waiting for you when you change your mind."

Then he hung up.

I looked at the phone, shocked. I knew he wouldn't be thrilled with the news, but I never imagined that he'd be so upset about it.

I rolled up tight into a ball and began to cry. I had Noah back, and Hunter didn't mean that much to me—so why did I feel terrible, as if my guts were being pulled apart?

The feeling of having forgotten something trickled into my mind slowly and then hit me with the force of a train. I bounced out of bed, racing for the door.

I was scheduled to work at the clinic that morning. Even if I'd left ten minutes ago, I'd still be late.

My crazy soap opera life was going to get me fired.

Running out the front door, I decided that I didn't have time to slow down to lock it. Noah was way too paranoid. Who would wander into a house in a nice tract like this in broad daylight?

I tried to slow my movements down as I backed out of the driveway. The last thing I needed was a speeding ticket.

Taking a deep breath, I put on my game face. At least a day at the clinic might help me forget about my problems, for a while, anyway.

I only half noticed the older model, dark Monte Carlo parked across from the house. Something about it struck me as odd, making me look in the rearview mirror at the car.

Strange...I'd never seen that car before. I slowed my truck down and thought about turning around, but only for a second. I didn't have time to go back. The creepy feeling left me as I got farther away from the car.

Turning on the radio, I forgot the car and focused on my driving—and the faces of Noah and Hunter.

34

Noah

Father's head hung like he'd been shot in the chest. Mother was standing at the kitchen sink, her hands braced on the ceramic, her eyes focused on the drain.

It wasn't that bad. You'd think I'd just told them someone had died.

When Father finally spoke, his voice was deflated, almost empty. "Son, what have you gone and done to yourself now? Can you not be content with the fine woman that you've asked to be your wife? Why must you stir up the devil's games?"

"But this wasn't my fault—or Rose's. We were doing everything right, and her father and brother ruined it for us." When Father's head snapped up and I had his gaze, I forged on. "I never stopped loving her. *You know that.* Why would I abandon her now?" My own voice was steady. I'd already made up my mind. Regardless of whether my family supported me, I'd have Rose as my wife, and no other.

"Because it's not the right thing to do—you're committed to Constance now. Both you and Rose moved on with your lives and discovered that there were other people in the world that could fulfill your needs. How many girls' hearts are you going to break before you get it through your thick skull that Rose is not the one for you?"

His words shot to my heart, waking my anger. "I wouldn't have fooled with any other girls if it weren't for the fact that so many people have been meddling with Rose and me from the beginning. But none of you succeeded—we still love each other."

"I don't doubt your love for her, Noah. I never did. But this is about what is in your best interest. Constance will make the perfect wife for you, and she'll be happy and complacent in that role. With Rose, you'll always have trouble in your life. She will never be content with our Plain ways."

"She was doing just fine until her father took her away." I slammed my hand on the solid oak table, the sound waking Mother from her fixation with the drain.

Mother turned and said, "I love Rose also. I understand how deep your feelings go with that girl, but *how can you do this to Constance?* She is the woman that you owe your allegiance to now."

Mother's voice was sad and pleading at the same time. It hit me how much my decisions had affected my folks, had hurt them, and I felt guilt well up inside of me. But, regardless of those feelings of remorse about my actions, I would not be deterred from Rose this time. Father and Mother must understand that Rose was the only woman for me.

I took a breath, and after swallowing my fear, I told them, "Rose may be with child—my child."

The silence in the kitchen was complete. The warm breeze ruffled the curtains, pushing the smell of the lilac flowers from the bush outside to my nostrils. Somehow, the awakenings of nature after the long winter made everything seem a little less drastic. The hot season was approaching, the time that reminded me so much of Rose. I could handle anything that my parents threw at me…as long as I had Rose in the end.

Mother sat down, shaking her head feebly. Father, on the other hand, was pumped with fresh energy at my announcement.

"How could you do this to her—how could you do this to yourself? You've gone and made a proper mess of it this time," he said, rubbing his beard as if he wanted to pull it off.

My mother's calm voice pulled my focus back to her. "This news changes everything then, Amos. Noah has an obligation to take care of his child…and its mother."

Father barked, "We won't know if there is a child for weeks yet."

Mother stood up and faced Father with such a hard face that I leaned back a little.

I hadn't seen Mother with that kind of a look directed at Father since the time Jacob nearly got killed when the team of four Haflingers got away from him out in the cornfield. Jacob had only been nine at the time, and Mother had been fit to be tied that Father had given him the reins.

"You listen to me, Amos Miller. Noah has taken that girl's purity and he must now marry her." Glancing at me, she added, "And it's a right good thing for you, Noah, that you're so crazy in love with her, because as far as I'm concerned, you'll be spending the rest of your life with Rose."

Father sighed in resignation. He wasn't going to argue with Mother when she was in such a state. He knew better.

The door burst open. Jacob came in breathing hard. Katie was on his heels, dragging Ella by the arm behind her.

"What's amiss?" Father was as startled as I was when he spoke to Jacob.

Jacob took a second to catch his breath and looked between

Father and me before he said, "Ella just told Katie something that I think you should know. It's about Rose—and her safety."

"What's going on?" I shouted, confusion making my insides clench.

"Hold on, Noah. Jacob, you must calm yourself and explain." Father moved closer to Jacob, his body tight as a bow.

Jacob nodded to Katie, who finally let go of Ella's struggling arm, probably figuring that the rest of us would run Ella down if she made a move for the open door. Even in my anxious state, I couldn't help but notice that Katie looked plumper in the face and around the middle. *She was pregnant...* and I hadn't a clue until that moment. It was the type of thing that Amish women kept quiet about until they bloated to the point of no denial, but shucks, you'd think someone would have filled me in on the news.

It was Katie who spoke, the friction in her voice touchable. "Ella came to me, just a little while ago. She said that she did something that she wished she hadn't. I didn't pay much mind to her. After all, Ella is always having her drama, but when she said that she'd been talking to Levi Zook on the phone, I began to listen. Somehow, he'd contacted her from that place he's at." She paused, glancing back disapprovingly at her sister before continuing. "It seems that Levi was obsessed with Rose. Always asking Ella what she was doing."

When Katie paused again, Father became impatient, saying, "How does this affect Rose's safety—? Out with it, girl."

Katie composed herself and said, "A while back, at the church service you held here last, Ella had seen Rose's address in Cincinnati..."

My heart stopped, and I moved toward the door, but Father's hand shot out, holding me back while Katie finished speaking. "...and she called Levi, and told him things about Rose." Katie's voice was almost hysterical now and Jacob closed the gap, putting his arm around her, pulling her into his chest.

Mother said, "What does this mean? Why would you do such a thing, Ella?"

Ella didn't meet Mother's eyes. Instead, she talked to the floor. "I...I never did get on well with Rose. If you all remember, it was me that Noah was going to court. And then to have an Englisher come into the community and become so popular—it didn't seem right."

Ella's voice cracked, and for the first time since we were kids, real emotion poured forth from the ice princess. "But I never meant her any real harm. *I didn't*."

I shouted, "What did you do, Ella? Tell us."

Ella raised her face, and tears were streaming down her cheeks. "I gave Levi her address. *Noah, he's going there.* He told me that he could study road maps on the computer at the library with no trouble at all. He said he was going to teach Rose a lesson for setting him up."

My heart froze—the chill crawling all over me.

I looked at Father, who met my eyes at the same time. "I have to go to her."

"Yes. And I'll go with you," Father said, picking up his hat and placing it on his head.

Jacob said, "But Mr. Denton has already left to haul those cows for the Yoders. He's not supposed to be back until nightfall."

"I know who to call," I told them all, my words racing as fast as my heart.

I silently prayed that we got to Rose before Levi did.

35

Rose

"Rose, come on. You need to think this out before you go doing something stupid."

Summer's voice sounded more mature than usual, but I didn't like her words much.

Watching the cars hustle by the vet clinic, I fiddled with my car keys. I didn't like driving and talking on the phone; I hadn't mastered that ability yet—thus the reason for me hanging out in the clinic parking lot for the past half hour.

"I get what you're saying, but I love him so much. How can I not be with Noah?"

"Yeah, yeah, I know. But you were doing pretty well these last few months with your new guy. You've been having fun being English again...dancing, doing your drill team, and all." Summer's voice came through the invisible wires, scratchy with frustration.

"That stuff isn't so important," I said quietly, not sure I believed myself.

"What about Hunter...don't you like him anymore—at all?"

I couldn't help but see Hunter's handsome face float into my vision. He'd been really good for me—the guy who came out of nowhere at the crisis point and helped me make it through. But was there more to it than friendship?

I didn't want to know.

"Course I still like Hunter. He's been great. But I *love* Noah. Nothing is going to change that."

"Look, Rose, all I'm saying is you should think long and hard before you jump back into the Amish community with him. Wrack you brain, and try to remember all that hard work and those dumb rules. Do you really want to live like that for the rest of your life?"

She was right.

I was conflicted. It wouldn't kill me to wait a little while, finish up my junior year in Fairfield. I wanted to follow through with the spring dance recital—and my drill team performances. The clinic needed me also.

Maybe Noah could wait a while.

"And, don't you go thinking that since you had sex with the guy, you owe him anything...'cause you don't," Summer tossed in for good measure, bringing a grin to my mouth.

"Thanks for the advice, Summer. All your worldly knowledge is very helpful." I giggled into the phone.

"Yeah, and you're lucky I'm not charging for it."

"I need to get home. I haven't taken Hope for a walk in a few days, and she's digging up all Aunt Debbie's tulips in the back yard from boredom."

"Oh, sure, drop me for the dog. I see how it is." Summer tried to sound hurt, but I could tell she was messing with me.

"My phone's about to go dead, anyway—I'll call you later on tonight. That is, if you're not busy doing something with my brother." I smirked to myself.

"Sam is in time-out, far as I'm concerned. I might allow him the pleasure of my company next weekend...so I'll be available to talk tonight. You better call me."

"Okay. Later."

When I hung up, my whole body felt lighter. Talking to Summer always brought things into perspective. She had a way of taking any problem down a couple of notches.

Turning the key and hearing the engine roar to life, butterflies spread out in my belly. Driving my truck was as fun as kissing—*almost*. I turned the radio up, listening to my favorite station and trying not to think about how Noah would handle the news that he'd have to wait a little longer for me.

What's that car still doing there?

My mood darkened when I saw the old car parked in front of the house.

Taking the initiative, I circled the cul-de-sac, cruising slowly up behind the black Monte Carlo. Strange, it had Indiana plates. Peering in as I crept by, I saw no one.

Maybe who ever owned the vehicle was visiting one of the neighbors?

I hesitated for a minute, staring at the car. I could check around the neighborhood.

No, I was just being dumb. Shaking off the weariness, I pulled into the driveway and parked.

If I planned my timing right, I could take the dog for a run, visit Lady at the barn for a few minutes and still meet up with Amanda and Brittany somewhere later tonight. Having some friends around when Noah called would be a good thing.

Slipping in the front door, I dropped my purse on the table in the foyer and headed for the kitchen. *That's odd,* I thought, when I saw the mayo and deli ham slices on the counter. I didn't remember leaving the food out—or even having a ham sandwich.

I picked up the butter knife and studied the smudge of white goo at the end of it. A little chill breezed over me. I might be dealing with a whole lot of crap right now, but I knew that I hadn't done this.

"Hello, pretty."

The voice behind me froze me to the tile floor.

My eyes saw Hope through the window, digging madly at one of my aunt's newly planted saplings, but my mind was far away—*screaming.*

This could not be happening. I knew that voice. It belonged to Levi Zook. He was in my aunt's kitchen, standing behind me. Close enough that I felt his breath on my hair.

My brain started rattling off strategies as his hand touched my hair, softly for a few seconds, and then yanking me backward with nasty force.

Just as my back hit his chest, I swiveled, trying to jab at Levi with the only weapon I had, the blunt-ended knife. He was too quick, and I suddenly recalled his hidden strength when I'd wrestled with him in the Weavers' barn.

He twisted my hand, forcing me to drop my only chance to the ground.

"Aren't you happy to see me, Rose?" Levi's voice was deceptively sweet, but his eyes were black, crazy pools. The contrast between those eyes and his pale skin made him seem not quite human.

My brain registered that his orange hair was longer, the strands clinging together with greasiness. He was wearing regular street clothes—a T-shirt with a skull that had a guitar popping out of an eye socket and plain old jeans—as if he were a normal, regular kind of guy.

He might fool some people, but I knew differently.

I'd watched enough crime shows to realize my best bet was to talk him down. And, if that didn't work out, judging by the not-really-there look on Levi's face, I was dead.

"Hey, this is a surprise. Did you drive here all by yourself?"

Only my eyes moved as I checked to see if there was another psychopath in the house.

Levi had my hands clamped tight in his own between us. Since he couldn't touch me with his fingers, he used his face instead, rubbing it alongside my cheek, as he said, "Clever girl. But that's exactly what I'd expect from you."

He buried his nose in my neck, breathing in, and then letting out a disgusting breath of enjoyment. The grossness of him touching me made me feel as if I was going to vomit. I had to swallow the hot juices that rose in my throat.

"Did you steal that car?" I hoped that my voice was steadier than the rolling of my insides.

He pulled back, his gaze focused again.

"Guess you could say I borrowed it from a friend. But that's not really important," he said, his eyes prowling over my face and body as if I were a juicy steak.

My hands were hurting, and the fact that I couldn't move much made my heart drop into my belly. I had one more idea, but I knew that if it didn't work, Levi was going to hurt me bad, so I gave the talking plan a little more time. Time for what, I wasn't sure. Maybe, Amanda would stop by…or Hunter.

How I wished that he would break the damn rules and show up with the intention of trying to win me back from Noah. *Then he could rescue me…* But that kind of thing only happened in the movies.

"What *is* important?" I tried to distract him, looking up with a friendly face, even though it was difficult.

"Seems to me that you did me a bad turn a while back—you need to make it up to me."

Levi's voice was not right. He was speaking differently now, as if he was pretending to be someone else, someone older. The craziness in his eyes had changed to an even more terrifying, hungry look.

I panicked just as his mouth slammed onto mine. He bru-tally bit at my lips, forcing my mouth open as his snakelike tongue slithered in.

The talking option was over.

Lifting my knee as fast and hard as I could, I brought it into his groin. I was too close to him to do any real damage, but I did get him to let go of my hands for just enough seconds for me to bring up my balled fist into his jaw. That separated us, giving me the space I needed to dart past him.

I was heading for the door, but he got a hold of me before I reached it. I fought with everything I had, giving Sam and Justin a mental *thank-you* for the combat training.

Clawing, swiping, kicking—but I still couldn't get him off of me. My long hair was my biggest downfall, giving Levi a flying target to grab on to and control my body with. The hair pulling hurt more than the return kicks and punches he was giving me combined.

My adrenaline was up, and even though I was in a dream-like state, the sharp jabs of pain I was feeling drove me to an anger that I'd never experienced before.

I was not going to make it easy for Levi.

When his arm was close enough, the one connected to the hand that had my hair jerked high, I bit down. Tasting his salty blood in my mouth, I let go and spit at the same time that he howled back in fury.

"Damn it, you little bitch."

He had me trapped in the stairway, so I turned and worked my legs into a run up the steps. He caught my leg before I reached the top, pulling me down a few of the steps with thuds. The carpet rubbed hard against my chin as I bounced down the steps, instantly becoming wet with blood. His body crawled onto me, pinning me facedown onto the stairs. His weight on my back smashed my chest, cutting off my ability to breathe.

Levi brought his face down to mine and spoke into my bleeding ear. "You little whore. I'm going to take my time with you, have my fun, then I'm going to squeeze the life out of you..."

His words swam around in my head.

I was going to die.

He whispered, "...so that Noah will never have you again."

Levi's words seeped in. My brain was slowing, maybe going into shock from lack of oxygen. Besides the burning on my chin and the pain shooting through my ear, I also was aware of the jab to my hip from the car keys in my pocket, which were pressed into the stair.

As Levi shifted his weight and rolled me over, I reached into my pocket and pulled them out. The slash to his face was a blur in my mind, until I made contact with the soft flesh of his eye. The squirt of liquid onto my face told me I'd hit the mark.

Levi let go completely to clutch his ruined eye, and I worked my bruised body into a fast climb up the stairs with my hands and knees.

His painful scream behind me pushed me into an upright position when I reached the top, and I dashed into Aunt Debbie's bedroom. My mind had cleared enough to know I had one more option on the table.

Slamming the door behind me, I locked it and ran to the wardrobe in the corner. Flinging the doors open I started pulling the small drawers out, madly feeling through them, throwing lingerie and scarves everywhere.

Levi hadn't given up—he banged on the door with unreal strength. As I searched, the door shook and shuddered.

A great bang against the door finally burst it wide-open just as my hand closed over the cold steel of Aunt Debbie's purse revolver. It was only the length of my hand, and I didn't know if it was loaded, but it was all I had.

I will never forget the sight of Levi's bleeding face, distorted in rage and pain, coming full speed into the room. I found some inner place of calm and aimed.

I pulled the trigger before he even saw the tiny thing.

36

Noah

"Can't you go any faster?" I asked Sam, pushing my body from the backseat into the front.

"I'm damn near going twenty miles over the speed limit as it is—so back off."

I knew that Sam was just as frustrated as I was with the traffic, and the distance to cover to get to Rose. He'd readily jumped into his truck and picked us up when I'd called him.

Sam slammed his phone against his thigh and breathed out in frustration. "Damn it, she's not answering her phone." He gazed over at Father and said, "Maybe I should go ahead and call the Fairfield cops and ask them to check the house out for us?" Sam asked, while he swerved in between the cars on the busy highway.

Father said, "Oh, I don't think that will be necessary. Chances are that Levi isn't even in the state. I find it hard to believe that the boy would be able to get away from the house for our troubled teens and hire a driver to bring him to this city."

Father smoothed out his beard and added, "Then he'd have to find her house in this maze of humanity."

"Levi is resourceful, Father...and obsessed with Rose. He'll find a way to get to her, if he can."

My heart was thumping so hard, I could hardly catch a proper breath at times. I hated the feeling of helplessness.

"What the hell does this guy have against Rose, anyway?" Sam growled. He took the exit from the highway a little too fast, and we were swept to the left side of the vehicle.

I righted myself and told him, "Back in the fall, he tried to have his way with Rose at a benefit auction. Summer was there, and she videoed what he did until I got there and beat the crap out of him."

I couldn't help but think about what I'd do to Levi this time if he went near Rose. I'd kill him.

Sam's voice rose. "Why didn't anyone tell me and Dad about this?"

Father answered, "The bishop and the ministers handled the situation. Since we had the video as proof, Levi was punished and sent away to the special home in Indiana. He needed counseling."

"It sounds like he needed a jail cell. Damn, this is completely nuts, you know that?" Sam turned again.

Father was probably right. It would be impossible for Levi to find where Rose lived here. I wouldn't know myself how to get back to the highway, as crowded and confusing as it all was.

"So what's the plan?" Sam asked, still using a loud anxious voice.

"We bring Rose back to Meadowview tonight," I said with no question in my mind.

"Whoa, wait a minute—Dad isn't going to like that one bit. Rose lives here now. She has school and dancing. Hell, she even has a job."

"She'll need to be protected, Sam. Can't you get that through your thick head?" I said harshly, definitely not wanting to hear all Sam's reasons for why I couldn't bring Rose home with me.

"Now, hold on, son. Once we locate Rose and make sure she is all right, we can contact the police and put them on alert. Your mother was going to visit the Zooks and inform them of the problem. I'm sure they can get a hold of the home in Indiana and verify that Levi is there," Father said.

Sam said, "That's a better plan than yours."

We were silent for the next few minutes while he turned onto several roads, entering a residential area that was filled to the brim with house after house after house. I never could understand how people lived so tightly packed as this. It wasn't natural.

"We're here." Sam pulled into the driveway of the attractive, two-story brick colonial that I'd already been inside of. But Sam didn't need to know that right now. My eyes noted Rose's red pickup—and the older model black car at the curb. I didn't like the look of the car one bit, and just as I was going to tell Father and Sam about it, we all heard the loud pop of a gun going off.

The sound was sharp and out of place in the otherwise quiet neighborhood. My brain exploded with the sound, triggering my legs and hands to work frantically to free myself from the vehicle.

I covered the yard, running full tilt over the thick carpet of grass, with Sam right behind me.

Grabbing the knob, I flung the door open and barreled into the house. Sam went into the family room, while I took the stairs two at a time. I remembered where her room was—I'd never forget that room.

"Rose!" I screamed. Sam and Father's voices echoed mine downstairs.

I called to her again and burst into her room. One quick turn of my head and I saw she wasn't there.

Running back into the hallway, my heart cold as ice, I moved toward the door that hung off its bottom hinge.

Please, Lord, don't let Rose be dead.

I covered the space in a few steps, but it seemed as if I were crawling through thick mud as I crossed into the room.

The sight that met my eyes gripped my insides. Levi was on the ground, writhing in pain. Blood covered his swollen face, making him almost unrecognizable. Since I'd only heard one shot, my mind quickly figured out that his thigh was where the bullet must have met its mark, hitting an artery, if the bright red, spurting blood was any indication.

I had a couple of seconds to process what I saw before I stepped over Levi who was only inches from Rose's curled-up body. I grabbed Rose up into my arms, carrying her away from the room, and Levi's wailing profanities. The sounds and words slipping from Levi's tongue made me think the devil was among us.

Sam nearly smashed into me as he flew through the hallway.

"Holy shit," Sam said. He had a cell phone plastered to his ear. I vaguely heard him tell whoever was on the other end that an intruder had been shot, and then he rattled off the address.

Father paused to place a hand on Rose's face. "Is she all right?"

"She's in much better shape than Levi is." I said the truth.

Father nodded, his face grim, as he swept by us toward Levi.

I took Rose to her room and laid her carefully on the bed. There was a smear of blood on her chin that stretched up the side of her face to her right ear. Her other cheek was bruised dark red and swollen. All that didn't still my breathing as much as the way her glazed eyes stared out from the ashen skin of her face.

"Rose, sweetheart, I'm here."

I brought my face to hers, "Please talk to me, Rose. Come on, snap out of it."

I only half noticed Sam on the other side of the bed searching around Rose's head with his hands and then going over her body.

"She appears to be in shock," Sam offered, before he shouted at her, "Rose, you better start talking or I'm going to tell everyone how you fainted at the sight of some blood."

Astounding me, Sam's words did the trick.

"You're…a…prick, Sam," Rose stammered out between breaths. "Did I really get him?"

"You sure did, sweetheart," I said pulling her up into my arms again. Even with the smell of her blood, there was still the scent of warm flowers underneath.

I thanked God as I held her trembling body.

"I'm glad," she said into my neck.

"Good job, sis. Looks like you didn't even need us." Sam's relief was evident as he blew out a long sigh.

The sound of the sirens got Sam back up again. "I'll go meet everybody," he said, sprinting out of the room.

"Is he…dead?" Rose whispered.

I listened to the house; the sound of the sirens and the voices bursting around downstairs were clear to my ears, but I didn't hear Levi's screams any longer.

I smoothed Rose's tangled hair down, as I said, "Reckon I don't know. He was very much alive when I took you out of there."

Rose's eyes narrowed, and the words from her mouth sent a shiver over me.

"I hope he's dead."

Before I could say anything, there were three officers sweeping into the room, along with two paramedics.

"Move over, young man," the oldest officer commanded me.

The guy's no-nonsense tone was enough to get me away from the bed and up against the wall.

The big guy cleared an area so that the paramedics could sail right over to Rose. I was glad they were there caring for her. My mind worried that when she calmed down, she'd be hurting all over.

"Noah, don't leave me," Rose called out, holding her hand to me.

I slid over close enough to reach out and grasp it, even though the head policeman frowned at me.

"Are you related to her?" the officer asked.

"I'm her boyfriend."

Sam squeezed in, seeming comfortable to bump past the lawmen until he reached Rose's head. I had to give him credit for his audacity.

"I'm Rose's brother," Sam told them.

"Then you'll be the one riding with her to the hospital," the chubby officer said, taking the time to look squarely at me in warning.

What did I ever do to him?

Sam, reading my thoughts, told me, "Ah, Noah…Dad talked to the sheriff about the situation with Rose and you a while back… You aren't supposed to be here."

"Don't you dare make Noah leave—Sam, please tell them it's all right now," Rose pleaded with her brother. The lady paramedic spoke soothingly to Rose as she held her down to the bed while the man tried to see into her eyes with a light that looked like a pen.

"Yeah, don't worry about it. It's okay now," Sam said, eyeing the chubby guy, apparently the sheriff of this busy town.

The commotion in the hallway made me look up in time to see Levi being carried away by another group of medical workers, with several officers following behind. I didn't see much of Levi because of the mask on his face. He was just a blur going by to my eyes.

I was glad that he wasn't speaking any longer.

"We're ready," the man said.

In no time at all, a slender, cotlike device was beside the bed. I had to let go of Rose in order for them to move her, and I did, but only after I bent down and kissed her forehead.

"Can't he come?" Rose looked to the sheriff.

"Sorry, but only one other person can ride with you to the hospital—and that'll be your brother."

I could see Rose was preparing to argue, and she didn't need to waste her energy. "It's all right, sweetheart. I'm sure one of these kind officers will give Father and me a ride to the hospital. I'll be right behind you."

Everyone took that as a cue to quickly get Rose on the cot and whisk her out of the room. Sam held her hand, hovering near her while she craned her neck to watch me until she disappeared into the hallway.

Before I got out the door, Father stayed me with his hand.

"How serious are her injuries?" Father asked. His face was flushed and his voice jumpy.

"She was beat up pretty bad, but I believe they are all the type of cuts and bruises that will heal well." I hesitated, not sure if I wanted to know, but asking, anyway, "What about Levi?"

Father shook his head wearily and sighed. "He was alive when they took him out, but he'd lost so much blood it's hard to say whether he will survive."

I remembered Rose's wish, and I couldn't say that I didn't feel the same way. It served Levi right for attacking Rose. And, if he did die, we'd never have to worry about him again.

"We have to go to the hospital to be with Rose," I said, surging forward and forgetting about everything else.

Father slowed me by stepping into my path. His face was bright with concern as he said, "Noah, what happened here today was inexcusable. Levi will face justice from the authorities…and God. But you must not let your heart turn to stone toward him. It is our way to show forgiveness in all things."

I thought about Levi hitting Rose, scratching her and cutting her. I remembered his vile cussing, and I thought about how terrified Rose must have been.

No, he would not get any forgiveness from me.

"I feel that God is the only one in the position to forgive that bastard. Now, please, can we go to Rose?"

Father hesitated for some seconds, then nodded and moved aside. I hoped that one of the officers would indeed transport us to the hospital. As I walked out into the dim evening light, the sight of many police vehicles assaulted my vision. There were also a dozen neighborhood people standing around, pointing and gawking at me and Father as we made our way across the yard.

I didn't need to worry about the police leaving us behind— several of them were walking to us briskly.

"We have some questions for the two of you," the sheriff said.

I only half paid attention to the conversation flying back and forth between Father and the sheriff, my mind was so distracted by the crowd and flashing lights.

I was also remembering Levi's destroyed face—and the look of disapproval on Father's when I had told him I would not take the way of Grace where Levi was concerned.

It seemed as if it was hours before we stepped into the lobby of the hospital. Our questioning had moved from the yard to the sheriff's office, where we'd recounted our story several times, before the large man finally had allowed us to leave.

At least he had instructed the younger patrolman to drive us to the hospital. It was amazing that the sheriff even showed us that courtesy, as unfriendly as he'd been. Obviously, Dr. Cameron had given the man an earful about the Amish. Now that he had to deal with one of us who'd attacked a girl in his own backyard, his impression of our people was probably sullied forever.

The patrolman led us to the emergency waiting area and then disappeared behind the doorway for some minutes before returning with Dr. Cameron in tow. Rose's father had made a quick journey to the city.

My heart stumbled at the sight of him—one more obstacle to keep me from seeing my love.

Dr. Cameron did not offer his hand to my father, nor did he look my way. The patrolman, who had been engaging enough on the ride over, was stone-still, avoiding our eyes altogether.

We had no one on our side in these parts.

"How's Rose?" I spoke to David, anyway.

David glanced my way dismissively and focused his gaze on my father.

"Rose is doing well. Her outer scars will heal much more quickly than her inner ones. I appreciate your concern for her. And the fact that you coaxed Sam into bringing you to the city was admirable, but I will reiterate what I told you before. Rose will not be having anything to do with your community while she is still a minor—especially after all this. I hope you will respect me in this matter, Amos, and keep your son away from her."

Father stood silently staring at David. At that moment I wished I could have spied into my father's brain to see what he was thinking. He was obviously weighing his words carefully before he spilled them. After all, he knew that Rose could be pregnant, and what David wanted might not even be an issue in a couple of months.

I remained silent. I trusted Father to represent me.

Finally, Father spoke, his voice level and resolved.

"So be it, then, David. But the forces of nature may affect your decision in time. Until then, we will patiently wait for Rose, for I do believe that regardless of your wishes, Noah and Rose will be together in time."

Father tipped his hat and turned, walking straight out the front doors. I hesitated, wanting desperately to see Rose, but the look David gave me told me he'd never allow it. As I went to follow Father, I saw a wisp of sympathy pass over the patrolman's face before I left.

I tried to leave with the same confident manner that Father had used, but I probably didn't pull it off as well. My heart was breaking that I would again be kept away from Rose.

How long could this go on? I quickly counted in my head, seven months until her birthday…or earlier if her belly began to grow.

For Rose's sake I didn't want her to be with child, but for my sake, I silently prayed that she was.

no end. Even
Levi was rec
a mental i
And t
Sin
alw
th

I wondered what Noah was doing right then. Absently, I stroked Hope's head, which was flopped on my lap like a rag doll.

The darkness outside the front windows was complete, and I couldn't help but stare out into it, zombielike. The trickling of Summer's country lingo occasionally reached my ears, with Sam's voice popping up here and there, a bit more abruptly.

The two of them sat on the couch side by side, looking as if they were a couple of straitlaced Amish kids. I hid a smile, thinking about how Sam had attempted to pull Summer's legs onto his lap, but she'd have nothing of it. She had said something to the effect that she was in no way going to get all cozy with Sam in front of his entire kin, and then added that it was rude, besides, with Rose not able to cuddle up with her guy and all.

That had instantly brought an image of Noah's worried face to mind. The discomfort I was feeling because of the bruises and scrapes to my body were nothing compared to the throbbing hurt my heart was dealing with.

Why was Dad being such a dictator?

It had been a week since the psycho Levi had tracked me down to give payback for getting him kicked out of his community. The fact that the worm was still alive bugged me to

...hough the sheriff had assured me that once ...overed enough to leave the hospital, a jail cell or ...stitution awaited him.

...at he'd be in one of those places for a very long time. ...e he hadn't died, no matter where he ended up, I would ...ys be looking over my shoulder. I would forever worry ...at he'd sneak up on me some dark night after he'd escaped from wherever the powers-that-be stuck him.

This was not the sort of stuff a seventeen-year-old should have to deal with. But here I was, the honoree for the get-well party Aunt Debbie was throwing, thinking about how I wished the guy I shot would have died. And, since he hadn't, I decided I would have to get a permit to carry a concealed weapon when I turned eighteen. Next time, if there ever was a next time, I would aim higher.

Aunt Debbie and Tina were busy in the kitchen whipping up my favorite, chicken and dumplings, to cheer me up. Their voices sounded so normal, which just added to the weirdness of the evening. How could they be talking about the weather after everything that had happened? Were they nuts?

On the other end of the spectrum were Dad and Uncle Jason. They were sitting in the overstuffed recliners gazing at a news program in complete silence.

I hadn't talked to Dad much since I'd gotten out of the hospital. After the begging didn't get me anywhere closer to seeing Noah, I just gave up and slunk into my own self-induced miserable trance.

Would I really have to wait until November to see Noah again? And would Dad immediately write me out of the family when I jumped ship and headed to Meadowview?

I let my eyes wander over to Dad for a split second before I looked away again quickly. He'd been watching me with that vague look of incredulity on his face.

The ringing doorbell jolted me upright.

Amanda was working and Brittany had other plans, so it wasn't one of them. My mind began racing through the possibilities.

"Why don't you get the door, Rosie?" Dad said, all nonchalantly, triggering a warning alarm in my mind.

Then the room became brighter, and I pictured Noah on the other side of the door. Jumping up, I ran and opened it.

My eyes probably popped out. Instead of Noah, it was Hunter, smiling sheepishly on the porch.

"Hey, aren't you going to invite me in?" he said, with an air of confidence that I was immediately bugged by. Didn't he get the memo—we were broken up!

I was seriously thinking about shutting the door and walking away. I already had way too many complications in my life. I certainly didn't need Hunter stirring up trouble. Especially when I'd finally stopped thinking about him every few minutes.

Unfortunately, I wasn't alone and didn't have the option of being a rude B.

"Hey, dude. Come on in," Sam shouted out from the background.

Hunter continued smiling as he waited for me to step aside. The lift of his eyebrow was the only indication that he might be getting annoyed. He was always such a good sport about my bad behavior.

I stepped back. He purposely passed by me closely, his chest nearly rubbing my boobs. The near contact made my heart sputter a bit—not a good thing at all.

I decided right then and there that I needed to talk to Hunter and explain to him in person, and in very thick detail, that I was with Noah now, even though I technically wasn't with Noah, so that he'd back off and go away.

If Hunter left me alone, then I could forget about him and focus on Noah. I was not going to fool around with two guys—even though it seemed as if that was exactly what my sick father wanted at the moment.

Before Hunter was too many steps into the family room, I looked at Dad and asked, "Is it okay if I take Hunter upstairs to talk in private?"

Unsurprisingly, Dad's eyes perked up. "Of course you can. It's good to see you, Hunter."

"Yeah, it's nice to see you, too."

Before Hunter had the opportunity to make a great impression on my close family and friend, I grabbed his hand and pulled him up the stairs.

On the way up, we passed Justin coming down. The poor kid's mouth gaped when he saw us. I was definitely not setting a good example for his future dating practices.

Once in my room, I shoved Hunter in and closed the door with a thud.

Staring at him, I decided Dad was *insane*. That he was all for me and Hunter sequestering ourselves in a room alone together just proved how desperate Dad was to get Noah out of my life for good.

Actually, it was a good plan, but Dad was not figuring how much I loved Noah into the equation.

Hunter seated himself on the bed. He looked relaxed, resting against the backboard, his legs stretched out on my light green comforter. He also didn't leave any room for me to sit down—unless I wanted to be real cozy with him.

Nice try, Hunter.

I remained standing with my hands folded under my breasts and said, "We have to talk."

A smile played at the corner of his mouth. The little twitter of his lips caused a warm flush to fill my face.

Hunter drawled, "Why don't you sit over here next to me and get comfortable? You're wired like a hand grenade."

"No way—I don't know what game you're playing at, but your behavior has me on edge." I narrowed my eyes, trying to make him mad at me. After all, it would be easier to get him to leave if he was pissed off.

"Sorry that *me* being friendly has confused you. I just don't see why you and I can't still be friends and hang out, even with you dating Noah." Then he smirked a little, really making me annoyed. "If you can even call it dating. From what I've heard, you won't be seeing much of him for a long while."

I took the few steps needed to place me right beside him, and stared with the meanest face I could manage.

"You and I have broken up, Hunter, so it doesn't matter one iota how much time I spend with Noah. The fact that you're clearly enjoying my restricted relationship shows that you don't care for me at all."

Hunter was standing so fast it nearly made my head spin. One minute he was casually lounging in my bed, the next he was glowering down at me, his hands on the sides of my arms.

He lowered his face to mine and growled, "The problem is, I care way too much. And as much as I'd like to walk away from you, and not have to deal with this infatuation you have with a guy from another lifetime—I can't. And I won't."

"You have to—you don't have a choice in the matter," I seethed back.

"I most definitely do," Hunter said, and in the blink of an eye, his mouth was on mine. He wasn't being exactly forceful, just a little pushy with his mouth.

I fought my response to him for a few seconds, with a very vivid image of Noah in my mind, but Hunter's mouth softening and working against mine clouded the thoughts of Noah.

Everything was so easy with Hunter.

My family approved—heck, my Dad *loved* the guy. I could hang out with him whenever I wanted, pretty much do whatever I liked around him. Hunter was definitely the easy path—and his kisses were really nice.

But after a few seconds, I got control of my senses and tore myself away.

I stepped back, wiping him from my mouth.

Hunter looked at me smugly and said, "See, there is something more between us than just friendship. I can give you what Noah can't—everything."

I began to open my mouth with some kind of comeback, but he closed the distance again, only this time he didn't touch me. His surge forward did shut me up.

"I love you, Rose...I really do. And right now it's enough for me to know that you do have feelings for me, because I'm sure that eventually I can wash Noah from your mind once and for all. I'm a patient sort of guy."

Feeling all torn up inside, I whispered, "No, you can't. I'm sorry."

He smiled confidently and said, "I'm heading downstairs to hang out with your family. I'll try not to distract you too much with my presence."

Before he walked by me, he softly cupped my face with his hand, his eyes piercing mine. Then he broke away from me.

The click of the door made me feel a little bit lonely.

When it came to Hunter, I didn't know what to think. There was no doubt that I liked the guy. But I didn't think he was the love of my life.

You could only have one of those, and Noah already had the job.

But Hunter was going to make things more difficult than I originally thought.

38

Sam

I rubbed my face vigorously with my hands. I was sitting uncomfortably on the floor outside of Aunt Debbie's upstairs bathroom, but even this uncomfortable position was much better than the chaos in my head at the thought of what was going on behind the door at my back.

Things could change a lot in one month.

The last time I'd been in Cincinnati was for Rose's party, and I'd come away that weekend feeling that she was on the way to getting back together with Hunter—and moving in the right direction with her life.

Now this—*damn it.*

The soft scurrying and conversation of the girls behind the door was too quiet for me to gauge how things were going.

The whole day had a surreal feel, and I kept attempting to blink myself awake from the nightmare. Hell, a couple of hours ago I'd been getting ready to go for a run, when I'd gotten Summer's frantic call that I needed to take her to the city to be with Rose.

I didn't hesitate. When your girlfriend, who you've finally admitted has your heart totally in her grip, begged you to do something, you did it.

It had taken a full hour of the drive for me to pull the information out of Summer about what was going on.

Now, I wish I didn't know.

Rage filled me at the knowledge that Noah would do this to my little sister. Was he an absolute moron?

Then again, probably not—this was a calculated way to rip my sister away from her family and her goals to trap her with him. I was sure of it.

When the door opened, I found myself falling backward into the bathroom, cool tiles against my back.

Summer was beside me in a heartbeat, her eyes meeting mine. I didn't need to even ask, the news was plain from her green stare.

She held up the pregnancy test in front of my face, anyway, and I only glanced at it. Shit.

Standing up, I made my way over to Rose who sat on the vanity, her head dropped into her hands. The bobbing of her head and the gurgling sniffs told me that she was crying.

When my hands touched her shoulders, she looked up, and her light blue eyes were washed out with tears.

"Sam...I'm...sorry. How stupid...stupid," she sobbed out.

I pulled her into my arms and hugged her more tightly than ever before while her body rocked against me.

Summer leaned in, placing her head on Rose's shoulder and her arms around the both of us.

Maybe the three of us together could work this thing out.

But I knew one thing for certain—I was going to kill Noah.

★ ★ ★ ★ ★

What's next for Rose and Noah?
Turn the page for a sneak peek at the stunning conclusion of
the TEMPTATION series.

Sarah

Glancing sideways, I quickly looked back into the laundry basket and blushed. Micah had been watching me.

Oh, goodness, what should I do?

Trying to ignore what my eyes had just told me, I reached into the basket and pulled out a pair of pants heavy with dampness. Snapping them onto the line, I nearly jumped out of my skin when Micah spoke close behind me.

"Would you like some help with that?"

His words were fuzzy in my mind and his face blurred for a second. Did the brown-haired boy with the prettiest green eyes I'd ever seen just ask me if I needed help hanging the laundry? Surely, I must be dreaming.

Coming to my senses as quickly as I could, I looked around for anyone watching, before facing Micah.

"Uh, no...but it sure is nice of you to offer—none of my brothers ever have," I said before turning back to the work.

As much as I wanted his company, I wished he'd leave. If Father or Mother caught him talking to me, I'd be in trouble for sure. Especially with everything so mixed up with our families and all. Oh, if only Noah had never gotten involved with Constance. He hadn't taken my advice, and now we all were paying the price—especially me.

Micah chuckled softly and said, "My mother and sisters trained me well." He paused and took a wet work shirt from the pile and began hanging it before saying, "Actually, I don't mind helping you at all."

I turned quickly and grabbed the shirt from his hands and tugged. "You mustn't do that. Someone might see and then questions will be raised."

Micah was strong and he wouldn't let go. He pulled the material back and argued, "There is nothing wrong with me assisting you. I hardly see why anyone would complain."

Nearly frantic, I glanced around and yanked hard. The rip was loud and I didn't need to see the shirt to know a seam had been broken. The material came loose from his hands and I stepped back.

My cheeks felt warm when I said, "Now look what you've gone and done. You're supposed to be helping Peter build the fence. And with all the trouble brewing, you should be happy that Father invited you to do so."

Micah must have lost his mind, I thought, when he came forward and whispered close to my face, "If you hadn't refused my help, that wouldn't have happened. Besides, the only reason my father allowed me to come over here was to spy on you all."

I suddenly felt light-headed and ignored the possibility of others watching us.

"What are you talking about?"

Micah did a quick scan of the area and said, "I shouldn't have said anything, but I don't guess you'll tell anyone. You used to talk to me and smile sometimes and now you won't even glance my way. Is it because of your brother and my sister?"

Sighing with worry that he'd even asked, I said, "Of course, silly. I'm not sure why we became friends, but the things that your father has said about Noah and my family have made it impossible for it to continue. It wasn't proper, anyway. I'm going to begin courting Edwin."

His hand shot out and grabbed my arm lightly. The heavy feel of it made the blood drain from my face. "What? Are you crazy, Sarah? You don't even like him."

"Course I do. And who are you to say so?"

Micah leaned in and said with a sureness that made me believe him, "'Cause you like me, that's why. This thing will eventually settle down between our families. Don't do something that we'll both regret."

He left me and went back to the fence across the yard. A part of me wanted him to come back, but the other wanted him to stay far away. He was dead wrong about our families. When the bishop announced Noah and Constance's separation on Sunday, it would get worse.

Wiping the wetness from my eyes quickly, I went back to work. I had to get Micah Schwartz out of my mind.

He was nothing but trouble.

Acknowledgments

Many thanks to the professional people who've been instrumental in bringing Rose and Noah's story to the public: Christina Hogrebe, my wonderful agent from the Jane Rotrosen Agency, and T.S. Ferguson, Natashya Wilson and the rest of the spectacular editorial team at Harlequin Teen. I'm truly blessed to have the guidance of such an amazing group of people on this project.

Special and heartwarming thanks to my five children, Luke, Cole, Lily, Owen and Cora, who made it possible for my frenzied days of writing by helping out with the cooking, cleaning and basic requirements of survival; my mother, Marilyn, who has been an avid promoter of all of my work and spent countless hours on the phone sharing her sound advice and suggestions; my father, Anthony, brother, Tony, and nephew, Jamey, who are always there to lend a helping hand. I love you all.

I also want to thank a few of my friends who've been there for me during the strange journey that has been my life over the past few years: Jay, Carey, Opal, Devin, Kelsey, Kendra, Marian, Brooke, Tyler, Jackie and Eric. Everyone should have friends like these.

The seasons in the sleepy Amish community I live in are measured by the planting and harvesting of crops, the spring and autumn schoolhouse benefit dinners, and the smell of wood smoke in the air during the wintertime. I'm thankful that I found this place of buggies, open fields and honest, hardworking people and for the inspiration it's given me in my writing.